A Perfect Scoundrel

Heather Cullman

Ø

A SIGNET BOOK

SIGNET
Published by New American Library, a division of
Penguin Putnam, Inc., 375 Hudson Street,
New York, New York, 10014, U.S.A.
Penguin Books Ltd, 27 Wrights Lane,
London W8 5TZ, England
Penguin Books Australia Ltd, Ringwood,
Victoria, Australia
Penguin Books Canada Ltd, 10 Alcorn Avenue,
Toronto, Ontario, Canada M4V 3B2
Penguin Books (N.Z.) Ltd, 182–190 Wairau Road,
Auckland 10, New Zealand

Penguin Books Ltd, Registered Offices:
Harmondsworth, Middlesex, England

First published by Signet, an imprint of New American Library,
a division of Penguin Putnam Inc.

First Printing, February 2000
10 9 8 7 6 5 4 3 2 1

Copyright © Heather Cullman, 2000

All rights reserved

 REGISTERED TRADEMARK—MARCA REGISTRADA

Printed in the United States of America

In memory of our precious Siamese cat, Trey

For being company when I was lonely. For giving sympathy when I was sad or sick. For Indian dances in the morning and for cuddling on chilly nights. For bug-busting, wigginess, and safety. For the imagination you fueled. For simply being you, a gentle presence in our lives. We love and miss you.

and

For little one-eyed Oscar

*Because you made me smile,
and I cared.*

Chapter 1

S he had loved him from the very first moment she saw him.

Jane Wentworth clasped her hands in her lap, her heart leaping as the majordomo ushered Lord Quentin Somerville into the drawing room. Oh, but he looked handsome this morning, so handsome that the sight of him quite stole her breath away.

Always impeccably dressed, today his lordship was the picture of urbane elegance. His coat, tailored to perfection and cut in the latest bobtail style, was a deep azure blue, and beneath it he wore a bright red waistcoat and immaculately starched linen. Hungry, as always, to view every magnificent inch of him, she furtively dropped her gaze lower to admire the fit of his nankeen trousers and the way his gleaming Hessians molded to his strong calves.

Perfection. Utter perfection. She had just shifted back up to his watch fob and was admiring its jeweled design when he stopped before the tête-à-tête upon which she sat with her stepsister, Clarissa Edwardes.

"Miss Edwardes. Miss Wentworth," he murmured, sketching a bow.

As always happened when in his dazzling presence, the

normally outspoken Jane was struck speechless and was thus unable to respond but for a stiff nod.

Her stepsister, however, suffered from no such bashfulness. "Why, Lord Quentin, how very kind of you to call on us," she exclaimed, smiling the smile that had captured the hearts of the entire *ton*.

Had Jane been able to smile herself, she'd have done so at Clarissa's use of the word "us." Though the dear girl would no doubt have denied the fact until she was blue in the face, Lord Quentin, like the other nine gentlemen in the room, had come to see Clarissa, and only Clarissa.

Lovely, vivacious Rissa, as her stepsister was called by her friends and family, was the undisputed success of the Season, while Jane—well, she had begun to hear the terms "last prayer" and "on the shelf" used in conjunction with her name of late. And with good reason. This was her fifth Season, and as with her first four she had again failed to attract a beau.

That wasn't to say she completely lacked male attention. With her rich dowry there was always a debt-ridden wastrel or two eager to make her acquaintance. But Jane, being of the opinion that no husband at all was better than one she could neither love nor respect, always discouraged such fortune hunters out of hand. Besides, she had no interest in marrying any man save one, and at the moment he was gazing at her stepsister with the adoration she dreamed he would one day direct toward her.

Oh, she knew it was a hopeless dream, for never once in almost five years, years in which she and his lordship had moved in the same circles, attended the same soirees, musicals, and balls, had he indicated so much as a spark of romantic interest in her. Yet she continued to dream, clinging to the hope that he would someday come to love her as she loved him. And though she knew she was a fool for doing so, she couldn't help herself. Besides, where was the joy in living without dreams?

Aching with bittersweet yearning, Jane watched as he sat among Clarissa's bevy of admirers, awed, as she always was, how the other men seemed to pale, and then fade, beside his masculine beauty. And Lord Quentin Somerville *was* beautiful, undeniably so.

Lowering her lashes to hide her interest, Jane continued her infatuated scrutiny while Rissa dazzled her beaux with her much-admired wit. She studied him not to memorize his form or features—those were engraved upon her heart. She did so because she simply couldn't keep her eyes off him.

Thus she passed the time as she always did when he called, first examining his person, then remembering how he had looked in past Seasons, and now marveling at how he grew handsomer with every passing year. This Season his appearance had taken on a decidedly artistic, and in her opinion, romantic, quality. His hair in particular.

Like all the gentlemen in his set, a set currently absorbed in the rage of composing poetry, Lord Quentin had grown his hair until it just swept his shoulders. Unlike those other gentlemen, however, who managed to look merely unkempt, his hair curled naturally, creating a glorious mane of dark mahogany ringlets. Those ringlets, so fat and glossy, framed his handsome face and tumbled over his brow, emphasizing his amethyst eyes in a way that was nothing short of stunning.

As Jane admired the effect, he laughed at something Rissa said, flashing strong, white teeth and a rakish pair of dimples. Instantly she was besieged with a faint, familiar fluttering deep in her belly. Disturbed by her response, she tore her gaze away. After a beat during which she frantically looked everywhere except at Lord Quentin, she dropped her gaze to her hands. The moment she did so, she almost groaned aloud.

Hateful things! They were wringing together like those of

the overwrought heroines in Mrs. Smith's novels. Praying that no one had noticed their telltale motion, she pried them apart and commanded them to lie still. They had just begun to obey when she heard her stepsister utter her name, as if in query.

Anxious at being called to attention, certain that she would be struck dumb or, worse yet, say something stupid, she reluctantly looked up.

"Lord Quentin asked if we are looking forward to Lady Kirkham's masqued ball next week," Rissa said, giving her an encouraging smile. Aware of Jane's feelings for his lordship and wishing to help further her cause, Clarissa had taken to deferring his lordship's questions to her. Though Jane appreciated her stepsister's good intentions, she lived in dread of such moments as this.

Not, of course, that she would ever tell Rissa of her feelings. Rissa was a dear, sweet girl who would be beyond wretched if she learned that she'd caused her stepsister even the smallest measure of distress. And because Jane loved her so, she'd sooner die than say anything that might bring her grief. Thus she forced herself to return the other woman's smile and croak, "Yes."

There followed a pause, during which the gentlemen politely waited for her to elaborate. As she miserably grappled for something to add, Rissa gave her hand a quick squeeze and came to her rescue. "Our Jane has created the *most* original costume for the ball. Clever girl that she is, she has decided to go as—" she broke off with a small laugh. "Oh, but of course I mustn't tell. I shan't. It is a masqued ball, after all, and you gentlemen are supposed to guess at the ladies' identities."

"You can disguise your beautiful face, Miss Edwardes, but I shall know you the instant you walk into the room. You float like an angel upon the clouds of heaven." The duke of Goolding waxed poetic, his jowly face as rapturous as his words.

"And I should know your voice. 'Tis like the sweetest of celestial music," interjected Viscount Dutnall, not to be outdone by his rival.

One by one, the other gentlemen rushed to add their flowery tributes, praising everything from the tilt of Rissa's head to the way she carried her fan. All except Lord Quentin.

Jane stole a glance at him. He lounged in a Sheraton chair, his eyebrows raised and his arms folded across his chest, looking immensely amused by the other men's fawning. For the first time since being in his presence, she smiled. For all his dedication to poetry, he wasn't given to cooing insipid, prosy praise. No. When he flattered a woman, he did so in a straightforward yet gallant manner, one that left little doubt as to the sincerity of his esteem.

At least that is what she'd heard said by women who had received his compliments, and they weren't inclined to lie. Indeed, so admired was Lord Quentin by those ladies, and a good many others in the *ton* as well, that had he not been a second son they would have been tripping all over themselves in their rush to set their caps for him. As it was, more than one had professed a willingness to forgo the titles and greater fortunes of their other suitors for the sheer pleasure of being his wife. To Jane's eternal relief, he had yet to declare himself to any of them.

When at last the poetry duel ceased, leaving Rissa prettily flushed from the glut of flattery, Lord Quentin finally spoke. "As you can see, ladies, your attempts to disguise yourselves shall be quite in vain. Hence, you might as well spill the bag and save us poor gentlemen the torment of wondering at your costumes."

Jane felt a surge of gratitude at his use of the words "ladies" and "yourselves." He was being gallant, of course. For she knew perfectly well that none of the gentlemen, most probably including himself, had the least bit of interest in learning her disguise. Indeed, she doubted if, the day after the ball, any of them would even be able to answer correctly whether or not she had attended.

Not that she cared to be noticed—well, except by Lord Quentin, of course. No, she was perfectly content to sit alone, observing those around her. She'd found that one learned a great deal about people by watching them, and after five seasons of doing little else, she probably knew more about the members of the *ton* from her observations than their confidantes knew from their conversation.

"Well, Jane?" Rissa queried, interrupting her musings. "What do you say? Shall we tell them?"

Though Jane would have preferred to keep her costume a secret, being hopeful that Lord Quentin might notice it and be intrigued enough to ask her to dance, she nodded. She could see from the sparkle in her stepsister's eyes that she was bursting to tell. No doubt she wished to ensure that she was asked to stand up for every dance, though Jane felt certain she had nothing to fear. As the men said, it would be impossible for Clarissa to hide her charms.

"Well, in that instance . . ." Grinning impishly, Rissa slanted her suitors a glance.

All the gentlemen, save Lord Quentin, leaned forward, eager to learn her disguise. They no doubt planned to use the advantage to claim all her dances before her other admirers had a chance to identify her.

"As you know, the theme of the ball is 'An Evening on Mount Olympus,' " her stepsister began, "and . . ."

"And a devilishly fine theme it is," boomed Lord Witley, or Lord Witless, as the harebrained young man was referred to by his peers. By the exasperation on the other men's faces, it was clear that they thought his interruption yet another justification for his unflattering nickname.

"Very fine, indeed, as shall be the ball," Rissa concurred. "I hear tell that Lady Kirkham is having her ballroom transformed into a glittering Grecian temple set among clouds. The host and hostess are to reign over the merriment from bejeweled thrones, disguised as Zeus and Thetis. Thetis, as you might recall, was the sea nymph whom Zeus loved but didn't dare wed. Lady Kirkham said that she chose to portray her, rather than Zeus's wife, Hera, because she finds the tale deliciously romantic."

"You don't say?" murmured the flame-haired Lord Henson, exchanging a look of dismay with the stout, yet immensely wealthy, Lord Beveridge.

Jane was hard-pressed not to laugh aloud. What a minx Rissa was, tormenting the poor gentlemen like that. The sly-boots knew that they were in an awful stew to learn of her costume, and she had chosen to tease them by changing the subject.

Nodding, her stepsister rattled on. "There is to be an oracle beneath the oak tree in the garden, from which shall fall golden stars bearing the answer to whatever question one chooses to ask. The answers are to be written in riddle, which Lord Gramshaw, who shall be dressed as a mystical priest, will interpret."

"Er, how very amusing." This was from Viscount Dutnall.

Rissa nodded again. "More amusing yet, the menu is to be comprised entirely of foods described as ambrosia, though I simply cannot imagine what sorts of foods those might be." She paused a beat to ponder. "Hmm. If I am not mistaken, there is a dessert of oranges and coconut called ambrosia. Perhaps all the dishes shall contain either oranges or coconut, or a combination of the two. What do you think, Lord Fitton?"

The earl of Fitton, a smug, rather pompous sort of gentleman who more than made up in wealth for what he lacked in looks and personality, preened like a peacock beneath her regard. "I think your guess quite clever, my dearest Miss Edwardes."

Rissa graced him with a beatific smile, then slanted a meaningful glance at Jane. "And what say you, Lord Quentin?"

Rather than answer with the eager-to-please immediacy that the other men demonstrated, Lord Quentin took his time to consider her question. After several moments, during which Jane didn't dare breathe for fear of missing a single word of his response, he slowly smiled and replied, "I agree with Lord Fitton that your guess is quite clever. Since, however, the Kirkham cook is decidedly lacking in both skill and originality, my prediction is that we shall be served his inevitable menu of beef Tremblant and pickled grapes."

The corpulent Lord Beveridge groaned aloud at that prospect.

Rissa laughed. Except for Lord Quentin, who merely continued to smile, the other men laughed with her, stopping abruptly when she did. "No doubt you are right, my lord," she said. Then she fell silent, leaving her admirers to glance at each other helplessly.

Jane bit her lip to keep from giggling. The men were growing visibly uneasy, most probably wondering if Rissa was going to reveal her costume and trying to think of a way to broach the subject should she continue to stray off course. If the game continued true to form, they would start dropping hints any moment now to nudge the conversation back in the desired direction.

It was the balding, sharp-featured Mr. Cuddimore who dropped the first hint. "The menu aside, the ball should prove an excellent affair. It shall be most amusing to see the disguises and guess at the identity of their wearers."

"Most amusing," Rissa serenely agreed.

Another glance among the gentlemen, one that eventually

funneled to Lord Henson. Having been thus elected, he delivered the second hint. "*A-hem!* I, for one, am having difficulty deciding whether to go as Helios, the Sun God, or Hephaestus, God of Fire. Which do you ladies think most fitting?"

"Hephaestus," Jane surprised herself by replying. "With your red hair, you shall make a wonderful fire god."

Rissa eyed him thoughtfully, then nodded. "Yes, I do believe you are correct, Jane." She nodded again, then transferred her gaze to the man seated to the would-be fire god's left. "And what about you, Lord Beveridge? Who shall you be?" As he opened his mouth to reply, she cut him off with a wave of her hand. "No. On second thought, let us guess. You go first, Jane."

Not daring to look away from Rissa for fear of seeing Lord Quentin and losing her tongue, she promptly said, "King Midas."

"By jove, that is correct," Lord Beveridge exclaimed, sounding genuinely surprised. "How ever did you know?"

Rather than point out his obvious fondness for gold, which today was evidenced by a pair of gold watches, gold fobs, gold buttons, a gold-topped cane, three gold rings, and an enormous gold cravat pin, she replied, "I can assure you that it was nothing more than a lucky guess."

That statement was greeted by a soft chuckle, one that she instantly recognized. "Very lucky, indeed," Lord Quentin drawled. By his tone it was apparent that he knew exactly how she had come by her so-called guess. "And since you seem to have such luck at this game, let us see if you can guess whom I have chosen to portray."

His challenge left her with no choice but to look at him. Hoping that her face wasn't as red as it felt, she reluctantly glanced his way. He returned her gaze with a smile, his cheeks dimpling in a way that always wreaked chaos on her emotions . . .

And her tongue. Oh, dear! However was she to reply when he smiled at her like that?

"Well, Jane?" Rissa murmured, giving her hand a squeeze. "Who do you suppose Lord Quentin shall be? Heracles, the hero god, perhaps? Or maybe the valiant Perseus?"

His smile broadened into a devastating grin.

"Adonis," she blurted out. "He is a perfect Adonis." The instant the love-struck words left her mouth, she wanted to die, especially when the gentlemen chuckled.

Always the mistress of every situation, Rissa again came to her rescue. "I think that a perfectly wonderful guess, Jane. With his curls and dimples, Lord Quentin does bear a remarkable resemblance to Lady Saxby's garden sculpture of Adonis."

To Jane's relief, his lordship appeared to accept the explanation. "Indeed? Well, in that instance, I shall keep your observation in mind the next time I am called upon to disguise myself as a mythological character." He nodded. "Since, however, I was unaware of the resemblance, I have chosen to portray not Adonis but Morpheus, God of Dreams."

An even better choice, for did he not rule her dreams, both sleeping and awake?

"Now that you know my disguise, might I guess at yours?" he smoothly inquired.

Jane didn't miss the looks of gratitude the other gentlemen shot his way.

"But, of course. Fair is fair," Rissa replied.

"Do guess Aphrodite, Somerville," chimed in Lord Witley. "If anyone can properly portray the Goddess of Love, it is our beauteous Miss Edwardes."

"No. She should be Pandora, the first and most beautiful woman," Lord Goolding interjected worshipfully.

"Eos." This was from Mr. Cuddimore. "With her flame-blushed golden hair, Eos, Goddess of the Dawn, is the most logical choice."

"I cast my vote for the incomparable Andromeda," volunteered the thus far silent Lord Endicott.

"Helen of Troy," Viscount Dutnall inserted, while Lord Henson and the bashful Mr. Betton added votes for Psyche and Artemis.

As for Lord Quentin, he merely listened, shaking his head at each suggestion. "No, no," he finally said. "Miss Edwardes is far too clever to chose anything so obvious. My guess is that she shall be one of the Graces."

Rissa laughed. "You are all wrong, though Lord Quentin came closest. I shall be attending as one of the Muses." She glanced at Jane. "Shall I tell them which one?"

"You might as well," she replied, amused by the men's competitive zeal. "They shall eventually plague you into telling, you know."

"Indeed we shall," Lord Henson gaily concurred. "We shan't give you a moment's peace until you spill the bag."

Rissa glanced from one gentleman to the other, each of whom nodded his accord with Lord Henson. Finally she sighed and said, "You win. I shall be disguised as Urania, Muse of Astronomy." As the men released a collective sigh of relief, she added, "Now, you must all guess at Jane's costume."

A long, leaden silence greeted that command. After several uncomfortable moments, during which no one looked even the least bit inclined to venture a guess, Viscount Dutnall glanced at the mantel clock and exclaimed, "My word! Will you look at the time? I was due at my mother's house ten minutes ago."

"And I am due at my tailor's," chimed in Lord Fitton.

One by one the gentlemen excused themselves until only Mr. Cuddimore and Lord Quentin remained. That the former stayed surprised Jane; that the latter had done so warmed her soul.

"Well now, Miss Edwardes. What shall we discuss? The theater, perhaps? I know how fond you are of plays," Mr. Cuddimore said, once the last farewell had been tendered.

"You gentlemen were guessing at Miss Wentworth's disguise," she reminded him, smiling at Jane.

He looked as pained as if he sat on a pin. "Yes. Of course."

"And your guess, sir?" Rissa prompted.

He gave a disinterested shrug. "I can't begin to imagine."

"Indeed?" Both Rissa's utterance and her gaze were like shards of ice—frigid and sharp. Instantly seeing his mistake in slighting her stepsister, he scrambled to make amends by declaring himself a dull fellow. But it was too late, Rissa had already transferred her attention to Lord Quentin.

"And what is your guess, my lord?" she sweetly inquired. "I do hope you are more imaginative than poor, dull Mr. Cuddimore."

Jane tensed as she waited for him to reply. Would he act the gallant she believed him to be and grant her the courtesy of a thoughtful guess? Or would he disappoint her with a random, disinterested response?

As she waited, his arresting gaze slowly moved to her face. After several beats of contemplation, beats during which her heart remained firmly lodged in her throat, he said, "Is she to be a Muse as well? Euterpe, Muse of Music, perhaps? As I recall, she is quite skilled on the pianoforte."

Jane managed a shy smile. Of course he hadn't disappointed her. What a goose she was to have imagined that he might. For while it was true that he'd never paid her any special notice, he'd always been kind, which was more than she could say for most of the men in the *ton*. That in itself was one of the qualities that so endeared him to her.

True to his charming manner, he returned her smile. "Did I guess correctly, Miss Wentworth?"

There was something so gentle, so very encouraging about his smile that she found the confidence to reply, "I am afraid not, my lord, though I thank you for the compliment on my musical skills."

"No need to thank me. I speak only the truth." Having thus fulfilled his gentlemanly duty, she expected he would return his attention to Rissa. Instead, he tipped his head to one side and said, "Well?"

She blinked, taken aback. "My lord?"

His smile broadened, displaying his dimples in all their tongue-tying glory. "Are you going to reveal your disguise? Or are you going to continue to torment us with suspense?"

It was all she could do to keep her jaw from dropping in her astonishment. Beyond flattered by his interest, and the ability to speak, she simply returned his gaze.

Once again Rissa rescued her. "Oh, no, you don't, Jane. I shan't allow you to keep your disguise a secret after convincing me to reveal mine." Giving Jane a fond hug, she announced, "My dearest stepsister shall be going as Iris, the Rainbow Goddess. And a more cunning costume I have never seen."

"I look forward to seeing it," Lord Quentin murmured, and to Jane's delight he sounded sincere.

Could it be that he had noticed her at last?

Quentin Somerville stalked into the drawing room of his bachelor quarters, badly in need of a drink. Damn Miss Edwardes's legions of suitors; damn them for courting her and damn them for the tenacity with which they did so. Most of all, damn them for their titles and superior fortunes. How the hell was he, a mere second son with only a tumbled-down estate in Worcestershire and twelve thousand pounds a year, to win her against such competition?

His mood growing fouler by the second, he marched to the sideboard and seized the nearest decanter. Without bothering to identify its contents, he poured himself a double measure of the intoxicant and tossed it down in a single gulp.

"That bad, eh?" came a sardonic voice from nearby.

Quentin choked on the gin?—or was it whiskey?—in his surprise. His throat burning and his eyes watering, he swung around to glare at his best friend and fellow house tenant, Julian Palmer, Viscount Oxley, who lay sprawled on the worn crimson sofa, imbibing as well.

"What are you doing here? I thought you were off dancing attendance on Miss Talcott," he growled, not particularly pleased to see his friend. Though Oxley was the best of companions in most instances, he dismissed love as missish twaddle, thus making him the last person with whom he wished to discuss his problem.

Oxley heaved an exaggerated sigh. "Alas, it didn't go any better for me than it apparently went for you. I was turned away from Miss Talcott's door with news of her engagement to Lord Buchner." Another sigh. "Ah, well. I shall just have to set my sights on another well-dowered chit. I was thinking on Miss Wilkins, though her ears are rather large and stick out too much." He paused a beat to drain his glass, then added, "I suppose I could grow used to those ears for the forty thousand her guardian is offering to have her taken off his hands."

"Always the romantic, eh, Oxley?" Quentin muttered, eyeing the decanter from which he'd poured his drink. No wonder his throat felt blistered. He'd drunk the cheap gin they kept on hand to serve their foxed, and hence less than discriminating, visitors.

Oxley stared at him in genuine astonishment. "What is this? You, the King of Rakes, chiding me for a lack of sentiment? Don't tell me that you've been felled by Cupid's arrow?"

"It seems so," he reluctantly admitted.

There was a long pause, one during which Oxley gaped at him as if he'd sprouted horns. Then he sighed yet again and murmured, "Oh, my. How very unfortunate."

Quentin shoved aside the gin with a force that made the decanter stopper rattle, and reached for their best brandy. "It is unfortunate only in that I haven't a thief's chance in heaven of winning the girl's hand."

Another pause, then, "Do you really wish to wed her that badly?" This was uttered softly and in a tone free of irony.

"Yes. I do." Quentin filled his glass with the brandy, after which he held up the decanter in mute offering.

The other man nodded his acceptance. "I must say that I'm surprised by all this."

Carrying his glass in one hand and the decanter in the other, Quentin moved to where Oxley lounged. As he deposited the decanter on the cluttered tea table before him, he replied, "I can assure you that no one is more so than I. Like you, I always believed love to be nothing more than a delusion prompted by the reading of too many romantic novels. But now—" he broke off, shaking his head.

"Are you certain you're truly in love and not just suffering from frustrated lust? I saw your mistress in the park yesterday, and she complained that you have neglected her quite dreadfully of late. Perhaps all you need is a quick tussle between the sheets to restore your senses."

Quentin more fell than sat in the chair opposite his friend. "Trouble is, I have no interest in bedding anyone but Miss Edwardes. Indeed, I doubt I could become aroused enough to do anything with anyone else."

"Surely you jest?" Oxley looked as appalled as if his friend had just confessed to murder.

Quentin's only response was to drain his glass.

Oxley shook his head, his expression sympathetic. "You poor, poor fellow. You truly are in a bad way."

"You can't even begin to imagine," he muttered, pouring himself a refill.

Oxley eyed him gloomily for a beat, then sat up and followed suit. When he had resumed his lounging position, full glass in hand, he said, "It seems that the only thing for you to do is to marry the chit. There is nothing to restore a man's appetite for his mistress and the pleasures of Town quicker than a wife."

Quentin snorted. "If I thought that I had even the slightest chance of winning her, we wouldn't be having this conversation."

"What makes you so certain she would turn you down? I've seen the way she and her stepsister—uh"—Oxley snapped his fingers twice, then made a dismissive hand motion—"whatever her name is, whisper and watch you every time you're in company together. If that doesn't signify interest, I don't know what does."

"Jane Wentworth. The stepsister's name is Jane Wentworth," he miserably supplied, "and mere interest in my person doesn't necessarily indicate a desire to wed. Hell, I've had chits all but give up their maidenheads to me and then cast me aside in favor of a title. And as you know, Miss Edwardes has at least a dozen titles vying for her hand, all with impressive fortunes attached to them."

As he always did, Quentin cursed his wretched luck in being born second. Were he the current earl of Lyndhurst and heir to the mighty marquess of Beresford, Miss Edwardes would skip to the altar hastily enough. Unfortunately such was not the case, and since his obnoxiously perfect brother, Nicholas, was in equally perfect health, his lot in life wasn't likely to change anytime soon.

"Are you so certain that Miss Edwardes is after a title?"

"Aren't all women?" he retorted bitterly.

"If I remember correctly, there have been several dozen chits over the years who have been more than willing to forgo the grandeur of a title in their infatuation with your person."

"Pshaw. Those misses were either silly beyond endurance or being courted by titled men three times their age, neither of which is the case with Miss Edwardes. And even if she were inclined to choose my face over her other suitors' titles and fortunes, I doubt very much if her parents would indulge her in her foolishness."

Oxley sipped from his glass, his gaze never leaving Quentin's face as he considered his words. Suddenly a sly smile curved his lips. "Well, then, I suppose you must compromise the girl."

Again Quentin choked on his drink, this time in his shock at his friend's suggestion. While he wasn't above employing an occasional unsporting tactic to sway things in his direction, it had never crossed his mind to use such a ploy on Miss Edwardes.

"If matters are as hopeless as you profess, it's the only way," Oxley continued, ignoring his companion's startled reaction. "Besides, where is the harm in it? You love the girl and shall no doubt make her happy enough."

Indeed he would. In fact, between his twelve thousand a year and her generous dowry, he would be able to spoil her in the manner she deserved. And unlike her titled suitors, who would most probably dump her in the country once they had their heir and spare, he would see that she never had reason to regret their marriage. Hmm. When viewed that way, it seemed that he would be doing her an enormous kindness by entrapping her.

Having thus rationalized the admittedly unscrupulous action, he slowly acknowledged, "The idea has merit."

"Of course it does," Oxley shot back. "We have only to decide how you shall compromise her, and when."

"Well, it had best be soon. I overheard Goolding tell Endicott that he was going to declare himself to Miss Edwardes the day after Lady Kirkham's masqued ball. And as you know, Goolding is a duke."

"An enormously wealthy one with a hot head and a steady hand with a pistol," his friend added thoughtfully. "Yes. You must definitely make your move before he proposes. Can't have Goolding calling you out for dallying with his fiancée. As to when . . . " He drummed his fingers on the side of his glass, frowning as he mulled over the question.

Quentin considered it as well. After a moment, he snapped his fingers in inspiration. "But of course! I shall do it at the ball. Miss Edwardes said that there is to be an oracle set up in the garden. What if I lure her outside under the pretext of visiting it, and instead escort her somewhere for a kiss?"

Oxley continued his drumming for several more seconds, then nodded. "That might work, yes—if you can discover her disguise. It wouldn't do at all to be caught kissing the wrong woman."

"I already know her disguise," Quentin replied with growing confidence. "She is to be Urania, Muse of Astronomy."

"Well, then, our only remaining obstacle is finding a way to ensure that you are discovered together."

"That, and getting Miss Edwardes away from her stepsister," he interjected, making a face. "She insists on dragging that dreary creature with us everywhere we go."

"Perhaps she does so because she is attracted to you and is afraid of being alone with you, for fear of doing something improper," his friend suggested.

Quentin paused to consider the notion. Could that indeed be the reason Miss Edwardes clung so to Miss Wentworth every time he approached her? After several beats, beats in which his hopes soared, he sighed and said, "If what you say is indeed true, our plan is doomed to failure. She most certainly will not allow me to escort her to the garden alone."

Oxley too looked nonplussed. True to his cunning nature, however, he quickly recovered and said, "Well, then, we must lead her to believe that you shan't be alone."

"And how, pray tell, are we to do that?"

"Simple. We shall implore someone in our set, someone witty and dashing like Bancroft or Salvidge, to escort Miss—ur"—an impatient flick of the wrist—"oh, you know, the stepsister, outside with you and Miss Edwardes. Once there, you will conveniently part company in the shadows. If the stepsister is kept properly amused, she shan't notice that Miss Edwardes has been led away, while Miss Edwardes shall be unaware of the fact herself, since we shall make certain that the stepsister walks behind you."

"Perfect!" Quentin exclaimed. Damned if things might not work out after all! "Now all that remains is finding a way to ensure that Miss Edwardes is compromised."

Oxley chuckled wickedly. "I shall leave the manner in which she is compromised to you. As for ensuring that you are discovered, well, we will designate a place for your seduction to which I shall lead members of the *ton* under some other pretext. Voilà! Miss Edwardes is compromised. Gentleman that you are, you will naturally propose and she shall gratefully accept. As for her parents—"

"Puget," Quentin interjected abruptly. "Yes, the Puget. Of course."

His friend eyed him as if he had lost his mind.

"Don't you remember Lord Kirkham bragging about his new garden statue at White's last week? It is supposed to be an exact replica of Pierre Puget's *Perseus Rescuing Andromeda*. He is inordinately proud of the piece and invited everyone to see it at the ball."

"By Jove! You are right!" Oxley exclaimed, easily following his train of thought. "The Puget it shall be. I will wait ten minutes after you leave the ballroom, then ask Lord Kirkham to show me and several of the more scandalmongering members of the *ton* the statue. When we arrive, we shall find you and Miss Edwardes indulging in a most—*ahem!*—scandalous display of affections. You will, of course, have unmasked her during your seduction, so that her identity will be unmistakable."

"Brilliant!" he exclaimed, unable to bridle his enthusiasm.

"Yes. I am," Oxley smugly concurred.

Quentin raised his glass. "A toast to genius."

His friend shook his head as he followed suit. "No. We shall drink to your upcoming marriage. May it restore your wits and deliver you from this madness called love."

Chapter 2

It was a fine morning for riding. The late-April breeze stirred soft and cool, the air swirled golden with sun-gilded haze. Every plant, flower, and tree along Rotten Row looked vibrantly alive, with dew-studded petals and leaves glimmering like fairy jewels as they strained toward the newly risen sun.

This was the time of day Jane loved best, the dawn hour that woke the earth to the promise of the boundless possibilities and opportunities of the newborn day. This was her time to think and dream, to plan and wonder, and to simply be alone. And aside from the groom, who cantered behind her at a discreet distance, she was completely alone. It was marvelous.

For as long as Jane could remember, dawn rides had been a part of her day; first astride her father's horse as he inspected the tea fields near their home in India; later over the country roads of Lincolnshire, where she and her older brother, Philip, had lived with their grandparents after their mother's death from fever.

She had been seven and Philip thirteen at the time. Despite the passage of fifteen years, the memory of that terrible time still had the power to devastate her. For not only had she lost the gay, beautiful mother she adored, she had been torn from her beloved papa and the country of her birth to be sent to a cold, foreign land to live with relatives she knew only from letters and her father's stories. Though she had grown to love her kindly grandparents and the quaint village of Oxcombe, of which her grandfather was vicar, not a winter day passed that she didn't long to feel the hot Indian sun on her face and breathe the sultry, spice-laden Indian air.

Feeling suddenly homesick, Jane guided her dappled gray mare through Hyde Park gate and around Hyde Park corner, heading down Piccadilly toward her family's town house in Berkeley Square. It had been a long time since she'd last seen India. So long, that she sometimes wondered if her memories were not really memories at all, but wishful dreams of a fanciful paradise, created to lighten the darkness of the tragedy she had suffered there. Now that her father had returned to England to live and had settled into a comfortable new life with his second wife, Elizabeth, it was doubtful that she would ever learn the truth.

That, of course, didn't mean that she begrudged her father his newfound happiness, nor did she rue the day her stepmother entered her life. No. Though it was true that she was at first intimidated by the woman's beauty and elegance, Elizabeth had soon won her over with her warmth and gentleness. Indeed, she couldn't have asked for a more wonderful stepmother. Instead of trying to replace the mother she had lost, as many women might have done, Elizabeth had assumed the role of friend and mentor, always there for Jane should she seek her counsel, yet respectful enough to let her make her own decisions and learn from her own mistakes. As for Clarissa . . .

Jane urged her mare left onto Berkeley Street, her lips curving into a smile. Darling Rissa. What a blessing she was! Though she dearly loved Philip, who now managed their father's tea-trading business in India, she'd always longed for a sister to whom she could confide her girlish hopes, dreams, and secrets. She had found that sister in Clarissa.

Though four years her junior, pretty, vivacious Rissa was beyond sophisticated for her age. Unlike Jane, who had been educated first by her mother and then by her grandparents, Clarissa had attended the finest schools in England. Her father, Sir Francis Edwardes, a landed baronet, had adored his only child and had lavished attention upon her in a manner that would have quite spoiled a girl of lesser character. Thus Rissa had been a woman, refined and self-assured at twelve, while Jane was still an awkward girl at sixteen. It was only through her stepsister's encouragement and her stepmother's guidance that she'd acquired the polish to enter the *ton*.

The *ton*. Jane sighed, her smile faltering. She'd been only vaguely aware of its existence when Elizabeth had informed her that she must join its exalted ranks. Indeed, all she'd known or cared to know about its grand denizens was what she had observed when they stopped at the village coaching inn on their way to their country estates. And though she'd enjoyed peeking into their elegant vehicles and scrutinizing their London finery, she'd harbored no desire to be like them.

She still didn't. In truth, the only reason she'd consented to a London Season at all was because it meant so much to her father that she have one.

Having amassed an enormous fortune in the tea trade, he had spent the past six years trying to make up for what he viewed as her dreary childhood in Oxcombe. Thus, he'd indulged her with every luxury under the sun. With all that luxury came the rather dubious advantages of a court presentation, courtesy of the patronage of Elizabeth's sister, Mary, who'd had the good fortune to hook a duke, vouchers to Almack's, and instant entrée into the *haut ton*.

Though Jane would have much preferred to pass the Season at the vicarage, spending her days ministering to the poor, tending the sick, and engaging in lively debates with her grandfather, she loved her father and would sooner have en-

dured the torments of hell than hurt him by rejecting his offerings.

Hence, she had spent a year being "finished," as Elizabeth
so delicately termed the grueling process of refinement, and
almost five years suffering the rigors of London society. Talk
about torment! So tedious did she find the *ton* that she would
have begged off attending her fifth Season had Rissa not been
coming out . . . and had she not still harbored hope that Lord
Quentin might notice her.

Her heartbeat tripled, as it always did when she thought of
his lordship. Had her hope at last paid off? Had he finally noticed her? Judging from his interest in her disguise for the
masqued ball, it seemed he had. Would tonight, the night of
the ball, be the night he declared his intentions?

Her mind was working rapturously in that direction when
she arrived home. With her head in the clouds, dreaming
dreams of impassioned declarations and stolen kisses, she
more floated than walked into the house. She was drifting
across the entry hall, imagining a particularly romantic scene
where he pledged his eternal love, when—*smack!*—she col-
lided with something very solid. For a moment she teetered
precariously, her arms flailing wildly as she fought to regain
her balance. Then that something grabbed her and steadied
her.

"Jane." My dear. I am so sorry. I didn't mean to run you
down," she heard her stepmother say through the shattered
haze of her dream. "Rissa awoke with a most dreadful cold,
and I'm afraid I didn't see you in my rush to fetch liquorice
for her sore throat."

That bit of news instantly cleared Jane's mind. "Rissa is ail-
ing?" she squeaked. This was the first time in all the time she
had known her stepsister that she'd taken ill. In view of that
fact, she could only conclude that whatever ailed her must be
very serious indeed. It had to be to have felled one of such a

hearty constitution. Beyond alarmed, she clutched Elizabeth's arm, and inquired urgently, "Have you sent for the doctor?"

Her stepmother smiled faintly and gave her a quick hug. "What a dear you are to worry so."

"Of course I'm worried. How could I not be?" she retorted, returning the hug. "I count Rissa not only as a sister but as my best friend. Why, I would simply die if anything happened to her."

"Well, never you fear. Nothing is going to happen to her," Elizabeth replied in a soothing tone. "All that ails her is a cold, which I can assure you merits neither your concern nor a visit from the doctor. With a bit of rest, she shall be right as rain in a few days' time. Of course, she is terribly disappointed at having to miss the ball tonight."

The ball! Jane had forgotten all about it in her concern over Clarissa. Naturally, she wouldn't go either. She couldn't, not without her stepsister. Promising though the evening was, she knew she wouldn't enjoy herself if Rissa was home in bed, ill and feeling blue over missing the fun.

Sincere though her good intentions were, Jane still couldn't help feeling a twinge of regret as she murmured, "Of course I shall stay home as well and do my best to cheer her," though how she would do that she didn't know. The ball was the event of the Season.

Elizabeth gave her arm a fond squeeze. "If anyone can lift Rissa's spirits, it is you." With that, she was off.

As was Jane. Tossing the train of her riding habit over her arm, she dashed up the stairs to look in on her sick stepsister. Stopping in her own chamber only long enough to wash and change into a simple striped morning gown of blue, pink, and white, she headed for Clarissa's room.

"What!" came her stepsister's uncharacteristically ungracious response to her knock.

"It's Jane. I've come to offer you my company, if you want it."

An explosive sneeze, followed by the sound of nose blowing. "Of course I want it. Always. Do come in."

Promptly, Jane did as directed. Unlike her own bedchamber, which she had chosen to furnish for comfort rather than style, her stepsister's room was a vision of feminine opulence. Decorated in delicate shades of green, coral, and ivory, Rissa's favorite colors, the chamber was appointed with masterpieces selected from Sheraton's drawing book. Though all the furnishings were undeniably splendid, the most spectacular of all was the extravagantly fringed and festooned "Duchesse" bed upon which Rissa lay. It was to that bed that Jane flew.

"Oh, Rissa! You poor, poor dear!" she exclaimed, alarmed anew by her stepsister's pallor. "I am so sorry you are unwell."

"Yes, well, isn't this just the most wretched bit of luck?" Rissa muttered, sitting up. "I go nine years without so much as a sniffle, only to come down with a wicked cold on the day of the most thrilling event of the— the"— she sneezed— "century!"

"I doubt it will be so thrilling as all that," Jane consoled, sitting on the edge of the bed. "Why, the menu shall most probably be just as dismal as Lord Quentin predicts, and I shan't be a whit surprised if the rumors of golden temples, fleecy clouds, and oracles are just that—rumors. We mustn't forget that Lady Kirkham is the hostess, and she is notorious for her cheeseparing ways."

"Only in regards to food," Clarissa retorted, not about to be mollified. "And you know that I never eat at balls."

"That's because your suitors never give you the chance. Indeed, you have yet to leave a ball in slippers that haven't been danced to shreds." She shook her head. "No wonder you're ill. You are no doubt quite as worn out as your slippers."

Rissa emitted a noise halfway between a sneeze and a snort. "I can assure you that I am not at all tired. And if it weren't for this"—she pointed an accusing finger at her red nose—"I would count myself perfectly fit to attend tonight. But, of course, I cannot go looking and sounding so dreadful." She sniffled to illustrate her point.

Dreadful? Jane couldn't help but to feel a twinge of envy as she gazed at her stepsister, a twinge she promptly banished. Even in her current diminished state, Clarissa was beyond beautiful. Like her mother's, her hair was a glorious shade of golden-red, graced with a natural curl that never required paper and tongs. Her eyes, almond-shaped and lushly lashed, were a stunning shade of aquamarine, set in a face as enchanting as it was perfect. Then there was her lovely complexion, which had inspired at least a dozen sonnets thus far that Season. And her figure—

Jane glanced down at her own meager bosom and was struck anew with envy as she compared it to her stepsister's magnificent one. It hardly seemed fair for one person to be blessed with such an abundance of charms while others were left so woefully lacking.

Instantly shamed by her covetous thoughts, she took Rissa's hand in hers and honestly declared, "Your nose could be as red as a cherry and honk like a goose, and you would still be the most sought-after girl in the *ton*." She stared at Clarissa's exquisite face for a beat, then added in a soft, rather wistful voice, "Sometimes I wonder if you realize how truly lovely you are."

Clarissa returned her gaze for a moment, then sighed. "Don't you think that I often wonder the same about you?"

She frowned. "Me?"

Rissa nodded. "I often wonder how you can be so blind to your own beauty."

"Me? Beautiful?" Jane released a shaky laugh. "What stuff and nonsense. I am not the least bit pretty, and we both know it."

"But you are!"

"No, I am not," Jane shot back with finality. "And unless fashion sways toward skinny women with speckled noses and drab brown hair, I am not likely to be considered so anytime soon."

"You are not skinny, but elegantly slender, like a sylph," Clarissa indignantly retorted. "And no one in their right mind would ever pronounce your hair drab. It's an enchanting shade of chestnut, and I shan't hear you utter a single word to the contrary. As for your freckles, they have all but disappeared since you have been using Roman Balsam, and you've completely neglected to take into account your lovely brown eyes. In case you haven't heard, dark eyes are all the rage these days." She shook her head, her expression mulish. "You are quite beautiful. Were you to lift your head long enough to show your face and display the wit I know you to possess, you would steal every heart in the *ton*."

"Rissa," she began, flushing beneath the other girl's praise.

Clarissa slapped her hands over her ears. "No. I shan't listen. Nothing you can say will ever convince me to see you as you see yourself. Indeed, the more you disparage yourself, the more resolved I shall grow to show you and everyone else in the *ton* how very wonderful you are."

Since nothing made her feel quite so pathetic or uncomfortable as when her stepsister promoted her in company that clearly had no interest in her, Jane instantly bit off her ready protest.

Rissa grinned and dropped her hands from her ears. "Good. Now that you've seen the right of the matter, we must decide how you will wear your hair tonight and what you will say to Lord Quentin when he admires your disguise."

"Oh, but I'm not going to the ball," she replied, her voice catching on her regret. "I shall stay home and entertain you. I thought we would play a few rubbers of whist and then—"

"Not go?" Rissa eyed her as if she had just committed an unforgivable faux pas. "But of course you are going. You shall don your lovely rainbow gown and go dazzle Lord Quentin."

"I couldn't," she demurred, halfheartedly.

"Rubbish. You can and you will. I am counting on you to go so you can tell me all about it tomorrow."

"Your mother can do that just as well as I," Jane countered, though the argument sounded weak, even to her own ears.

Rissa shook her head. "Mama isn't nearly as observant as you, and I want to know every little detail—who wore what, who danced with whom, who is gossiping about whom or what, how the ballroom was decorated . . . everything!" She latched on to Jane's arm and peered earnestly at her face. "Do say you will go. I shall be ever so desolate if you do not."

Jane returned her gaze, hating herself for the joy she felt at Rissa's insistence. Guiltily vowing to note every last tidbit about everyone and everything at the ball, she yielded. "As you wish, but I shall stay only long enough to see and hear what is what, then I will return home and amuse you with the particulars."

Rissa nodded and lay back on her pillows, visibly pleased by her victory.

Jane smiled. Tonight might be her dreamed-of night after all.

"What do you think, Miss Wentworth?" Miss Parson, Jane's abigail, indicated her mistress's elaborately coiffed hair.

Jane nodded and smiled, relieved that her hairstyling ordeal had at last come to an end. Unlike most of the women of the *ton*, who spent hours every day being curled, combed, and pinned, Jane found primping tedious and flatly refused to endure it. Hence, she wore her long, wavy hair simply knotted atop her head for all but the most formal of occasions. It wasn't the most becoming of styles, true, but as she had learned from disappointing experience, the resulting improvement of anything fancier was far too minute to merit the effort of its creation.

Or so she'd thought. As Jane examined her reflection in her dressing-table mirror, she wondered if she'd perhaps been too hasty in dismissing the virtues of primping. For while it was true that she would never be a great beauty, her eyes did look rather nice framed by those curls. And the ringlets dangling over her shoulder, didn't they make her neck look a bit longer and more swanlike?

Feeling rather pleased with herself, she turned to Clarissa, who lay elegantly draped upon the nearby chaise longue, directing the proceedings. "Well?" she inquired breathlessly.

Rissa tipped her head first this way, then that, a small frown creasing her brow as she examined Jane. Then she grinned and replied with a laugh, "But of course you look beautiful. All you need to be utterly exquisite is a soupçon of powder, rouge, and lip paste."

"Paint?" Jane gaped at her stepsister, appalled. "Oh, but I cannot!"

Rissa made a dismissive hand motion. "Of course you can. All the ladies paint, even those who claim they don't."

"But I have never—"

Another wave of the hand, this one accompanied by three sneezes. "There is always a first time for everything. Besides, this is a masqued ball. It is perfectly acceptable for one to paint one's face as a part of one's disguise."

Jane dubiously eyed the collection of boxes, pots, and hare's feet her abigail had laid before her. "Well—"

"Have I ever directed you wrong in these matters?"

She had to admit that if anyone knew the rules of fashion, it was Rissa, and Rissa would never steer her wrong. Though still plagued with misgiving, she nodded.

Oh, well, she sighed to herself, as Miss Parson attacked her face with rice powder and puff. It shall be easy enough to remove the paint should it not be to my liking.

But she did like it, very much. Her freckles had all but disappeared beneath the dusting of powder, leaving her skin looking as lustrous and creamy as Rissa's. As for the rouge and lip paste, well, were those really her cheekbones, so high and elegant? And when had her lips become so fashionably full?

"Perfect!" Rissa crowed, clapping her hands in delight. "You are a regular pink of the *ton*, Jane. Indeed, I shan't be at all surprised if your success at the ball tonight serves as prime gossip on the morrow."

Jane smiled at her own reflection, feeling pretty for the first time in her life. Perhaps she wasn't so very wrong in believing that tonight might be the night his lordship would start paying her his much-longed-for court.

"I have been telling her for years that she could be attractive, but she refused to allow me to show her," Miss Parson declared, visibly pleased with her handiwork. "Perhaps now she will let me do my duty without protest."

Clarissa laughed. "After tonight, Jane shall no doubt be eager and begging for your services. The costume now, if you please, Miss Parson. I simply cannot wait to see how she looks in it."

As the abigail went to Jane's adjoining bedchamber to fetch the gown and headdress, Rissa rose from the chaise and moved to the bench on which her stepsister sat. Still smiling,

Jane moved to one side, making room for Rissa to sit beside her.

For a long while they sat there in silence, arms twined affectionately around each other's waist, Clarissa's head resting on Jane's shoulder as they admired the pretty picture they made in the mirror. Finally Rissa gave her a hug, murmuring, "We must have a portrait made of you just like this, so you and Lord Quentin's"—another squeeze—"grandchildren can marvel over how very lovely their grandmama was in her youth."

Jane met Rissa's sparkling gaze in the mirror, her smile growing pensive. "Perhaps I am a fool, but I have the queerest feeling that tonight will be the night I win his lordship's heart."

"Then you shall," Rissa declared. "You can do anything you wish if you truly believe it possible. Haven't I always told you so?"

"Yes. Unfortunately my tongue has thus far remained unconvinced of that theory." She sighed. "Oh, Rissa, whatever shall I say to his lordship if he does notice and admire me? You know what a stammering ninny I am in his presence."

Clarissa sneezed, then sniffled. "You needn't say anything. Stand with your head held high and simply accept his tributes as your due."

"But I will have to say something eventually."

Her stepsister blew her nose. "Perhaps, but not until after he has thoroughly extolled your charms. At that point you must slap his arm lightly with your fan and coyly protest his praise by murmuring something like, 'You are far too kind, my lord,' or 'I shall blush if you continue going on so.'"

Jane considered her instructions for a beat, then slowly nodded. She should be able to manage those few words and the slap easily enough . . . unless, of course, she froze completely, which was always a dreadful possibility.

As if reading her thoughts, Clarissa reassured her, "You shall do splendidly, I just know you shall. If, however, you begin to feel overwhelmed and find yourself in need of a moment to gather your wits, fan yourself, as if suddenly overheated, and beg his lordship to fetch you a glass of punch."

"And if I'm still in a state when he returns?" she queried, all too aware of the paralyzing effects of her nerves.

"Why, you shall drink the punch and tell yourself that you are not shy, retiring Jane Wentworth, but bold, dazzling Iris, Goddess of the Rainbow. As Iris—" Whatever she was about to say was abruptly cut off by a shriek from the next room, followed by shouts of, "Bad puss! Wicked, evil puss!"

"Scratch!" Jane groaned, as she and Clarissa rushed into her bedchamber. Scratch was the skinny black kitten the neighbor's cook had tossed out in the street a month earlier, contending it to be as wicked as Old Scratch himself. Unable to bear the thought of it starving or being run over by a carriage, Jane had promptly adopted it as her pet. Though the animal had proved every bit as mischievous as the cook claimed, she'd instantly loved it and was now seldom without its company.

When she saw what it had done this time, she almost regretted her charity. Her costume was ruined, utterly and irredeemably. The gown, fashioned of silk the color of the rain-washed sky and cunningly embellished with a fall of paste diamond raindrops, lay in a rumpled heap before the fireplace, its delicate bodice shredded by tiny claws.

"Oh, Scratch, how could you?" she wailed, running to where the kitten and Miss Parson were engaged in a tug-of-war over her headdress. The abigail had won possession of the jeweled rainbow crown, while Scratch, who had sought refuge beneath the bed, retained two-thirds of the attached six-foot-long rainbow veil.

Muttering several grisly threats under her breath, Miss Parson dropped to her knees and hauled the wayward kitten out of its shelter by the scruff of its neck. With the furry vandal dangling from one hand and the remnants of the headdress from the other, she rose, exclaiming, "Perhaps you will listen now when I tell you to get rid of this—this"—she gave Scratch a fierce shake—"menace!"

The kitten meowed piteously in its terror, its scrawny legs flailing impotently in the air as it struggled to escape.

Jane's heart, and anger, melted at the sight of its panic. Snatching it from Miss Parson, she clutched the tiny animal protectively to her breast, stroking its trembling body as she countered, "You mustn't blame poor Scratch, none of this is his fault. Not truly."

"Oh?" The abigail braced her hands on her hips, eyeing her cynically. "And who, pray tell, is at fault if not *poor* Scratch?"

"I am. I was careless in leaving the costume lying on the bed. I should have remembered his fondness for attacking anything that glitters, and put it back in the clothespress when I had finished admiring it."

Miss Parson made an exasperated noise. "It's a sad day indeed when a household must revolve around the vices of one wicked cat."

"Scratch is not wicked, and using prudence to circumvent a regrettable incident hardly qualifies as the sort of indulgence you imply," Jane shot back. She was well versed in this argument. "All I am saying is that we must exercise the same sort of caution with Scratch that one would employ in keeping forbidden objects out of a small child's grasp."

"Yes, well, and small children are usually spanked when they willfully destroy such objects," Miss Parson retorted. "A practice that I strongly suggest exercising on that animal."

Jane clasped the kitten yet tighter. "I shall not! Under no circumstances will I spank Scratch, and I most certainly shall

never allow my children to be struck, no matter their crime.
I—"

"You will simply have to wear my costume," Rissa cut in.

Jane tore her gaze away from Miss Parson to stare blankly
at her stepsister. "Pardon?"

Rissa held up the ruined gown. "You must wear my costume to the ball. This one is beyond all prayer, I fear."

The ball. Of course. She had forgotten all about it in her
rush to defend her pet.

"It should fit you well enough," Rissa continued, sweeping
Jane with an assessing look. "We are the same height, and the
color shall be quite becoming to you."

Jane returned her stepsister's regard dubiously. "The color
and length might suit, but"—she dropped her gaze lower to
cast a meaningful look at Rissa's bountiful bosom—"our figures are in no way similar."

Rissa shrugged. "It should be simple enough to make the
necessary adjustments. What say you, Miss Parson?"

The abigail seemed to consider her suggestion, then nodded. "I will do whatever is possible."

"Impossible," Miss Parson declared, eyeing Jane's bosom
with an air of defeat.

"At least impossible without three days' work," concurred
Miss Stephens, Rissa's abigail. "All those stars must be removed before the bodice can be taken in, and then reapplied
in the pattern of the constellations of the zodiac."

Jane peered down at the sagging midnight-blue velvet
bodice, more miserably aware of her shortcomings than ever.
Even if there were time to take it in, there would never be
enough room left to replace all twelve constellations. No. If
ever there was an eight-constellation bosom, it was hers, and
that was an optimistic assessment. Her spirits sinking to the

dregs of despair, she sighed and said, "Well, that is that, then. I suppose I have no choice but to stay home."

"Of course you have a choice," Rissa countered, abandoning her post beside the cheval mirror to approach her stepsister. "A most amusing one."

"Indeed?" This was from Miss Stephens, who was all too familiar with the often disastrous results of her charge's schemes.

Rissa came to a stop before Jane, nodding. "We will pad the bodice and you shall go as me."

"Pardon?" Jane said with a frown, wondering if her stepsister had taken a fever and was now delirious.

"We will pad the bodice and you shall go as me," Rissa repeated. "Just imagine everyone's surprise at the unmasking when they discover that the girl they assumed to be me disguised as Urania is in fact you disguised as me. Why, the entire *ton* will be abuzz over your cleverness. And you, dear Jane, shall be the success of the evening." She clasped her hands together, clearly enthralled by the idea. "Do say you will do it."

"I-I am certain it will never work," Jane demurred, daunted by the notion of impersonating her stepsister. "No one could ever mistake me for you."

"They could and they shall. The headdress will completely conceal your hair, though it will be a terrible shame to hide that lovely style." She shot Miss Parson a regretful look. "And the mask will cover most of your face. You have only to do and say as we discussed earlier, and no one will be the wiser."

"But even with the mask, people will note the difference in my eye color," she argued. She couldn't pose as Rissa, she simply couldn't . . . could she?

Rissa plucked the headdress, a fabulous creation of shooting comets and swirling constellations, from a nearby chair and held it up. "Your eyes will be shadowed by these," she ran her finger across the face-framing fringe of silvery stars, "hence, no one will think twice about them appearing dark. Besides, as you, yourself, pointed out, Lady Kirkham is a cheeseparer. She shall no doubt scrimp on candles, which will leave the ballroom far too gloomy to accurately note the color of anyone's eyes."

"Well—"

"Say yes, Jane. Do say yes," Rissa begged, imploring her with wide, pleading eyes.

Jane returned her gaze somberly as she considered. She had often wondered how it would feel to be Rissa, to be flattered and admired and sought after by the *ton*. Tonight was her chance, most probably her only one, to satisfy that curiosity.

It was also a chance to be a success. Lord Quentin couldn't help but to admire her if the plan went as well as Rissa imagined. A thrill of excitement tingled down her spine at the thought of his lordship praising her cleverness and gazing at her with the accompanying adoration.

Could she do it?

"Tonight is your night," Rissa murmured, enticing her like the serpent tempting Eve. "Do it, and it could change your life forever."

Dare she?

"Say yes, Jane," Rissa urged.

"Yes," she whispered, responding not to her stepsister's prompting, but to that of her heart. It, too, told her that tonight could be the night . . . the beginning of a forever with Lord Quentin.

Chapter 3

"I cannot recall ever having to sit in such a tiresome crush of carriages," Jane's father muttered as their barouche crawled nearer to their destination. For three blocks and the better part of an hour they had inched through the long line of vehicles, awaiting their turn to be deposited before the Kirkham mansion. Now that they were almost there, Jane felt queasy with nerves.

What in the world had possessed her to consent to this daft charade? No one with eyes in their head was going to believe that she was her stepsister, not ever! They would take one look at her and instantly see beyond her padding, paint, and mask, and know exactly who she was and what game she played. Then—then—why, then she'd be laughed from the ballroom, disgraced and branded as the brass-faced ninny she was.

All in front of Lord Quentin.

Her queasiness deepened into nausea at that thought. She couldn't do it. She simply could not! She would plead a headache and beg to be taken home immediately. Of course Rissa was bound to be terribly disappointed, but—

The creeping carriage lurched to an abrupt stop, jolting her mind from her musings and her body to the edge of the seat. Anxiously worrying her lower lip with her teeth, she peered out the window.

Everywhere she looked she saw masqueraders milling

about. Some laughed and frolicked; others clustered in gossip-mongering groups; here and there a person struck a playful pose, gaily showing off a fetching costume. Beyond the throng, darkly silhouetted in the blazing windows of the grand Kirkham house, were the dancing figures of what looked to be the whole of London. Certain that she was about to be sick, Jane looked away.

"At last," her father grumbled, lifting his domino from his lap and slipping it over his head. Unlike his gay wife, who was fancifully attired as Nike, the winged Goddess of Victory, her father's only concession to what he grumpily viewed as "the damfool spectacle" was a double-sided domino with a half-mask depicting comedy in the front and a full one depicting tragedy in back.

"Well?" he muttered, turning to his wife for an inspection.

Elizabeth laughed at the incongruity between the smiling mask on his upper face and his scowling mouth below. Dropping a kiss on his down-turned lips, she teased, "Such a bear. With that fierce frown you should remove your mask and go as ill-fated Callisto."

As always happened when she kissed him, his lips instantly curved into a boyish grin. Growling like the bear she accused him of being, he drew her into his embrace and retorted, "Callisto, if you recall, was a woman before becoming a bear. And I, madame, am every inch a man. Or must I remind you of the fact?"

"Please do refresh my memory, sir," she murmured, to which he responded by thoroughly kissing her.

Jane smiled wistfully at their tender game. How many times had she dreamed of playing so with Lord Quentin? Of being kissed by him with such passion? She'd had such hopes that Rissa's scheme would prompt the beginning of a forever of such frolics, but—

Her smile faded. But she had lost her nerve to enact it.

And most probably her only chance to dazzle his lordship.

Loathing herself for her cowardice, she alternately scolded and pleaded with herself, desperately trying to buoy her courage. But, alas, it was no use. She simply hadn't the pluck to risk the charade. Bleakly resigning herself to a lifetime of regret, and a severe scolding from Rissa, she opened her mouth to excuse herself from the ball.

Before, however, she could utter a word, the door was flung open and a head of thick, coppery hair crowned with a circlet of gilt laurel leaves popped in. Lord Henson, of course. No doubt he'd been lying in wait of their carriage, hoping to gain an advantage in the evening's race to woo Rissa.

"Mr. and Mrs. Wentworth. Miss Edwardes. Recognized your carriage and wanted to be the first to welcome you to Mount Olympus." He spared the elder Wentworths the briefest of nods before eagerly turning his attention to Jane. "Say, Miss Edwardes. I was wondering if—" Whatever he was about to say was cut off as he was roughly jostled aside.

Lord Beveridge's fleshy head, resplendently adorned with an enormous gold crown, appeared in his place. "Greetings! Greetings from good King Midas!" he boomed, extending his hand to Jane.

She gaped at the hand, her eyes wide with astonishment. Each plump finger bore an enormous ring, the middle one two, all magnificently wrought in gold and set with precious gems. No doubt they were part of the legendary Beveridge jewel collection, worn in hopes of tempting Clarissa to favor his suit.

"Ah, Miss Edwardes. Mr. and Mrs. Wentworth. A pleasure. A very great pleasure indeed." This was from Mr. Cuddimore, whose balding blond head appeared over Beveridge's shoulder.

Beveridge snorted. "If you don't mind, Cuddimore, I was having a word with Miss Edwardes."

Lord Henson reappeared over his other shoulder, the purple of his angry face clashing violently with his red hair. "I was speaking to her first. So if *you* don't mind, Beveridge—"

"Miss Edwardes is here, you say?" Lord Witley's head, festooned by goat horns, materialized in the space above Beveridge's, knocking the other man's crown askew.

Beveridge shot him an infuriated look and straightened his crown in one wrathful motion, while the other two men eyed each other as if in doing so each could make the other vanish.

Elizabeth laughed. "My, my! Such a reception! As you can see, it has left the muse Urania quite speechless."

Jane froze as the men turned their attention to her, breathlessly awaiting them to see through her disguise and denounce her for the impostor she was. Instead they smiled the ingratiating smiles they always wore in Rissa's presence and gazed at her as if she were indeed a mythical deity.

Her jaw slackened in her amazement. Goodness! Could it be that she had actually fooled them? Another glance at their faces, worshipful and full of yearning, assured her that she had.

Her confidence rose a notch. Perhaps there was hope for the scheme after all. Of course, the light in the carriage wasn't the best. And she had yet to speak. Still—

Beveridge waved his bejeweled hand beneath her nose again, making the gleaming gems dance in the lamplight. "If I might be so bold, Miss Edwardes, I wish to beg the honor of escorting you into the ball."

"I was about to beg that very thing when Beveridge so rudely usurped me," Lord Henson interjected, glaring at the adversary in question.

"No. You must allow me to escort you," Cuddimore cut in. "There is a matter of some importance that I most urgently need to discuss with you."

"No. Me. I learned to play a merry tune on my pipes, just for you." Witley waved his pan pipes in the air, again displacing Beveridge's crown.

Jane glanced from one hopeful face to the other in dismay, uncertain what to do or say. Though part of her still longed to plead a headache and scurry home to safety, another part was tempted to throw caution to the wind and play the game through.

Could she?

Should she?

It was Elizabeth who settled her indecision. "You shall all escort her," she declared. "It is the only fair way I can see to resolve this."

Though the gentlemen looked far from pleased, they all nodded and murmured their assent.

"Well, then, unless you wish to keep us trapped in our carriage all night, I suggest that you all move away from the door and allow us to step down," her father snapped, clearly annoyed by the whole scene.

"Yes, do move away," a new, exceedingly superior voice drawled. It was the pompous duke of Goolding, who had appeared next to Witley. "How am I to hand Miss Edwardes down with you all blocking the way?"

"You!" the other men echoed in unison.

"But of course," he returned, unperturbed by the murderous glances being stabbed his way. "I am of the highest rank, you know."

"But I have the plumpest pockets," Beveridge protested, waving his ring-laden hand to illustrate his point.

"You are also the most vulgar, to mention money in the

presence of ladies," Goolding countered. "Far too vulgar to keep company with a lady of Miss Edwardes's sensibilities."

"Now you wait just one blasted moment, Goolding," Henson snarled, his face now darkened to the color of an overripe plum. "If you think you can waltz in here—"

"Enough!" roared her father.

Lord Henson fell abruptly silent, as did Witley, Cuddimore, and Beveridge, who stood airing their views in a blathering chorus. As for Goolding, he crossed his arms and eyed the other men with visible disdain.

For a long moment her father simply looked at the now hushed assembly, his eyes narrowed and his lips set in a hard line as he sternly glanced from face to face. Finally he emitted an irritated noise and declared, "I shall hand her down. And if I hear another quarrelsome word from any of you, I shall also escort her into the ball and claim all her dances for myself. Do I make myself clear?"

"Abundantly," Goolding retorted with a sniff, while the others nodded vigorously.

He nodded back. "Excellent. Now please step away and wait by the walkway. I wish a private word with my daughter before relinquishing her into your company."

When they had done as bidden, leaving a dazed and trampled-looking footman in their wake, Jane's father turned to her and growled, "I hope you know what you are about, my girl. If you ask me, this deception is nothing but a design for disaster."

Her stepmother made a clicking noise behind her teeth. "Gloomy bear." She cast him a fond but exasperated look, then leaned forward and took both Jane's hands in hers. "You ignore him, dear, and go have a marvelous time. There is no doubt whatsoever in my mind that your joke will be a triumph."

"I-I don't know," she murmured, stricken anew with uncertainty. "Perhaps Father is right. Perhaps I should plead a headache and go home."

"Go home?" Elizabeth released a short, musical laugh. "Nonsense. You deserve a bit of fun, and you shall have it if I have to drag you into the ballroom myself. Besides, just imagine Rissa's disappointment were you to arrive home with nothing to report. She is so counting on you to attend the ball so that she might experience it through your recollections." She gave Jane's hands a squeeze. "Do it for Rissa, if not for yourself."

Jane gazed first at her stepmother, who smiled and nodded, then out at the waiting gentlemen. The last thing in the world she wished to do was disappoint Rissa, especially after she'd promised her a complete account of the ball. Besides that, she rather liked the idea of being a success. Lord Quentin couldn't help but to notice her, really notice her, should she triumph this evening.

It was that last that made her pull her hands out of her stepmother's and extend her right one to her father. "If you please, Papa, I am ready to go inside now."

Elizabeth clapped her delight. "Very good, Jane. Excellent decision. Just you wait and see. Tonight shall be a night you will remember for the rest of your life."

"I have an unsettling suspicion that you are correct," her father muttered, taking his daughter's hand.

"She has arrived," Oxley whispered to Quentin. He nodded once, then continued trailing the hopelessly silly, but brilliantly dowered Miss Sibble through the crush.

Quentin glanced toward the door, hungry for the sight of his beloved. On the threshold stood not Miss Edwardes, but a tiny girl disguised as Atalanta, who giggled while a swain dressed as Hippomenes tossed golden apples before her. Smiling faintly at their romantic play, he scanned the crowd to their left. No Miss Edwardes there, either. He sighed. Where was she, anyway?

Group by milling group, he continued to search the glittering assembly, his eyes narrowing as he scrutinized every costumed form and skimmed the sparkling forest of headdresses. He paused once to examine a particularly shapely young lady, only to dismiss her in the next instant. Not only was the girl not disguised as Urania, she lacked Miss Edwardes's elegance and grace.

When at last he was certain he'd combed the entire crowd, he worked his way across the room to Oxley to inquire as to her whereabouts.

"Will you look at that?" his friend muttered, scowling at Miss Sibble, brazenly flirting with a Trojan warrior. "And after she wheedled me into coming as Apollo to her Daphne."

Quentin shrugged one shoulder. "She probably forgot she wheedled you. Miss Sibble isn't exactly the most wide awake of females, you know. Indeed, I heard tell that she climbed into Lord Bedell's *green barouche* after the Jeppesons' soiree last week, thinking it to be her father's carriage. As you know, Sir Sibble owns a *white landau*."

Oxley chuckled. "She also gets lost in the Burlington Arcade, and believes a shilling to be worth more than a pound."

"And you're actually considering courting her?" he exclaimed, incredulous.

Another chuckle. "Well, they do say that a shatterbrained wife is more easily controlled than a clever one. Speaking of wives, have you spoken with Miss Edwardes yet?"

Quentin shook his head. "Are you quite certain she's here? I seem unable to find her."

"That's because she is hidden by her usual gaggle of goose-brained suitors." His friend nodded toward Beveridge, splendidly garbed as King Midas, and a man whom Quentin recognized as Witley, dressed as Pan. "There. If you look just to the right of Witley's horns, you shall see the top of a head-dress of stars. That, my dear fellow, is Miss Edwardes." A wicked grin. "Or should I say, the future Lady Clarissa Somerville?"

Quentin smiled, liking the sound of that last. "Did you find the statue?"

"It is exactly where you said it is. I thought—"

Whatever his friend said was lost on Quentin, for at that moment Miss Edwardes's throng of admirers parted, distracting him with a glimpse of her. She looked magnificent tonight. Glorious. A vision of dark spangled velvet and pale silken skin. The sight of her left him quite breathless and taut with desire.

As he watched, she laughed at something someone costumed as Heracles said, and he was certain he heard the sultry music of her mirth drift through the crowd. It beckoned to him, beguiling him with a sudden, burning urgency to possess her. Without conscious thought he moved toward her, drawn like Odysseus to the enchantress Circe.

"Somerville?" Someone grasped his arm, halting him.

He glanced at that someone in bewilderment.

Grinning, Oxley grasped his chin and snapped his mouth shut.

Quentin frowned. What the—?

Then his wits returned and he felt himself flush. "Bloody hell. Was I gawking?"

"Like an unlicked cub at a Cyprian ball," his friend replied with a chuckle.

He groaned. "Good God. I must be losing my mind."

"Yes, well," Oxley gave his arm a sympathetic pat, "never fear. I hear tell that such insanity is instantly cured by the marriage bed. Speaking of marriage, I was informing you of the change in our plan when you went all slack-jawed and calf-eyed."

"Change?" Quentin echoed, unable to resist stealing another glance at his beloved. The wall of her suitors had closed again, leaving him with a decidedly uninspiring view of manly backs.

"Somerville, please." Oxley snapped his fingers beneath Quentin's nose. "Plenty of time to gape at the girl once you are wed."

He met his friend's gaze with an apologetic smile. "Sorry."

The other man grunted. "Yes, well, you will be even more so if our plan doesn't succeed, so I suggest that you heed what I say."

"You have my complete attention," he solemnly vowed. And it was true. With Miss Edwardes out of view, there was nothing in the room to divert him.

His friend eyed him skeptically, clearly expecting him to fall into another moonstruck daze. When it was apparent that he indeed had Quentin's attention, he moved nearer and murmured, "I have decided against asking Kirkham to play guide."

"Oh?"

A nod. "As you might recall, his lordship has an inordinate fear of scandal and would no doubt go to great measures to avoid having his name attached to this one. Thus, he would most probably herd everyone away from you and Miss Edwardes should he spy you engaging in an—*ahem!*—exchange of affections."

Quentin considered for a moment, then nodded. Kirkham was a prig. "So, what do you propose to do instead?"

"I thought that I would strike up a conversation with Aldgate, Wylde, and Pickett, all of whom, you know, are notoriously loose-tongued, and invite them to view the statue with me. That way I can make certain that we catch you and Miss Edwardes in the—uh—act."

"Hmm . . . yes. I do believe that that shall be for the best." He nodded. "Good. Then it appears that all is ready. I have only to lure Miss Edwardes to the garden for us to begin."

"Any thoughts on how you will do that?"

"As you know, she has her suitors assigned to a fixed order of dances. Mine are the Scotch reels and the first waltz. I thought to extol the glories of the oracle as we waltz, then offer to escort her outside so she can try it for herself."

"And when she discovers that there is no oracle?"

"Why, then I shall declare my love and confess the lie for what it is: a ploy to get her alone. From there, well," he grinned, "you shall just have to use your imagination."

Oxley frowned and glanced about him. "Speaking of being alone, where is Crowley? He agreed to squire the step-sister, didn't he?"

"He hasn't arrived yet, and yes, he did agree to squire her . . . to the tune of ten pounds." Ten pounds he could ill afford. As Quentin had discovered years ago, twelve thousand a year was a woefully inadequate amount when it came to enjoying the Season. He heaved an inward sigh. Ah, well. If all went as planned it would be money well spent, for not only would he have Miss Edwardes, he would have her generous dowry as well.

His friend snorted. "I do hope you had the wits not to pay him in advance?"

"Of course. I know what a wastrel he is."

"Then we needn't worry about him not showing. Desperate as he is for funds, he'd go to hell and woo the devil himself if someone promised him ten pounds to do so." Oxley paused, again looking about him. "By the way, I don't believe I've seen the stepsister this evening. You said she was to be disguised as—ur—" He snapped his fingers as he sought to recall.

"Iris, Goddess of the Rainbow," Quentin supplied.

"Right. Iris. Then we must look for a girl dressed like a rainbow hovering near Miss Edwardes."

"Or watching from the chairs along the wall. She often sits aside, observing the *ton.*"

Oxley arched one eyebrow in sardonic wonder. "You seem to know rather a lot about the little frump."

Quentin shrugged. "Only because it pleases Miss Edwardes for her suitors to notice the girl. Indeed, the only advantage I can claim over her other beaux is that Miss Wentworth seems to approve of me."

"Well, if she dotes on the chit as much—ah, there is Crowley now." Oxley gestured to a tall, exquisitely dressed dandy who had just entered the room. While not of the most steady nature, Viscount Crowley was exceedingly charming and thus quite popular with the ladies. "I see that he has spent his fee in advance," he added, holding his quizzing glass to the eye slit of his sun-shaped domino. "Isn't that a new waistcoat he's wearing?"

Quentin signaled to the viscount, who nodded and pushed his way through the crowd toward them. "I couldn't say. He has at least a hundred of them."

"Somerville. Oxley," the viscount hailed, coming to a stop before them. "A wonder I found you. Can't recall the last time I saw such a crush. Must be half of England here."

"Mmm. Yes. Splendid turnout, very splendid indeed," Quentin agreed, searching the room for Miss Wentworth.

"Do you see her yet?" Oxley murmured.

"See who?" Crowley inquired.

"Miss Wentworth, of course." This was from Oxley.

The viscount frowned. "Who?"

"Miss Wentworth. The chit you are to amuse," Quentin reminded him.

"Right. I had forgotten her name." Crowley reached beneath his nondescript domino to scratch the bridge of his nose. "Hmm. Can't say I know the girl. However, I might be able to help spot her if you tell me what she looks like."

"Brown hair," Quentin said.

"No figure," Oxley contributed.

"Disguised as Iris," Quentin added.

The viscount blinked. "Who?"

"The Rainbow Goddess," he and Oxley snapped in unison. "I already told you about her disguise," Quentin adjoined irritably. Bloody hell. Perhaps they should have chosen someone with less charm and more wit for the task.

"Oh. Right. Sorry." Crowley looked momentarily nonplussed, then turned and began to scrutinize the crowd.

Quentin and Oxley followed suit. After several moments they turned back to each other and exchanged a shrug. "Hell if I see her," Oxley muttered. "Perhaps she is in the retiring room."

"Or maybe she didn't come." This was from Crowley, who looked exceedingly down in the mouth at the notion of losing ten pounds.

"She always comes," Quentin said, glancing about the room again. Where was the blasted chit, anyway? It would never do to lure Miss Edwardes out to the garden only to have the stepsister scurry out of some dark corner and ruin the whole plan. After scanning the crowd three more times, he emitted a frustrated noise and gave up. If she didn't appear soon, he'd have no choice but to—

"Why, I shall ask Miss Edwardes where she is," he finished out loud.

"Pardon?" Oxley murmured.

"I shall go to Miss Edwardes and inquire after her stepsister," he said with a meaningful lift of his brows.

Oxley stared at him for a moment, then chuckled. "Now why didn't I think of that? Not only will your inquiry serve to gain the information we seek, your feigned concern shall further your cause with your beloved."

Quentin's smile broadened into a grin. "Exactly."

Chapter 4

Jane had never dreamed that being a success would be so very exhausting. Having danced almost constantly during the hour she'd been at the ball, she now held a new appreciation of her stepsister's stamina. For all her delicate looks, Rissa must have the constitution of an ox to have survived a month of such rigors before falling ill.

Feeling on the verge of collapse herself, she smiled wanly at something Lord Dutnall said and discreetly shifted her weight from one aching foot to the other. Oh, what she wouldn't give to sit by herself for a moment to gather both her strength and her thoughts. But, of course, she couldn't. She was Clarissa Edwardes tonight, toast of the *ton*, and toasts of the *ton* never sat at balls, especially not alone. Besides, if her joke turned her into the success Rissa anticipated, she would have to get used to dancing the night away. Might as well start doing so now.

"I say, Miss Edwardes, you look fetching this evening," cooed Lord Aldgate, as he and his friend Mr. Pickett sidled up to her. Both wore intricately tucked gold-and-white tunics with gilt laurel leaf crowns atop their fashionably coiffed heads.

"Fetching," Pickett echoed, lifting his quizzing glass to peer at her cleavage. "Mmm. Yes." He licked his thin lips as if in anticipation of a tasty treat. "Very fetching indeed."

Discomfited and more than a little affronted, Jane snapped

open her fan and indignantly blocked his view. Dreadful . . . hateful! . . . man. Not only was his leering insulting in the extreme, if he stared hard enough, he was bound to discern her padding and know her to be an impostor. Then her joke would be spoiled, for next to Lord Aldgate, Pickett had the loosest tongue in London and would no doubt spread word of her deception throughout the ballroom.

Though she now felt certain that the disclosure wouldn't bring her disgrace, the fact that she'd been unable to maintain her charade until the unmasking at midnight would most definitely disqualify the joke as a triumph. And she so wanted to be a triumph for Lord Quentin.

Her heart missed a beat at the thought of his lordship. Though he had yet to seek her out, he had numbered among the seven other couples with whom she and Lord Beveridge had danced the first cotillion. Talk about being flustered! So handsome did he look, garbed all in black, as befitted his disguise as Morpheus, that she had been rendered quite clumsy in her awe. Indeed, it was a wonder that no one had realized her deception then, as she'd tripped through the changes, for Rissa danced with the grace of an angel.

Jane felt herself blush at her remembrance of her poor performance. No wonder his lordship had yet to claim her for a dance. He probably feared for his toes.

"Are you overly warm, Miss Edwardes?" This was from the notoriously unimaginative Lord Fitton, whose entire disguise comprised a generic black domino.

"Warm, yes. Your face is the color of raw liver," piped in the less than tactful Witley.

"Of course she is warm, you dolts. She's fanning herself, isn't she?" Pickett snapped, moving to her side to resume his leering from a new angle.

She shifted her fan, again foiling him. He took a step back and continued his lascivious inspection over her shoulder.

At wit's end, she glanced at the musicians, hoping to be rescued by a dance. Though most of the men had finished the beverages the footmen had served them, it was apparent from the way they chatted among themselves that it would be several minutes before they resumed playing. Blast!

"Er, perhaps some punch might help cool you," suggested Lord Henson, eager, as always, to ingratiate himself to Rissa.

Jane started to shake her head, revolted by the thought of the Kirkham's inferior Negus. Then inspiration struck and she nodded instead. "A glass of punch would be very nice indeed." She smiled sweetly and looked over her shoulder at the lewdly engrossed Pickett. "Might I impose upon you to fetch it for me, Mr. Pickett?"

"But it's my turn," Witley protested, pouting like a babe denied a sweet. "Endicott fetched it last time, which makes it my turn. I always follow Endicott in the punch order, remember?"

Jane sighed. She'd forgotten all about Rissa's punch order, of which, unfortunately, neither Pickett nor Aldgate were a part. To be included in her stepsister's rotation of privileges a man must be officially courting her. Pickett and Aldgate were far too busy with their gossip and debauchery to court anyone.

Seeing no other choice, she nodded her concession to the order. As she did so, she wondered if there was one for fetching cake. Since Rissa never ate during balls, perhaps—

"Miss Edwardes." The voice, rich as port and smooth as claret, washed through her like a flush from fine wine, warming and stimulating her in a way that left her breathless. It was the voice she had longed to hear all evening. Lord Quentin, at last.

Helpless to do more, she looked up and smiled at the glorious man before her.

He sketched a courtly bow and smiled back.

Sinful, that's what it is, sinful that one man can be so very beautiful, she thought, captivated by sight of his dimples and strong white teeth.

As she stood spellbound, greedily drinking in the sight of him, he lifted the hand dangling at her side and pressed a lingering kiss to her palm. Even through her gloves she could feel the heat of his lips, and something inside her melted at the sensation. As she continued to stare at him, helpless to look away, he lifted his heavy fringe of lashes and met her gaze.

The melted something within her instantly turned molten. His eyes had darkened from their usual vibrant amethyst to a deep, passion-drugged violet, and for the first time in her life Jane knew the heady thrill of seeing a man look at her with desire.

Lord Quentin desired her. An unfamiliar sensation swept through her at that realization, one of fierce, feminine power that quite banished her shyness. Thus emboldened, she released a throaty laugh and lightly scolded, "My dearest Lord Quentin, at last. I was beginning to fear that I had lost your heart to another."

He lifted his lips from her hand, smiling faintly. "And would you have mourned the loss, Miss Edwardes?"

"Keenly, my lord, very keenly, indeed," she whispered, speaking from the depths of her soul. "For there is nothing I cherish more than your heart."

"Then I pledge it to you forever," he declared, pressing her hand to his chest.

"Say, Somerville, do release her hand so she can drink her punch." It was Witley, bearing the Kirkhams' typically meager ration of watery Negus.

"Yes, do release it, Somerville. It isn't at all sporting to monopolize Miss Edwardes in such a manner," Goolding growled, visibly resentful of the other man's favor.

"Not sporting," echoed Pickett in a distracted tone.

Jane glanced over her shoulder, her awareness of him renewed. To her dismay, he still studied her breasts as though they were a curious display at the British Museum. Wanting nothing more than to slap the quizzing glass from his eye, she resumed shielding herself with her fan and returned her attention to Lord Quentin.

He stared at Pickett, his eyes narrowing behind the slits of his black winged mask. "Speaking of sporting, Pickett," he murmured, releasing her hand, "Lady Rimell is sitting alone in the chariot near the windows. She looks in need of company." Lady Rimell was a widow with an enormous bosom and questionable morals.

The quizzing glass dropped from Pickett's eye. "Indeed?"

Lord Quentin nodded.

Pickett grinned in a manner that was nothing short of lecherous. "Well, then, I must rush to her rescue." Without bothering with the courtesy of leave-taking, he was off.

Aldgate made an exasperated noise and trailed after him.

Jane shot her rescuer a grateful look.

He nodded and said, "Now then, Miss Edwardes, I believe that the next dance is mine. It is to be a waltz, and your order grants me the first waltz at every ball." He offered her his arm with a graceful flourish.

"Miss Edwardes is overly warm and is thus in no condition to dance," Goolding snapped. "Do go ask another lady."

"No!" Jane blurted out, far more urgently than she intended. Blushing, she repeated in a softer voice, "No. I-I am feeling much better. I would very much like to dance, my lord."

"I must protest, my dear," Goolding pompously declared. "I would be remiss in my duty as your suitor were I to allow you to take to the dance floor when you are clearly in no state to do so."

Pointedly ignoring him, Jane took Lord Quentin's proffered arm. As he led her onto the dance floor, Witley called after them, "But Miss Edwardes, your punch!"

Lord Quentin grinned and flung back over his shoulder, "Give it to Goolding. It is he who looks warm now."

Jane couldn't help giggling at the comic look of outrage on Goolding's face as Witley handed him the glass. "You, my lord, are a rogue," she murmured as they took their place among the couples assembling on the dance floor.

"And you, Miss Edwardes, are beautiful. Have I told you how much I admire your costume?" he countered, taking her right hand in his left one and encircling her waist with his free arm.

Oh, but she liked the feel of his arm, so warm and strong, around her. And the way he looked at her—

Her confidence rising to dizzying new heights, she playfully chided, "No, you have not. You have said next to nothing to me the entire evening. In truth, you've quite neglected me. I should be exceedingly angry with you."

He looked momentarily stunned by her response, then smiled a slow, almost unbearably sensual smile. "Then allow me to beg your forgiveness. I can assure you that the neglect wasn't intentional." The music began then, and they started to whirl. "Surely you must know by now that I would never purposely slight you."

"And you must know that I would forgive you anything," she retorted, honestly.

Again he looked taken aback. After several beats during which he gazed at her in wonder, he murmured, "I had no idea that you hold me in such regard."

Jane felt the heat rise in her face as she realized the rashness of her admission. Good heavens! Whatever had possessed her to reveal her feelings so freely? Rissa would never—

Rissa. There was a sinking feeling in her chest. For a mo-

ment she had forgotten that she was supposed to be Rissa; that
it was Rissa Lord Quentin's gaze worshiped; Rissa that he
held tenderly in his arms; Rissa that he so clearly adored.

She hung her head, feeling suddenly deflated. Oh, what had
she been thinking? She must be mad to have imagined that
she could ever win his affections from her stepsister. Rissa
was lovely, gay, and witty, while she—

Her heart contracted painfully in her chest. While she was
plain and bookish and shy. In truth, the only advantage she
had over Rissa in regards to his lordship was that she loved
him.

"Miss Edwardes?"

Miserably, she looked up.

"Did I say something amiss?"

She shook her head. "No. I—I'm sorry. I was just thinking
of—of—" Oh, what was the use? She sighed and blurted out
the truth. "I was thinking of my stepsister."

"Indeed? What a coincidence. So was I."

Jane blinked in her surprise. "You were?"

He nodded. "Yes. I am most anxious to see her rainbow
costume, but I cannot seem to find her in the crowd."

She missed a step. He had been looking for her. Could it
be—

"Did she accompany you tonight?" he persisted.

Oh, it was! He had taken an interest in her, Jane Wentworth. Her confidence rebounded. Though it was obvious that
he harbored feelings for Rissa, the fact that he thought to ask
after her, Jane, gave her new hope. Perhaps, just perhaps—

She smiled. Perhaps she had only to encourage his affections and show him her own to sway his feelings in her favor.
After all, she'd never dropped so much as a hint that she cared
for him. She'd never had the courage to do so, at least not as
Jane Wentworth. But as Rissa—

She squeezed the hand he held, delighted when he

squeezed hers back. As Rissa, she felt strangely free to say and do what was in her heart. So why not use that courage to further her cause with him? True, he might be angry and disappointed when he discovered her deception. Then again, he could be flattered and intrigued, perhaps enough to grant her a chance to win his love.

Should she take the gamble and risk her heart?

Could she?

She met his gaze then, and the tenderness in his eyes melted the last of her reserve. She would. She would venture anything for the chance at a lifetime of seeing him look at her so.

Thus resolved, she finally replied, "She is ill and was unable to attend tonight. It quite broke her heart to miss the fun."

"I do hope it is nothing serious?" he inquired, his voice ringing with concern.

He did care. He did! She stifled her urge to smile, for, of course, it would never do to smile at another's illness. "Just a cold. She shall be fine. It is kind of you to inquire."

"Not at all. I find your stepsister quite agreeable. Please do convey my wishes for her swift recovery."

Agreeable? All urge to smile vanished. Agreeable was hardly the term a man used to describe a woman for whom he had feelings. Jane heaved an inward sigh. Oh, well. Agreeable was a start, she supposed. Besides, Lord Quentin was a gentleman, and a gentleman never revealed his interest in a woman when with another. Praying that such was the case now, she murmured, "I shall convey your wishes with pleasure, my lord."

For several moments thereafter they remained silent, swirling past golden temples and plaster-winged horses, dipping beneath spun fleece clouds as they danced among the denizens of mythology. Finally his lordship asked, "Have you visited the oracle yet?"

Jane shook her head. "I'm afraid that I have been too busy dancing to explore the wonders of Mount Olympus. Is it wonderful?"

"Very," he replied, his well-shaped lips curving into an enigmatic smile. "Perhaps you would allow me to escort you outside to try it for yourself?"

"Well—" She frowned as if trying to decide, though, in truth, it was all she could do to hide her excitement. "There is the dance order to consider, though I do admit that I could use a breath of fresh air. It is frightfully close in here, and I am feeling rather warm." That last was no lie—she was warm, disturbingly so.

"In that case, I insist that you allow me to take you outside. If the man whose dance turn is forfeited protests, well, then he is no gentleman and is thus unworthy of your notice."

Before Jane could reply, the music ended and he whisked her out the side door, using the confusion on the dance floor as a cover to spirit her away from her horde of admirers.

Jane, of course, voiced no protest. Indeed, the thought of doing so never crossed her mind. She was too intoxicated with anticipation. Lord Quentin was taking her for a stroll in the garden, and from what she had discerned from the whispers of other, more popular women, men oftentimes used a stroll in the garden as an excuse to get a lady alone. And the most common reason they wished to be alone with her was to steal a kiss.

Did Lord Quentin intend to steal one from her?

She shivered at that titillating prospect. How many nights had she lay awake dreaming of his kiss? How many times had she gazed at his lips and wondered how they would feel moving against hers? Would they be tender and gentle, or rough with passionate demand?

She shivered again. Perhaps she was about to find out.

"You're shivering. Are you cold?" he murmured, pausing on the steps that led to the torchlit garden.

She looked up at him, smiling. "No. Not at all. I was shivering—" why? Ah, yes. Of course. "I was shivering in anticipation of asking the oracle my question." .

He smiled back in the way that always made her feel all warm and bubbly inside. "Indeed? And what do you hope to learn that makes you tremble so?"

"About love," she replied breathlessly. "I hope to learn if I shall find true and everlasting love."

His smile faded abruptly and he grew suddenly solemn. "Is love what you long for? Do you wish it above riches and a title?"

"Yes," she softly replied, seeking his gaze through the flickering shadows of the torchlight. He tipped his head down to meet it, his eyes gleaming through the slits in his mask as they caught and entrapped it. "Oh, yes," she repeated, bewitched by the dark magic of those eyes. "I desire it above all else."

His face inched nearer to hers. "If that is indeed what you wish to know, then we needn't visit the oracle."

"Oh?" The word was little more than an enraptured sigh.

"I can tell you what you wish to know." His face moved yet nearer. "It is a gift, you see. I have only to kiss a woman to know if there is love in her future . . . true love." His face was so close now that she could feel his breath fanning across her cheeks. "Shall I kiss you and find out?"

"Please do, my lord," she whispered. This was it.

At that instant the ballroom door burst open and three foxed gentlemen tumbled out, all more howling than talking about opening Pandora's box and enjoying the wickedness within.

Lord Quentin uttered a mild curse and pulled away. "Not here," he growled, grasping her arm. "We must go somewhere more private." With an urgency that matched her own, he led her down the path and into the garden of mazelike topiary hedges.

Past flowers, trees, and statues they rushed, all of which melded into a gloom-smudged streak as they raced toward the heart of the labyrinth. When, at last, they stopped, it was before a statue of a half-naked man with an equally scantily clad woman who appeared to be chained to a stone. At either side burned three torches and before it stood a low stone bench, as if the owner was inordinately proud of the piece and wished to draw notice to it.

"*Perseus Rescuing Andromeda,*" Lord Quentin stated, nodding at the tableau. "Do you know the tale?"

Jane smiled. "Of course I do. It has always been one of my favorite stories. Silly though it sounds, I used to play at being Andromeda when I was a child. I would stand as if chained against the large stone near my—" She broke off abruptly, suddenly remembering herself. She had been about to say near her grandfather's vicarage, but, of course, she was supposed to be Rissa, and Rissa hadn't lived at a vicarage. No doubt he knew that.

After a beat during which she remained awkwardly silent, he ducked his head to peer at her face. "Is something amiss?"

"No. I was just—" She made a helpless gesture, her near slip again causing her to doubt the wisdom of her game.

He tipped his head to one side, viewing her thoughtfully. As he did so, torchlight spilled across his dark curls, burnishing them in a way that reminded her of fire against a silken midnight sky. Beautiful—so very beautiful. His splendor merely served to deepen her doubt.

Oblivious to the vision he made, and the havoc it played upon her senses, he softly inquired, "Are you feeling homesick?"

"Yes. Homesick," she concurred, though, in truth, what she

felt was guilty. Was she wrong to deceive him into kissing her? What if, at the unmasking, he perceived her trick not as the act of love it was, but as a game in which she'd played him for a fool? He would be angry for certain, and all would be lost.

She was trying to absorb that wretched thought when his arms wrapped around her and she was crushed against him. "My lord," she gasped, half in shamed protest, half in wishful plea. She knew she should pull away, yes, pull away and confess—

"Quentin," he whispered huskily. "You must call me Quentin."

But she couldn't, she couldn't pull from his embrace. She liked the feel of his body, so strong and deliciously warm, far too much to draw away. Weak with desire and powerless against her longing to be loved by him, Jane melted against him, mindlessly echoing, "Quentin."

His arms tightened around her.

She nuzzled nearer, delighting in the feel of his heart thundering against her cheek as she rested it against his black linen–clad chest. Not only did he feel like heaven, he smelled like it too . . . a deliciously spicy heaven of musk, cloves, vanilla, orange-flower, and—

Hmm. Her nostrils flared as she sought to place the elusive underlying scent. It was earthy . . . and masculine . . . and, mmm, completely seductive. It was a perfume unlike any she'd ever smelled before, one of which she couldn't seem to get enough.

It was only after taking several more deep, questing breaths that she realized its source: it was the manly essence of Quentin Somerville himself. That realization made her knees go weak.

"Look at me, love," he whispered.

Feeling like she was in a dream, Jane slowly raised her

head and met his gaze. As had happened when he'd kissed her
hand, something inside her melted, this time at the naked desire she saw glimmering in his eyes.

Smiling in a way that was frankly sensual, he dipped his
face toward hers. "Not only do I have a talent for telling the
future, I also possess the power to banish homesickness." He
was so near now that his lips caressed hers as he finished. "All
with a single kiss."

"Then kiss me," she commanded on a sigh.

Promptly, he complied.

At first his kiss was gentle, little more than a soft melding
of lips. Then it gradually deepened. Now he licked, tracing
and parting her lips with a tickling sweep of his tongue; now
he nibbled, seductively teasing her lower lip with his teeth.
And now—oh, now!—he eased his tongue into her mouth, his
movements slow yet urgent, as he probed the sensitive re-
cesses. The resulting sensations made her shudder and moan
with delight.

She had known that his kiss would be wonderful, miraculous even, but this—this!—why, this was beyond all imagining. Innocent that she was, she'd thought that one kiss from
him, just one, would be enough to satisfy her longing for him
forever, that its memory would be enough to last her whole
life should it be all she ever had of him.

But she'd been wrong. The feel of his mouth against hers,
so hot and hungry and demanding, made her want more.
Much, much more. Every inch of her tingled and burned, bedeviling her in a way that made her flesh cry out for his touch.
And she wanted him to touch her, to stroke and caress her all
over, to somehow ease the throbbing ache that radiated from
deep within her and stirred her in the most bewildering places.

Almost frenzied with need now, yet uncertain as to what
that need was, she moaned into his mouth and clung to his
neck. As if possessed by a will of its own, her body began to

move against his, rubbing and undulating in a way that was nothing short of wanton.

Quentin too moaned, his body jerking and twitching in inflamed response. God, but she was a passionate little creature, far more so than he'd have ever believed possible. Never in his life had he had a woman respond as she did, with such joy and abandon. She was like a dream come true . . .

And she would soon be his wife. His mind drugged with thoughts of the pleasurable nights to come, he grasped her buttocks and lifted her hard against his arousal. She gasped and molded her body to his, clinging yet tighter to his neck. Certain that he would die if he didn't take her, Quentin sank onto the bench beside them, pulling her against him until she sat straddling his lap.

"I love you. How I love you, Quentin," she cried, pulling her mouth from his to meet his passion starred gaze.

"And I you, my darling," he growled, reclaiming her lips with his. Desperately wishing that their mouths were other, more intimate parts of their anatomy, he thrust his tongue deep inside.

Jane emitted a soft sound, then returned the favor. As her tongue moved against his, she felt his hand glide up her back. After pausing several seconds to gently knead her shoulder, it lightly traced down the bare slope of her breast. Somewhere deep in her brain, a warning bell went off, but she was too enraptured to pay it much mind. She wanted him to touch her breasts, to fondle her nipples, which were now taut and aching for his caress.

For what felt like an eternity of sensual torment, he stroked the flesh at her neckline, then his hand slipped into her bodice. A second later his fingertips grazed her nipples. She stiffened and moaned, electrified by the resulting sensation; a sensation that deepened and then exploded into jolting pleasure as he cupped her breast.

"Good heavens! It's Somerville and Miss Edwardes!" someone exclaimed.

Jane gasped and sprang from his lap, panting as she gaped at the intruders with stunned horror. It was Oxley, Aldgate, Wylde, and Pickett, all of whom gaped back. Beyond embarrassed and more than a little panicked, she looked to Quentin for rescue.

He sat staring at a wad of something in his hand, looking as flabbergasted as she felt. It took her but a second to realize what the wad was. When she did, she wanted to die. Her padding. He held one of the pink silk stockings Rissa had used to pad her bosom.

All four interlopers lifted their quizzing glasses to peer first at the damning evidence of her deception, then at the now sagging left side of her bodice.

"Well I'll be damned. Who'd have ever guessed?" Wylde snickered. "The eye-filling Miss Edwardes pads herself."

Jane frowned her confusion at his comment. Miss Edwardes?

"Who, indeed?" Pickett echoed with a smirk. "Such a tasty bit of scandal broth. Miss Edwardes's much-toasted bosom is a fake."

"But—" Jane began.

"Sorry, dear girl, but the truth is out now," Aldgate cut in, "as is what appears to be most of your bosom." He gestured to the stocking in Quentin's hand.

All four gentlemen guffawed.

Why, they still thought that she was Rissa, and they were about to ruin her. "No!" she blurted out, unable to bear the thought of her stepsister's name being bandied about with such derision. "No," she repeated, this time more softly. She would not let Rissa suffer for her foolishness. "I-I am not Miss Edwardes," she confessed.

She stole a glance at Lord Quentin to gauge his reaction. If ever a man looked shocked, it was his lordship. As if in a daze, he stood. "Not Miss Edwardes?" he repeated hoarsely.

She shook her head.

A rapid play of expressions danced across his face: disbelief, dismay, and finally cold, implacable fury. "Then who, pray tell, are you?" he growled, dropping the stocking.

When she didn't instantly reply, he stalked forward and ripped the mask from her face. The headdress came off with it and her long hair tumbled forth.

The four quizzing glasses were up again, this time trained on her face.

After a beat, Wylde shook his head and murmured to Pickett, "Who the devil is it?" Pickett looked to Aldgate who shrugged.

"Dear heavens! It's the stepsister, Miss—" Oxley snapped his fingers as he sought to recall her name.

"Wentworth," Quentin spat. Looking as though he wished to throttle her, he tossed aside the mask. His eyes narrowed, and with bared teeth he snarled, "I demand an explanation now, girl. And for your own sake, it had better be a good one."

In a broken, halting voice she confessed the joke and her reasons for playing it, finishing with a whispered, "So you see, my lord, I did it in hopes of gaining your notice."

"Well, you have most certainly succeeded in doing that, my dear, though not in the manner you wished," Aldgate chortled. He rubbed his hands together in glee. "Oh, but this is rich. I can't wait to see the faces of the rest of the *ton* when they hear."

"Aldgate," Quentin growled, advancing upon the smirking man. "I appeal to your sense of honor to keep silent on this matter. No need to ruin the girl over what amounts to nothing more than a regrettable misunderstanding."

Aldgate shook his head. "Sorry, Somerville, but this is the

first truly delicious scandal of the Season. As such, it is my duty to submit it to the *ton* for their amusement."

"And even you must admit that it is amusing, Somerville," piped in Pickett. "Indeed, I daresay that this is farcical enough to earn a lampoon in the *Tatler*."

Wylde nodded. "Yes, and what shall be even more diverting is watching the outcome of this little comedy of errors." His quizzing glass was on Jane now. "Say, girl. You don't happen to have a brother who's likely to call Somerville out, do you?"

Jane shook her head, her throat too clotted with misery to reply. If Philip shot anyone, it would be her for being such a goose. Not only had she disgraced herself, she'd dishonored her family. She stifled the sob that rose in her chest, determined to hold on to what little remained of her dignity. Perhaps she would save Philip the trouble and shoot herself.

"Pity. Nothing adds luster to the scandal of a compromise like pistols at dawn. Ah, well." Wylde dropped the glass from his eye with a sigh. "I suppose we shall just have to make do with the game of guessing at the outcome of this debacle. I, for one, intend to enter a wager in White's betting book predicting that Somerville will wed the chit before the end of the month."

"Indeed?" Quentin gritted out.

Wylde nodded, his expression smug. "In case you haven't heard, your father arrived in town the night before last, and we all know what a stickler for propriety he is. My guess is that he'll force you to the altar the instant he hears the scandal."

His eyes now narrowed to burning slits, Quentin slowly raked Jane with his gaze. Then he snorted and looked away. "Prepare to lose your wager, Wylde."

Chapter 5

"**Y**ou're really in the basket this time, boy," boomed a wrathful voice.

Ripped from his sleep, Quentin sat up with a start, only to fall back upon his pillows again, groaning at the nauseating hammering in his head. Beside him he heard a squeak of alarm from—well, he'd been too foxed last night to inquire as to his bed partner's name—and felt her plump, naked body shrink against his.

His skin crawling, he flinched and rolled away, a little shamed and a lot disgusted as the sordid details of the night before played through his mind. Good God, what had he come to, picking up a common street trollop and making her pleasure him in the crudest of manners?

"You, girl. Go," the voice commanded.

Quentin didn't have to open his eyes to know that the voice belonged to his father, just as he didn't have to see his face to know that he was in for a monstrous dressing-down.

"But me pay!" his companion squawked.

In the next instant there was the unmistakable clinking of coins, followed by the sensation of silver pelting the coverlet.

"There. That should more than compensate you for your services." A brain-piercing clap. "Now go."

It was all Quentin could do to hold on to his stomach at the motion of the bed as his companion scrambled from beneath the covers and gathered up the coins. There followed a blessed moment of stillness, during which the girl no doubt bit one of the pieces to confirm its authenticity, then another series of gut-churning lurches as she scampered across the bed to retrieve her clothes. When that last was accomplished, she hopped out of the bed with a saucy, "Pleasure doin' bizness wit' ye, me lord," and padded from the room.

His father emitted a humorless chuckle. "Well, well, Quent. Developed a taste for the gutter, have we?"

Quentin opened his eyes a crack to shoot his father a belligerent look. "Of course not. I was three sheets to the wind when I accepted her offer." Behind his father hovered his distraught-looking valet, Andrew, who was shadowed by his visibly flustered majordomo, Mr. Scotbrook. It was apparent by both men's expressions that the marquess had stormed into the house without regard for either etiquette or their protests, and that they now expected the worst.

As did he. Quentin moaned and closed his eyes again. Of course he'd known that his father would call when he heard the scandal. Indeed, he'd even prepared for the unpleasant visit, rehearsing his defense over and over again until he was certain of swaying his parent to his point of view. He just hadn't expected him to call so indecently early in the morning, and most certainly not while he was in such a disadvantaged state.

And at that moment he truly was disadvantaged. For not only did the mere act of thinking make his head threaten to explode, his stomach roiled precariously and his bladder felt ready to burst. All and all he was in a thoroughly wretched state.

"Drunk or not," his father was saying, "you should count yourself very lucky indeed if you don't find yourself plagued with the Covent Garden ague after last night's episode." He shook his head, as if he couldn't quite believe his own son's stupidity. "But that is neither here nor there. Your taste in whores isn't the reason for this visit."

Wanting nothing more than to rid himself of his father and to nurse his miseries in private, Quentin forced his eyes open again and growled, "I know why you are here and what you want. I, however, have no intention of discussing Miss Wentworth at this time, so you have wasted your time in coming."

"We shall discuss her, and we shall do so whenever I say. And I say we do it now." The response was like the crack of a whip.

Quentin winced as it ricocheted through his head. Gritting his teeth against the pain, he spat, "In case it has escaped your notice, I am a grown man and no longer subject to your dictates."

"In case it has escaped *your* notice, it is I who pays the allowance that enables you to get into scrapes such as the one in which you now find yourself, which gives me every right to dictate to you when and how I see fit."

As much as it galled him to do so, Quentin had to concede the point. The bastard did hold the purse strings, and as he'd learned through bitter experience, his father wasn't above tightening them to gain his way. Thus he bridled his tongue and forced himself to satisfy his seething resentment with a glower.

After several beats of tense silence, his father gave a curt nod. "Good. Glad you see things my way. Now get up and make yourself respectable. I have no wish to conduct our business with you laying in sodden sheets, reeking of whores and whiskey." After gracing Quentin with a look that perfectly matched his disdainful tone, he whirled around and barked at the valet, "You, man. Prepare a bath for your master. And make certain you add plenty of scent to the water. He smells like a wharfside bawdy house. And you"—he directed a gloved finger at the majordomo—"fetch tea and toast. And send someone around to the florist for a nosegay." As the servants hurried off to do his bidding, he stalked over to the heavy damask drapes and yanked them open.

The effect of the bright morning sunlight on Quentin was like having red-hot pokers rammed through his eyes and into his brain. Cursing Oxley for coaxing him to drown his woes in drink the night before, and the blasted Miss Wentworth for causing those woes in the first place, he rolled over and buried his face in his pillow.

"Come, come now. Enough lolling about in bed and feeling sorry for yourself. The day is a-wasting, and you have a full program of tasks to complete before nightfall," his father chided, ripping the covers off the bed. Ignoring the fact that Quentin was naked, he grasped his arm and hauled him into a sitting position.

Quentin moaned aloud, almost losing the contents of both his stomach and his bladder at the abruptness of the motion. Pushed beyond all dignity in his discomfort, he clutched his belly and groaned, "Chamber pot . . . now."

To his relief, his father refrained from comment, instead handing him the urgently needed necessary and turning his back to allow him to alleviate his misery in a modicum of privacy.

He'd just completed his business, and was feeling somewhat better for having done so, when he heard a footman and Andrew enter the adjoining dressing room, and the sounds of water being poured into the tub. In the next instant there was a scratch at the door.

It was Mary, the chambermaid, bearing the requested tray of tea and toast. Quentin hastily pulled the sheet up over his nakedness. It wasn't that he was modest about the girl seeing him nude—she had done so more times than he could count. It was that he was certain his father would never approve of such a casual display before a female servant. And the last thing he wanted at that moment was to court more disapproval from his father.

After the tray had been set on the table by the window and Mary had retreated, his father again turned to face him. Tossing him the dressing gown that had been draped over a nearby chair, he said, "I suggest you take as much tea and toast as your stomach will tolerate. We most probably shan't have time for nuncheon."

"Oh? And what exactly do you have planned that will keep us so very busy?" he inquired, rising unsteadily from the bed. God, but he was dizzy.

"Our first order of business shall be to pay my old friend, Cecil Sheldon, a visit at the Doctors' Common."

Quentin paused in slipping the dressing gown over his shoulders, his eyes narrowing at the mention of the Common. As all men knew, it was where one obtained special marriage licenses. "I do hope our visit has nothing to do with what I am suspecting," he ground out, though he had an appalling feeling it did.

"And what do you suspect?"

"I shan't marry the girl. Everyone knows that she tricked me, and I refuse to be caught in her trap," he declared, not bothering to justify the question with an answer. He knew his father far too well not to know what he was thinking.

"Is that so? Well, it takes two to perpetrate a compromise, and from what I hear you weren't exactly a reluctant participant in the situation. Indeed, from the accounts of the witnesses, you appeared to be enjoying yourself a great deal."

"I thought I was kissing Miss Edwardes, whom I love and wish to wed," he flung back, unable to deny the accusation. As much as he hated to admit it, even to himself, he had enjoyed kissing Miss Wentworth, and not just because he thought he kissed his beloved. No. Despite his loathing for her and her deceit, he had to admit that she was a sensual little thing.

"Fooled you, did she?" A dry laugh. "Must be a cunning little wench to dupe a man of the town like you."

Bristling at his father's amusement, he shot back, "Miss Wentworth knew of my affection for her stepsister and deliberately used my feelings to trick me into marrying her instead. In case you haven't heard, the chit is a bran-face frump with no figure and even less conversation who is long past her last prayer. I shan't be shackled to such a creature, do you hear? I shan't!" He practically shouted the last words, which did nothing to improve his aching head.

His sire's features hardened to stone. "You shall and you will. For years now, I have pulled you out of one scrape after another, turning a blind eye while you blithely sullied the Somerville name with your dissolute ways. But not this time, my boy, not this time. This is one scrape from which I shan't rescue you, and a sully I will not ignore. By not offering for the girl, you have shown yourself to be without honor. And while I must tolerate you being labeled both a wastrel and a rake, I shall not stand by and let it be said that a son of mine is completely lacking in honor. To a Somerville, honor is everything."

He stalked a few feet nearer to Quentin. "You shall do the honorable thing and marry the girl, or by God I will cut you off. I shall forever turn a blind eye to you, even should I see you starving in the gutter, and declare to the world that I have but one son—a son, I might add, who would never disgrace the family in such a manner."

Quentin's gut twisted at the mention of his older brother, Nicholas, the saintly earl of Lyndhurst. All his life he had been compared to his perfect brother, and every time had been found wanting. He'd been constantly chided to look to Nicholas, or Colin, as he was so fondly called, as a model of all that was good and right, and encouraged to emulate his example. From his earliest memory it had been darling Colin this, dearest Colin that, all uttered in the most fawning of tones. While he—

Quentin glared bitterly at his father, who so resembled his brother—the same towering height, the same strong, handsome features, the same dark eyes and burnished brown hair—resentment festering in his chest. He had learned long ago that he could never live up to his brother's example. Never, no matter what he did or how hard he tried, would he outshine or even come close to equaling him. He would be forever overshadowed by Colin's sterling character and impressive accomplishments, second not only in birth but in his parents' hearts and eyes.

The second son, always second in everything.

Quentin's gut twisted a fraction more. It was a dreary, unenviable position, that of second son, one without either prestige or advantage. And as always happened when he thought of his position, he raged against society and the inequity of its inheritance laws.

Damn it to hell! Why should Colin, by virtue simply of being born first, inherit everything, while he was entitled to nothing save what scraps his father chose to toss him? Granted, he was more fortunate than most second sons in that his maternal grandfather had left him an estate. Still, in view of what his brother stood to gain: the marquess of Beresford, six fine estates, one of the largest fortunes in England, and the undying adoration of both the *ton* and his parents, it was mean consolation.

Hating his brother, the laws of England, and most of all his father, for so painfully calling to mind his inadequacies, he hissed, "Of course you realize that you leave me with no choice but to wed the Wentworth creature?"

His father shrugged one shoulder. "There is always a

choice. You could retire to Worcestershire and attend to your estate. The place was once quite profitable and could be so again if properly managed. That, of course, would mean much hard work on your part, and we both know how much you abhor work. Question is: Which do you abhor more? Work or the notion of marriage to Miss Wentworth?"

Quentin glared at him with all the pain and resentment he felt inside. "Neither! I abhor the thought of giving you the satisfaction of denouncing me as your son."

Apparently his voice—or was it his face?—reflected his hurt, for his father's expression suddenly softened and he slowly moved forward, stopping only when he stood before his son. After a beat, he reached out and clasped his shoulders. "Whatever am I to do with you, my boy? Don't you know how very precious you are to me?"

Quentin snorted.

His father sighed. "Whether or not you choose to believe me, it's true. You are as dear to me as my own life. I shall never forget the day you were born, it was the happiest day of my life. Well," a faint smile, "next to the day I wed your mother, of course."

Another snort from Quentin. "Next to the day Colin was born, you mean."

His father shook his head. "While your mother and I greatly rejoiced at your brother's birth, the event didn't begin to approach the pleasure we felt when you arrived. With your brother we fully expected and got a fine, strong babe at the end of nine months' time. But with you . . . well, as you know, your mother lost several babes after he was born."

He paused then, his expression one of remembered pain, as if he relived the heartache and disappointment of those miscarriages and stillborn infants. When at last he continued to speak, his voice was a shattered whisper.

"How we longed for another child . . . all of us. When

Colin was old enough to understand, he too wept when he lost yet another hope of a little brother or sister. Thus when you were born, you were like a miracle, so strong and healthy and beautiful. You were the answer to all our prayers, and we loved you from the instant you entered our lives. Whether you believe it or not, we still do."

When Quentin merely grunted, his father's face hardened and he gave him a vicious shake. "Damn it, Quent! Why can't you see that I only wish the best for you? All I want is to help you become the fine man I've often glimpsed beneath your bitterness and rage."

"And I suppose that you think that forcing me into marriage will miraculously transform me into that man?" Quentin spat, ignoring the way his heart ached at his father's words.

For a long moment his father simply stared at his face, his eyes glittering with warring emotions. Then he dropped his hands from his shoulders and turned away. "I never wanted to have to force you. I had hoped that you would see reason and agree to do the honorable thing." He ran his hand through his thick, dark hair, now liberally streaked with gray. "By the way, I spoke with the girl's father."

"You did what! How could you—"

His father held up his hand to silence him, though he remained turned away. "He says that his daughter did what she did because she fancies herself in love with you. She has for some time now, it seems. And despite what you think, she never meant to trap you into marriage. She simply wished to know what it was like to kiss you."

Quentin made a derisive noise. "So she claims. Well, her father must be enormously pleased with the outcome of her curiosity. No doubt he danced a jig when he learned that you intend to coerce me into wedding her."

"Hardly. I got the distinct impression that he is none too eager to be rid of the girl, nor is he keen on having you for a son-in-law." His father chuckled. "Rather an odd volume, that Wentworth. Have to admit that I like him." A head shake. "At any rate, he has no intention of allowing his daughter to wed you unless he's certain that you will properly cherish her. As for the girl, well, she has declared that she shan't marry you unless she truly believes you want her for a bride."

For the first time since the beginning of the interview, Quentin felt a niggle of hope. "Are you saying that my suit will most probably be rejected?"

"Of course not."

"But if Wentworth knows that I am being forced—"

"He doesn't know."

"Well, then, surely neither he nor the girl is fool enough to believe that I wish to wed her after waiting three days to come up to scratch?"

"I explained that point away quite neatly."

"Oh?" The utterance was more groan than query.

"Yes. I told him that as a fledgling poet, you are in the throes of artistic agony over composing the perfect proposal. That you want to make certain it is one that his daughter simply cannot refuse."

"And he believed you?" He couldn't keep the incredulity from his voice.

His father turned then and looked at him. That one look was more threat than all his words combined. "No. But he will. You shall convince him."

Whatever was happening?

Certain that she would burst with impatience at any moment, Jane held up her tambour to examine her needlework. Oh, drat! In her distraction she'd unwittingly worked the left wing of the butterfly motif in a Roman stitch instead of the encroaching satin stitch she'd used on the right wing. Of course the threads would have to be pulled and the stitches re-done.

Muttering several mild oaths that would most probably have earned her a frown from Elizabeth and sent Rissa into a fit of giggles, she reached into her sewing basket without looking and fished about for her scissors.

"Ouch!" Something latched onto her hand, something small and furry with tiny needlelike teeth and claws. "Scratch?" She peered into the basket. The kitten wallowed within, gleefully making a snarl of her costly Persian silk floss. "Scratch! Bad, bad puss!" she chided, scooping her naughty pet out of his tangled nest.

Though she knew she should be furious, Jane couldn't help but smile, so droll did he look with a skein of white floss hanging off one ear and a scarlet thread draped over his nose. He rather resembled her old dancing master, Monsieur Fortier, with his powdered court wigs and scraggly red whiskers.

It was thinking of Monsieur and how grateful she'd been for his instruction when she'd danced with Lord Quentin that made her smile fade and prompted her to whisper, "Oh, Scratch. Whatever is taking so long? He's been in Papa's study well over an hour now."

He, of course, was Lord Quentin. She'd been sitting on the morning-room window seat, stitching away, when the elegant Somerville carriage had pulled up to the door and his lordship had stepped down. And oh! Had he looked handsome . . . every inch the bridegroom-to-be, in his Spanish blue coat with a nosegay in hand. Since she had yet to see him leave, it could mean only one thing: his mission matched his appearance. Well, either that or her father had murdered him. Her papa had been furious at his lordship for his part in her dis-grace.

"What do you think?" she asked her pet, plucking the length of floss from his nose. "Has Father ripped his lordship limb from limb? Or are they negotiating a marriage contract?" She fervently hoped it was the latter. Of course, in order for it to be so, Lord Quentin would have to convince her father that he bore a true and sincere desire to wed her. And knowing her father, well . . .

She sighed and rescued her white skein from the kitten's ear. Perhaps his lordship was dead after all.

Now devoid of his disguise, the kitten squeaked his disinterest in the affair and squirmed out of her grasp. Pausing only long enough to bat at the drapes, which had the misfortune to stir in the noonday breeze, he skittered off and promptly attacked the toy mouse she had made him.

For several moments Jane watched as he tossed the brown velvet toy in the air and deftly caught it in his mouth. Then she shook her head and resumed searching the kitten-jumbled contents of her basket for her scissors. She had just located them when the door opened and Nathan, the second footman, announced, "Your father requests your presence in his study, Miss Wentworth."

A wedding contract. They had to have been discussing marriage. Why else would her father now wish to see her? Filled with nervous excitement, she practically flew to the mirror that hung on the opposite wall. Blessing Clarissa and her dogged faith in his lordship, she inspected her appearance.

Beyond hope herself, it was only because of her stepsister's insistence that Jane had allowed herself to be curled, powdered, and dressed for a proposal every morning since her disgrace. For unlike Rissa, she'd had no expectation whatsoever of his lordship's coming up to scratch.

And why should she? He had been furious upon discovering her deception. And shocked. Oh, but he'd been shocked, and rudely so. Then there was the little matter of how he had publicly declared that he would never be forced to wed her.

No. All in all, she'd been left with no reason to hope for,

much less expect, a proposal. And in her heart, she couldn't blame him for turning his back on her. After all, it had been she who had teased and tempted him, she who had deceived him. What had happened had been all her fault, and she deserved to suffer the consequences.

Yet, incredibly, he was here.

Desperate to look her best, Jane anxiously straightened a face-framing curl, then neatened the triple fall of lace at the neckline of her yellow muslin round dress. After another moment of critical evaluation, she puffed the top of her short bishop sleeve a fraction more. There. Perfect. Well, at least as close to perfection as she could get—

Which wasn't so very close at all, she decided, miserably. Ah, well. At least she looked better than she usually did, which was something. Heaving a soft sigh, she turned from the mirror and headed for her father's study.

Never had a journey seemed as long as that short trek across the entry hall and down the east hall. Never had she been plagued so by conflicting feelings.

While she wanted to marry his lordship—more than anything in the world!—a part of her questioned her wisdom in wishing to do so. He had, after all, made it perfectly clear at the time of her disgrace that he harbored no tender feelings for her. Indeed, by all appearances, he detested her to the utmost degree.

Then again, he had been in a state of angry shock at the time, and everyone knew that a person often acted rashly when in such a state. Not, of course, that she held any illusions about his actually loving her. No. Even she wasn't that big a fool. Yet, surely—surely—he couldn't loathe her as much as he had appeared to do when he'd unmasked her? Surely he wouldn't ask her to wed him if he truly despised her— would he?

No. No! Of course not. He had most probably come to his

senses after his shock had faded and remembered that he
found her agreeable. He confessed to doing so as they danced.
He'd said that he found her, Jane Wentworth, not just agreeable, but *quite* agreeable. Surely he'd meant it or he wouldn't
have said it. Besides, her father would never allow him to present his suit to her had he any doubt that he truly wished to
wed her—would he?

Not quite certain what to think, Jane stopped before her
father's study, nodding at the footman as she fought to tamp
down her nerves. Nodding back, the man scratched on the
door.

"Enter!" came her father's voice. By his tone, she could tell
he was far from pleased.

Heavens! Perhaps he had murdered his lordship after all.
Perhaps—

"Miss Wentworth?" The footman tactfully indicated the
door he had opened.

"Oh, yes. Thank you," she croaked, her throat suddenly too
dry to speak in a normal voice. Praying that all was well and
his lordship lived, she stepped into the spacious buff-and-
brown room.

"Jane, my dear," her father exclaimed, rising behind his
massive mahogany desk. A tall, imposing man, he appeared
even more so this afternoon in his black coat and equally dark
expression.

Lord Quentin, who sat rather stiffly in one of the Trafalgar
lounging chairs before the desk, stood as well, a polite smile
curving his well-shaped lips. After an awkward beat of silence, he came forward and took her hand.

"Miss Wentworth. How very delightful you look today," he
said, lifting her hand to his lips. As he kissed it, his jewel-
bright gaze met hers, and his smile broadened into all its dimpled glory.

The effect of that smile was instantaneous, and as had happened when he'd kissed her hand at the ball, something inside her seemed to melt—that mysterious and disturbing something that lay deep in her belly. Suddenly breathless and dizzy, she slowly returned his smile.

An odd expression crossed his face then, and his eyes took on a hungry, almost predatory gleam. Slowly his charming smile faded, displaced by one that was undeniably sensual. Mesmerized, she swayed toward him, her mind void of everything but her desire to kiss him.

He, too, seemed caught up in the moment, for he clasped her hand to his chest and inched his face nearer to hers, his compelling gaze never leaving hers.

"My lord," she whispered huskily, lifting her head to invite his kiss. Oh, but her lips felt strange, all quivery and aching to feel his moving against them.

"Well, well, well." A harsh laugh. "Perhaps you two just might suit after all."

Her father! Oh, heavens! Jane gasped and sprang back, her face burning as time and place came flooding back.

Quentin too started, disturbed and more than a little shocked by his reaction to the chit. Bloody hell! What was wrong with him, responding so to a woman he loathed? Only once before had a female he disliked prompted such lust from him, but she had been beyond beautiful and as tempting as Eve . . . virtues that Miss Wentworth decidedly lacked.

Bewildered, he stole a quick glance at her from beneath his lashes. No, Miss Wentworth wasn't beautiful. Why, she wasn't even pretty, not with that heart-shaped face and those freckles. As for being tempting, well, there wasn't a thing about her that he found remotely enticing. At least not now. As Miss Edwardes she'd been the most alluring creature in the world.

It was remembering his beloved and the wrenching fact that she was forever lost to him that slammed him back to his senses and the grimness of his task. Ah, well. Whatever the chit stirred in him, it had to be of a base nature, no doubt brought on by the fact that he'd been unable to find his release the night before, despite the dollymop's enthusiastic efforts. Indeed, after the amount of fruitless fondling he had endured, it was little wonder that he was now haunted by frustrated lust.

His mood not improved by the thought of his dismal performance, Quentin forced himself to smile and return to the business at hand. "As I said, Wentworth, I find your daughter a most appealing young lady. That is why I wish to marry her." Such a smooth, convincing lie. His father would be proud of him.

The other man grunted. "So you say."

Remembering the nosegay in his hand, Quentin shifted his attention back to the blushing Miss Wentworth and presented it with a bow. "A token of my great esteem, my dear."

By the pleasure on her face, you would have thought that he had offered her the crown of England rather than a simple bouquet of roses, carnations, daffodils, and lily of the valley.

As for Jane, she couldn't have been more pleased had he offered her the sun, moon, and stars. This was the first token she had ever received from a man, and the man who offered it was the one she desired most in the world. It was like a dream come true.

After a beat, she realized that her dream was coming true. Lord Quentin Somerville truly did want her. She had seen it in his eyes and face only moments ago. He wanted her, and he had said that he wished to wed her.

More happy than she'd ever dreamed possible, Jane accepted the flowers and lifted them to her nose to inhale their scent. Mmm. From now on, every time she smelled the spicy sweetness of carnations or the honeyed perfume of lily of the valley, she would remember this moment and how happy she was.

"Well, don't just stand there, Somerville. You have my permission to ask her," her father barked.

Never in her life had Jane felt so awkward. What did one do with one's hands and feet while receiving a proposal? And how should she look? Should her expression be shy and demure? Or should she smile her encouragement? She was trying to decide when his lordship seized her free hand and clasped it between both of his.

So much for wondering what to do with her hands.

"Miss Wentworth," he murmured, his stunning violet eyes again capturing hers. "Though I know that this is rather sudden, I find that I have developed a strong affection for you and cannot live without you. Thus, I would consider myself the luckiest man in the world if you would do me the honor of becoming my wife."

Tongue-tied with joy, Jane stared up at his beloved face, stunned by his expression. Why, he looked almost uncertain, as if he half expected her to decline and would despair if she did. The sight made her heart flutter wildly in her breast. He wanted her. He truly did.

As she opened her mouth to reply, her father cut in, "You needn't marry him, you know. The scandal will blow over in time. And if it doesn't"—he shrugged—"you, yourself, have said that you prefer the peace of the country to the hustle-bustle of Town."

At her startled glance, he came from behind his desk, continuing, "As you know, Jane, I am not pleased by Somerville's actions, nor do I favor this match. Unpopular as my view may be, I am of the opinion that a woman is better off without a husband than married to a man who does not love her and will not make her happy. Despite his protests to the contrary, I have grave doubts as to whether his lordship will make you happy."

Lord Quentin not make her happy? Why—

Jane opened her mouth to protest, but her father silenced her with a wave. "Oh, he claims to care for you and pleads his case quite prettily. Still . . . " His gaze drifted to his lordship, narrowing as it came to rest on his face. "I cannot help wondering at the truth of his words. After all, he didn't exactly dance attendance upon you in the past, and it did take him three days to come up to scratch."

"I believe that my father and I both explained that last quite satisfactorily, sir," his lordship retorted stiffly. "I simply wished to present my case in the most attractive manner possible, and it took me time to decide how best to do so. As for your former point, well, I admit that my shift in affections is rather abrupt, but"— his gaze met Jane's again and he smiled gently—"I myself didn't realize how I felt about your daughter until after I kissed her. The instant I did, I knew that she was the only woman for me."

Jane returned his smile, her whole being rejoicing at his admission.

Her father snorted. "What you speak of is passion, not love. And while passion is unquestionably an important part of marriage, it is hardly a firm foundation upon to which to build one's life together." He shook his head. "But we have already been through all that. To get to the heart of the matter, Somerville, Jane has professed a fondness for you, and a deep one at that. Yet, despite her feelings, she has determined that she shan't wed you unless she is certain that you aren't being forced to the altar and that your proposal isn't merely a bow to the dictates of propriety. It is for that reason, and that reason only, that I have allowed you to present your suit. Sensible girl that she is, I trust my Jane to make a wise choice." He paused a beat, then boomed, "Well, daughter? What say you? Will you have him or nay?"

Jane felt his lordship's hands tighten around hers and heard the trembling plea in his voice as he whispered, "Say yes, Jane. Say that you will be mine." His smile had faded and his expression was tense, as if his life hung in the balance of her reply.

Her throat thick with tender emotion, she drew her hand from his and gently cradled his cheek in her palm. "Of course I will wed you, my lord. I shall be yours, for forever and a day. And you shall be mine."

Chapter 6

Jane smiled as Elizabeth removed the aigrette of pearls from her bridal coiffure, feeling as though she were in a dream. Only four hours earlier, at exactly six o'clock that evening, she had stood before the Honorable Reverend Gerald Baker in the grand salon of the marquess of Beresford's palatial town house and become one with Lord Quentin Somerville.

The wedding had been a private affair with only her family and Lord Quentin's parents to bear witness, but to Jane it couldn't have been more perfect had it been held at Westminster Abbey before the entire *ton*. Indeed, it didn't even matter that she hadn't had time to have a proper wedding gown made, or that they were married on Friday, a monstrously unlucky day for weddings, not when the groom was Lord Quentin.

No, not *Lord* Quentin, she reminded herself, the reality of her blissful new state beginning to dawn. He's simply Quentin, or even Quent, if I prefer, my husband.

Her husband.

And he would soon be coming to the chamber to claim his husband's rights. Thrilled yet apprehensive, she clasped her trembling hands tightly in her lap, trying to imagine exactly what those rights entailed. She knew that they involved sharing a bed and letting him do things to her body. She just wasn't quite certain what those things were.

As she sat lost in troubled thought, Elizabeth, who had remained silent except to issue the most summary instructions and comments, murmured, "You're probably wondering why I insisted on preparing you for bed myself."

Jane started at the sound of her stepmother's voice, then looked up to meet her gaze in the mirror, smiling faintly. "I imagined it was because I am spending my wedding night here, at Lord and Lady Beresford's house, and you didn't wish me to be tended by a strange servant."

"That is one reason, yes," her stepmother said, pulling the pins from Jane's intricately coiled hair. "The other is that I wanted to find out if anyone had ever discussed the more—intimate—aspects of marriage with you."

Wondering if Elizabeth had read her mind and mortified by the thought, Jane blushed and shook her head. "Uh . . . no . . . yes . . . er . . . not exactly. I mean, my best friend in Oxcombe, Maria Huddlestone, and I used to speculate about . . . about . . ."—another head shake—"you know, but, well, neither of us was certain as to the truth of the matter. We were both rather sheltered, you see, what with me living at the vicarage and her living with her maiden aunt, and well—" She broke off, shaking her head yet again.

Her stepmother paused from her pin pulling to stare at her, her brow furrowed in a frown. "Are you telling me that you know absolutely nothing of the ways between men and women?"

"I . . . ah . . . I know a few things," she stammered, chiding herself for feeling shame at her ignorance. After all, the secrets of the wedding bed wouldn't be called secrets at all if they were meant to be known before marriage. At least that was what her grandmother had told her when she was thirteen and had broached the subject.

Elizabeth gazed at her for several more beats, then sighed. "Perhaps you should tell me what you do know," she murmured, resuming her task.

Talk about kissing and touching, and all the other wicked things she dreamed of doing to Lor—uh, to Quentin? Heavens! She couldn't! She would die of embarrassment.

As if again reading her thoughts, her stepmother reassured her, "You're a married woman now, dear. It is quite right and proper for us to speak of such things. Indeed, it shall be for the best if you do. That way I can lay to rest any fears you might have." She smiled wryly as she removed the last pin, releasing Jane's hair to tumble down the back of her white cambric dressing gown. "How I wish someone had spoken to me on my wedding night. I was only sixteen at the time and so frightened of the marriage bed that I locked myself in my dressing room to avoid my new husband."

"What were you frightened of?" Jane inquired, growing alarmed. Was there something truly terrible about the marriage bed that young Elizabeth had known, and consequently sought to escape?

Her stepmother laughed. "I had heard tales about the ways between men and women, silly, harrowing ones." She shook her head as if at her own foolishness. "At any rate, I refused to come out until my abigail explained the truth of the matter to me. When she did, I promised myself that were I ever blessed with a daughter, I would make certain that she knew what to expect on her wedding night. Since I intend to keep that promise, well"— she shrugged—"that is why I ask what you know of the subject. I want to make sure that you aren't harboring the same misconceptions I did."

"I see," Jane murmured, feeling all the more stupid for having heard no tales at all, harrowing or otherwise.

"Well?"

Bowing her head to hide her abashment, she mumbled, "I know about kissing . . . and, uh, hugging."

Her stepmother chuckled. "After what happened in the garden, I daresay you do. What else?"

"Er . . ." she bit her lower lip to stop it from trembling so that she could continue. "I—I know that married people sometimes lie naked together and—and that they t-touch each other."

"Correct. What else?"

Frantically she searched her mind for more. Oh, drat! That was all she knew . . . except . . . ah, yes. "Lying together often results in babies."

"Yes. Good." There was a pause, then Elizabeth inquired, "You aren't frightened of the act of making babes, are you?"

Jane shook her head without looking up. She wasn't what one would precisely call frightened, just a bit uneasy. It was, after all, going to be embarrassing to the extreme to have Quentin stick his finger between her legs to plant one of the magic baby seeds she and Maria had concluded all men carried in their purses. At least that is where they assumed men planted them, since they both knew for a fact that babies came out of that place.

"Good." Her stepmother gave her shoulder a squeeze of approval. "I can assure you that you have nothing to fear. While it is true that the act hurts a bit at first, the pain fades quickly and most women find it pleasurable thereafter."

"It hurts?" she echoed, looking up in shock.

"The entry does, yes," Elizabeth replied, beginning to brush Jane's hair. "It is usual for a woman to feel some pain and even bleed a bit when a man enters her."

"Bleed?" The word came out in a squeak of panic. "Why?"

"Because the maidenhead is broken." Her stepmother paused in her brushing to frown down at her. "You do know where a man enters a woman and with what?"

Jane released a shaky laugh, hoping that she sounded more confident than she felt. "Of course I do. A man uses the middle finger of his left hand to plant a magic baby seed between a woman's legs."

There was a moment of silence during which Elizabeth's face turned very red and she choked, as fighting laughter. Then she smiled gently and set down the brush. "Come, dear. Let us sit over there." She motioned to the blue velvet sofa before the dressing room fireplace. "I can see that there is much I must explain."

More acutely aware of her ignorance than ever, Jane did as directed. When they sat side by side, Jane with her head hung in disgrace, her stepmother looped her arm around her shoulders and gave her a hug. "You mustn't feel badly about your innocence. It is a most admirable trait in a bride. If I seemed surprised by it, it's just that, well, I assumed that being from the country as you are you had seen the animals—" She broke off, shaking her head. "Well, never mind. I shall tell you all you need to know."

"Animals are involved?" Jane squeaked. Goodness! Things were getting more complicated by the second.

Elizabeth looked momentarily nonplussed, then burst into laughter. "No, no, dear! No! I didn't mean that animals are involved in the act between a woman and her husband. I simply meant that farm animals sometimes do the act in public, and that country children often learn about it from their display."

"Oh, I see," she said, though in truth she didn't see at all. Could it be that she'd observed the act and not known what it was?

"Now, then," her stepmother began after a moment of consideration. "You do know the difference between men and women, don't you?" She glanced hopefully at Jane.

Jane felt what was quickly becoming a chronic burning in her cheeks deepen. "Um . . . yes. A man has a . . . er . . ." She pointed at her belly and made a vague shape with her hands. "You know. And a woman doesn't. M-my brother and I used t-to"—her face was on fire now—"sneak off and swim naked when we were children."

Rather than look scandalized by her confession, Elizabeth looked relieved. "Yes. Well, fine, then. And have you never wondered at the differences in your bodies?"

Certain that her face was charred to cinders, she nodded. She was curious. However, the one time she'd asked her grandmother about her brother's—er—she had been told that it was an exceedingly immodest question, and that had been that.

Elizabeth, however, had no such reservations, and promptly and thoroughly explained all about—ers—including what they were used for. By the time she had finished, Jane felt not embarrassed or apprehensive, as she knew she most probably should be, but strangely excited.

Indeed, now knowing that it would bring him immense joy, she actually looked forward to having Quentin put his—er—inside her. The only thing that troubled her now was that she still wasn't quite certain what to do up to that point. Elizabeth had said that a man needed to be aroused for his—er—to stiffen, which was the state it must be in in order for it to enter her, and she wasn't quite certain how to prompt arousal.

When she shyly voiced her concern, her stepmother chuckled and assured her, "Most men don't need much help in that regard, especially young, virile ones like your husband. However, should he be nervous, as some bridegrooms are, and have trouble, it will move matters along if you kiss and caress him. Indeed, you should do so in any instance, since it will greatly enhance his pleasure."

It would enhance hers, too, for she could think of nothing more thrilling than kissing Quentin's marvelous lips and stroking the splendid body she was certain lay beneath his clothes. Just the thought of seeing that body naked sent the most delicious shiver of wanting trembling through her. As for the notion of touching it . . .

She hugged herself in her eagerness. She could barely wait.

"Yes, Jane. It will be the most wonderful experience of your life," her stepmother murmured, accurately reading her thoughts. "It can't help but be so when a woman loves a man as much as you love his lordship."

Love? Her anticipation dimmed a fraction. She loved Quentin, yes, but he—he—well, he'd said that he felt passion for her—and affection, but he'd never claimed to love her. A niggling fear that he never would bled from the corner of her mind. Instantly she stanched it. He would learn to love her, he would! She would teach him to do so.

And his first lesson would be tonight.

Anxious to begin, she met her stepmother's gaze and said in a soft voice, "Thank you, Elizabeth. I believe that I am ready for my husband now."

Her stepmother searched her face for a moment, then nodded and kissed her forehead. "Yes. I can see that you are."

Leg-shackled. Buckled. Spliced. Shut up in the parson's pound. Anyway you phrased it, he was wed.

Uttering a foul oath, Quentin drained his glass, then lifted the decanter from the drum table at his elbow to refill it. The decanter, which had been full of fine, aged brandy less than an hour earlier, was down to its last dram and it was with another curse that he emptied it into his glass. The way he felt, he would need at least another bottle, maybe two, before he'd be foxed enough to go upstairs to his bride.

His bride. That bran-faced, scheming, bare-boned excuse for a female, Jane Wentworth.

Bloody hell!

Grimacing his distaste, he tossed down the last of the brandy, then stalked over to the library sideboard to search for something stronger, something much, much stronger. Hmm. Canary. Port. Sherry. Ah, yes. Gin. The very thing. Nothing like a bit of sooth-syrup to numb a man to the ugly realities of life.

Heedless of how particularly ugly his reality would feel in the morning, he downed a healthy portion where he stood, then carried the decanter back to his seat before the fireless hearth. He had just filled his glass and settled into a serious drinking pose, his body sprawled in the "curricle" chair with his feet propped up on a footstool, when his father entered the room.

Instantly his father's expression of surprise at finding him there tightened into one of disapproval when he saw what he was about. Pausing in the middle of the room to view him with censure, he growled, "Drinking again?" A disdainful snort. "Now why am I not surprised?"

"Could be because you, too, would be getting foxed if you had what I have waiting for me in your bed," he retorted flippantly.

"What you have," his father ground out, striding to where he sat, "is a perfectly charming and lovely wife. One who, as you yourself pointed out, is lying in her bridal bed waiting for you to come to her." He stopped before Quentin's chair to glare down at him, his eyes narrowed and his mouth thin with displeasure.

Quentin returned his gaze coolly for a beat, then shrugged one shoulder and took a slow, defiantly deep quaff of gin. "Well, she shall just have to wait a bit longer," he murmured, at last lowering his glass. "It's going to take at least six draughts of this"—he raised his drink in mock salute—"and perhaps a dram or two of whiskey as well, before I'll be drunk enough to bed her." He chuckled, a dark, brittle sound, and took another swig. "As they say, Even a goat looks fetching if a man is fuddled enough."

"Damn it, Quentin. It is your wife you speak of," his father hissed, his eyes now little more than burning slits. "You shall do so with honor and respect, or so help me I shall—"

"What?" Something inside him snapped at the prospect of yet another threat and he lunged to his feet, his resentment spilling over as he glared at his father, eye to eye. "You shall do what? Cut off my allowance? Will you force me to suffer the humiliation of begging my wife for funds?" He gritted his teeth, his hands clenching in his outrage as he thrust his face nearer to his father's. Nose to nose now, he snarled, "You knew, didn't you? You knew about the contract Wentworth made me sign before he would allow me to propose."

His father's brow furrowed. "Contract?"

"The bloody sheet of paper giving his daughter sole right to her dowry until I've proved myself a proper husband," he shouted, wishing that his opponent was anyone else so he could hit him. "And do not try to tell me that you knew nothing about it. You knew, and saw it as yet another way to control me." Certain that he'd explode if he didn't unleash his violence, he downed the remainder of his gin and smashed the tumbler against the hearth. Amid the crash of splintering glass, he spat, "Tell me, Father, was the contract all that bastard Wentworth's idea, or did you suggest it?"

Always a model of control, his father returned his gaze, undaunted by his outburst. After several beats, during which he clearly awaited Quentin to compose himself, he shook his head and calmly replied, "No, Son, I had nothing to do with the contract, nor did I know of it."

When Quentin opened his mouth to argue, his father cut him off by adding, "That is not to say that I fault Wentworth for making you sign it. In truth, I rather admire him for doing so. Were Jane my daughter and set on marrying a man of your reputation, I, too, would take measures to protect her."

Again he sought to speak and again he was silenced, this time with a chuckle and, "Never fear, dear boy. I shan't leave you at the mercy of your wife, at least not financially. I promised not to cut you off if you wed her, and I intend to honor my word. Do not think, however, that that leaves my hand completely empty. I still hold a winning card or two."

He snorted. "Of course. You always control the game."

A shrug. "Not always. Just in matters concerning my sons."

Quentin's eyes narrowed at his father's plural use of the last word. "Sons?" he repeated, drawing out the end *s* on a hiss. "We both know how often you use your cards to trump your dear Colin."

"I use them as I deem necessary," his father returned shortly. "But enough of this. My discipline of your brother has nothing to do with the matter at hand."

His mouth pulled into a sour grin. "Right you are. Saint Colin needed no prompting in bedding his wife . . . before or after the wedding. We both know that he lifted her skirts—"

"I said enough, damn you!" Roughly seizing his arms, his father barked, "I shan't hear another word against your brother or his wife. Do I make myself clear?" He gave him a vicious shake. "One more word, and I swear upon my honor that I shall give you the thrashing I should have given you years ago. You, Quentin Isaac Somerville, are an insolent, un-principled scoundrel, and by God you shall mend your ways."

Quentin returned his father's menacing gaze for several beats, then jerked himself free of his grasp, jeering, "A thrash-ing? Is that your winning card, then?" He released a humor-less grate of laughter. "You are going to have to do better than that."

His father continued to stare at him, a faint smile tugging at his lips. When at last he spoke, his voice was as cold and sharp as a sword blade in winter. "Fine, then. Either you be-have like the gentleman you were raised to be or I shall see that you are banned from every fashionable club, drawing room, gaming hell, and yes, fancy house, in London. You will be left without any entertainment, save that of the lowest kind. And even you, for all your dissolute ways, aren't likely to seek amusement in those quarters."

Quentin snorted. "You have a mighty high opinion of your power over the *ton*. Is it indeed so very great?" He swept his father with a measuring glance, one meant to be as galling as it was insulting. "I wonder."

His father returned his look in kind. "Shall we test it and find out?"

For a long moment they stood dueling with their gazes—his challenging and belligerent, his father's unwavering and certain. It was Quentin who looked away first. He knew when he was defeated, and he was prudent enough not to invite the kill.

Balling up his hands in impotent rage, he resentfully retreated a step, growling, "As always, you win, Father."

His father nodded once in curt acknowledgment. "Then I shall bid you a good night so that you can go to your bride."

Quentin bowed stiffly in response, then pivoted on his heel to do as directed.

"Quentin?"

He paused, but didn't bother to turn or speak.

"Be gentle with her." It wasn't a request, it was a command.

He smiled darkly. Be gentle? Ha! He didn't intend to touch her. Ever.

Jane looked at the clock for what must have been the millionth time that night, wondering where Quentin was. She had been waiting for him for more than two hours now, and she was beyond restless . . . too restless to remain lying in the graceful pose in which Elizabeth had left her.

Careful not to disturb the pink and yellow rose petals scattered around her, she climbed out of the silk-draped bed and strayed to the white marble fireplace, where she stood staring at the flickering flames within. Though it was the end of April, the day had been wet and cold, and she couldn't help shivering at the sound of the rain pelting the windows, despite the coziness of the chamber.

Rain. Yet another bad omen for her wedding. It was beginning to seem as though everything and everyone was against this marriage . . . including the groom, perhaps?

Chilled all the more by that nagging thought, she drew nearer to the fire, holding out her trembling hands to warm them. As loath as she was to admit it, it did seem rather queer that Quentin had kept her waiting so very long, especially if he'd been as moved by her kisses as he claimed. Indeed, shouldn't he be eager to collect on the promise behind them?

Plagued by misgivings, she frowned. Could it be that he had lied about his passion for her? That he had wed her for some other, less romantic reason?

The instant the suspicion entered her mind, she vehemently denied it. No, of course not, she chided herself, sinking to the floor to sit upon the toasty hearth rug. He'd been detained, nothing more. No doubt there had been a few more details regarding the marriage contract to work out. Either that, or— or—

She smiled abruptly, tenderness swelling in her chest as she remembered Elizabeth's words. Maybe he was nervous and was having trouble finding the courage to come to her. As her stepmother had explained as she'd helped her into bed, even men who were experienced in love, as were most bachelors in the *ton*, suffered some apprehension when it came to bedding their brides. They worried about the pain they would cause in taking the maidenhead.

Could that be what now kept Quentin?

Jane's smile broadened at the notion of her groom suffering from such tender concern. Well, if such were the case, she'd best await him in bed. Were Quentin to find it empty, he might think her afraid of the marriage act and thus lose his hard-won confidence. And the last thing she wanted to do was discourage him.

As she stood up, stretching stiffly, she caught sight of her fire-kissed reflection in the gilt-frame chimney glass. Clad in a filmy white nightgown, with her unbound hair about her shoulders, she looked every inch the maiden bride.

The gown, a gift from Rissa, was embroidered all over with pale pink roses, their stems curling scrolls of misty green. The neckline, which was cut in a flattering scoop style, was embellished by fine Mechlin lace, a theme carried out both at the hem and at the edges of the tiny puffed sleeves. In deference to the rose pattern, Elizabeth had banded her head with a pink satin ribbon, the ends of which she'd tied in a bow at her temple. All in all, even Jane had been pleased by the results of her efforts.

Feeling almost pretty and hoping that Quentin would find her so as well, she returned to the bed, where she arranged herself in what she hoped was an elegant yet inviting pose. She had just started to relax when the door opened.

Her husband, at last. He had changed out of the dark blue tailcoat and fawn-colored breeches he had worn for the wedding and now wore a patterned dressing gown in jewel-tone shades of emerald, ruby, and topaz. Standing in the candlelight with his dark curls haloed in copper, he was the most beautiful sight she'd ever seen.

Wanting nothing more than to hold all that magnificence in her arms, she stirred upon the bed and softly called his name.

He started at the sound of her voice, a frown creasing his brow as he glanced toward the bed, upon which she lay. "You're not asleep?" he murmured, crossing the room—not to the bed, as she hoped, but to the fireplace. "You should be. It is very late."

Jane frowned, taken aback. What sort of bride would fall asleep while awaiting her groom on their wedding night? What kind of groom would expect her to do so?

Her frown deepened as she was abruptly struck by a new and extremely disheartening thought. Could it be that he'd not only expected but *wished* to find her sleeping? Had he delayed coming to her in hopes that she would doze off before he got there, thus freeing him of his husbandly duty?

Was he really so very anxious?

She watched for several moments as he picked up the poker and stabbed at the fire. When it burned to his satisfaction, he returned the tool to its holder, then leaned against the mantel to study his handiwork. After observing him for several more beats, ones during which he neither moved nor spoke, she decided that he must indeed be overcome by nerves and that it was her duty to ease them. The question was, how?

Hmm. Well, her stepmother had said that kissing and caressing one's groom would help him should he have trouble getting aroused. Would it also help him relax?

After a short debate, she deemed it worth a try. That left her with the puzzling problem of how to go about it. In her eagerness to lie with Quentin, she had neglected to ask how one approached the coaxing business. Should she simply go over and start kissing him? Or would it be best if she talked to him a bit first?

Timidly judging the former to be too brazen, she sat up and instigated the latter, saying the first thing to come to mind. "This is a lovely chamber." And it was. Decorated in pale purple and white with expensive furnishings and lavish appointments, it was the epitome of upper-class luxury.

Quentin, however, was apparently less than impressed, for he merely shrugged. Either that or he'd lost his tongue to his nerves. Hmm. Probably a bit of both.

Jane shook her head at her conclusion. Goodness! Who'd

have guessed that Quentin Somerville, with his glib banter and easy charm, would be reduced to such a state on his wedding night?

Then again, what did she really know about him except what she'd observed? As she knew from her own dismaying gaucheness in company, appearances weren't always an accurate reflection of the person within. If such were the case with her husband and he was indeed as reticent as he now seemed, she must take bolder steps.

Glad for the cover of the shadows, she forcibly swallowed her own shyness and somehow managed to murmur, "As you said, it is late. Why don't you come to bed now?"

His whole body stiffened visibly at her invitation.

Her heart went out to him. Poor, poor man. He was positively rigid with fear. Well, if anyone knew the pain of feeling awkward and uncertain, it was she, and she would be damned before she allowed the man she loved to suffer in such a manner. Her confidence thus bolstered by her compassion, she gently coaxed, "It is all right, darling. Come. Please?"

For a long moment he didn't respond, then he slowly turned. When he at last looked at her, she smiled her encouragement and held out her arms. "Come."

No, damn it. No! He would not go to her. Quentin gritted his teeth and looked away. He may have been forced to wed her, but he would not bed her . . .

No matter how tempted he was to do so. It was all he could do to bridle his urge to smash his fist against the mantel in his frustration with himself.

Bloody hell! What was wrong with him? Why did he desire her so? While it was true that he was lusty by nature, he'd always adhered to the highest of standards when selecting his inamoratas. Indeed, aside from the regrettable episode with the Haymarket whore, he'd never once bedded a woman who had been judged less than passing fair by the *ton*. He'd never had to, nor had he wanted to . . .

Until now.

"Quentin?"

Against his better judgment, he looked at Jane again.

"Please?" she whispered, rising from the bed. As she stood the candle at the bedside back lit her gown, silhouetting her slim but surprisingly shapely body in a manner that was nothing short of provocative.

His groin tightened savagely at the sight. Drunk, I must be drunker than I thought, he told himself, forcing himself to view her with critical eyes. Mmm, yes. Now that he really looked at her figure, it wasn't so very enticing. Indeed, while she wasn't as spare as he'd imagined, she wasn't what he'd call voluptuous either, and he'd always favored women with lush bosoms and rounded bottoms. All in all, she was rather . . . boyish.

Well, at least she would be if boys had such sweetly curved hips and thighs, he amended, his gaze dropping to her lower body. That observation wrenched his belly with a force that almost brought him to his knees. Disgusted by his response, he tore his gaze away.

You do not want her, he commanded himself firmly. She is nothing but an unappetizing old maid with neither face nor figure to recommend her.

Her face. Yes, of course. One look at those plain features and speckled complexion should dampen his lust quickly enough. Verging on desperation now to prove that he indeed harbored no desire for her, Quentin glanced at Jane's face.

To his disconcertment, and increased discomfort, his gaze fell on her lips. The sight of them, so soft, moist, and pink, promptly recalled the episode in the garden and how very stimulating it had been to kiss her. Mesmerized by the memory, he stared transfixed, consumed with longing as she walked across the room toward him.

Oh, but she had a wonderful mouth, so warm and sweet and responsive. The way she'd returned his kiss, melting and moving against him—

He moaned at the intensity of his burgeoning need. God help him, but kissing her had been the most sensual experience of his life. In her, he'd felt something that he had never before felt in a woman . . . a wildness, a wanton and joyful sort of abandon that had awakened something fierce and primal within him. That something now stirred, clawing at his loins and roaring for its release.

Aching in ways he'd never before imagined, Quentin took a step toward her, hating himself for doing so. Damn it, no! He'd promised himself that he wouldn't touch her, and if he never honored another promise as long as he lived, he would honor this one. She would be his wife in name, and nothing else. The lying little jade didn't deserve any more than that. She most certainly didn't deserve the part of his soul that now commanded his body.

"Quentin. Come," she murmured huskily, opening her arms to him again. Her voice was like a caress to his senses, luring and beguiling him.

"No!" he choked out, more to himself than to her as he turned away. "No," he repeated in a broken whisper.

There was a beat of silence, then her arms coiled around his waist. "There, there, now, Quentin. It's all right," she crooned, pressing her body against his backside. "Everything will be fine."

He sobbed aloud and flung his head back, his eyes closed and his teeth gritted in agony at the feel of her feminine softness nestling against him. God, how he wanted her! He yearned to turn around and toss her on the floor, and shove his inflamed male flesh deep inside her. He wanted to thrust again and again, and taste the passion on her lips as she eagerly returned his kisses. The very thought of her moaning and writhing beneath him snapped what little control remained.

Emitting a groan that gave voice to his torment, Quentin turned around and roughly pulled her into his embrace. Without so much as looking at her, he crushed his lips to hers, ruthlessly assaulting her mouth with a brutal, desperate kiss. Hungry, more sexually ravenous than he'd ever been in his life, he forced his tongue between her lips and thrust it deep into her mouth, ignoring her gasp of . . . shock? . . . passion? . . . or was it protest? Whatever it was, he didn't care, he was far too aroused to do so.

It was shock. Jane was utterly and completely shocked by the fierceness of his ardor. So much so that she stood paralyzed in his embrace, too stunned to do more than yield to his onslaught of passion. This wasn't at all how she'd expected things to be. She'd expected Quentin to kiss her gently and woo her with tenderness, as he had in the garden. But this . . .

She gasped again, this time louder, as his hand slipped down the neck of her gown and convulsively grasped her breast. Too fast! He was moving too fast. She wasn't ready to go so far, not yet. When she tried to pull away and tell him, he clamped her face yet harder to his and ravished her mouth into speechlessness.

As his mouth plundered hers, his hands moved over her breasts and despite her growing panic, Jane found herself moaning as his fingers found her nipples. Unlike his lips, his hands were gentle, his touch soft yet deliciously sensual as he fondled and caressed the sensitive peaks into hardness. It felt more wonderful than anything she'd ever imagined.

The molten sensation in her belly, which had so plagued her of late, now exploded, making the place between her legs feel heavy and hot. In the next instant there was an unfamiliar rush of moisture there.

Not certain what the moisture was and embarrassed by it, she tried to pull away, but he held her firmly. As she squirmed against him, struggling to free herself, he grasped her buttocks and slammed his groin against her belly. She stilled instantly, electrified by his hardness.

He was aroused. She had aroused him without even trying. The knowledge gave her an odd thrill of power, one that instantly eased her fear. Exhilarated by it, she twined her fingers through his thick curls and forcibly wrenched his mouth from hers. Breathing hard, she sought his gaze with hers.

For a long moment they simply stared at each other, their gazes turbulent and simmering with untamed passion. Then instinct took over and she thrust her hand downward, boldly cupping his hardness through his dressing gown.

A hoarse scream tore from his lips, and his pelvis jerked against her palm. She, too, cried out, but hers was the sound of victory edged by a plea she was helpless to explain. In the next instant he bared his teeth and tore her hand away. His breath coming in harsh, ragged rasps now, he wrestled her back into his embrace, his mouth reclaiming hers as he lowered her to the rug.

God, but he needed her. Now. At this moment. Tortured beyond reason by the throbbing of his sex, he shoved her nightgown up around her waist and roughly opened her legs with his knee. His hands clumsy with need, he parted her woman's flesh, his suffering deepening when he found it wet.

That she desperately wished to be teased there was undeniable, what with the way she moaned and moved against his hand, but for the first time in his life he gave no thought to his partner's pleasure. He didn't dare. He would lose himself if he indulged her, and he had no intention of humiliating himself in such a manner.

Thus maddened by urgency and frenzied with need, he fell upon Jane like a wolf on a lamb, giving no thought to anything save his own release. Parting her again to ease his way, he took her in one hard thrust.

She screamed, her body stiffening beneath his as he ripped through her maidenhead. The next instant she began pounding on his back, tearfully begging him to stop. The sound of her pleas, broken and strangled with pain, immediately shocked him back to sanity.

He tried to stop then—heaven help him, he truly did try— but he couldn't. As if by a will of its own, his body kept thrusting. Once, twice, thrice, he shoved into her, each move accompanied by an agonized cry from Jane and one of shame from him. Then he spilled himself.

What Quentin felt as he climaxed wasn't pleasure, just release, a mere easing in his male parts. Humiliated by his loss of control and hating himself for his weakness, he rolled off her.

For a long while thereafter he simply lay there, his back to Jane and his face buried in the carpet as he listened to her weep.

He'd raped her. She was a virgin, and he had taken her in the cruelest possible manner.

Feeling like the world's biggest brute, he turned onto his back where he lay staring at the coffered ceiling above, bleakly trying to rationalize what had happened.

That she had provoked him into taking her was undeniable. Indeed, she had all but thrown herself at him the moment he'd stepped into the room, cooing and coaxing and tempting him in a manner that would have sorely tested a saint. Yes, and he mustn't forget how she had grabbed his sex. Women who wished to repel a man's advances most definitely did not do such things, especially to men who were so obviously aroused. No, and they didn't encourage those same men to stroke their intimate parts either.

Trembling faintly at the remembrance of the latter, he ran

his hand over his face. She had been wet down there, wet and ready and practically begging to be taken. By moaning and opening to him, she'd wantonly goaded him into doing as she wished.

Again she had manipulated him to her will.

Abruptly his shame turned to rage and he sat up, ignoring the virgin blood staining his nightclothes. First she had tricked him into marrying her, then she'd baited him into taking her. Now she laying sobbing, trying to cover her regret in doing so by making him feel guilty.

It was all he could do not to bellow at her in rage. Well, it wouldn't work. He'd given her what she wanted, and if she didn't like the manner in which he'd done so, she had only herself to blame. Indeed, she could count it as her first lesson in learning that she couldn't direct his life, at least not without suffering unpleasant consequences.

He smiled sardonically then. No doubt she thought to parade him through every ballroom in London, triumphantly flaunting him to the *ton* that had long ago relegated her to the shelf.

Well, she thought wrong. He had no intention of spending the remainder of the Season playing the dutiful husband. In truth, he had no intention of altering his life in the least, despite his father's threats. What he did intend to do was exercise the rights that the law extended a husband and banish her to the country.

A year or two alone at his dreary estate in Worcestershire would teach her smartly enough who was in charge.

Chapter 7

Her dream had died, and with it all hope for happiness. Quentin had killed it on their wedding night.

As she had done for the past three days, as she traveled the storm-ravished countryside to Worcestershire, Jane fought to expel the memory of that devastating night from her mind. As always happened, it remained starkly etched in her brain, mocking her for her foolishness in believing that he could ever love her.

Oh, how could she have been so stupid, so very blind? And why hadn't she listened to her father? Unlike she, herself, who had been dazzled by Quentin's beauty and silver-tongued words, her father had looked past appearances and questioned his lordship's sincerity. He'd suspected all along that Quentin lied about the reasons he wished to wed her, and he had tried to urge her not to go through with the marriage.

He had been right. Quentin had proven him so in both the churlishness with which he'd taken her and the callous way he'd treated her afterward.

The knot in her chest, which had plagued her since her wedding night, gave a savage wrench. No, she revised, her eyes welling up with tears, he'd been beyond callous. In the aftermath of their fierce mating, as she lay weeping on the hearth, desperately in need of a kind word or a gentle touch, he had been nothing short of cruel. First he'd accused her of trying to manipulate his life, then he'd curtly informed her that he was sending her away.

When she'd tearfully asked him why he'd wed her when it was so bitterly clear that he despised her, he had confessed his true motive. He'd married her to save himself from being cut off. And that had been that. Without so much as taking his leave, he had left her alone. That was the last she'd seen of him.

The next morning she had risen to find his coach waiting to take her to his estate in Worcestershire and a note informing her that he had dismissed Miss Parson. Since she was to live in the country, it said, she would no longer require the services of an abigail. That she knew no one in Worcestershire and could have used a companion to ease the loneliness of her days there was a consideration that had apparently never entered his mind.

Or perhaps it had. Perhaps he'd dismissed the woman with the express intent of making his wife feel her isolation all the more acutely. Whatever the case, that final blow had shattered her already fractured world.

The only thing that had saved her from dying of desolation right then and there was the sight of her darling Scratch, peeking out of a basket on the seat. From the perky red ribbon tied around his skinny neck, it was clear that it was Rissa's thoughtfulness that had made certain that her pet accompanied her into exile.

Miserably Jane wondered if Rissa, or any of her family, knew that her trip was an exile. She hoped not. The last thing she needed was the added sorrow of knowing that they worried about her and grieved for her new lot in life.

Sighing at that troubling new thought, she gently stroked Scratch, who slept on the seat beside her, and took comfort in his familiar presence. Ah, well. Once at her destination, she would write them and put to rest any concern they might harbor over her sudden departure. She would tell them . . . hmm. Yes. She would tell them that the trip was her idea. That she'd begged Quentin to let her return to the country, where she was more at ease, and that he'd kindly indulged her wishes. Exactly how she would explain the fact that he hadn't accompanied her she didn't know, but she would think of something.

Too exhausted from her emotional strain to consider the matter further, Jane rested her cheek against the coach window and watched the scenery roll by. After three days of delays from rain-flooded roads, washed-out bridges, and lanes rendered impassable by mud, the skies had at last cleared, and they had finally reached Worcestershire. Despite her despondence, Jane had to admit that it was a pretty county.

As far as the eye could see stretched emerald meadows and fields, gilded with sweeps of buttercups, dandelions, and gorse. Over there grew a copse of hawthorne trees, their branches laden with deep pink blossoms; here flourished a silver birch, fringed with yellow catkins. Now and again they passed orchards of cherry trees, all garbed in springtime splendor of frothy pink and white.

On they drove, past rolling pastures of black-faced lambs, past hedgerows edged with speedwell and ivy. Then the cantering horses slowed to a walk, and they entered the outskirts of a town.

Little Duckington, of course. When they had last stopped to change horses, the coachman had told Jane that the next town they reached would be Little Duckington, her husband's village.

Roused from her apathy by curiosity, she straightened up to study her surroundings. Except for their names, she knew nothing about either the village or the manor that was to be her new home. Quentin, of course, had been unavailable for questioning, and though kindly enough, neither the coachman nor the footman was inclined toward conversation. Thus she viewed the scene without expectation or prejudice.

After her first glance, she judged the place a delight. While not as large as Oxcombe or as obviously prosperous, the tiny town had a quaint, timeless charm that instantly endeared it to her. Like Oxcombe, Little Duckington was made up of a series of narrow, branching roads, edged by neat cottages. But unlike Oxcombe, whose dwellings were harmonious in both construction and style, these streets were lined with a queer hodgepodge of structures.

Over there stood a half-timbered house from Elizabeth's time; across from it was a Jacobean one of weathered red sandstone. On the corner, behind a neatly pruned hedge of yews, was a rather decrepit yet attractive example of medieval architecture. All the houses, she noted with a faint smile, had tiny gardens full of the sweet, simple country flowers she so loved.

For the first time since beginning her sad pilgrimage, Jane felt a lightening of her heart. Surely people who lavished such care on their flowers must be of a good and kind nature? Perhaps, just perhaps, she would find the contentment here that she'd found in Oxcombe.

She was certain of it when they progressed to the center of the village and she caught her first glimpse of the townspeople. All looked hale and jolly, and by the way they stopped amid their tasks and conversations to stare at the coach, they were clearly as intrigued by her as she was by them. The community was not on one of the regular coaching routes, and so strangers were most probably a rarity here, no doubt exciting endless speculation.

Unlike the citizens of many such isolated towns, who regarded strangers with chilly suspicion, the people of Little Duckington seemed inclined toward friendliness. Indeed, several of them smiled and nodded as she passed. One boy even waved. She was about to wave back when the coach hit a rut that almost pitched her out of her seat.

Crack! The vehicle listed crazily to the left.

Gr-r-r! Hiss! Scratch flew to her chest, where he clung to the bodice of her green merino carriage dress, his ears flat and his golden eyes round.

"Bloody hell!" the coachman bellowed, followed by a series of thumps as the footman and posting boy jumped down from the servant's seat in the rear. After several seconds of peering at the front left wheel, the footman looked up at the coachman, shaking his head.

Crooning in a soothing manner, Jane pried Scratch from her bodice and set him on her lap. After petting him a moment, she opened the window and inquired, "What has happened, Malcolm?"

Malcolm, the dour-faced footman, gave his box-cloth topcoat a cursory dusting with his hand, then came over to reply. "It's the wheel, my lady. It broke when we hit the rut."

Yet another delay. She sighed. "Well, I suppose we must find someone to mend it." A crowd had begun to gather around the coach, and it was to them that she now looked. Nodding cordially to a small knot of men nearby, all of whom instantly removed their battered hats and bowed, she called, "A good day to you, gentlemen. I was wondering if you might be kind enough to direct my man to your wheelwright?"

The men looked from one to another, as if trying to decide who should speak, then a stocky young man of about twenty stepped forward. Clutching his wide-brimmed hat nervously to his chest, he said, "We ain't got no wheelwright, my lady, but Bertie, the blacksmith, should be able to fix your wheel up right 'nough."

Jane smiled her most gracious smile, hoping to put him at ease. "Very well then, Mr.—?"

"Crawford, my lady." He bowed again. "Simon Crawford. Apprentice butcher. At your service."

She inclined her head in acknowledgment. "Pleased to make your acquaintance, Mr. Crawford. I am Lady Jane Somerville."

By the expression on his face, one would have thought that she'd punched him in the belly rather than introduced herself. The rest of the crowd, who had been smiling just seconds earlier, also looked stunned.

"Somerville?" a grizzled man croaked, exchanging a narrow-eyed glance with his equally aged neighbor.

She nodded, not quite certain what to make of their response, but suspicious that it had something to do with her husband—something disagreeable, if she didn't miss her guess. "Yes." She nodded again and forced her smile wider. "I have come to live at Swanswick Abbey."

There was a pause at that announcement, then a young woman with a broad, pleasant face and thick russet hair, meekly inquired, "Are ye *his* wife, then?"

Disagreeable. The something to do with her husband was most definitely disagreeable. She broadened her smile a fraction more. "If by *his*, you mean Lord Quentin's, then yes, I am his wife. We were wed four days ago."

A buzz arose at that revelation. As quickly as it began, it ceased, and the same woman said, "Pardon me fer askin', me lady. But we was wonderin' if yer husband were comin' too?"

Jane's smile faltered at that question. When they learned that Quentin had no plans to join her, they would probably assume that she was a nagging shrew of a wife whose presence he couldn't abide. Blast. And she had so wanted to make a fine impression.

Hoping that they would be just and reserve judgment of her until after they knew her, she replied softly, "No. I am afraid not, at least not anytime soon. I do hope, however, that you will all look upon me as a friend and feel free to call upon me should I ever be able to be of assistance." That last came out sounding more plea than invitation.

There followed another pause during which they all eyed her, though whether with disappointment or disapproval, she couldn't say. Then Simon Crawford smiled again, a warm and genuine smile, and stepped nearer. "Please let me be the first to welcome you to Little Duckington, my lady. I hope you'll be happy here." With a nod to underscore his greeting, he beckoned to the boy who had waved to her.

Upon closer view it was obvious that they were brothers. When the boy had doffed his cap, revealing a shock of unruly black hair, Simon directed, "Fetch Bertie for our lady. Tell him to hurry."

Rather than dash off to do his brother's bidding, the boy remained rooted in his tracks, his cheeks growing redder by degrees as he gaped at Jane.

"Willy?" his brother murmured, giving him a push.

"Gar! She's a pretty one," he whispered loudly. "Are all fine ladies so pretty, then?"

Pretty? Her? Why, she must look a fright after three days on the road. Absurdly pleased by the compliment, Jane grinned and replied, "Thank you for the praise, Willy, but there are many ladies a great deal prettier than I."

When he merely continued to stare, looking unconvinced, she added with a laugh, "When you are finished fetching the blacksmith, would you please go around to the village stable and see if I might hire a vehicle? I am exceedingly anxious to see my new home."

Someone snorted at that, while another person muttered, "She'll be anxious ta getta 'way when she sees it."

Ignoring their outburst, Simon said, "I'm afraid there ain't no stable, my lady. Most people in need of transportation hire the wagon at the Duck's Rest Inn, but the horse came up lame yesterday and won't be goin' nowhere for a week."

Jane considered that discouraging information for a moment, then sighed. "Well, then, I suppose I shall just have to wait for the wheel to be mended."

"Simon can take you," Willy piped in, looking exceedingly proud of himself. "He were abouts to deliver some meat at the abbey."

"Willy," Simon growled, casting her an apologetic look. "Ladies don't go ridin' about the countryside in tradesmen's wagons, 'specially not ladies from London. It ain't fittin'."

Jane laughed. "It so happens that I lived half my life in a village not much larger than yours, and have ridden with its butcher countless times. My grandfather was vicar, you see, and he often sent me to visit the surrounding farms. The butcher was always kind enough to give me a ride if he happened to be going in the same direction." She smiled and nodded at Simon. "In truth, Mr. Crawford, I would be much in your debt if you would take me and my footman to the abbey. I have a wish to arrive there before dark."

"Imagine that," a stout, merry-looking woman exclaimed. "*Him* taking her, a slip o' a country lass, for his bride." She cackled and shook her head, as if she couldn't believe his foolishness.

Jane felt her smile slip a fraction. Oh, dear. She supposed she really wasn't what one expected the lady of the manor to be.

Another cackle from the woman. "Well, well, well. Maybe there's something behind his lordship's pretty face after all." Meeting Jane's gaze with twinkling blue eyes, she said, "I'm Sarah Claypole, my lady, wife to the owner of Duck's Rest Inn. Welcome to our village. I can see that you'll be a fine addition."

With a friendly wink, she turned to the footman, who stood

conferring with the coachman, and snapped, "Well, don't just stand there, man. Help your lady down. She could no doubt do with a bit of refreshment before starting out for Swanswick." Jane couldn't be certain, but she thought she heard the woman add beneath her breath, "She's going to need her strength when she sees the place."

Oh, dear! Could matters at the abbey really be so dreadful? Before she could muse upon the question, Malcolm opened the door.

"Careful of the rut, my lady," he cautioned, jerking his head to the right. "Might not find you again if you fall in there."

Jane clutched the squirming Scratch to her bosom, her eyes widening at the sight of the furrow in question. It was at least two feet deep and five feet wide.

One of the men guffawed. "If ye think this un's bad, man, ye outta see the one by the church. Five cows, a wagon an' a whole flock o' ducks disappeared in it last week, an' they ain't been seen since."

Apparently this was a village joke, because everyone laughed.

"Well, that ain't nothin' compared to the hole on Blue Mallard Lane," chimed in a rawboned woman of middle years. "Ben Watney's mule fell in there yesterday, and he still ain't figgered out how to git it out again."

Not to be outdone, the woman next to her contributed, "And the one on the far side o' Three Duckling Bridge is even worse. Ain't been able to use that bridge for over a year now because of it."

Jane frowned, appalled that such problems could go unattended for so very long. "Have you not informed my husband of the need for repairs?" she queried.

Again everyone fell silent, this time to pass an uncomfortable glance among themselves.

It was Simon who finally spoke up. "In truth, we ain't seen his lordship in almost four years."

"Yes. And the last time he came, he only stayed for two days." This was from Mrs. Claypole, who shook her head, frowning her censure. "Had a couple of fine young swells with him. Not a one of them was sober the whole time they were here."

That bit of information did nothing to improve Jane's opinion of her husband. "Well, then what of his agent, Mr.—" she glanced to Simon, hoping that he could provide the man's name.

"Benjamin Maxwell," he supplied with a nod.

She nodded back. "Mr. Maxwell, yes, thank you. And what has he to say?" She looked to the innkeeper's wife for an answer, deeming her the most outspoken member of the crowd.

The woman shrugged. "He told us that his lordship said that we were to deal with matters as they are or go live somewhere else. Those of us that could afford to do so did just that."

Jane's wounded heart hardened at the revelation of yet another grievous flaw in her husband's character. Quentin Somerville was a villain. There was no getting around the fact. For only a villain would disregard the needs of the people who depended on him.

More incensed than disheartened by the knowledge, she gazed first at the people—her people now—then at the street around her. Now that she really looked at the cottages and shops, she saw definite signs of neglect. All the thatched roofs were furrowed with age; those made of slate were cracked and missing tiles. The timbered houses she had so admired all needed whitewash and daub; the stone and brick ones suffered for a mason. Then there was the matter of the streets, and heaven only knew what other troubles lurked behind the idyllic facade of Little Duckington.

Jane's jaw tightened, as did her resolve. Her husband might not care about these people and their village, but she did. And she would see to it that both got the care and consideration they deserved, no matter what it took.

Securing her hold on Scratch, who seemed determined to wriggle out of her arms and attack the flock of ducks that now stood quacking at the crippled carriage, she looked back at the crowd. "Please make a list of all the needed repairs and present it to me. I shall see that they are made, I promise. This is my home now, and I intend to see to its welfare."

"But what of yer husband?" someone called out.

"And Mr. Maxwell?" queried another.

She smiled grimly. "Leave them to me."

It was worse than she'd imagined. Far worse. And she had expected it to be bad. Simon had warned her of Swanswick's frightful state as he drove Malcolm and her to the house. Still, nothing he'd said had fully prepared her for the sight that now met her eyes. The place was a shambles!

Built two hundred years earlier in the gabled style of the time, the blue-gray stone house loomed before her, forlorn and unloved, a moldering ghost of its former glory. And it had been glorious once, that much was apparent from its elaborate heraldic roof finials, ornamental entry porch, and clusters of highly decorated chimney stacks.

Now, however, some of the finials were either missing or broken, the chimneys were crumbling, and the porch sagged dangerously on one side. To make matters all the more dismaying, what windows weren't overgrown with ivy were cracked and missing panes. Completing the sad portrait of neglect were the grounds, which grew wild and corrupted by weeds. In truth, were it not for the thin curl of smoke spiraling sullenly from one of the chimneys, Jane would have thought the house long abandoned.

"Mind the steps," Simon cautioned Malcolm, who was prepared to march up the porch stairs and announce his lady's arrival. "The mortar's cracked away and the stones've come loose."

Malcolm, who bore an injured air at having been required to ride in a butcher wagon, cast Jane a long-suffering look, then sighed and cautiously picked his way to the door, shaking his head and grumbling to himself as he went. Once at his destination, he removed his hat and lifted the door knocker to knock.

It came off in his hand. For several beats he simply stared at it, as if he couldn't quite believe his eyes, then he shot Jane another affronted look and deposited it on the sagging wood settle nearby. With as much dignity as he could muster at that point, he pounded on the door with his immaculately gloved fist.

No answer.

He banged again, this time louder.

Still nothing.

"Are you certain someone is here?" Jane asked, frowning. Perhaps the smoke she had seen was the final exhaust from a recently banked fire.

"Aye. Jemma lives here. So do Owen and Martha. They should be expectin' you." Simon tipped his head, peering at her in query. "They are expectin' you, ain't they?"

After what she'd learned of Quentin's character, she doubted that he'd bothered to notify the staff of her arrival. Embarrassed by his thoughtlessness, she murmured, "Perhaps the message was delayed by the storm."

"But—"

"Who are Jemma, Owen, and Martha?" she interrupted, not wanting to pursue the topic.

He gazed at her for an instant, frowning, then blinked and looked back at the house. "Jemma's sort of a maid of all

works, and Martha's the cook. Owen, well"—he shrugged—
"he's Martha's husband. He used to be head carpenter back in
the days when Swanswick had a carpenters' shop. Now he
does a bit of this 'n that to keep the place from fallin' down.
Both he and Martha have lived here for nigh onto thirty
years."

"And my husband's agent, Mr. Maxwell, where does he
live? I thought it customary for an estate agent to live at the
manor for which he is responsible?"

"Oh, him." A snort. "He lives in the dowager cottage on
the other side of the park." He pointed in the direction of the
wooded deer park. "If he had the servants spend as much time
tendin' this place as he does his own, it'd look a whole sight
better. He—" He broke off abruptly, his expression changing
as if he'd been struck by a new idea. "Hmm. Now there's a
thought. Owen and Jemma might be slavin' away for
Maxwell. Martha should be here, though. He'll be wantin' her
to roast up this beef for his supper."

"Perhaps she went to his house to cook and expects you to
deliver it there?" Jane suggested, incensed by what she was
hearing. No doubt the agent, like most men in his position,
was well compensated for his services and could easily afford
his own servants. He had no excuse or right to monopolize the
ones at Swanswick in such a manner.

Another snort from Simon. "Nah. Maxwell don't allow
cookin' in the cottage. Says the odors hang around and turn
his stomach."

"Well, then—" She glanced at Malcolm, who stood on the
porch awaiting instruction, then back at Simon.

He shrugged and called to the footman, "Is the door unlocked?" As the man turned to check, he added to Jane,
"Seein' as how you're mistress here now, it ain't trespassin'
for you to go on in."

Malcolm tugged at the door, then turned back to them, shaking his head.

"Oh, dear." She considered for a moment, then said, "I suppose we shall just have to enter through the kitchen. If Martha is indeed expecting you, the servant's entrance should be unlocked."

"The kitchen!" By Simon's tone, you would have thought that she'd suggested visiting a bawdy house.

She laughed at his shocked expression. "I hardly think it likely that I'll fall into vapors at the sight of pots and pans. In truth, I've been known to scrub a few in my time. My grandparents weren't ones for coddling children. They insisted that my brother and I help with the daily chores."

At that instant, Scratch, who was imprisoned in his basket beneath the seat, let out an indignant yowl. She laughed again and added, "Besides, poor Scratch could do with a saucer of milk, and what better place to find one than in the kitchen?"

With a nod to emphasize her resolve, she beckoned to the footman, who looked even more horrified than the butcher had when she told him of her plan. Mindful of his place, however, he refrained from comment and resumed his seat in the back of the wagon.

As Simon drove them around to the servants' entrance, Jane was able to get a more comprehensive view of the manor. With some relief she noted that the sides and back were in no worse condition than the front. Well, at least as far as she could tell. The actual state would, of course, have to be determined by the workmen she intended to hire on the morrow.

It was thinking of all the work to be done that turned her mind to financial matters. She must ask the agent for the estate ledgers as soon as possible, so that she could assess what funds were available for the repairs.

And if they proved inadequate, as she suspected?

She gave her head an impatient shake. She would just have to write to her father and request a portion of her dowry.

Her dowry. Yet another bone of contention between her and Quentin.

She sighed. Ah, well. It didn't really matter anymore what he thought or how he felt. He'd made it perfectly clear that he wished no part of her, and she'd be damned before she'd waste any more time thinking about a man who didn't want her. From here on out, her sole concern would be Swanswick and its tenants. Despite her disappointing marriage, her life would be both meaningful and satisfying. She would make it so.

"I'm sorry things ain't nicer, my lady, but we wasn't told ye was comin'," Jemma apologized for what must have been the tenth time in the past half hour.

The pretty blond maid had been in the laundry starching Mr. Maxwell's neckcloths when they arrived, and at Jane's request now showed her about the house. Like the exterior, the interior proved in dire need of refurbishment, though to Jemma's credit, everything appeared at least somewhat clean.

Turning from her examination of the mildewed drawing room drapes, caused, no doubt, by rain coming in through the missing windowpanes, Jane smiled tightly and said, "You have done just fine, Jemma. It isn't your fault that the house is in such bad repair." No. The fault lay entirely with Mr. Maxwell. It was his job to attend to each problem as it arose, a duty he had clearly shirked. Wishing that Simon would hurry up and return with the man so she could grill him on his laxity, she added, "I believe I'm ready to see the upstairs now."

The maid wrung her apron, her gray eyes growing so large that they seemed to encompass her entire face. "I'm 'fraid it's even worse up there. Mr. Maxwell told us we wasn't to bother wi' the bedchambers, so they ain't been aired out for well on a year now."

"Indeed?" Jane murmured, her own eyes widening as a mouse popped its head out of a hole in the once fine sofa. "And what would he have you do with your day, then, if not attend to your duties here?" Though she already knew the answer, she wanted to hear the maid's account of the agent's transgressions to make certain that it agreed with those she'd received from Martha and Simon.

The girl, and she truly was little more than a girl, nervously wrung her apron a fraction tighter. "He . . . he says it's my duty to care fer him 'n the cottage," she stammered out. "Well, me 'n Owen, that is. I do all the cleanin', washin', 'n ironin' 'n all them sort o' things, 'n Owen does the fetchin' 'n carryin'. If we finish wi' all that 'fore ten, we's to work here."

"I see," she said, wandering over to a conspicuously empty space in the center of the room. By the shape and depth of the impressions in the stained Wilton carpet, it appeared that a pianoforte had once graced the spot . . . and recently, if she didn't miss her guess.

When she quizzed the maid in her suspicion, she replied, "It were sold last month to pay Benny Crofts, the coal man. That, 'n the two portraits from the upstairs hall, 'n the last o' the silver candlesticks in the dinin' room."

Jane whirled around to stare at the girl in astonishment. "What? Surely the bill couldn't have been that much in arrears? Why, my father's country house doesn't use nearly that much coal in a year, and he keeps sixteen servants in residence."

Jemma bit her lip and looked away, a faint blush staining her fair cheeks. "Me'n Martha 'n Owen was wonderin' about it too, 'specially seein' as how the fancy crystal dinin' room chandelier, 'n the other three candlesticks was sold just three months ago fer the same reason."

Jane could do little more than stare at the maid, not trusting herself to speak for fear that she would vent her rage. The agent was a thief. He had to be. There was no other explanation for her husband's valuables being—

A-hem! Both women started, then turned in unison. At the sight of the tall, foppishly dressed man standing just inside the door, the maid fell into a curtsy, squeaking, "Mr. Maxwell, sir."

He snapped his fingers and waved her out of the room, his gaze never once leaving Jane as he did so. As the maid scrambled to do his bidding, he sketched a shallow bow and uttered, "My lady. This is indeed a surprise." It was clear from his tone that he didn't find the surprise a particularly pleasant one.

She nodded stiffly in acknowledgment. "Mr. Maxwell, thank you for coming so promptly. As Simon no doubt told you, there are several matters I wish to discuss with you."

"He did, my lady, though I must profess bewilderment at your request. I cannot think of a single issue of mutual concern," he said, eyeing her with the same patronizing amusement one might direct at a five year-old demanding pudding for breakfast.

"Indeed?" she retorted, galled by his manner. "How very queer. I can think of at least a dozen such issues, not the least of which is the disappearance of the pianoforte and several other objects of value."

"Ah, yes. The pianoforte." His pale green eyes narrowed and his thin-lipped mouth curved into a chilly smile. "I shall be happy to explain the matter to you . . . tomorrow."

"Now will be fine, thank you," she countered, folding her arms. As Jane knew from her experience in Oxcombe, evasiveness was the sure mark of a thief.

His smile faded and his eyes narrowed a fraction more. "I think not. It is clear that you are tired from your journey, and I have learned from regrettable experience that females are—

a-hem!—well, let us just say that they are less than reasonable when tired." He shook his head. "No, my lady, it shall be best for us both if I send around my carriage to take you to the inn, where we shall discuss matters after you have rested."

"I can assure you, sir, that I am not the least bit tired, nor do I need you to tell me what is best for me. You also needn't bother sending your carriage, as I have no intention of going to the inn."

"But of course you will stay at the inn. We received no word of your coming and are thus unprepared to receive visitors." It wasn't a protest or a plea, it was a command, a high-handed one.

It wasn't his tone, however, but his use of the word "visitor" that stiffened Jane's spine. Deciding it high time he learned his place, she reminded him in her most cultured voice, "I am the mistress of Swanswick, not a visitor. Please be good enough to remember that fact in the future, Mr. Maxwell. As for being unprepared, well, the word 'unprepared' hardly begins to describe the dreadful state in which I find this household. Indeed, from what I have seen and heard of your management, you have a great deal to answer for."

He shrugged one expensively garbed shoulder, clearly unperturbed. "I shall be perfectly happy to answer any questions his lordship might have."

Her back went up even more at his insolent dismissal of her authority. Arrogant wretch! If he thought her a green girl whom he could bully, cow, and then dismiss, well, he had better think again. Knowing that to show her anger would give him the upper hand, she forced herself to smile and reply calmly, "As an agent of some experience, I expect that you know that a wife has the right to act on her husband's behalf in his absence. That includes asking questions and directing his affairs as she sees fit."

He inclined his head in acknowledgment of her point, revealing a thin spot in his carefully coiffed hair. "That is true, yes, provided, of course, that the wife in question has the sense and experience to do so."

"Oh, you needn't worry on that account," she replied, her hand itching to snatch the spot completely bald. "I can assure you that I have more than enough sense and experience to deal with an estate this size. Indeed, I kept my grandfather's vicarage accounts when I was just fourteen and oversaw the parish relief. I think you will find me quite capable, sir."

His eyes began to narrow again. "Indeed? Well, then, his lordship must count himself fortunate to have such a clever wife. Tell me, my lady, when exactly were you and Lord Quentin wed?"

"Friday last."

His brows rose in mock surprise. "So recently? My, my. How very odd that he should allow you from his side so soon."

Jane saw instantly what he was about, and she refused to be shamed into retreat. Deliberately lying, and not feeling the least bit guilty for doing so, she retorted, "My husband is currently involved in a business transaction that is expected to keep him in town for some months. Therefore, when he voiced concern over matters here, I naturally insisted on coming myself. As everyone knows, it is a wife's duty to help her husband in any way possible, even if the wife is a wife of only a few days' time and in helping him must travel from his side."

"How very commendable," he rasped, staring at her in a manner that was no doubt meant to unnerve her. "I do profess to find it queer, however, that your husband should take such a sudden interest in Swanswick. As you most probably know, it has been years since he's bothered to visit." By his expression, he clearly expected her to know no such thing.

She returned his stare in kind. "It has been a long time, yes, almost four years," she said, remembering Simon's saying so. "He told me all about it. He came with several friends who grew tired of the country rather quickly and insisted on returning to town."

"Yes." The man's eyes were pale slits now, and for the first time since beginning the interview, he looked alarmed.

Seizing her advantage, she added, "It was one of those gentlemen, Lord Oxley, I believe"—as Quentin's best friend, she assumed he would have been among the visitors— "who drew Swanswick's deterioration to his notice. It seems that he passed by here on his way to Worcester a fortnight ago and was shocked by what he saw. Naturally, my husband was most distressed by the news."

"Naturally," the agent muttered.

Jane smiled pleasantly and nodded. "Since it was obvious to Lord Oxley, as it now is to me, that the profits from the estate are going to something other than the maintenance of the house and lands, my husband shall, of course, wish a full accounting of where the monies were spent."

"Of course," he bit out from behind gritted teeth. "And he shall have it. I will write a full report and send it to him posthaste."

"Oh, that shan't be necessary," she replied sweetly. "The last thing either of us wishes is to put you to any trouble." She shook her head. "His wish is that I look at the estate ledgers and ascertain matters for myself. As you yourself said, my husband counts himself fortunate to have such a clever wife. I shall expect you to present the books to me within the hour."

"Impossible!" The instant the word was out, he clamped his mouth shut, as if regretting his outburst.

"Why is it impossible? You do have the books, I assume? It is, after all, your job to keep them."

"I most certainly do not need you to remind me of my duties, madame," he snapped.

"Apparently you do," she flung back, her patience at an end. "A single glance at Little Duckington and Swanswick is enough to prove that."

"It is obvious by that remark that you know nothing about business, my dear, despite your ministering of village charities." He uttered the word "charities" as if the institutions were beneath contempt. "The running of an estate is a complex and difficult affair, far too much so for a chit with your limited capabilities."

Suddenly weary and determined not to be drawn into the argument he so clearly wished to provoke, she icily replied, "My capabilities or lack of such are none of your concern, sir, nor is it your place to question them. You shall have the books here within the hour, or I will send the parish constable to fetch them."

"Fine." He slapped his gray beaver hat on his head. Pausing only long enough to shoot her a look of unadulterated hatred, he turned on his heel and stormed out of the room.

Just over an hour later, Owen returned bearing the books.

As Jane had suspected, the agent was a thief, and after she sat up well into the early hours of the morning to confirm the fact by examining the books, it hardly came as a bolt out of the blue to learn that Mr. Maxwell had fled during the night.

Chapter 8

One week flew by, then another and another. The showers and rainbows of late April surrendered to the sunshine of May, leaving the countryside awash with spring colors. May faded quickly into June, bringing the warm promise of summer.

For Jane, the days flew by in a blur of bustling activity as she worked to restore the house and oversaw repairs to the village and farms. They were daunting tasks, sometimes seeming nothing short of impossible, but it was work that brought her immense satisfaction with every obstacle she surmounted. And while it was true that her new life wasn't perfect, what with the disappointing state of her marriage, it was closer to being so than she'd ever imagined possible.

She was content, and that was enough.

Today, however, as she drove through the village, viewing the improvements, she soared past contentment and landed squarely in happiness. With the aid of a little paint here, some mortar there, a bit of cobblestone, and wagonloads of thatch, the promise of Little Duckington's charm had at last been realized. It was as neat and pretty a hamlet as one could hope to find in all of England.

As she drove her gig down Red Drake Road, her heart swelling with pride, an elderly woman paused in her broom-making to call, "A very fine mornin' to ye, my lady!"

Jane waved and reined her docile roan mare to a stop. "A

good day to you too, Mrs. Jeffries. I do hope your husband is feeling better this morning?"

The woman nodded her cottony white head, her withered lips stretching into a gap-toothed grin. "Right as a trivet, thanks to yer physic."

She smiled back, her already buoyant mood soaring at the news. "I am indeed glad to hear it," she replied, leaning out of the vehicle to hand the woman a jar. "Please give him this with my sincerest wishes for his continued good health. It's quince jelly. It will help his throat should he have any lingering soreness."

"Bless ye, Lady Jane. Bless ye fer the angel ye are," the woman exclaimed, giving Jane's hand a grateful squeeze as she took the offering.

Jane felt herself blush with pleasure at the woman's heartfelt tribute. "And bless you for being a part of our village, Mrs. Jeffries. The brooms you made for Swanswick have made the cleaning ever so much easier. Why, my maids have all declared that they shall never again use a broom made by anyone else."

"Lady Jane! My lady!"

She looked up to see Jacob Flixton, the glovemaker, rush out of his shop next door, followed at a more sedate pace by his pet ducks, William and Mary.

"Look, my lady!" He waved a rumpled paper excitedly in the air. "My first London order. That shop where you sent the samples says my gloves are the finest they ever saw, and they've ordered twelve dozen pairs in assorted colors. Twelve dozen! Why, that's more gloves than I sold in the past three years!"

Jane laughed, every bit as thrilled as he. "No doubt they will be ordering a great many more once the ladies of the *ton* see your excellent work. Congratulations, Mr. Flixton. You look to be on your way to being a very successful man."

"All thanks to you. It was your idea for me to sell my gloves to the London shop and you who sent the samples," he declared, his dark eyes nothing short of adoring as he gazed up at her.

She grinned, her gaiety bubbling over into another laugh. "Nonsense! The success is entirely yours, sir. It is your superb skill that prompted the orders. I did nothing but write a letter and post a parcel."

"Well, it's more than anyone else ever did for me, and I thank you for it." He paused, looking as if he wished to say more. Then he reached into the pocket of his work apron and drew out a pair of gloves, prettily tied up in a yellow ribbon. "I hope you don't think me too forward, my lady, but I made these for you . . . uh . . . in thanks. They're not much, but I want you to have them."

Jane reached down and took the gloves, gasping her delight. Made of fine buff leather, they were exquisitely worked around the cuffs in a design depicting the wildflowers she so loved. "Oh, Jacob, thank you! They're beautiful," she cried, removing her driving gloves to try them on. Of course they were a perfect fit.

"They're for working in the garden . . . to protect your hands. I heard that you like to help with the planting and such, and well, it wouldn't do for our lady's hands to get rough and ruined. I treated the leather special to help keep them nice for you."

"They're wonderful," she murmured, not looking up from her admiration of his gift. "I shall treasure them always."

Mrs. Jeffries, who had been watching the exchange with approval, said, "As I were tellin' our lady, she's a godsend. Everyone's sayin' so. A real angel, she is."

"An angel," the glovemaker echoed, gazing up at her as if she were indeed a celestial being.

Jane felt her cheeks grow warm again. "Oh, posh. I'm simply doing what any good mistress should. Now, as much as I would like to tarry, I must bid you both a good day. I still have several more visits to make." She nodded first to Mrs. Jeffries. "Please do give my best to your husband." Then to the glove-maker, "Congratulations again, Mr. Flixton," and with a snap of the reins she was off.

Down every street she traveled, she experienced a similar scene—people rushing out to greet her and to relay their latest news, all good. Thus it was early afternoon before she reached her final destination, the Duck's Rest Inn.

"My lady, what a pleasure!" Mrs. Claypole called, waving her welcome as she stepped from the kitchen door into the stable yard.

"It's wonderful to see you too, Sarah," she replied, smiling at the woman who had become a surrogate mother of sorts. "I brought the celery seeds I promised."

"Bless you, child. I can certainly use them. I don't know what got into my kitchen garden this spring, but it surely was partial to celery." She paused to signal to her fourteen-year-old grandson, Joel, who stood near the stable, broom in hand, watching them with bright-eyed interest. "I was just setting the kettle to boil. You will take a cup of tea with me, I hope?"

"Why, yes, thank you. Tea sounds very nice. I'm feeling rather tired all of a sudden, and it should be just the thing to refresh me," she replied, relinquishing the reins and two of Martha's freshly baked gingerbread men to Joel. The carrot-topped youth grinned his delight and promptly bit the head off one of the men.

Frowning, Sarah moved to the gig to help Jane down. When she was safely on solid ground, the woman took her face in her hands and peered at it with concern. "Goodness, but you're looking peaky today—pale as Old Man McKellan's white drake. Best you come in and rest in the parlor."

Sitting in Sarah's cool, comfortable parlor did sound nice,

thus Jane voiced no protest as the woman hustled her inside, clucking over her like a hen with one chick.

"There now, my lady," she crooned, settling Jane into a chair with thick, soft cushions. After hovering a moment, she fetched a footstool and insisted that Jane put up her feet. Her fussing thus completed to her satisfaction, she bustled off to the kitchen to prepare refreshment.

Grateful for a few moments of peace, Jane sank yet deeper into the cushions, watching with heavy eyes as a bright blue butterfly floated through the open window and landed in the pot of pinks on the sill. After several minutes of watching it flutter from blossom to blossom, she closed her eyes, lulled by the soft clanging of pans and the murmur of voices drifting from the kitchen.

Comfortable, so very comfortable. She took a deep breath, savoring the inn's homey aroma of baking bread and dried lavender. Ah. Lovely. She exhaled on a sigh of contentment.

She couldn't say exactly when she dozed off or how long she slept, but when she awoke she did so to find the innkeeper's wife peering at her with worry.

"Oh, Sarah, I'm so sorry," she murmured, smiling sheepishly. "I don't know what has gotten into me of late. I seem to fall asleep at the blink of an eye."

The woman clucked and began to pour tea. "It's no small wonder you're fagged out, what with the way you've been working. And you being a such a tiny, delicate little thing!" She shook her head as she plopped two lumps of sugar into the cup.

Jane yawned, stretching as she straightened up. "In truth, I haven't been working hard at all the past week. Most of the truly difficult work is done, and there has been little for me to do but select wallcoverings and decide what vegetables to plant in the kitchen garden." She yawned again. "Goodness! I feel as though I could sleep for a week."

Sarah paused amid doling out cakes to stare at her with narrowed eyes. "Have you been sleeping well at night?"

She blinked drowsily. "Well enough, I suppose, though I've been plagued by a touch of dyspepsia of late that awakens me rather early." She shrugged. "No doubt it's caused by all the macaroons I've been eating. I seem to have developed a sudden fondness for them."

The other woman stared at her for a beat, frowning. Then her brow cleared and she chuckled. "Macaroons, is it? It was marchpane with me."

It was Jane's turn to frown. "Excuse me?"

"When I was expecting my daughter, Rachel, I had a fierce craving for marchpane."

"What?" She blinked in confusion, then the meaning of her friend's words dawned. "Oh, heavens, no! I'm not in the family way. I can't be!"

Could she?

Sarah smiled gently. "Are you so very sure?"

"I-I . . . do you think it possible?" she murmured, not certain whether to wish for it to be true or not.

"You have the signs," the older woman replied, taking the tea and cakes to Jane.

"Signs?" she whispered.

"Feeling sick in the morning, sleepiness and cravings, and . . ." Sarah paused, gazing at Jane as if considering something. "Pardon me for being forward, but when were your last menses?"

She thought for a moment, trying to remember. "Um . . . let me see now. The first week in . . . yes, the first week in April." Heavens! She'd been so busy, she hadn't even missed them.

"Two months." The woman's mouth broadened into a very wide, very pleased grin. "If I don't miss my guess, dear girl, you will be presenting Little Duckington with their future lord or lady some time in January." She clapped. "Oh, but this is happy news!"

Happy? Jane set aside her plate and gingerly laid her hands against her still flat belly. A baby. She closed her eyes, imagining that she could feel its tiny heart beating against her palm. She smiled. A little boy or girl. Someone whom she could love and share her life with.

Happy?

Slowly she opened her eyes and met Sarah's sparkling gaze. "Yes," she said softly. "Oh, yes! It is very happy news indeed."

No doubt she would be resentful . . . and querulous . . . a veritable shrew. It had, after all, been over two months since he'd exiled Jane to his estate, and she was probably half mad with boredom by now . . . as he, himself, would most likely be after spending the months mandated by his father there.

Making a face at the thought of his father, Quentin took a long pull of whiskey from his silver flask. The bastard! When his father had found out that he had banished Jane to the country, he'd been furious and had delivered a most unreasonable ultimatum: Either bring her back for the remainder of the Season and play the fawning husband, or suffer the consequences. The consequences, of course, were that he would be banned from London society.

Enraged by this new demand, he'd refused. He had, after all, done as the bastard had commanded and married the chit, and to his way of thinking that was quite enough. It was certainly far better than the scheming baggage deserved. For though his father stubbornly refused to see the truth of the matter, it was he, Quentin Somerville, who was the victim in all this, not Jane. She'd gotten exactly what she wanted, a husband, while he'd lost forever the only woman he'd ever loved.

As it always did of late when he thought of beautiful Clarissa, a knife seemed to turn in his heart. He'd had such hopes for their life together, such marvelous plans and dreams. With her there would have been no need for ultimatums. He'd have gladly and proudly escorted her about London, or anywhere else she wished to go. For her, he'd have played the adoring slave.

But those dreams were all dead now, killed by Jane and her deceit. And he'd be damned before he'd be party to sustaining it. Thus he'd held firm to his resolve to punish her and had defied his father.

Within a month thereafter, all invitations from the *ton* ceased. By the six-week mark, he'd been turned away from the doors of every fashionable bastion of amusement in London. As his father had promised, he'd been effectively shunned from society. It was after the seventh week, during which he'd had no diversion save the increasingly scarce company of Oxley, that his father had again called on him.

Like the devil Quentin was beginning to suspect him of being, he'd offered him a deal: If Quentin went to the country and stayed with his wife until after Christmas, hence giving his marriage a chance at succeeding, he would see Quentin restored to the good graces of the *ton* and allow him to return to Town the following Season.

Though Quentin would rather have died than again play the pawn in his father's despotic game, he saw no choice. To him, a life without the *ton* and its endless rounds of amusements was a fate worse than death. And so he now traveled to the country . . .

He snorted. Correction. He was in the country. Raising the flask to his lips, determined to drown both his sorrows and the stabbing pain in his flank in a numbing wash of whiskey, he gazed out the window at the village they had just entered.

A frown knit his brow at the sight of it. Where were they,

anyway? He couldn't recall passing through this pretty little town on either of his two journeys to Swanswick Abbey. Of course, he hadn't paid much mind to his surroundings on his first trip, having been traveling in the company of a particularly delectable and lusty bit of muslin. As for his second visit, well, he, Oxley, and their friend, Lord Dutnall, had been foxed the entire way.

Desperate to achieve a like state now, Quentin again tipped the flask to his lips, this time bent on draining its entire contents. As he drank, ignoring the burning in his throat as he gulped, the coach came to a jarring halt. "What the—"

Crash! The vessel flew from his hand and dashed against the coach floor.

"Oomph!"

His body followed suit.

For a long moment thereafter he lay crumpled between the facing seats, too stunned to do anything else. Then he slowly rose to his knees, carefully testing his limbs for damage. Nothing seemed broken there. Experimentally, he flexed his spine.

"Ow!" Gritting his teeth in agony, he dug his fist hard into his left flank. He'd had a most wicked pain there for the past two days, and though he'd tried to ignore it, hoping that in doing so it would go away, it was now apparent that he had another of the stones that had caused him such misery just last year. Groaning his dread at the torment that lay before him, he snatched up the flask.

It was empty. All the whiskey had spilled out and now soaked into the carpet. Expelling the coarsest oath he knew, he tossed it aside. Just his rotten luck. Cursing again, he dug his fist yet deeper into his flank and gingerly eased himself into his seat.

As Quentin sat massaging the inflicted area, muttering his discontent, the trapdoor above his head opened and the weathered face of his coachman appeared. "Sorry about the sudden stop, my lord. You all right?"

"Do I look all right?" Before the man could reply, he snapped, "What the devil possessed you to stop like that, anyway?"

The servant bit his lip and looked away. "Er—*ahem!*— ducks, my lord."

"Ducks?" he echoed with a snort.

"A whole flock of 'em, my lord."

Another snort. "Why the hell didn't you just run them over? Would've served them right for standing in the road."

The man's face darkened into something suspiciously like a blush. "Uh—they're—um—they're wearing hats, my lord."

"Hats?" He drew back, scowling. Certain that the driver had lost his wits, he glanced out the window.

Three ducks of assorted shapes and colors waddled by, all decked out in the most ridiculous headgear he'd ever seen. One, a queerly speckled monster of a fowl, wore a tall conical creation with a scrape of sheer cloth that suggested a medieval hennin. Another, a dainty brown wood duck, flaunted a foil crown bejeweled with bits of colored glass. Still another was arrayed in what appeared for all the world to be a bridal veil, complete with a wreath of orange blossoms.

"What the devil?" he muttered, glancing up at the coachman in bewilderment. The man nodded and disappeared, then reappeared several moments later, saying, "It's a parade, my lord. The annual Little Duckington Duck March."

Little Duckington? His village? He glanced out the window in disbelief. Why, this couldn't be Little Duckington. Little Duckington was a shabby, dreary hamlet with rutted roads and dilapidated cottages. This place . . . why, it was charming—well, as far as villages went, that is. It most definitely couldn't be his Little Duckington.

Yet, it had to be. There couldn't be two Little Duckingtons

in Worcester. Besides, now that he looked about, the ancient stone church did look rather familiar . . .

As did the small figure in pink in the forefront of the crowd gathered on the green beside the church.

His eyes narrowed as he homed in on the woman, and sudden anger gripped his insides as he recognized her. It was his wife, and she was behaving in a most unseemly manner. Indeed, she appeared to be leading the villagers in their cheering of the passing ducks.

Outraged that she'd not only allowed such foolishness to take place, but encouraged and participated in it as well, he wrathfully rapped his blackthorn cane against the roof of the coach, signaling the driver, who had, to his increased chagrin, again disappeared.

The man instantly reappeared, looking sheepish. "My lord?"

"Instruct the footman to bid my wife to come to me this instant," he bit out. It would be a cold day in hell before he allow a wife of his to make such a spectacle of herself.

Through the window he could see that the crowd had spied his vehicle and now silently gaped at it. As for Jane, she stood very stiff and still, as if frozen with shock.

And with good reason, he thought, eyeing the scene with tight-lipped fury. She couldn't help but recognize both the coach and the approaching footman, since they were the same ones that had brought her here. No doubt she guessed that he was in the vehicle and was horrified that he'd witnessed her ill-bred behavior.

As Quentin watched, the footman came to a stop before her and delivered his message. After staring at the coach a moment longer, she looked at the man and replied. He appeared to start to speak again, but she shook her head and interjected something. After glancing at the coach, as if uncertain what to do, the servant bowed and returned.

"Well?" he barked, yanking open the window.

"She—uh—" The footman shot Jane, who had turned back to the parade of ducks and now applauded their progress, an anxious look. "She says that she will speak with you at the house when she has finished judging the duck disguises."

"She what!" he bellowed. Why the incorrigible little—little—hoyden! How dare she dismiss his orders in such a manner!

"She said that—"

"I heard you the first time," he snapped. Seething with mounting rage, he watched through narrowed eyes as she again coaxed the villagers into a frenzy of cheers. If she thought she could do whatever she pleased, whenever she wished, and naysay his commands at every turn, well—

"Open the door," he barked, slapping on his hat. He would take the insolent baggage in hand and do it now. She would learn who was in charge once and for all. Giving his yellow silk waistcoat a savage tug of adjustment, he stepped from the vehicle.

"Oomph!" *Quack Q-ua-q-uack!* He tripped over an enormous white duck wearing a cocked military hat.

Smack! "Oww!" He fell backward, bruising both his dignity and his hip, and provoking yet another stabbing pain in his flank.

"My lord!" The horrified footman rushed to help him up. As he reached down to grasp his master's arm, the enraged duck darted forward and launched a pecking attack on Quentin's boot.

"Damn it, Malcolm, get that blasted beast away from me!" he spat, kicking in an attempt to repel its advances. It changed strategies and lunged at his arm.

Always the faithful servant, the footman grabbed for the animal. It quacked furiously and redirected its charge at him. Flailing one arm to ward it off, he snatched up the cane

Quentin had dropped in his fall and lifted it to beat off his attacker.

"No! Don't you dare hit that duck!" cried a feminine voice, a warning echoed by several youthful shrieks.

The footman froze, giving the beast the opportunity to dart forward and peck his knee.

Quentin looked up from his seat on the ground to see Jane, her bonnet awry and her muslin skirts hitched immodestly high above her ankles, tearing across the green, her steps shadowed by two sturdy boys and a skinny little girl.

"Drop that cane this instant! Do you hear me? This instant!" she commanded, coming to a skidding stop before the footman.

Without giving him a chance to respond, she yanked the weapon out of his hand and tossed it into the coach. Signaling to the children, who stood watching with wide eyes, she said, "Take poor Wellington over by the cross and calm him. Here," she dug a small sausage out of the basket over her arm and handed it to one of the boys. "Lure him with this. These are his favorites."

Wellington the duck promptly ceased his attack at the sight of the treat, and his beady black eyes were riveted on it as he waddled after the boy, who used it to coax him away from the coach. The other two children brought up the rear, shooing him along.

When both fowl and children were well out of earshot, Quentin stiffly rose to his feet, hissing, "What the hell possessed you to make such a spectacle of yourself?"

"Me?" She recoiled slightly, as if taken aback. "It was not I who fell on my backside and had to be rescued from a duck."

"No, but it was your vulgar behavior that prompted the incident," he gritted out, again pressing his fist into his sore flank. God, but he felt wretched. Wanting nothing more than to go to Swanswick, where he could upbraid her over a palliative glass of spirits, he finished, "But enough. I refuse to argue with you in public. We will discuss your disgraceful conduct at home, in private. Now get in the coach."

To his annoyance, she folded her arms across her chest and stubbornly shook her head. "As far as I am concerned, we have naught to discuss. I have done nothing wrong, and thus see no reason to indulge you in your ill humor." Setting her mouth in a mutinous line, she reached up and straightened her frilly bonnet. "Now, unless you care to join me in judging the ducks, I shall bid you a good day." With a nod, she turned and started to walk away.

Something inside him snapped in the wake of her defiance, making him grab her and roughly jerk her around again. Seizing her shoulders, he snarled, "Damn it, Jane, I am your husband and you will obey me. As my wife, it is your duty to do so."

She emitted a noise that sounded suspiciously like a snort and yanked herself free. Her dark eyes flashing with indignation, she flung back, "To my way of thinking, I have no obligation to play the dutiful wife until you act the part of husband."

He snorted back. "You have every obligation, regardless of what part I choose to assume in this farce of a marriage. Do not forget that it was you who tricked me into the parson's trap, and you who were so eager to vow to love, honor, and obey me for the rest of your days."

She sputtered her outrage for several beats, then spat, "You know perfectly well that trapping you was never my intent. I—"

"You wanted to know how it felt to kiss me." He chuckled, a harsh, bitter sound. "Yes. So you claim. Well, I hope you enjoyed your kisses, my dear, for they are the last we shall ever share. Indeed, I give you my full permission to completely disregard the love part of our marriage vows, since I neither wish nor have I any use for your love. As for the rest, well, those vows I fully expect you to keep. You shall honor all my wishes and obey my every command or suffer the consequences accorded me by law."

For a long moment Jane simply gazed at his face, a riot of emotions playing through her mind: pain and longing for what might have been, sorrow and regret for what would never be, and finally, hollow acceptance for what was.

Suddenly unable to bear the sight of him for fear that she would either weep or slap him, or perhaps both, she looked away and quietly replied, "I made those vows to a different man, a man whom I loved and who gave me hope that he might someday share my affections. When, and if, that man, my true husband, ever returns, I shall gladly honor and obey him."

He made an impatient noise. "The only husband you have is the one whose name is written on the marriage license. Unfortunately for us both, that name happens to be mine. And since I see no remedy for the situation in the foreseeable future, I suggest that you try to make the best of it."

Forget weeping. She definitely longed to slap him, and hard. Grasping her skirt to keep from acting upon her violent urge, she tartly demanded, "And what exactly do you think I've been doing these past two months, if not making the best of the situation?"

He scowled and massaged his lower back, as if he'd hurt it in his fall. "It seems quite obvious."

"Indeed?" To her shame, she rather hoped that he was in pain.

A nod, a brusque one. "Yes. Judging from your conduct just now, it is obvious that you have been busy disgracing my name with displays of vulgarity and indecorous fraternization with the commoners."

Again her hand twitched to strike him. Again she clutched her skirt. "I can assure you, my lord, that you've managed to sully the Somerville name quite admirably all by yourself."

"Oh? And how, pray tell, have I managed such a feat? I haven't spent outside a week here in the entire seven years I've owned the estate."

A sniff. "Exactly."

He sighed and shifted positions, his hand pressing his left flank. Gritting his teeth, as if the area was indeed as sore as she hoped, he snapped, "If you have something to say, then for God's sake just say it. I'm tired of standing in the street, trying to make sense of your rattlebrained babbling." He eyed her with haughty disdain. "I do hope that your liaisons with the lower classes haven't made you forget how civilized people communicate?"

"If by 'civilized communication' you mean the pretentious, condescending sort of dialogue favored by the *ton*, then, no, unfortunately I haven't." Her grip on her skirts was almost painful now in its intensity. "And to clarify my last remark: You have discredited the Somerville name through your indifference. Have you any idea of the condition in which I found your estate?"

He shrugged. "Judging from the last report I received from the agent, matters seemed well enough in hand."

"Oh, he had them in hand, all right," she retorted heatedly. "A few more years under his hand would have—"

"What do you mean, 'would have'?" he interjected. "Is Benjamin Maxwell gone, then?"

"Yes, and I say good riddance. He fled in the night like the thief he was when I demanded the estate ledgers."

"Thief?" His eyes took on a dangerous glitter. "Are you saying that I've been robbed?"

She made an exasperated noise. Now who was being rattlebrained? In a tone that clearly reflected her thoughts, she replied, "You and your people, yes. I'm astonished that you didn't discover the fact for yourself. Did you never ask to see the books?"

He waved the question away with an angry slash of his hand. "Why would I? Maxwell came highly recommended."

"But—" She shook her head, barely able to credit what she was hearing. "Did you never look at the fields and compare the richness of their crops to the poverty of the cottages? The discrepancy between the two should have prompted some suspicion in your mind. And then there is the matter of the abbey. I cannot believe that you never wondered at its dreadful condition."

Another wave. "I always attributed the state of the house to its age. As for the rest, well"—he shrugged one elegant shoulder—"as lord of the manor, I hardly think it seemly for me to visit the fields and hobnob with my tenants."

"Quite the contrary, my lord. What is unseemly is that you neglected to do so. Had you spoken with the farmers and villagers, you'd have instantly seen the trouble here and saved yourself thousands of pounds, and them years of misery."

"Impossible. Such fraternization is utterly impossible." He flinched, as if stabbed by a sudden, intense pain. "Unlike yourself, dear wife, I come from nobility, which—" He broke off abruptly, gritting his teeth. His face growing pale, he sucked in a hissing breath and finished, "My nobility makes it inherently impossible for me to communicate with the farmers with the same ease that you apparently experience."

Had it not been for the pomposity of both his words and his tone, she might have pitied him for his suffering. Instead she felt nothing but outrage and bristled as she replied, "Then I suppose I should view my lack of nobility a blessing, for the farmers and villagers are fine, intelligent people, and I feel most fortunate to be able to count them as my friends. In truth, my lord, I find them much better company than most members of the nobility."

"Indeed?" A dry chuckle. "Well, as they say, 'Blood does tell.'"

"Yes, and what it tells me is that the common people who work hard and make an honest living are far more deserving of my respect than the worthless peers who live off the sweat of other people's brows." Loathing him for his arrogance, she demanded, "Tell me, my lord, how would you live without the farmers and laborers to provide you with food, warmth, and shelter? Do you truly think that you and your exalted nobles could survive without them?"

"We most probably shall never have to find out, and do you know why?" he countered, casting her an imperious look down his perfect, aristocratic nose.

Wishing that she were taller, and her nose longer and more elegant so that she could adopt a like pose, she returned, "Please do enlighten me, my lord."

"Because, my dear wife, despite your poor opinion of us nobles, we are superior in both mind and body to your beloved commoners, which makes us the natural leaders. Thus, we shall always command, and they will always obey. It is their lot to do so, and they understand it, even if you cannot."

"Ah, but you contradict yourself in acknowledging my lack of understanding, my lord," she retorted, bridling her uncharitable urge to smile at the spasm of pain crossing his face. "For as you pointed out, I am of common blood, thus it only stands to reason that I should understand a commoner's lot."

He seemed to wait until his discomfort passed before responding. "As with nobles and their varying degrees of nobility, there are also levels of commonness, which, of course, determines a commoner's lot. You, Jane, come from the highest level, which makes you closer in intellect to us of the peerage than to the farmers and laborers for whom you profess such a penchant. Such being the case, you can no more be expected to understand their instinct to serve than you can mine to lead."

"Hmm. Let me see, now." Jane made a show of frowning. "If I was born neither to serve nor to lead, then what, pray tell, is my lot in life?"

"Oh, do not mistake my meaning. You are meant to serve, but in a more genteel manner. Take your father, for example. I believe that he made his fortune in the tea trade?" At her nod, he continued, "Tea, the fine type which I understand your father imports, is the drink of nobility. Thus, in his own way, he is serving our needs, as does a merchant of silks, furs, and anyone else who purveys fine goods or in any way caters to the peerage. The fact that your father became so very wealthy at his trade shows him to be a man far and away above the average commoner."

"I see," she murmured, momentarily at a loss as to how to respond to his latest nonsense. Then inspiration struck. Carefully choosing her words, she inquired, "If I am meant to serve, and you to lead, what, I wonder, will be our child's lot in life?"

"He shall—" His jaw dropped. "What!"

"The child I am carrying, my lord. What is to be his—"

He shook his head, silencing her with an impatient wave of his hand. "What do you mean, the child you are carrying?"

"For one of noble intellect, the meaning should be quite evident," she replied, thoroughly enjoying his disconcertment.

"But . . . how could such a thing have happened? We only—"

"My lord, please! The servants." She nodded toward the footman and the coachman, who studiously pretended to ignore their conversation. Lowering her voice to a whisper, she reminded him, "Do not forget your own theory, sir. No doubt your seed is as superior as both your mind and your body, thus it should come as no surprise to you that it bore fruit so easily."

His brow creased. "Yes. Of course. But . . . are you certain?"

"Oh, yes."

"Er—" He shook his head again, as if trying to clear his mind. "When is it to be born?"

"Considering that we—" She slanted him a meaningful look. "Well, you know— only once, it should be simple enough for a man of your superior intellect to do the calculations."

"Yes, um, that would make it near the end of January, I believe." His frown deepened.

"Correct, my lord. Very good. It seems that—"

"Uh, Lady Jane?"

Jane glanced around to see Willy creeping cautiously toward them, eyeing Quentin much as she would expect him to eye an ogre set on ravaging the village. Smiling gently, she beckoned him to approach. "It's all right, Willy. I can assure you that his lordship has never devoured a child. Well, at least not to my knowledge." She glanced at her husband as if seeking his concurrence, winking saucily at the boy in the process.

Willy relaxed and even managed a wan smile, while Quentin simply stood there, visibly lost in his thoughts.

After waiting a beat for a response that she didn't expect to receive, she shrugged and asked, "Is there something I can do for you, Willy?"

"We was wonderin' if you was still gonna judge the ducks. They're all lined up and waitin'.'"

Jane looked to the gaily bedecked birds which were, if not precisely lined up, at least gathered together and being contained on the green near the ancient Saxon village cross. "But of course. I look forward to doing so." Nodding, she turned back to her preoccupied husband. "Now, my lord, I really must return to my task. I will be home at dusk and shall be perfectly glad to continue our discussion then if you wish."

"What?" He frowned, as if annoyed by her interruption.

She repeated her speech.

"Oh. Of course." He excused her with a lordly wave.

She turned away, grinning. For all his superior intellect, he had underestimated the cunning of the common mind.

Chapter 9

He couldn't decide which hurt worse, his head or his groin. The stone, which had felt firmly wedged in his flank for the past three days, had now passed into his groin, an event resulting in a most devilish increase in his discomfort. To combat his misery, he'd taken to drinking steadily throughout the day, starting from the moment he awoke, usually around noon, and stopping only when he at last fell into a restless, sodden sleep.

The outcome of his attempts at anesthesia was splitting headaches, such as the one he now suffered, which eased only after he'd had his first drink of the day.

Something which he presently awaited his valet to bring him. Peevishly wondering what kept the man, Quentin gingerly unfolded himself from his current favored position, curled on his side with his arms and legs pressed against his beleaguered groin, and carefully eased onto his back. Andrew, who had arrived from London with his trunks two days earlier, had been gone more than half an hour now, which was twenty minutes longer than it had taken him to fetch a bottle yesterday.

As he lay there, pondering how he could feel so wretched and still live, he heard the hallway door of his adjoining dressing room open and the splash of water as the footmen prepared his bath. After several minutes, during which there was more splashing and a murmuring debate, the noise ceased and all was silent again.

Though Quentin knew that he should rise and bathe while the water was hot, the thought of doing so without whiskey to numb the pain of his motions made him cringe against the mattress with dread. And so he waited.

And waited. When it became apparent that he could wait no longer, unless, of course, he wished to multiply his suffering with a dunk in cold water, he gritted his teeth and sat up.

For several moments he sat slumped on the edge of the bed, grimly eyeing the chamber pot, then he grimaced and rose to his feet. Later. Unable to stand up straight and feeling like an advertisement for pain, he shuffled into the adjoining room, not even bothering to cover his nakedness with a dressing gown.

Once there, he promptly sank into the long, marble-painted wooden tub, relieved to feel a slight easing in his groin as the warmth of the musk-scented water washed over him. Gradually his teeth unclenched and he relaxed against the backrest, the top of which one of the footmen had thoughtfully cushioned with towels.

As he lay soaking, his eyes closed against the harsh noonday sunlight that filtered through the window overhead, there was a scratching at the door. "Yes?" he growled, hoping that it was his delinquent valet with his badly needed bottle of whiskey.

It was the valet, and when he entered the room, Quentin opened his eyes just enough to shoot the man a look of icy displeasure. When he saw that he carried not the requisitioned bottle, but a tray of what looked to be tea and toast, they flew the rest of the way open. "What the hell is that? And where is my whiskey?" he snapped, rising to his elbows to treat the man to the full heat of his glare.

"It's, uh, breakfast, my lord. I was, um—" The normally

pasty-faced valet's cheeks were suffused with a rare flush of color, and his prominent Adam's apple bobbed in a way that always boded ill. "Er, a thousand pardons, Lord Quentin, but I was unable to get you your bottle. Your wife has locked all the spirits in the wine cellar and refuses to relinquish the key until she's spoken with you."

"She what!"

The man turned a shade redder and nervously shifted the tray. "She—"

"I heard you the first time, damn it! Where is she now?"

"In the library, my lord. She has requested that you attend her there when you are dressed."

Quentin sank back into the tub and again closed his eyes. Oh, he would attend her all right, and this time he *would* take her in hand. He wasn't about to let any woman, especially a bran-faced little termagant like Jane, dictate when and how much he would drink. She would learn her place, and nothing she said or did was going to stop him from delivering to her a much-needed lesson in wifely obedience. Not this time. After the shock she'd dealt him with the news of his impending paternity, there was nothing she could say that could possibly throw him into a muddle.

Well, at least not into the same sort of slack-jawed, addlepated muddle he'd suffered at her announcement of her pregnancy. Nothing—nothing!—in the world could be so jarring as that. Truth be told, he still felt a bit dazed and confused and . . . frightened—yes, *frightened*, at the prospect of a child.

Exactly what he was frightened of, he couldn't say. The feeling was just there, a queer sort of panic that gnawed at his belly and squeezed his chest every time he imagined himself with a babe. After all, what did he know about children? Admittedly nothing. And he was none too sure that he cared to learn about them, not from what he'd seen of other people's offspring.

To him, children were noisy, smelly nuisances, to be fobbed off on nannies and kept out of sight as much as was humanly possible. They were a necessary evil, true, but one he'd never cared to contemplate. He had always thought them something to be experienced later in life, when he was old and had tired of the pleasures of Town. He'd always imagined that when he finally sired them it would be with someone he loved, and that his opinion of them would change because of that love. But this babe . . .

Could he love it?

Would he? It would be, after all, half his. A Somerville. As for its mother, well, would he feel differently about her once the baby was born? He'd heard tales of how babies prompted changes of heart in people, how couples who despised each other were sometimes drawn together in love at the birth of a child.

Would such a miracle happen to them?

Did he really wish to love Jane?

Sighing, Quentin sank deeper into the tub, savoring its renewed warmth as his valet added another bucket of steaming water.

He knew little more about his new wife than about children, and he wasn't certain that he wanted to. Apparently the feeling was mutual, for he'd seen next to nothing of her since his arrival at Swanswick Abbey. She was always off visiting this farmer or nursing that cottager, or helping with one of the bewildering array of village charities. The situation suited him fine. The less he had to deal with the incorrigible chit, the better.

Yet, despite his unfavorable opinion of her and his aversion to her company, he had to give credit where it was due. She had worked wonders on the village and the house.

Under Jane's capable hand, the abbey, which he'd so dreaded occupying, had been transformed from a gloomy pile of moldering stones into a warm, elegant home staffed with pleasant, smiling servants. The village, though he'd seen it only once since arriving, and that being the chaotic day of the duck attack, had appeared equally improved. If the farms had been transformed in a like manner—and he suspected that they had—he now possessed an estate of which he could be proud.

As Quentin sat up to allow his servant to wash his hair, he sourly wondered where she'd learned such excellent management skills. From what he'd seen, her competence far exceeded that of most men he knew. The fact that beside it his own skills paled into nonexistence, and that she'd made no bones about pointing out his inadequacy in the area, did little to further endear her to him.

Still, despite his reluctance to do so, he couldn't help but feel a grudging niggle of respect for her. Indeed, for all her faults, she really was rather amazing. Instead of pining away from boredom here, as most women he knew would have done and as he'd fully expected her to do, she'd busied herself with improving her lot and that of everyone around her. And from the bits and pieces he'd heard from the servants, all of whom seemed to adore her, she'd enjoyed doing it.

"My lord?"

Quentin glanced up, frowning. At the sight of the ewer in his valet's hand, he ducked his head to permit the soap to be rinsed from his hair. Blasted woman! She'd always seemed such a weak, timid creature, the sort to crumble beneath the slightest adversity. In view of that fact, he'd been certain that exile to this dreary house would be just the thing to teach her her place. He'd assumed she would be so wretched here that she would forever after tread lightly, for fear of again arousing his ire and provoking another such banishment.

Clearly, he'd been wrong.

He'd also been a fool not to have seen past her hen-hearted

facade and identified her as what she truly was—a shrew disguised as a mouse.

His frown deepening at his own stupidity, he lifted his dripping head, silently cursing himself and his devious wife as the servant blotted his curls with a linen towel. He should have guessed her true nature after the way she'd deceived him, and known that she would need precise, and yes, harsh, discipline to bring her to heel.

"If you please, my lord?"

Quentin looked up again, this time to see his valet holding a large towel in one hand and extending the other to him in an offer of assistance in rising. Gratefully accepting his aid, he let himself be helped out of the tub, gritting his teeth against his unmanly urge to sob as an excruciating pain knifed through his groin.

Yes, he thought, gingerly massaging the area. Jane needed discipline, the kind that came from a strict and unforbearing husband.

And she was about to get it.

"Scratch! No!" Jane chided, disengaging the kitten from her pen. Pouncing on her quill while she wrote was one of his favorite games, one that she found exceedingly vexing this afternoon as she struggled to make order of the mayhem that was the estate accounts. Indeed, his latest attack had sent a spray of ink splattering across the ledger page, which meant, of course, that it would have to be completely redone.

Sighing her exasperation, she scooped her pet from the desk and for what seemed like the tenth time in as many minutes, put him on the floor. "Here. Play with your mouse," she ordered, picking up the toy by its yarn tail and dangling it over the kitten's head.

Scratch crouched down, his gold eyes round as he stared up at the velvet mouse, then he tensed and sprang at it.

She jerked it up just out of reach. "Oh, no. You can play at the other side of the room. I've had quite enough of your mischief for one day, thank you very much. Giving the mouse one final, tantalizing wave near the tip of Scratch's shiny black nose, she flung it in the general direction of the hearth.

"What the hell?" muttered a voice Jane knew so well.

Her head came up in a flash—*Smack!*—"Ouch!"—slamming into the edge of the desk. For several beats she sat rubbing her abused skull and squinting at her husband through a swirling haze of stars. Then her vision cleared and she saw how very awful he looked.

His smooth skin, which was usually tanned and flushed with health, was blanched to a sickly ashen pallor. A sore-looking red rimmed his eyes, the whites of which were bloodshot and tinged with yellow. Everything about him, from his hunched stance to the faint lines of fatigue marring his handsome face, bespoke a man suffering the aftereffects of jug bite.

And it is no wonder, she thought uncharitably. He'd done nothing but drink since arriving at the abbey, and it had caused considerable talk among the servants. If the sympathetic glances being shot her way in the village were any indicator, the news of his drunkenness had traveled there as well.

Wondering how she could have been blind to such a conspicuous vice, she watched as Quentin stiffly bent down to pluck Scratch from his Hessian. Apparently her aim had been woefully off, for the mouse had landed between his feet and the kitten now stood arched on his gleaming boot, wildly batting at it.

Frowning fiercely, as if the animal were a soiled chamber pot rag instead of a cat, he hoisted Scratch by the scruff of the neck, growling, "What in God's name is this?"

"It's a kitten, of course," she replied lightly, refusing to be intimidated by his scowl.

He graced her with a black look. "I know *what* it is. What I want to know is what the blasted thing is doing in the house. Didn't anyone tell you that I despise cats?"

"No one here knows enough about you to tell me anything at all." She shrugged. "As for the kitten, his name is Scratch and he happens to be my pet. Knowing now how you feel about cats, I shall endeavor to keep him out of your sight in the future."

"See that you do so," he snapped, stalking toward her. Unceremoniously dumping the squirming animal on the desk, he added, "Be warned, wife. Should I find this beast anywhere near me in the future, I shall order it taken to the river and drowned."

Jane gasped in horror and snatched up her pet. "You wouldn't!" she exclaimed, pressing it protectively to her breast.

Bracing his hands on the edge of the desk, he leaned over and whispered with a grim smile, "Try me."

She squeezed Scratch so hard that he yowled in protest. "Oh! You horrid, wicked man! How dare you make such an evil threat? Scratch is my pet and I love him. I would sooner see you drowned than him!"

Quentin chuckled and straightened up again. "No doubt you would, dear wife. Unfortunately, drowning me isn't an option you have. For though you seem to have forgotten the detail, I am still master of this house and my word is law. If I must sacrifice your pet to demonstrate that fact to you, then so be it. You will learn who is in command here, and you will show proper respect for my authority."

Despising him with all her being, Jane wrestled the squirming kitten more securely into her grasp and flung back, "Tell me, my lord. How am I supposed to respect something that doesn't exist? You have yet to exercise anything that remotely resembles command here. Indeed, aside from barking orders and drinking the cellar dry, you have done nothing at all."

"And I will continue to do so for as long as I bloody well please, while you, wife, shall bite your shrewish tongue and refrain from comment. It is not your place, or that of anyone else here, to question or criticize my actions." He leaned over the desk again, his eyes glittering like shards of ice as he stabbed his gaze into hers. "You will remember that if you truly love your pet, and you will spend your time keeping him in check instead of using it to undermine my authority and govern my life."

"Govern your life?" She stood up, the frantically wriggling and meowing Scratch still clutched to her chest, and steadily returned his glare. "I have done no such thing, and you know it. What I have done is take a wifely interest in your estate, an estate, I might add, for which you clearly care nothing. Indeed, by your own admission, you've barely spent a week here in all the years you've owned it. That being the case, how can you possibly accuse me of governing your life, when you have no life here to govern?"

"Oh? And what the hell would you call locking up the spirits and refusing me a drink, if not governing?" he spat.

"I would call it desperation." At that moment, Scratch squirmed out of her grasp and jumped to the floor. Watching anxiously as he scampered out of the room, she finished, "We haven't spoken once since that day in Little Duckington, and we have much to discuss. Things I would prefer to speak of while you're sober."

He snorted and straightened up. "I cannot imagine anything that we might have to say to each other."

"Can't you? Well, there is the matter of our child. Surely you have some thoughts on him . . . or her?"

A shrug. "Should I?"

"Of course you should. It is your child, too. It will bear your name, be of your blood, and perhaps even have your face. You should be giving some thought as to where and how it will be raised and what part it will play in your life."

"It will have no part in my life," he snapped, "at least not until it has grown into some semblance of a human being. As for where and how it will be raised"—another shrug—"I care not as long as it is nowhere near me and doesn't disturb my peace. There." He smacked the heel of his hand against the desktop. "We have discussed the matter. Now give me the cellar keys."

"No." She laid her hand over the ring of keys beside the ledger, stubbornly shaking her head. "We're not finished yet."

"We're finished when I say, and I say that we are finished now," he growled, lunging for her hand.

She snatched up the keys and held them behind her back, edging away from him as she said, "You may not care about our child, but I do. And I will not allow him to have a drunk-ard for a father."

"*You* will not allow?" he snarled, stalking around the desk toward her. "*You*, wife, have no say in what is or is not al-lowed in this house. That is my right as master, and mine alone. Now give me the damn keys."

She shook her head and took several more steps backward.

He shadowed them with his forward march. "You truly don't think you can keep those keys from me if I really wish to have them, do you?" he growled, looming menacingly be-fore her.

She took another backward step, again shaking her head. "No. I'm not fool enough to believe that you couldn't over-power me if you wished to do so."

"Then why this little show of resistance?"

"I'm hoping that you will remember that you are a gentle-man, a *noble* one, and not use the advantage of your superior strength to take them," she replied, again moving away. Her back butted up against the wall. Doggedly determined to hold her ground, she stiffened her spine and added, "I am hoping that, given time, you will see reason and listen to what I have to say."

"What you are hoping is that I will allow you to castrate me and turn me into a simpering slave to your petticoat government." Two long steps and he stood toe to toe with her. Slowly inching his face to hers, he hissed, "You hope in vain, madame. I happen to be exceedingly fond of my masculinity, and unless you wish to—to—bloody—hell!" The expletive was uttered on a ragged sob as he doubled over, convulsively grasping his abdomen. Another oath, and he crumpled to his knees.

Stunned, Jane stared down at him, crouching at her feet. Good heavens! He was ill, truly ill. And judging from his display just now, his ailment had nothing to do with jug bite.

Was failing health what had brought him to the country?

She'd wondered why he had come, especially since he'd made it so very clear how much he despised both Swanswick and her. That he might be sick had never occurred to her. Now that it did, it made perfect sense.

Her anger softened by her summation, she slowly sank down beside him. Thinking back, she remembered that he had seemed in pain when they had spoken in Little Duckington. And pain would explain his sudden fondness for the bottle. It was, after all, a common practice to dull the misery of disease or a wound with whiskey or brandy.

Was such the case with Quentin?

She considered for a moment, then decided that it was, especially in view of the fact that he wasn't counted a drunkard in London. Besides, illness would also explain much of his surliness these past days and the way he'd chosen to cloister himself in his rooms with his valet.

Compassionate by nature and unable to bear the sight of suffering, Jane laid her hand on Quentin's tense shoulder. Though she couldn't see his face for the thick fall of hair covering it, she could tell from his trembling that he was in a great deal of pain. Her heart instantly went out to him. Poor man. For all his faults, he didn't deserve to hurt so.

Wanting nothing more than to comfort him, she reached over and gently smoothed the curls away from his face. It was pale and drawn, a rigid mask of misery. Frowning, she lay her hand against his cheek to check him for fever. He was warm, very warm indeed.

"Oh, Quentin," she whispered in alarm. "Why didn't you tell me you're ill? I know you don't like me, but I'm here and I would gladly help you."

Quentin unclenched his teeth and opened his eyes slightly, prepared to tell her to go away, that he neither needed nor wanted her help. Then he saw her expression, and the words died on his lips.

The way she looked at him, so sweetly and with such genuine concern, touched something deep inside him, something needful and vulnerable, and he found himself suddenly wanting very much to accept her aid. It seemed a lifetime since anyone had looked at him like that, and forever since he'd been offered true compassion.

Of course, until that moment, he hadn't thought that he wanted or needed it. But now . . . now . . . well, he wanted— and yes, needed—it very much. Moreover, he was sorely tempted to take it. The only thing that gave him pause in doing so was the person offering it. As Jane had pointed out, he didn't like her. He didn't trust her either, and with good reason.

Oh, true. She had claimed her innocence time and again to the charges of trapping him into marriage; she'd said that she had tricked him because she loved him and had merely

wished to know how it felt to kiss him. He frowned at the remembrance. Thinking back, she'd seemed earnest in her
claims. Vehement even.

Could she have been telling the truth after all?

He opened his eyes all the way now to gaze at her in wonder. By her expression, he would be inclined to say yes,
though how she could look at him so kindly after the
wretched way he'd treated her, he didn't know. Still . . .

"Blast!" He clutched his groin yet tighter as he was assailed
by another stabbing pain.

She frowned, but in a way that conveyed worry, and laid
her hand over his squeezing ones. "Is this where you hurt,
then, low in your belly?"

"I—" He broke off, struggling to decide whether to confide
in her. To do so would mean an acceptance of her help. Could
he?

Should he?

He looked at her again.

She smiled gently and nodded her encouragement.

Damn it, he would. Glancing away, rather embarrassed by
the nature of his ailment, he muttered, "It's—I have a stone."

There was a pause, then she murmured, "You poor, poor
man. No wonder you're so miserable. Passing a stone is said
to be terribly painful." There was another pause, then, "It is
passing, isn't it?"

"God, yes. It's moved from my back to—" he indicated his
groin with a jerk of his chin.

He sensed rather than saw her nod. "Yes. Well," she patted
his arm, "that is a good sign. The fact that it is moving shows
that it is most probably small enough to pass completely on
its own."

"It doesn't feel small," he grumbled. Yet, he couldn't help
smiling at the scholarly tone of her speech. "Say, where did a
chit like you learn so much about stones?"

"From my grandmother. She's wonderfully skilled in physicking. The villagers in Oxcombe always call upon her to treat their ills, and I used to assist her."

"Indeed? And did she also teach you estate management?" he inquired, slanting her a curious glance.

"Oh, no. Grandfather taught me that. Well," she smiled and shook her head, "he didn't precisely teach me estate management, but he did show me how to keep accounts and direct parish affairs. I simply applied the same principles we used to keep order there to improve things here. But enough." Another head shake. "If you are truly interested in my methods of management, I will be glad to show you the books and tell you everything I've done thus far. But later. Right now we must get you off the floor and to someplace more comfortable." She paused to eye him in query. "Do you wish me to summon your valet to help you to bed?"

Quentin made a face and shook his head. The last thing he wished was to return to his bed, where he would lie alone with nothing to occupy his mind but his pain. Indeed, what he wanted was the distraction of company, and the company he wanted most right now was, oddly enough, hers. Thus he murmured, "What are your plans for the remainder of the day?"

"After getting you settled, I will make and administer a treatment for your stone, then I must finish the ledgers."

"In that case, I believe I shall stay here. I—" He paused, grappling for a reason to justify his wish for her company without having to confess his need for it. "I—I would very much like you to tell me all that you have done on the estate."

When she glanced away, he feared that she might deny his request. Then she gestured to the giltwood chaise longue by the windows and said, "All right, then. You lie over there and I will sit on a footstool beside you. That way you can look at the numbers while I explain."

Though looking at numbers was the last thing he wished to do, he nodded his agreement and allowed her to help him rise. With the same brisk efficiency she displayed in everything she did, she soon had him lying comfortably with his head and back propped up on a mountain of pillows. After a stern admonishment to rest, she left to prepare her physic.

Smiling faintly, Quentin watched her bustle out of the room. Now this sort of governing he could definitely learn to enjoy. Indeed, though he normally found feminine fussing annoying in the extreme, he was rather enjoying his wife's attention. For unlike most women he knew, who fussed over him because they wished to draw his notice or wanted something in return, she did so because she sincerely wished to improve his lot.

His smile broadened at that last. Now that he thought about it, improving the lot of others and making the world a kinder place seemed to be Jane's mission in life. Why hadn't he seen that right off when he'd noted the improvement in the estate and the happiness of everyone on it?

Why, indeed?

The instant he thought the question, the answer flooded his mind, bringing with it a profound sense of shame. He hadn't seen because he hadn't wished to, because he wanted to think nothing but the worst of her. Because . . .

He closed his eyes, as if in doing so he could somehow avoid recognizing the most devastating truth of all. He hadn't seen because to acknowledge her accomplishments would have filled him with feelings of guilt, because she had done for his estate and people what he knew he, himself, should have done.

Piqued at himself and amazed by his discovery of Jane's fine nature, he snorted. Of course, just because he now saw the benevolence behind her actions didn't mean that he suddenly viewed her as a saint. Far from it. She did, after all, have a most annoying tendency to behave like a hoyden, and she was without a doubt the most outspoken and provoking chit he'd ever met.

Yet, he was willing to admit that he'd been wrong to judge her solely by her faults, just as he'd been unjust in instantly dismissing her protests of innocence in the matter of their marriage. Yes, and he was also willing to concede that he owed it to her to be fair, no matter how angry he was, or how he resented their union. Honor compelled him to do so.

Honor? Quentin stiffened in shock, at last understanding what his father meant when he harped on honor. It meant, quite simply, doing what he knew in his heart of hearts was right. And if he failed to do so, whether through weakness, vice, or sheer stupidity, it meant acknowledging his wrong and accepting responsibility for it. And heaven only knew he'd wronged Jane. Why, when he thought of how he'd treated her on their wedding night—

He cringed at the memory of his boorish behavior. Well, if he remembered his boyhood lessons correctly, a part of honor was making restitution to a wronged person. Trouble was, how did one go about doing so?

Wishing, for the first time in his life, that he'd listened more closely to his father's lectures, Quentin nodded to Jane as she reentered the room. In her hands was a tray containing two cups, a teapot, and a small covered pan. A pretty, dark-haired girl whom he recognized as being one of the chambermaids followed at her heels, bearing a light blanket.

"You may set the blanket on the chair across from his lordship, then you are excused," Jane said, setting the tray on the small table near the chaise longue.

The girl bobbed a curtsy and did as directed. As she started to exit, Jane looked up and added, "Oh, and Hannah? Please be good enough to close the door on your way out. And tell the other servants that we are not to be disturbed."

When they were at last alone, she turned to him, smiling. "There, now, my lord. Are you ready for your cure?"

"I suppose. What is involved?" he inquired, eyeing the tray with suspicion. By the benign appearance of the objects on it, her treatment looked to be far and away more pleasant than the one he'd endured for his last stone.

"First we apply a poultice." She lifted the lid of the pan to show him a steaming length of muslin filled with something that gave off an aromatic, if medicinal, aroma. "The warmth will help ease your pain until the draught I made you takes effect."

He considered a moment, then nodded. "Fine. Please proceed."

"Ah . . ." her pink cheeks deepened a shade. "It needs to be . . . uh . . . laid directly on the skin over the pain. That means that you must . . ." She bit her lip and looked away. "Expose the area."

"Oh, I see." A frown knit his brow as he contemplated her blush. Whatever could be the matter with her that she would look so terribly distraught at the notion of him lowering his trousers? It wasn't as if they hadn't been intimate.

But, of course. He uttered a silent curse. She was terrified of him, terrified that he might pounce on her and take her as he had before, roughly and painfully. And he couldn't blame her. If someone had ravished him in such a manner, he'd be none too eager for that person to drop their trousers in his presence either.

Filled with an unfamiliar sense of self-loathing and wanting to assuage her fear, he softly said, "It's all right, Jane. I understand. I can apply the poultice myself, if you like."

Jane forced herself to smile and meet his gaze. "You will do no such thing. It must be positioned just so, or you run the risk of blistering. If you would just, well—" Feeling as if her cheeks were on fire, she gestured to his trousers.

Goodness! What a goose she was to be so embarrassed about asking her own husband to lower his trousers. True, she'd never seen what lay beneath them, what with the darkness of the room and the cover of his dressing gown when he'd taken her. Still, they were married, which made it right and proper that she see his body.

Repeating that last over and over again in her mind, and promising not to embarrass herself by looking at him any more than necessary, Jane turned away and pretended to fuss with the poultice.

Yet, despite her best intentions, she found herself sneaking a guilty peek at him as he unbuttoned his falls. To her bewildering frustration, he turned away, robbing her of the sight of anything more provocative than the sleek line of his hip and the muscular curve of one buttock as he pulled down his trousers.

When at last he lay still, he murmured, "I'm ready."

Hoping that her face wasn't as red as it felt, Jane picked up the pan and carried it to him, not daring to look at him as she sat on the edge of the chaise longue. After a moment, during which she nervously tucked the muslin tighter around the linseed and mustard mixture, she at last forced herself to examine the area she was to treat.

That Quentin was athletic and frequently indulged in sports was readily apparent from the trimness of his waist and the rippling tautness of his belly; that he was one hundred percent male was evidenced by the dark line of hair leading from his navel down the hard contours of his abdomen.

Fascinated by his masculinity, she let her gaze follow the line, down to where it widened and finally exploded into a thatch of silken curls. To her shame-ridden disappointment, she saw that he'd modestly draped a portion of his trousers over his—er.

She sighed. Oh, well. It was probably for the best. It wasn't as though she wished to fondle him as Elizabeth had described and provoke him into repeating their wedding night. Still, she couldn't help slanting the fabric-covered mound a covert glance as she inquired, "Where does it hurt the most?"

He indicated an area very low on his pelvis, one directly abutting the mound. Hoping that her hand didn't quiver as she did so, she lightly smoothed the curls that grew there, preparing to lay the poultice.

His belly visibly tightened beneath her touch, and he sucked in a hissing breath.

She glanced at his face in sympathy, certain that he was in the clutches of another pain. By his expression, that most certainly seemed to be the case. Not only were his teeth clenched, he wore a shocked look, as if he couldn't quite believe what was happening to him.

Making a soft, soothing noise beneath her breath, she carefully set the poultice in place. As she adjusted it, her trembling hand clumsily slipped beneath the fabric mound and brushed against his flesh.

He jumped, emitting a strangled moan.

"Sorry. Sorry," she murmured, giving his bare hip a pat.

He made another smothered sound and squirmed as if burned.

Burned? It was her turn to gasp. "Oh, Quentin. Don't tell me that the poultice is too hot?" She reached down again. "Here, I'll remove—"

"No!" He more yelped than said the word as he grabbed hold of her wrists, stopping her. "No. Don't—touch it. It feels—fine." Heaven help him if she touched him again. Who would have guessed that he would be able to get aroused in his current state? But aroused he was, a fact that confounded him to no end. What the hell was it about the woman that so excited him?

"Yes. All right, Quentin. I won't touch it again until it's

ready to be removed. By then you shouldn't hurt so badly," she murmured, gently disengaging his hands from her wrists. "I'll just cover you up, in case someone comes in."

As Jane tucked the blanket around him, murmuring soothing nonsense as she worked, Quentin studied her features in an attempt to understand his attraction to her.

She was no great beauty, and never would be. No. But perhaps, just perhaps, she wasn't as plain as he'd first imagined.

Hmm. No. Indeed, now that he really looked at her, he saw that her eyes were a rather pretty color . . . a warm, velvety brown with just the slightest hint of green and gold. Yes, and their almond shape was nice, too, as were the thick lashes fringing them.

Engrossed in his quest of discovery, he let his gaze drop lower, to consider her nose. While unremarkable, there was nothing really wrong with it—well, barring the splatter of freckles across it. And even those didn't seem such a flaw now, as he noted the fine texture of the skin beneath them.

He glanced briefly at her mouth, then looked away. Her lips, of course, he didn't need to consider. He already knew that they were spectacular.

As she reached over to the table to lift one of the cups from the tray, he tipped his head and observed, really observed, the sum total of her features.

She wasn't beautiful, no, not in a conventional sense, but she most definitely wasn't ugly either. Indeed, there was something almost charming about her small heart-shaped face, especially when it was lit by the sweet smile that currently curved those all too luscious lips.

"Quentin?"

He found himself smiling back. "Yes?"

"You need to drink this now. I know it tastes awful, but it truly will help your pain. Old Mr. McFindley, the Oxcombe cobbler, used to say that it wasn't so bad if he took it in one long gulp."

"Did he, indeed?" Quentin murmured. No, she most definitely wasn't ugly, not by a country mile. Lifting the cup in mock salute, he said, "Then I bow to old Mr. McFindley's wisdom," and tossed back the contents as directed.

It did taste terrible, so foul in fact that it was all he could do to keep it from coming right back up again. Fortunately, Jane was prepared and instantly replaced his empty cup with one filled with a berry-flavored tea that promptly settled his stomach.

"There now," she crooned, gazing at him with bright-eyed approval. "You should feel much better within the half hour."

"That's it, then?" he murmured. Yes, she did have particularly clear, bright eyes.

"Not quite. You must drink this whole pot of tea and another besides. Even more if you can possibly manage it. We need to flush the stone out with liquids."

"Flush it out?" He made a face at the prospect. "How very pleasant."

She giggled at his droll expression. "No, I daresay that it shan't be pleasant at all. However, there is something in the tea, a secret something, that I promise will make it easier."

Smiling at him in a way that would have made him believe anything she promised, she rose and retrieved a petit-point footstool from across the room. After setting it beside him, she fetched the ledger.

"There," she said, sitting on the footstool and opening the book. "Now we shall distract your thoughts from your misery to more agreeable things."

"Such as numbers?" he countered without enthusiasm.

"Such as the grand profit you shall make this year, and the even grander one you stand to make the following one should we effect some improvements over the next few months."

"Profit?" Quentin frowned, taken aback. "The estate has never made a profit. Well, at least not since I've owned it."

"Oh, I can assure you that it has. Here." She turned back several pages and pointed to a column. "Look."

He tipped his head near hers and studied the entries. "Damned if you're not right," he finally said. "It appears that Maxwell was indeed robbing me, and on a very large scale. You were right about me being a fool not to have realized it."

She glanced at him quickly, as if startled by his admission. After a moment of staring at his face, she smiled her sweet smile and said, "Well, the man did come well recommended. I suppose it was reasonable enough for you to trust him."

"Maybe, maybe not." He shrugged and took a drink from his cup. "At any rate, it is a mistake that I shan't ever make again. I just hope that we can find Maxwell and bring him to justice. It would be a shame if he went on to rob someone else."

"A damn shame," she agreed softly.

He chuckled at her use of the expletive. "My, but I'm a fortunate man. Not only is my wife clever with figures, she has a most colorful vocabulary." To his delight, she flushed a most becoming shade of pink. Mmm. No. She wasn't the least bit plain.

All through the remainder of the afternoon and far into the evening they discussed the estate, all that had happened in the past, and what would most benefit it in the future. The only times they paused were when Jane fetched two more pots of her special tea and ordered dinner, which they ate from a tray delivered by a smiling servant. It was just past eleven when they finally ran out of conversation. Then they simply sat there, gazing at each other in the candlelight, their awareness of each other heightened.

It was Quentin who looked away first, discomforted by the powerful intimacy of the moment. There was something about Jane, a calm and gentle presence, that brought him the most soothing sense of peace. No longer did he feel wary or defensive toward her, nor did he feel the desperate need to guard himself as he always did when in the company of the *ton*. She had seen him at his worst—hell, she'd endured his worst—and she still cared about him. That unconditional acceptance gave him the strangest desire to take her in his arms and hold her close.

Bewildered by his impulse, he sat up and flexed his spine, which was stiff from hours spent lying on the chaise longue. Desperately longing to remain in her company, but unable to find a logical reason for doing so, he finally said, "It grows late. I suppose I should bid you good night now."

She smiled faintly and nodded. "I suppose. You do need your rest. I shall send one of the maids up shortly with another dose of the pain draught. It will help you sleep."

Returning her nod, he rose. When she didn't rise as well, he nodded again and walked to the door. Once on the threshold, he paused, wanting to say something but uncertain what.

The day, which had begun so wretchedly, had turned into one of serenity and pleasure, and all because of her kindness. What could he possibly say to convey his gratitude? Unable to think of anything grand enough, he simply smiled and said, "Thank you, Jane."

By the expression on her face as she met his gaze, he could see that she understood exactly what he meant.

Chapter 10

Jane arose with the sun the next morning, weary from a night spent tossing and turning. What had kept her awake was thoughts of Quentin, confounding and bedeviling thoughts that whirled and twisted like a dervish in her mind, making sleep quite impossible.

After weeks of despising him, of feeling hurt and lonely and betrayed, of vowing never to forgive him for his crimes against her heart, she had again felt a spark of what she'd thought was her long-dead attraction to him. That such feelings could be resurrected after all that had passed between them seemed impossible—impossible, improbable, and yes, beyond irrational. Thus she had lain awake, exploring her feelings and trying to make sense of them.

It was late, sometime in the black predawn hours, when she had at last drifted off to sleep, the matter still unresolved, only to be awakened again a short time later by awful sounds of torment. The sounds, she'd discovered, came from Quentin's room down the hall and were no doubt due to the effectiveness of her cure.

Though she had longed to go to him and offer him her aid, she was uncertain that he would want her there. And so she lay in the dark, cringing at his every moan and cry, praying that his ordeal would be short-lived.

To her eternal gratitude, it was, and when she finally returned to slumber, she did so soothed by the knowledge that the worst was over and that Quentin was on the mend.

Her peace of mind, however, like Quentin's ordeal, was short-lived, and morning found her again plagued by confusion, a state brought about by the memory of her anguish at his agony. What feeling did she harbor for him that made her despair so at his suffering?

What, indeed?

Sympathy, Jane decided, testing the heat of her curling tongs on the corner of a towel. It was sympathy, plain and simple. Nothing more.

She nodded, as much in approval of the temperature of the tongs as at her conclusion. Yes. It had to be sympathy. For even she, who had foolishly wasted five years pining for a Quentin who didn't exist, wasn't so very stupid as to allow tenderness for him to creep back into her heart.

Or was she? Carefully applying the hot tongs to the paper-wrapped coil of hair at her temple, she considered the likelihood.

It was possible, she reluctantly admitted, that she might have felt a stirring of something beyond sympathy for him yesterday. After all, he had been most charming and attentive, especially when she'd explained her methods of management to him. And when she'd voiced her ideas for future improvements, he'd listened carefully and discussed them with her in a way that paid compliment to her intellect. Then there was the matter of how he'd looked at her, his beautiful violet eyes soft with wonder and admiration.

How could she not have felt something in the face of such flattering attention? Despite his numerous faults, Quentin Somerville was a most handsome and—yes, she'd admit it— desirable man. Not, of course, that she desired him. Not now. Yet she had to give credit where it was due and acknowledge that there were many women, beautiful and fascinating ones, who counted him the most alluring man in the *ton*.

Wistfully wondering if he'd dallied with any of those women in her absence, Jane wrapped another tendril of hair in paper and applied the tongs.

Oddly enough, the thought of him lying with other women made her feel sore and bruised inside, though why it should, she couldn't imagine. It wasn't as if he loved her or she him, or as if he would be breaking a sacred trust between them. Besides, everyone knew that it wasn't at all uncommon for men to seek carnal pleasure outside marriage. Why, even men who were admittedly fond of their wives kept mistresses. That being the case, who was she to object if her unwillingly wed husband chose to stray?

Who, indeed? she mused, setting down the tongs. Yet, in spite of herself and her resolve not to care, she found that she did object. Strongly.

And she wondered. When Quentin took other women, did he do so with the tenderness and affection he had denied her? Did he kiss and caress them, and bring them the rapture Elizabeth had said often came from the wedding-bed act? And did he, in taking them, experience the pleasure from their bodies that he had been unable to find in hers?

She hoped not. She hoped that he'd forsaken all other women since wedding her, though deep in her heart she knew that she hoped in vain. Quentin Somerville was a sophisticated, urbane man of unearthly physical beauty, hardly the sort of man to deny himself the pleasures of the flesh.

Especially when they were so readily available to him. Growing more despondent by the moment, Jane remembered all the women she'd watched throw themselves at him over the years and recalled the heated whispers she'd heard regarding his prowess as a lover.

No, it was highly unlikely that he'd lacked feminine company in her absence, and that which he'd kept had no doubt been that of the most dazzling and desirable women of the *ton*.

Women far more beautiful and tempting than she could ever hope to be. Feeling suddenly like weeping, Jane removed the now cool papers from her hair and tugged the resulting curls into a simple arrangement of ringlets around her face. Gloomily wondering why she'd bothered, she studied the effect of her primping.

Lacking a maid to help her and seeing no need for vanity in the country, this was the first time she'd curled her hair and applied cosmetics since leaving London. Exactly what had possessed her to make the effort, she didn't dare contemplate, but of course it had something to do with Quentin and the rapport they had shared the day before. Now viewing her handiwork, she called herself every kind of a fool.

Even if she did want Quentin in her bed, which she decidedly did not, all the curls and powder in the world wouldn't be enough to tempt him there. Not with her impossibly plain looks.

Slowly she turned from the mirror, her vision blurring with tears. Oh, what a goose she was! How could she ever have been stupid enough to believe that Quentin could want her? And why should he? What had she to offer him, except a cure for stones and her services as an estate manager?

Aching in a way she'd thought no longer possible, Jane rose from the dressing table and donned the becoming coral print gown she'd purchased for her hoped-for but never realized wedding trip. No. She had nothing to attract a man, any man. That sad fact had been proved Season after disappointing Season. And despite the tentative truce she and Quentin had struck yesterday, she had no real reason to believe that matters between them had changed.

Well, at least not in regard to their marriage. There did appear, however, to be a possibility that they might become friends, that they might someday strike a harmonious balance that would allow them to live in peace and raise their child as a family.

With a sigh, she slipped on her dainty kid half boots and tied the ribbon lacings up the back. Though friendship wasn't what she'd envisioned when she'd wed Quentin, it would have to be enough. She would strive to make it so.

For the sake of their unborn babe.

She stood at a sturdy oak table, tucking a paper-wrapped parcel into a basket brimming with foodstuffs and flowers.

Quentin froze at the stillroom's threshold, arrested by the picture she made. Though the scene was ordinary enough, homely even, the way the morning sun spilled through the mullioned windows bathed it in a glistening haze of light, making Jane glow with otherworldly radiance. Seeing her thus left him oddly breathless.

Had her hair always been that glorious shade of chestnut, that rich, copper-shot brown kissed ever so slightly with gold? And her skin—when had it become so temptingly fine? Its texture, irresistibly smooth and dewy fresh, reminded him of the petals of a newly opened rose. Then there was her figure, which suddenly seemed fuller . . . more womanly somehow.

He blinked hard and shook his head, certain that her stunning improvement was a trick of his eyes.

It wasn't.

His mouth went dry. Good Lord. How could he ever have thought her plain?

He must have stirred in his astonishment, for she looked up, her face registering surprise at the sight of him. "Why, Quentin. Good morning," she softly exclaimed, her full lips curving in welcome. "I didn't expect to see you about until much later."

"Indeed?" he murmured, moving into the room. She was looking at him as she had yesterday, sweetly and with a gentle concern that made something inside him grow soft and warm.

She nodded. "I heard you early this morning and, well"—she gestured helplessly, as if not quite certain how to phrase her thoughts—"are . . . are you . . . all right?"

He nodded back. "A bit sore, but fine, thanks to you and your cure."

Her smile returned. "I'm glad. You were so ill and miserable yesterday. I was terribly worried about you."

"You were?" He came to a stop at the opposite side of the table, staring at her in bewilderment. "I cannot imagine why you would be. After the way I've treated you, I deserve neither your sympathy nor your concern."

"I—" A faint flush stained her cheeks, and she looked down at the basket. "I'm afraid that I'm rather too tenderhearted for my own good. A person has only to fall ill, or get hurt, or suffer some other misfortune to make me forget all past wrongs and come to their aid."

Quentin smiled at her charming confession. Had someone told him last night that he would look upon his stone as a blessing this morning, he would never have believed it. Yet, incredibly, he did. The torment he'd suffered with it seemed a small price to pay for the way she'd looked at him just now.

Wishing that he could tell her how much her kindness meant to him, but unable to find the words, he said, "I think your tenderheartedness quite admirable, Jane, and were it not for the care it prompted, I doubt I'd be feeling nearly as well as I do now. Please accept my most sincere thanks."

She made a dismissive hand motion, though he could tell from her deepening color that she was pleased by his compliment. "I did nothing but make you a poultice and a draught. Anyone could have done it."

"But no one did," he pointed out. "And no one else dared to brave my ill humor to keep me company and distract me from my pain. You did a great deal for me, and I am most grateful."

Her cheeks darkened a hint more. "You are most welcome. I am glad to have been of help."

At a loss as to what to say next, Quentin awkwardly watched as she straightened a violet knotted in the string bow of one of the parcels in the basket, then moved on to the next package to repeat the motion on a primrose.

In truth, he'd sought Jane out not just to thank her, but because he'd enjoyed her company and wished it again today. Indeed, it was the prospect of being with her, and that prospect only, that had enticed him out of his bed this morning after the wretchedness of the night before. Now that he was with her, however, he wasn't quite certain how to request her companionship.

Hell, he wasn't even sure she'd grant it now that he was on the mend. After all, she'd said that she forgave a person during their time of illness or tragedy. Whether that forgiveness extended past the crisis, he didn't know. Thus he settled for inquiring, "What are you doing?"

"I'm preparing to visit the Halidays."

He frowned, as much at the news of her plans as at the vague familiarity of the name. "The Halidays?"

"I told you about Samuel Haliday yesterday. He's the farmer I hired to oversee our home farm after Mr. Maxwell ran off. Remember?" She glanced at him in query. When he nodded, she smiled and tucked a geranium-festooned jar of jelly in among the parcels. "Anyway, his wife, Anna, gave birth to their first child last month, and today is the first day she is receiving visitors. Of course I must go and convey my best wishes."

"Of course," he muttered, bitterly disappointed. He should

have known that she would have plans to spend the day with her beloved commoners. After all, by her own admission, she much preferred their company to his.

Feeling like a nodcock for even imagining that she might want him for a companion, he nodded brusquely and growled, "No doubt you are anxious to be on your way, so I shall stop pestering you and bid you a good day."

As he turned away, dreading the day that now stretched before him in an infinity of boredom, she looked up and said, "You are welcome to join me, my lord."

Join her in visiting farmers? Him?

As if reading his mind, she hastily added, "I know how you feel about nobles mingling with commoners, Quentin, but I can assure you that the Halidays are a most excellent sort of commoner. Samuel is exceedingly intelligent and well-spoken, and Anna is perfectly charming. I am quite certain that you will like them immensely and have no problem whatsoever communicating with them."

When he didn't immediately reply, torn between the conflict of his lordly prejudices and his desire for her company, she appended, "You expressed an interest in the workings of the estate yesterday. If you were sincere in your interest, this would be a fine opportunity for you to see how things are run." There was a brief pause, then, "Besides, I would very much like your company, and I know that the Halidays would be delighted to make your acquaintance. You are, after all, their lord, and it would be a great honor for them if you acknowledged the birth of their child."

It wasn't her appeal to his vanity as lord that made up Quentin's mind, but rather her admission that she wished his company. And though the notion of spending the day among rustics ranked somewhere between a tooth extraction and a carriage accident on his list of preferred activities, he nonetheless said, "All right, then. I accept your invitation."

Half an hour later they were off, merrily jostling down the shady country lane with Jane at the reins of the small gig. It was a fine, warm, day, one made all the finer by Jane's pleasant yet edifying conversation. Now and again she stopped before a fruitful field or a sheep-populated pasture, all of which Quentin was stunned to learn were a part of his home farm. She pointed out improvements she had made or explained ones she felt they should make in the future. As she spoke, confidently and with startling expertise, Quentin couldn't help but to feel awe at her knowledge.

And discomfort at his own ignorance . . .

A feeling that grew with every passing mile. By the time they reached the Haliday farm, he felt beyond stupid and more than a little inadequate. Reining the horse to a halt, Jane nodded to her right, saying, "I think the land agent's cottage the loveliest on the estate. Why Mr. Maxwell preferred to live in the dreary old dowager house, I shall never understand."

One glance in the indicated direction was enough to make Quentin nod back in agreement.

Set within a rose-covered wall, behind which could be seen a well-ordered garden and a lime-tree walkway, the two-story, halftimber dwelling was the epitome of country gentility.

Hmm. Perhaps the Halidays might not be such oafs after all, despite the fact that they were farmers. As Quentin noted the freshness of the whitewash on the walls and the manicured perfection of the lawn, someone hailed, "Lady Jane. A good day."

That someone proved to be a roughly but neatly clothed old man, who rushed to Jane's side. By the smile on his weather-seamed face, it was clear that he was genuinely pleased to see her.

"And a good day to you, too, sir," she cheerfully replied. As the man relieved her of the reins, she smiled, and nodded to Quentin, saying, "Mr. Follows, please allow me to introduce my husband, Lord Quentin. My lord, this is Aaron Follows. Mr. Follows is in charge of the home farm animal husbandry, a job at which he has proved most admirable. Why, he's done absolute wonders in improving the weight of our hogs."

The man's smile faded abruptly at the introduction, and though he acknowledged Quentin courteously enough, you would have thought by his expression that he faced a villain come to rob him and run him off the land.

Is that how my people see me, then, as some sort of villain? Quentin wondered, taken aback by the man's response. Strangely enough, the notion that they might indeed view him as such bothered him more than he cared to admit.

Unsettled by the encounter, Quentin escorted Jane up the walkway to the house, only to suffer further discomfiture when she marched to the door and knocked upon it herself.

Though he knew that it was the way of gentry to go about without footmen and formal equipage when in the country, he still found the lack of pomp rather unseemly. Pomp, in his mind, was necessary in reminding inferiors of their place and in curbing their temptation to become too familiar . . . a point he felt justifiably proved by the maid who opened the door. Why, by the squeal of delight she emitted upon seeing Jane, you'd have thought that they were school friends, reunited after a particularly long holiday.

Jane, on the other hand, appeared to see nothing wrong with the greeting, for she laughed and said, "It's a pleasure to see you too, Millie." Ignoring his scowl of displeasure, she pulled him forward, breezily adding, "This is my husband, Lord Quentin."

As had Mr. Follows, the maid sobered instantly. Indeed, she looked nothing short of terrified as she collapsed into a curtsy. Finding her terror even more annoying than her impropriety, Quentin nodded curtly and deepened his scowl.

She gasped and shied back a step, as if fearful that he

would bite off her head. Her blue eyes practically bulging from their sockets, she sidled away, jerking her arm in a way that he assumed meant that they were to follow.

As she disappeared, Jane took his arm and whispered, "For goodness' sake Quentin, please do try to smile. Can't you see how nervous your visit has made poor Millie?"

Poor Millie? He cast her a sour look. Poor him for having to suffer the company of half-wits and rustics. If she thought that he was going to humor their hen-hearted nonsense by smiling, she—

"Please?" She gazed up at him, her guileless brown eyes wide and beseeching. "It would mean ever so much to me if you would at least try to smile."

There was something about her soft plea, a touching, wistful sort of earnestness, that instantly disarmed him, and he found himself surrendering to her wishes. Though it pained him immensely to do so, he smiled.

She beamed at him as if he'd just slayed a dragon. "Perfect." She gave his arm an ecstatic squeeze. "Oh, Quentin, absolutely perfect. You look so handsome and kind when you smile."

That he was handsome when he smiled was something he heard with monotonous regularity; that he looked kind was an entirely new notion. Oddly enough, it was a notion that he rather liked, especially since it seemed to please Jane. Thus, when they finally caught up with the maid, who waved them into a cozy parlor, he made a point to smile his best smile and say in his most gracious voice, "A thousand thanks, Mistress Millie."

Her jaw went slack and her eyes bulged a fraction more— hardly the reaction he'd expected. Though he was sorely tempted to frown, Quentin forced himself to continue smiling, sneaking a questioning glance at Jane from beneath his lashes.

Apparently she saw nothing amiss in the girl's response, for she nodded.

He heaved an inward sigh. Good God. What had he gotten himself into in consenting to pay this visit?

After what seemed like an eternity of remaining thus, during which his lips grew numb from strain and the maid evidenced no sign of wits, he was relieved when Jane cleared her throat and murmured, "You may go tell your master and mistress that we are here, Millie."

As if in a trance, the girl backed out of the room, her gaze still on Quentin's face. When she at last drifted out of earshot, Jane giggled and said, "Poor girl. She's positively moonstruck by you, my lord."

"Moonstruck?" he echoed in disbelief. How could the widgeon be moonstruck when only moments earlier she'd been on the verge of fainting from fright?

"Moonstruck," Jane confirmed. "It's your smile. I told you how very lovely it is. You have but to flash those enchanting dimples to win any lady's heart." She was beaming at him again. "Well done, Quentin. Very well done, indeed."

Warmed by her praise, he grinned and teased, "And does my smile have the same effect on you, wife?"

She made show of studying his face. "Mmm. Most assuredly, husband. I find myself quite helpless before it."

Before he could investigate her provocative remark, a pretty woman with curly black hair and lively brown eyes entered the room, followed by a fair-haired nursemaid carrying a baby. Like the servants, the woman too seemed unnerved by his presence. Unlike them, however, she quickly recovered herself and dropped into a curtsy that would have done a countess proud.

"My lord. My lady. This is indeed an honor," she murmured.

Remembering to smile, Quentin returned her curtsy with a

courtly bow. "I can assure you that the honor is all ours, madame."

Like magic, she relaxed.

He glanced at Jane to see if she'd noted the phenomenon.

Apparently she had, for she gazed at him with an approval that made him feel ten feet tall.

Feeling happier than he had for many a month, he stepped back and watched as Jane and their hostess exchanged pleasantries. Exactly why he felt such contentment, he couldn't say, but he didn't dare examine the feeling for fear of losing it.

When all the greetings were at last tendered to everyone's satisfaction, their hostess turned to the nursemaid and lifted the babe from her arms. Her pretty face aglow with motherly pride, she held it out to them, saying, "My lord. My lady. Please meet my son, James Joshua Haliday. Jamie, for short."

Quentin gazed at the babe for a beat, perplexed as to what to do or say. Then he glanced to Jane for help.

Talk about being moonstruck! She stared at the babe as if bewitched out of her wits. Damn. There would be no help forthcoming from that quarter, at least no time soon. Feeling impossibly gauche, he slowly looked back at Mrs. Haliday.

She gazed at him expectantly, clearly waiting for him to say or do something.

Hoping against hope that it was the proper thing to do, he took one of the infant's tiny hands in his and gave it a gentle but gentlemanly shake. "It is an honor to make your acquaintance, Master Jamie," he uttered gravely. As an afterthought, he smiled. Murmuring something about the child being a fine, handsome lad, he stepped away, again glancing at Jane.

She now looked at him, and by her expression you would have thought that he'd done something particularly heroic. The babe's mother appeared equally enchanted, though why, he couldn't for the life of him imagine.

After a moment during which the women exchanged an enigmatic smile and the babe burped, Jane moved forward and presented the lavishly packed basket. "Here. This is for you and your husband. I all but forgot about it in my infatuation with Jamie. It's to convey our best wishes at the birth of your son."

The woman looked genuinely pleased by their generosity. "Why . . . how very kind. Thank you," she exclaimed, nodding to the nursemaid to take charge of the gift. "You will stay for tea, I hope?" She glanced first at Jane, then at Quentin as she added, "My husband is due home soon, and I am certain that he would like to make your acquaintance, my lord."

"We shall be delighted to stay," Jane declared. She looked at Quentin again.

He dimpled on cue. "Delighted." The real delight, of course, was in seeing Jane's pleasure at his response.

Smiling in a way that communicated her own delight in their company, their hostess exclaimed, "Excellent. Please do make yourselves comfortable while I order refreshment." Curtsying as best she could with the babe in her arms, she turned to leave.

"Anna?" This was from Jane.

The woman pivoted back around, smiling in polite query.

"Might I hold Jamie for a while?" Jane asked, gazing at the infant with undisguised longing. "He is such a dear little fellow."

"But of course you may." Their hostess waited until Jane had settled in a plumply padded chair, then carefully handed her the babe. Her face the picture of maternal adoration, she said, "He really is a darling, isn't he, my lady?"

Jane nodded. "Indeed he is, isn't he, Quentin?"

Both pairs of feminine eyes were now trained on him. Secretly thinking that the babe, with his rumply face and red nose, rather resembled a drunken old man in miniature, he gamely murmured, "Darling."

Apparently the women found his abbreviated response acceptable, for they instantly lost interest in him in favor of cooing to the babe. When they had coaxed what they both deemed to be a smile from him, their hostess bustled off to see to refreshment, beckoning for the nursemaid to follow.

Once alone, Quentin and Jane sat in companionable silence—she, engrossed in the infant; he, content to watch her.

It was Jane who finally spoke. "Oh, Quentin. Will you just look at him? He's so beautiful," she exclaimed, her voice breathless with awe.

At that moment he was incapable of looking at anything but her. It was she who was beautiful, enchantingly so. She looked like a Renaissance Madonna, gentle and radiant, as she gazed tenderly down at the babe in her arms. Unable to speak for the emotion lodged in his throat, he simply nodded.

"Our child shall be beautiful too. I am certain of it," she continued. "Especially if it has your dimples. And your curls. Oh, and it would be ever so lovely if it has your eyes as well." She smiled shyly. "In truth, I hope it looks exactly like you."

"You do?" he croaked past the knot in his throat. At that moment, he rather hoped it resembled her.

She nodded. "I have spent a great deal of time imagining how it might look—the color of its eyes . . . the shape of its mouth . . . the texture of its hair. Every time I do, I somehow always picture it with your features."

She glanced up then, her gaze wistful as it met his. "What about you, my lord? Have you given any thought as to how it might look?" Before he could respond, a shadow crossed her face and she hastily apologized, "I'm sorry. I—I shouldn't have asked that question. It was unfair of me. I—"

At that instant the baby began to fuss, mewling in a way that augured tears. With an expertise that bespoke of practice,

Jane half rocked, half jiggled him, crooning, "S-s-h. Shush now, Jamie. Don't cry. There's a good boy. Yes. S-s-h."

To Quentin's amazement, the babe started to calm. After several moments, during which the only sound was Jane's soft, intermittent crooning, the infant at last lay still.

It was then that Jane again looked up. Smiling with a pensiveness that tugged at his heart, she said, "I have given what you said yesterday a great deal of thought, and now I see how unreasonable I was to expect you to be happy about our child. You don't love me, I know that, and after considering that fact and . . . well, everything . . . I think I understand why you feel as you do. Like—"

"Jane—" he interjected, his heart aching queerly at her words.

"No, Quentin. Just hear me out. Please?" At his reluctant nod, she continued, "Like every other man in the world, you wished your children to be born of a woman you loved and selected above all others. That I can never be that woman to you is something I understand. Truly I do, and I accept the fact. Still, I—" she swallowed hard and looked back down at the babe in her arms. "I cannot help but hope that you might someday forgive our child for having me for its mother, and learn to care for it in spite of the fact." That last was uttered in a raw whisper.

Quentin shook his head, his ache sharpening to a stabbing pain. "Jane," he whispered, then his words died, killed by his inability to read his own heart. Suddenly he was uncertain how he felt about her, their marriage, and their unborn child.

In truth, he no longer despised her, nor did he believe that she had tricked him into marriage. As for their marriage, well, that suddenly seemed less of a punishment than it had before. And their child? Well, he was rather beginning to like the idea of Jane, with her gentle ways and kind heart, mothering his babe. If ever there was a woman born for motherhood, it was she. If only he were as certain of his own ability to be a good father.

As he struggled to find the words to express his bewildering new feelings, wanting to scream his frustration when they eluded him, their hostess returned with tea, shadowed by Millie, who carried an enormous tray of cakes, scones, and jam. Rather than follow her mistress to the tea table, as she was no doubt expected to do, the maid strutted over to him and presented the tray.

Smiling coquettishly and fluttering her stubby eyelashes, she cooed, "Cake, m'lord?"

Had he been in the mood for humor, Quentin would have found her flirting amusing to the extreme. At that moment, however, he simply viewed it as annoying and wished that both she and her mistress would go away so that he could mend matters with Jane.

As he made to wave her away, her mistress cast him an apologetic look and chided, "No, no, Millie. You mustn't ask his lordship to serve himself. You must set the tray on the table and let me prepare a plate for him."

The maid's chin began to quiver, then a dull red flush swept her face. She looked as if she longed to die of embarrassment and stammered out an apology.

Feeling strangely sorry for her, Quentin helped himself to a slice of Queen cake, exclaiming, "Nonsense. You mustn't stand on formality for my sake. This shall do just fine." He nodded his thanks to Millie.

Instantly her chin stilled and she smiled, displaying two very crooked front teeth.

Satisfied that her feelings had been spared, something that he felt certain would please Jane, he looked to his hostess and added, "As for you, Mrs. Haliday, you should be resting instead of waiting on us. It is far too soon after the birth of your son for you to be bustling about. Do sit and let Millie tend to tea."

"Anna. Please do call me Anna, my lord," she said, sinking into a nearby chair with a grateful smile. "And thank you for your understanding. I am afraid that my staff has had little experience in entertaining gentry, well, except for you wife, of course." She cast Jane a fond look. "Her, we have come to view as a member of the family, and, as you no doubt noticed, we treat her as such."

"Which is as it should be, since I am equally fond of all of you," Jane said, relinquishing the baby to the nursemaid with visible reluctance. When she saw Quentin looking at her, she smiled and nodded faintly, as if she understood his turbulent state of mind and wished to reassure him.

Oddly comforted by her silent communication, he accepted a cup of tea and another slice of Queen cake from the fawning Millie. As he smiled and thanked her, a tall, barrel-chested man of about thirty entered the room. Looking neither right nor left, he strode over to Anna and tenderly kissed her cheek.

"Samuel, my love. Just in time for tea," she exclaimed, her pretty face alight with pleasure. "Just see who has come to visit, Lady Jane and Lord Quentin."

The man smiled and promptly rushed over to take Jane's hand. "Lady Jane. What a delight." He proceeded to add something, something that Quentin couldn't hear but that made her grin. Then he turned to face him. His fond smile fading, he sketched a bow and stiffly uttered, "Welcome to our home, my lord. We are indeed honored by your presence." As with everyone else on the farm, he seemed less honored than wary of his presence.

Quentin dimpled and politely inclined his head, hoping that like Anna and Millie, Samuel Haliday would thaw beneath his smile. He didn't, though he did unbend enough to sit down.

As he grappled for a way to put his host at ease, wanting to please Jane by doing so, Jane said excitedly, "Samuel informed me just now that the work on our gin house is to be completed this very afternoon."

"Indeed?" he murmured, stifling his impulse to frown. What in heaven's name was a gin house?

She nodded. "The new machinery will save ever so much time and labor in the dressing of our wheat this winter."

Dressing of wheat? Acutely reminded of his ignorance of farming, he again responded, "Indeed?" for lack of a better comment. As an afterthought, he added, "Excellent. Anything that saves both time and labor is a most worthy investment," then smiled and nodded for good measure.

To his surprise, Mr. Haliday, who had been eyeing him as one would eye a dog suspected of being rabid, smiled and nodded back. "Yes, my lord. My thought exactly. We have also replaced our hopper and riddles, and installed a most efficient device to help in the preliminary winnowing." His smile broadened into a grin. "I shan't be at all surprised to learn that Swanswick has the finest threshing barn in all of Worcestershire."

"Oh, and do tell him about those new baskets you discovered to aid in the removal of whiteheads," Anna piped in. "Why, we shall have the best chaffed grains in all of England."

Riddles? Winnowing? Chaff?

Never in his life had Quentin felt so humbled as he did at that moment. Exactly why he should feel so over something as inconsequential as a lack of farming knowledge, he didn't know, but he did. Perhaps it was because he saw, for the first time in his life, that he, with his aristocratic breeding and fine education, wasn't nearly as superior to the common man as he liked to believe he was. Indeed, as he sat listening to the others discuss the virtues of their new machinery, he felt nothing short of inferior.

So much for his theory about noble blood.

From there the conversation turned to a problem with the plough, which Samuel, who had relaxed enough to accept a cup of tea from Millie, deferred to Quentin. By his expression, he was truly interested in his opinion on the matter.

It was then, as he was left scrambling for a response, that Quentin resolved to learn all he could about farming so as never again to be put at such a disadvantage. He would do justice to his name and blood, and become the leader they demanded . . . even if it meant studying billhooks, slashes, and drags, whatever the hell those were.

In the end, it was Jane who rescued him from his embarrassment by saying that they were considering several new ploughs and then changing the subject to the couple's new baby. Like all proud parents, they promptly warmed to the topic and passed the remainder of the visit telling of their hopes, dreams, and plans for him.

When at last the time came for Quentin and Jane to take their leave, both Halidays had warmed to Quentin and seemed truly sincere in their wishes that he return soon. Left thoughtful by the visit, Quentin remained silent during most of the trip home, reflecting on the day's events. Jane, as if sensing his mood, graciously refrained from conversation.

It wasn't until they were within sight of the abbey that he finally spoke. "Jane?"

"Hmm?"

"What is chaff?"

She slanted him a glance, smiling faintly. "It's the seed coverings and bits of debris left sticking to grain after harvest."

"And winnowing?"

"Winnowing is the process used to separate the chaff from the grain. It is a part of dressing."

"I see," he murmured, though, in truth, he didn't really see at all. Wanting very much to do so, but not yet ready to surrender his pride by asking for an explanation, he waited a beat and then casually inquired, "I suppose there are books that explain about dressing . . . and ploughs?"

He thought he detected a smile at his query, but he couldn't be certain, for the expression disappeared as quickly as it had appeared. "There are books on the subject, yes," she replied. "In fact, we have several fine volumes in the Swanswick library. We also receive the *Annals of Agriculture*, which always contains the latest thoughts and methods of dressing, crop cultivation, and such. As for ploughs, *Farmer's Magazine* is full of articles and advertisements on all the newest innovations."

Satisfied, he smiled and nodded, then changed the subject to the weather.

He would read every last book, journal, and magazine on agriculture that he could find, and do so ten times if that was what it took for him to understand them.

The next time someone asked him about farming, he would be prepared to answer.

Chapter 11

The weeks passed, June gave way to July, bringing with it the long, fine days that Jane so adored. She'd always loved July best, the way it looked, so green and bright, the way it smelled, sweet with the fresh scents of summer. Most of all she liked the way it felt, hopeful and alive with promise. That particular July proved the most magical ever.

Never had she felt so vibrant and full of life as she did during that time, for it was then that she noted the first swelling of her flat belly, an occurrence that evoked a whole new, wonderful awareness of the miracle growing within her. She also found hope for her marriage.

True, she still didn't have the romantic, storybook marriage she'd envisioned when she wed Quentin, and she knew that she most probably never would. Yet, of late, they had fallen into an easy, lighthearted sort of companionship that she found promising in the extreme. Indeed, the very fact that they could live together as friends gave her hope for her dream of raising their child as a family.

Praying that that hope would flourish into truth, Jane carefully worked a stitch into the scalloped hem of the christening gown she embroidered. Though neither of them had mentioned the babe since the day at the Haliday farm, she sometimes saw Quentin look up from his reading in the evening and watch her, his expression thoughtful, as she sat stitching on tiny garments.

Such evenings had become a part of the pattern of their life. He would sprawl on the library chaise longue, reading anything and everything he could find about farming, while she sat opposite in the comfortable Sheraton easy chair, doing her sewing. Sometimes Scratch, with whom Quentin had struck a truce, joined them, and he would spend those hours merrily chasing the ghost-white moths that drifted through the open windows at twilight.

At such times Jane would pretend that their marriage was all she'd ever dreamed, and sometimes, just for a few heart-stopping moments, she would believe the dream to be true.

Tonight was one such night. Quentin lounged in his accustomed place, reading Sir Humphry Davy's *Elements of Agricultural Chemistry,* while Scratch, who was rapidly growing into a young tom, stalked something beneath the chaise upon which he lay.

As she gazed at the scene, thinking how much more handsome Quentin had grown during his month in the country, Scratch's prey, an errant damselfly, took flight. After executing several fluttering loops in the air, it came to a rest near Quentin's elbow. Eyeing it intently, Scratch hunched down, his skinny body tense and primed to spring. Then, with the charming exuberance of a kitten just learning to hunt, he bounded up after it.

"O-o-mph!" He landed squarely on Quentin's belly, causing him to drop his book in surprise and the fly to take wing again. As he poised to spring after it, Quentin seized him by his scruff and wrestled him against his chest. Holding him there with one hand, he wagged a finger before the animal's nose, warning, "Do not forget that I have a bag of stones with your name written on it, Master Scratch."

Always the unrepentant offender, Scratch batted his finger.

Quentin scowled, but in a way that Jane found more amusing than alarming. For all his protests over her pet, she knew him to be secretly fond of Scratch. Indeed, just yesterday, she'd caught him sneaking the cat a slice of bacon from the breakfast sideboard. Two days before that she'd spied them together in the stable, where he had appeared to be introducing Scratch to the new mouser . . . the pretty black-and-white *female* mouser. It had been all she could do to bridle her mirth at the sight of her elegant husband playing matchmaker to cats.

It had also further endeared him to her. Who would have guessed that Quentin Somerville, with all his sophistication and urbane ways, had a whimsical side? And who would have guessed that its revelation would touch her so? But touch her it had, leaving her heart a bit lighter and her head full of dreams of his someday sharing that side of himself with their child.

As Jane sat watching him scold the cat, smiling at his ludicrous threat to stuff a cherry in its mouth and roast it up for dinner, she felt a further awakening of her old feelings for him. Here was the man she'd once so admired—the gay, charming, gallant Quentin she had wished for a husband and had gladly vowed to love, honor, and obey. Seeing him thus made her suddenly long for him in ways, wifely ways, that were as frightening as they were impossible.

Wifely ways? Good heavens! She started in shock at her own desire, appalled that she could want him after the nightmare that had been their wedding night. How could she possibly crave a man who had hurt her so? How could she think to bear, much less yearn for, his touch?

Yet, strangely enough, she did yearn for it. She yearned to be kissed, caressed, and, yes, taken, by the delightful man who now sat across from her. This man was a different man from the one who had ravished her . . . a kinder, *better* man. And deep in her heart she knew that his touch would be gentle, that he would take her with tenderness and bring her the rapture a woman was supposed to experience from the marriage act.

Unfortunately, the man she now found so appealing didn't return her feelings in the slightest.

Oh, that wasn't to say that he hadn't been entirely agreeable, or that he hadn't expressed pleasure in her company. He had, on both counts. Since their visit to the Halidays, he'd been unfailingly courteous, and not just to her. Where he'd once scowled and barked at the servants, he now smiled and politely requested their assistance. They, in turn, responded with doting respect.

As for him enjoying her company, why, hadn't he said just last week that he'd never felt so at ease with anyone as he did with her? And didn't he often elect to be near her while she worked in the stillroom or the garden, his face animated and his eyes bright as he told of the things he'd read?

That he'd begun to view her as a friend was undeniable, and though she had initially thought that friendship would be enough, she now saw that she'd been wrong. Heartbreakingly so. With a man like the one Quentin was rapidly becoming, a woman couldn't help but long for love.

Aching with her new awareness, Jane watched as Quentin playfully tweaked Scratch's ear, then released him to resume his play. The cat promptly charged after his toy mouse, which lay beneath the desk. Grinning at his antics, Quentin shot her a droll look and quipped, "I shall no doubt have to drown that beast yet."

She forced herself to smile back, though her heart ached all the more at his easy display of charm. "Well, I most certainly cannot accuse you of not giving him ample warning should the day arrive," she replied, as lightly as she could.

"More warning than he deserves, wretched animal," he agreed. Chuckling, he looked back to the cat now lying upside down, savagely kicking and mauling its toy. After several moments of watching, he returned his gaze to her and said, "When I was so rudely attacked, I was about to ask when you planned to visit the Halidays next."

"Not for a week or so. I was just there on Monday, remember? I told you how disappointed they were that you didn't accompany me."

He nodded, smiling faintly. "Yes. I do remember."

"Samuel also asked if you had given any more thought to the purchase of a new plough. Ours has been repaired ever so many times, and he's uncertain that it will last out the coming harvest."

Another nod. "As a matter of fact I have, which is why I inquired as to your intentions to visit. I received a pamphlet from Ipswich today, describing Robert Ransome's renewable plough. It looks to be a fine piece of equipment. I thought that if you were going to the farm, you might take the pamphlet to Samuel and see what he thinks."

"Why don't you take it yourself?" she suggested, privately thinking that he might enjoy the trip, especially after all the reading he'd done on farming. "I'm sure he would love to discuss the matter with you. I also know that he wishes to give you a demonstration of our new threshing machine."

He returned her gaze as if seriously considering her proposal, then looked away. "Impossible."

Her eyes narrowed at his reply. Still clinging to his lordly airs, was he? Infuriated that he would snub the Halidays, especially after they had so graciously offered him their friendship, she demanded, "Why is it impossible? Because you are a high-and-mighty Somerville and Samuel is but a lowly Haliday?"

He lurched to his feet, scowling, and stalked to the window. "No. It is impossible because I would not know what to say or do. I'd be afraid to speak for fear of making a fool of myself."

Of all the responses he could have made, this was the last one Jane had expected. Lord Quentin Somerville, darling of the *ton*, intimidated by a farmer? Acutely aware of what it had cost him in pride to make such a confession, she went to him and gently laid her hand on his arm. Her chest swelling with tenderness, she murmured, "You, my lord, are a most charming and intelligent man. You need only to be yourself and speak exactly as you do to me for everything to go well."

He shrugged one shoulder, clearly unconvinced.

"It's true, Quentin. I promise. You and Samuel will have ever so much to talk about," she persisted. "Why, just look at all you've learned about farming these past weeks! I am certain that Samuel would be interested to hear your views on the latest innovations in agriculture."

Another shrug.

"Quentin," she began again, only to fall silent in the next instant, at a loss as to how to convince him. Wanting nothing more than to take him in her arms and reassure him, but certain that her embrace would be unwelcome, she decided that a change of tactics was in order and said, "The village wake is on Sunday. I shall be attending, as will the Halidays. If you like, you may accompany me and give him the pamphlet there. It is unlikely that he'll press you into serious conversation amid such gaiety. It would also be a fine opportunity for you to meet the rest of your tenants. Everyone will be there."

He made a frustrated noise. "My presence would just spoil everyone's fun. You have seen the effect I have on our people. The mere sight of me practically sends them into a swoon."

"That is because they don' t know you. In your absence they have built you up to be a jaded, ill-natured aristocrat whose sole purpose in life is to rob them. Mr. Maxwell's thievery simply supported that impression. I am certain that once they meet you, they will revise their opinion for the better and like you every bit as much as the Halidays do."

When he didn't reply, instead gazing bleakly out the window at the twilight-grayed landscape, she sighed and said, "See here, Quentin. I don't know how long you intend to stay at Swanswick. You never said, and I never asked for fear that you might think me tired of your company and leave again." The instant she confessed that last, she longed to cut out her tongue.

He glanced at her quickly, as if in surprise. "You like having me here?"

She nodded rather stiffly. "Of course I do. We have gotten on exceedingly well these past weeks. Don't you agree?"

He out and out grinned, dimpling in a way that left her quite breathless. "Indeed I do."

Tempted almost beyond resistance to touch those dimples, Jane hastily looked away. Awkwardly clearing her throat, she covered her discomfiture by saying, "Anyway, the point I was trying to make is that if you plan to stay here for any length of time, it would be best if you made peace with your tenants. The wake would be the perfect opportunity to do so. By attending, you will demonstrate not only an interest in village affairs but a willingness to be a part of their community. I know your views on nobles mingling with commoners, but—"

"Rubbish," he muttered.

She glanced back at him, frowning. "Pardon?"

He nodded. "Those views are rubbish. I was a fool to have ever held them. I know that now."

She smiled and nodded back. "I'm glad to hear that you have finally come to your senses."

"Indeed I have. I wasn't raised with such views, you know."

"I didn't think so. Not after meeting your parents at our wedding. For all their grandeur, they seem very unaffected."

He chuckled softly. "You shall never meet a more unaffected pair of nobles. Indeed, they think their tenants the most splendid people on earth, and never hesitate to say so." He shook his head. "My silly views came not from them but from my own arrogance and the prattle of my London set."

"Well, we all make mistakes," she commented lightly, giving his arm a squeeze. "The best way I can see to deal with this one is to make amends and put it behind you."

"And how, pray tell, am I to do that?"

"Simple. You must give your people the chance to know you, and yourself the opportunity to redeem yourself . . . not only in their eyes but in your own. The village wake presents the ideal time to do both."

He seemed to consider her advice, then tipped his head to one side, smiling down at her. "Tell me, sweet Lady Jane. How did you ever become so very wise?"

"By watching people and studying how they react in various situations." She shrugged her self-deprecation. "After almost five Seasons of doing little else, I have learned a great deal about human nature."

"Ah. So that is what you were doing. I sometimes wondered," he murmured, smoothing a strand of hair from her cheek.

Her knees went weak at his touch and it was all she could do to remain upright. "Y-You did?" she stammered, more affected by his casual contact than she would have dreamed possible.

He nodded. "Yes, and now that we have become better acquainted, I must confess to puzzlement at your reserve in company. With your rare intelligence and even rarer gift for engaging conversation, you could easily have been the toast of the *ton*. Why did you never reveal your talents?"

Jane gaped at him, unable to believe her ears. Her? Toast of the *ton*? She released a shaky laugh at the notion and said, "I never revealed it because I couldn't. I was terrified out of my wits every time I appeared in society." Another laugh. "As for me being a toast . . . posh! My freckles alone were enough to keep me from ever being a success, much less a toast."

"Indeed?" He dipped his face nearer to her, his expression solemn as he studied her face. "Hmm. I'm finding that I rather like freckles, especially when they are on skin as fine as yours."

"Really?" she croaked, captivated by the sultry light in his eyes.

"Really," he murmured, tracing the freckled bridge of her nose with his thumb.

She trembled faintly beneath his light touch, a delicious shudder heating her body.

Slowly he smiled, a smile as intimate and stimulating as a kiss. "So, you think that I should attend the wake?" he murmured.

Though breathless, she somehow managed to reply, "Most definitely, my lord."

"And you are absolutely certain that my presence shan't scare our people into an early grave?" His thumb was on her cheek now, stroking it in a way that set her pulse racing.

She swallowed with difficulty. "They cannot help but to adore you." As she did.

He chuckled, again softly and with a huskiness that vibrated through her soul. "All right, then. I shall place my trust in your word and attend . . . but with one condition."

"Which is?" Her throat was so dry now that it was a wonder the words came out at all.

He chuckled again and dropped his hand from her face. "That you remain by my side. People cannot help but think me tame if they see me being led about like a lamb by you."

For a beat she simply stared at him, still lost in the mesmerizing intimacy of the previous moment. Then his words penetrated her amorous fog, and she found herself laughing at

the droll image they prompted. "Done," she countered with
another peal of laughter. "Why, I shall even provide a leash if
you wish. I do, however, have one condition of my own if I
am to play shepherdess."

He raised one eyebrow in query.

She nodded. "You must promise to smile."

It was his turn to laugh. "Fine. I shall smile until everyone
wonders at the state of my wits."

At that instant, Jemma entered the room to inform her that
the kitchen maid suffered a toothache and required her
physicking.

Though Jane would rather have stayed with Quentin and
tried to recapture their previous intimacy, she couldn't ignore
the maid's pain. Not in good conscience. Thus, she followed
Jemma out of the room.

She had just reached the threshold when Quentin softly
called her name. "Jane?"

She turned to him, smiling.

"I shall be staying at Swanswick until after the babe is
born. Perhaps longer."

His words were like an answer to her prayers.

Jane hadn't exaggerated when she'd said that everyone
would be at the wake. Judging from the throng of gaily
dressed merrymakers, every single person from the village,
farms, and surrounding areas had come to join in the revelry.
Indeed, so crowded were the streets that Quentin and Jane had
no choice but to leave their gig with an elderly man who had
set up business tending vehicles on a bit of fallow ground outside town. At the rate of sixpence per rig, he looked set to
make a fine profit.

As for Quentin, this was the first time since the day of his
arrival that he'd come to the village, and it was with no small
feeling of self-consciousness that he allowed Jane to lead him

down a swarming street by the queer name of Dashing Drake Parade. Though no one fell into a swoon at the sight of him, as he'd feared, it was clear from the people's wary glances and the way they fell silent as he passed that they weren't exactly thrilled by his presence. All in all, he felt rather like a funeral procession passing by a wedding, so great was the pall his presence seemed to cast over everyone's gaiety.

It was a feeling that persisted until they came into view of the village green. Then he quite forgot his discomfort in his wonder at the sights before him. The center of the town had been completely transformed from the tranquil little hamlet he recalled to a bustling fair complete with a traveling roundabout and colorful stalls selling wares of every description.

"Oh, look! Quentin!" Jane exclaimed, pulling him abruptly to the right. There, in a clearing on the green, was a small brown bear in a jaunty red-and-yellow ruff, dancing a merry jig. Accompanying it on the violin was its exotically garbed keeper.

The surrounding crowd, which had been cheering and laughing only seconds earlier, fell silent as he was towed into their midst, though several of the people smiled faintly and nodded at Jane. As if sensing the audience's mood, the bear ceased its antics and scampered back to its keeper's side, and that personage in turn lowered his battered violin to peer at them with misgiving.

Unperturbed, Jane clapped her hands in pleasure and tossed the man several more coins. "Oh, please do continue," she begged. "I so love dancing bears." She glanced at Quentin with a smile. "Don't you think that bears look ever so cunning when they dance, Quentin?"

He forced himself to broaden the smile that had been frozen on his lips since entering the village. "Very cunning indeed."

She gave the arm she held a squeeze of approval and nodded at the bear warden.

"As you wish, madame," he replied, his swarthy face creasing into a smile.

"My lady," one of the villagers corrected him.

"Lady, ees it?" he responded with a bow. At her nod, he inquired, "And this ees your lord, yes?"

"Indeed he is," she replied, beaming up at Quentin as if they were the happiest couple on earth.

The man's smile widened into a toothy grin. "Ah, then my Ursula must do the dancing like a noble. The waltz, perhaps?"

Jane clapped her enthusiasm. "Oh, yes. Please. I have never seen a bear waltz before."

"Please," Quentin echoed, charmed by the animation of her rosy face. Never before had he seen a woman so openly express delight, and most certainly not with such exuberance. And though he knew that he should feel disapproval at her decidedly indecorous display, he didn't. He couldn't. It was too wonderful to see.

"Well, then," the man said with a nod, "for my Ursula to waltz, she must have a partner. A gentleman partner, since she ees Queen of the Forest." He made a show of scanning the crowd, then looked back at him, grinning. "You, my lord. You must partner my Ursula."

Him, a Somerville, dance with a bear like a common street entertainer?

"Oh, yes, Quentin. You must," Jane exclaimed, clapping yet again. "No one in England is nearly as fine a dancer as you."

Quentin stared at her as though she'd lost her wits, which, at that moment, he was certain was the case. Surely she didn't truly expect him to make such a spectacle of himself, especially before a crowd of people who clearly viewed him with trepidation? Why, he could just imagine the impression he would make, dancing about with a bear. They would think him either quite mad or an utter buffoon.

By the sweetly pleading expression on Jane's face as she murmured, "Please?" it was apparent that she did.

He groaned. Oh, bloody hell. How could he possibly deny her anything when she looked at him with those shining brown eyes? Sighing his reluctant surrender, he cast a sideways glance at the audience members nearest to him.

Several of them gazed at him with open curiosity, others with repressed anticipation, still others with nervous doubt. One, a grizzled old woman in a lovingly preserved court gown at least fifty years out of date, cackled and said, "That's right, m'lord. Show 'em 'ow it's done."

"My lord?" the bear warden said, gesturing for him to enter the clearing.

He shot Jane a helpless look.

She smiled her reassurance. "Everything shall be fine. I promise," she murmured, releasing his arm. "Now go. And don't forget to smile." She then nodded to the man and said, "Lord Quentin Somerville shall be honored to dance with Queen Ursula."

Seeing no way out of performing—well, at least not without behaving like the biggest bastard this side of creation— Quentin handed Jane the plough pamphlet he carried and stepped into the clearing. The bear lumbered forward, coming to a stop several feet away. When it simply sat there, staring at him, he frowned at the bear warden.

The man pantomimed a bow. "You must bow to her."

Bow to a bear? He shot Jane a disgruntled look.

She grinned in a way that could only be termed mischievous.

Secretly vowing to throttle her when they got home, Quentin sketched a shallow bow.

The bear promptly reared up on it s hind feet and returned

his bow with a clumsy caricature of a curtsy. Several people chuckled. That formality completed, the animal stood with its front paws outstretched, waiting for him to take them in his arms.

Gritting his teeth, he approached, praying that none of the *ton* ever caught wind of this indignity. After pausing a beat to eye the beast's enormous claws with alarm, he took a deep breath and took the final steps forward.

The bear instantly seized him and dragged him against its less than fragrant body in a rough hug. Though Quentin was counted tall by most people and the bear was but a small one, he couldn't help feeling a moment of panic at its intimate proximity. Were the animal to decide to gut him then and there, there wasn't a thing he or anyone else could do to stop it. Not that he expected anyone present would care if it murdered him.

Before, however, he could indulge in further reflection upon the gruesome notion, the bear warden began to play a waltz and his shaggy partner began to move. Helpless to do anything else, he fell into step—well, at least as best he could considering the bear's lack of dancing skill.

Round and round they waltzed, one ungainly rotation, then two. They had just begun their third circle around the clearing when a clarinet joined the violin, followed by a cornet. Thus serenaded, they danced two more rotations. Finally, after what felt like a millennium in circus hell, the music ceased.

As abruptly as the bear had grabbed him, it released him, again curtsying. Resigned to being a fool, Quentin bowed back, sketching his most elegant and courtly bow.

To his surprise the crowd burst into thunderous applause and cheers. When he turned to face them, he saw that they smiled at him. Him!

He looked at Jane in surprise, not certain what to make of their response. She too was clapping and looking at him with such unbridled pride that he couldn't help grinning. His grin seemed to please his audience all the more, for their applause intensified.

Feeling suddenly more lighthearted than he had in years, Quentin gave the bear warden several more coins and the bear a fond pat. As he started to turn back to Jane, a young voice piped in, "Wasn't you afeared of the beast, my lord?"

He turned to find the source of the voice and saw the boy he recalled Jane referring to as Willy, accompanied by several other rosy-faced children, peering at him with bright-eyed interest. Admiring the boy for his courage in coming forward, he chuckled and admitted, "Terrified. Fortunately, Ursula here"—he petted the bear again—"is a perfect lady."

"Well, we think yer awful brave ta get so close ta the beastie, m'lord," another boy interjected.

"And 'andsome, too. I think yer the purtiest man I ever seen." This was from a flaxen-haired girl of about thirteen, who instantly flushed scarlet and slapped her hand over her mouth.

He heard a low, husky laugh behind him, then Jane moved to his side and took his arm. "He is indeed a most beautiful man, Mavis. And brave. And as fine a husband as any woman could wish." She met his gaze then, with wide, admiring eyes, and at that moment he could have sworn that she meant every word of her praise.

Smiling a smile that echoed the emotion in her eyes, she looked away again, saying, "Now if you children will excuse us, there are many people who have yet to meet his lordship and are clamoring to make his acquaintance."

"There are?" he murmured, as she led him away.

"Of course. Your audience wishes to congratulate you on your fine performance." She looked back up at him, gazing at him in a way that made him feel like her hero. "Oh, Quentin. I was so very proud of you. You should have heard the whispered comments of the crowd as you danced. You quite won everyone's heart." To his astonishment, and pleasure, she paused to give him a quick hug. "I knew you could do it," she whispered, pulling away again. "I just knew that you could make your tenants see how marvelous you are."

Marvelous? She thought him marvelous? An odd warmth kindled in his chest at the notion. In truth, he thought her rather marvelous herself. That she could put aside the grievous wrongs he had done her and so generously befriend him made him feel a tenderness for her that he'd never before felt for any woman . . . not even Clarissa Edwardes.

Strangely enough, the thought of Clarissa provoked not sadness or regret, as it once had, but indifference. And though he still considered her beautiful, the glory of her red-gold hair and aquamarine eyes suddenly seemed less enticing than it once had. Suddenly he found that he much preferred the rich chestnut of Jane's hair and the dark, soulful brown of her eyes.

As she began to introduce him to his tenants, all of whom surged eagerly forward to greet him, it struck him: He now actually preferred Jane to her stepsister. In truth, he preferred her to any woman he had ever met. Somewhere, somehow, she had worked her way into his heart and he had begun to care for her.

Wondering when it had happened and what he should do about it, Quentin nodded and smiled, and shook the hands of what seemed to be hundreds of people. Now and again he glanced at Jane, who returned his gaze with a gentle pride that made him smile all the more charmingly in his fervent desire to please her.

Finally they came to the Halidays, Anna, who congratulated him on his grace, and Samuel, who chuckled, "Well done, my lord" and gave him a jovial clap on the back.

It was then, surrounded by his smiling people and warmed

by Jane's approval, that Quentin, for the first time ever, felt as if he had found his place in life. And that place was here, in Worcestershire, with Jane by his side.

Feeling as if he would burst with joy, he laughed out loud and swept Jane into his arms for a fierce hug. Her eyes widened in momentary surprise, then she too laughed and returned his embrace. Though he'd have been perfectly happy to remain like that forever, she pulled away and handed him his forgotten pamphlet.

"I believe you wished to give this to Samuel," she said.

He took it from her, though what he truly wished to do was carry her off to a quiet place and steal a kiss. Presenting the pamphlet to the other man, he said, "I wanted to get your opinion on Robert Ransome's plough, Samuel. I am particularly impressed by the fact that it has renewable parts. See?" He opened the front flap and pointed to the first sketch. "Worn or broken parts can simply be unbolted from the frame and replaced with new ones. Also—" He leafed over one page, then another. "Ah. Here." He pointed. "As you can see, there are sundry attachments available which can be affixed to the frame to convert it into tools suitable for hoeing, tining, subsoiling, and other such seasonal tasks, thus saving a need for separate equipment."

By the time he had finished his presentation, a large group of men had crowded about him, all marveling over the device and asking questions. As he answered, knowledgeably and easily, his confidence grew. Thus, when Samuel invited him to join the other men in a tankard of ale and a discussion of the coming harvest, he had the self-assurance to accept. The only thing that stopped him from immediately doing so was his desire to remain with Jane.

She, however, urged him to go, saying, "Please do join them, Quentin. I shall be quite all right, I promise. Anna and

I wish to shop at the stalls. I shall seek you out when it is time to award the prizes to the winners of the games."

He hesitated for a moment longer, then impulsively bent down and kissed her forehead. "As you wish, my dear."

"Young love," someone murmured indulgently, while everyone else looked on with dreamy-eyed approval.

As for Jane, she seemed to glow as she gazed up at him. More reluctant than ever to be parted from her, he allowed himself to be carried off by the ocean of farmers, all eager for drink and manly debate.

When the men were well out of earshot, Anna took Jane's arm and led her toward the stalls, saying, "Your husband seems to have made quite an impression on his tenants. Of course, I knew he would."

Jane, who was still stunned by Quentin's kiss, smiled faintly and murmured, "Yes. He did, didn't he?"

The other woman laughed. "He seems to have made an impression on you as well. My Samuel used to leave me just as flushed and moonstruck when we were first wed."

Jane blushed at having her feelings so easily read. She *was* moonstruck . . . more so than she'd ever been before. Indeed, the London Quentin she'd so adored paled into nothingness beside the Quentin she'd glimpsed today. Today's Quentin was beyond every dream of every perfect man she'd imagined. He was a man worth winning, regardless of risk or cost.

And she would gladly pay any price to make him hers.

Wondering exactly what that price was, she followed Anna from stall to stall, barely seeing the goods in her preoccupation with Quentin. It wasn't until they came to one stocked with sumptuous fabrics from London that her interest was piqued. What piqued it was a length of fine cashmere in a hue that perfectly matched the violet of his eyes.

Impulsively she bought the cloth, all ten yards of it. Quentin's birthday was in November; she would make him a dressing gown from it as a gift. Inspired by the notion, she purchased matching thread, rich gold silk for the lining, and a set of gilt buttons, all the while imagining how dashing he would look in her creation.

From then on, the remainder of the day passed in a blur of gay activity. Quentin, who had quickly caught the spirit of the wake, became an instant favorite with the crowd, especially after he partnered Willy in the blindfolded wheelbarrow race. Though they lost, taking a tumble that left both man and boy with the wind knocked out of them, they went on to win the duck race by cheering Wellington to victory.

As Jane sat on the sidelines, watching, she saw the last vestiges of his aristocratic arrogance slip away and the truly noble man within emerge. To her blissful pleasure, he seldom strayed from her sight the entire afternoon. When he did it was to perform service for her, such as fetching her food, or a shawl, or making purchases she had forgotten in her engrossment with him.

When, at last, they departed the festivities, long after dark, they did so to a chorus of fond farewells and invitations to visit.

"Well, then, sweet Lady Jane. Did you enjoy yourself?" Quentin inquired, gallantly lifting her into the gig.

"Immensely. I couldn't have had a better day," she replied on a sigh. She sighed not at the time she'd had, but at how handsome he looked in the torchlight, smiling up at her.

He chuckled. "I'm glad to hear it, since you appear to have bought out the stalls." One by one, he handed up her immense pile of parcels. When he came to the last and largest one, the goods she had purchased to make his birthday gift, he arched a querying brow at its size and murmured, "Whatever is this?"

She snatched it from his grasp. "It's just cloth and thread to make the baby some blankets. Nothing that would be of particular interest to a man."

"Ah. Yes. Speaking of the babe, I . . . made a purchase of my own." He smiled faintly and reached into his coat pocket for a small package. Handing it to her, he added, "It's not much, but I thought you might like it."

"Why, Quentin . . . thank you," she exclaimed softly, more pleased than she could express. It didn't matter what the gift was. The mere fact that he thought enough of her to buy it made it worth all the treasures in the world to her. Her heart in her throat, she opened the parcel while he climbed into the vehicle.

It was a string of coral teething beads, a beautiful one, from which was suspended the most exquisite silver rattle she had ever seen. That he would buy such a gift most certainly meant that he cared something for their child, didn't it? Wanting to weep at the significance of his offering, she met his gaze and whispered, "It's a wonderful surprise, Quentin. Thank you."

He returned her gaze for a beat, looking as if there were something he longed to say. Then he tipped his head down and studied the beads. After several moments during which he lightly traced them with his index finger, he cleared his throat and said, "According to legend, coral originates from the drops of blood that spurted from Medusa's head when Perseus chopped it off. As such, it is said to have magical powers and to ward off evil. It is a tradition of the Somerville family to buy something made of coral for each of their babes . . . to protect them."

"I see," she whispered, unable to force more from her emotion-clogged throat. He did care. He did!

Again Quentin looked as if there were something on his mind about which he wished to speak. Again he refrained from doing so, instead picking up the reins and urging the horse into action.

They didn't speak again until they had traveled several miles. Feeling their silence acutely and longing to hear his voice, Jane finally inquired, "How was your day, my lord? You never said."

He grinned. "Most excellent, thanks to you and Queen Ursula. Our tenants seem to have decided that I'm not such a wicked fellow after all."

She grinned back. "I told you that they were a wise and jolly group and that you would enjoy their company."

"As usual, you were correct. In fact, the farmers and I enjoyed our discussion so much that we have decided to meet once a month in the old tithe barn to mull over agricultural problems and to exchange ideas. Our first meeting is to be next Thursday."

"I think that to be a marvelous idea," she replied, studying his profile in the moonlight. It was beautiful. *He* was beautiful . . . both inside and out.

Here was a man with a heart worth winning.

And win it she would.

Chapter 12

Of late, everything seemed to remind her of Quentin. The primroses she now embroidered on their unborn child's cradle coverlet proved no exception.

Remembering all the times in the past month when she'd sat on the edge of the chaise longue gently coating Quentin's work-blistered hands with soothing primrose ointment, Jane gazed at it now, strewn with magazines. Since the day of the wake, Quentin had taken his interest in farming out of the library and into the fields, where he now spent most of his days. Indeed, so eager was he to do, see, and experience everything he'd studied that he had taken to leaving the abbey just after dawn, and he seldom returned before nightfall.

When he did return, he was always dirty, tired, sore, and sunburned from having worked the fields with their laborers, assisting in calving, or any of the other dozens of decidedly unlordly activities he favored these days.

He was also happier than she'd ever seen him.

To Jane there was no greater thrill than watching his face as he spoke of his day, relating with the greatest of satisfaction all that he'd learned and accomplished. If a person could truly glow, Quentin did at those times.

His smile, always brilliant, seemed a hint broader, brighter, and easier as he spoke; his laugh more sparkling and free. And then there was that dazzling new light in his eyes, the one that bespoke of soul-deep pride and contentment. All and all, his joy was a wondrous thing to behold.

Unfortunately for her heart, beholding it made her want him all the more. In truth, she was beginning to love him. So much so that when he dozed off in the evening while reading, which he often did in his exhaustion, she would sit exactly as she did now and watch him sleep, wondering . . . and dreaming . . . and longing.

She wondered how it would feel to sleep in his arms, with his long, elegant body spooned against hers. She dreamed of waking in the morning to find him beside her, his glorious curls spilling across her pillow and his slumber-drugged eyes burning with slow, sensual fire as he awakened beneath her kisses. Most of all she longed—oh, how she longed!—to have him take her in his embrace and make gentle yet passionate love to her.

Her body tingling at her thoughts, Jane glanced back down at the tambour in her hands. Ever since the wake, she'd found herself wishing that Quentin would seek her bed. For from that day forth, she'd known in both her heart and her soul that if he were to come to her again the experience would be everything Elizabeth said it should be, and more. Much, much more.

Oh, that wasn't to say that she now believed him to be in love with her. She didn't. However, she could see from the way he smiled at her, and from the genuine warmth in his eyes when he met her gaze, that he had grown fond of her. That fact, combined with the marvelous changes that had taken place within Quentin himself, gave her the conviction to believe that when, and if, he ever took her again, he would do so with tenderness and caring, thus making the act transcendent.

Saddened by the possibility that she might never get to sample such rapture, Jane worked another stitch into the stem of a primrose. The dismal truth was, unless she could find a way to spark his passion, it was unlikely that Quentin would ever come to her. And since she knew as much about seduction as she did about shipbuilding, well—

At that moment the library door swung open and the object of her hopeless longing strolled in. As always happened of late, his face instantly lit with a smile when he saw her.

Tonight, however, the smile quickly toppled into a frown, and instead of going to his usual perch on the chaise longue, he stalked over to the sideboard and snatched up the Argand lamp. Carrying it to where she sat, he gently chided, "You really shouldn't sew in the dark, you know. You shall quite ruin your eyes."

Jane glanced about her, surprised to see that it had indeed grown dark. Smiling rather sheepishly, she said, "I was so engrossed in my—uh—stitchery, that I didn't notice the nightfall. It was still light when I sat down."

"Was it indeed?" He deposited the lamp on a nearby table. "In that instance, you must be working on something exceedingly fascinating for it to have kept you so very rapt these many hours." Looking genuinely intrigued, he knelt beside her chair and examined her stitchery.

She, in turn, examined him, admiring the sun-kissed radiance of his skin and hair and marveling at the splendor of their contrast to his eyes and teeth.

Set in the newly bronzed frame of his face, Quentin's always remarkable eyes appeared brighter and more jewel-like than ever, his straight teeth pearlier and more perfect. As for his hair—

She let her worshipful gaze travel over his luxuriant fall of curls, noting the dramatic increase of fire in their mahogany strands. Those ringlets had grown during his stay in the country, and now coiled about his shoulders in a glossy tumble. To her eyes the effect was impossibly romantic. So much so that she fervently hoped that he would never cut them. Well, at least not until she'd had the chance to twist them about her fingers and bury her face in them to her heart's content.

She had just focused on his face again and was admiring the length of his lowered lashes, when he looked up. Meeting her gaze, he murmured, "Your workmanship is exquisite, Jane. What are you making?"

This was the first time he'd ever noticed her needlework, and it thrilled her that he did so now. Smiling with all the pleasure she felt inside, she replied, "It's a coverlet for our baby." Not *the* baby, as she usually said, but *our* baby. When he continued to look interested, she shifted the cloth to show him the Somerville family crest she'd embroidered in the center. "See here? I thought that with a border of flowers added around this, it can serve for either a boy or a girl."

"Indeed it can—a very fortunate boy or girl," he said, running his index finger over the padded contours of the crest. "I only hope that the cradle I ordered from Nathan Quinny shall be grand enough to do it justice."

Jane stared at his face in surprise, barely able to believe her ears. "You're having a cradle made for our babe?"

"I hope you don't mind?" he murmured, his gaze still on the coverlet. "Of course, if you would rather order one from London—"

"No! Oh, no!" she softly exclaimed. "Nathan Quinny is far and away a finer cabinetmaker than any to be found in London. It's just that—well—" She shook her head, at a loss for words to express how very touched she was by his thoughtfulness. Finally she settled on saying, "Thank you, Quentin. Your thoughtfulness means a great deal to me."

He looked at her then, his eyes dark with troubled emotion. "There is no need to thank me. It's the least I can do. The child is mine as well as yours, you know, and"—he looked away again—"I have decided that it is high time I started acting like the father I am about to be. Unfortunately, to my everlasting shame, I find that I don't know how."

Jane gazed tenderly at his profile, her heart bleeding at the note of self-loathing in his voice. Wanting nothing more than to hug him and reassure him, but too timid to do so, she murmured, "Don't feel badly, Quentin. There is no shame in being unprepared for parenthood, nor is it unusual to be so, especially in instances such as yours. After all, you neither wished nor planned to be a father." She smiled and nodded. "Personally, I think that you are doing admirably."

"But I feel so helpless . . . so lost. I truly wish to do what is right, but there is a part of me that is terrified of doing so and prevents me from acting as I know I should. I'm afraid of . . . of . . ." He shrugged and looked at her again, wretchedly, as if in desperate appeal. "In truth, I do not know why I am so frightened."

She smiled at that, but kindly and with gentle understanding. "You are frightened of the unknown, of the unfamiliar demands and responsibilities that come with parenthood. I know, because it is the same with me."

"You? Afraid?" He couldn't have looked more stunned had she told him that she was a changeling and her parents were trolls.

"Yes, me. I'm terrified that I shall do everything wrong in the care and rearing of our babe. Why, I'm even a bit afraid of holding it, though I've held at least a hundred infants over the years."

He shook his head, still incredulous. "But that is ridiculous. If ever there was a woman born to motherhood, it is you. There isn't a kinder, more sensible or nurturing soul in all of England."

"Perhaps. But simply being born to do something doesn't make the first time of doing it any less daunting. Besides, what makes you think that you weren't born to be a father? I saw the way you were with the children at the wake. They adored you, and by the look on your face, I would say that the feeling was mutual."

He smiled faintly. "In truth, I had never spent much time around children until that afternoon. I never cared to. I always thought them noisy, dirty, wicked little nuisances fit to be neither seen nor heard."

"And now?" she inquired softly.

He frowned and shook his head, as if he couldn't quite believe his conclusion. "I find that it is the pampered, overindulged children of my noble acquaintances that I dislike. The country children I met were quite enchanting."

She nodded. "Since your child is to be raised in the country with those same children for playmates, you shall no doubt find that he or she is equally as delightful."

He contemplated her reasoning, then tipped his head to fix her with a look of droll query. "Are you certain that it isn't their noble blood that makes my friends' children so disagreeable?"

"Quite," she replied with a laugh. "Besides, our child shan't be completely noble. It will have at least some of my common blood."

Smiling, he shifted his gaze back to the coverlet. "If our babe is anything like you, I shall enjoy it very much indeed."

Her jaw dropped at his unexpected compliment. "Really?"

"Yes, really. There is no one with a finer nature than you, sweet Lady Jane, and I would be exceedingly proud to have a daughter just like you."

Touched and pleased almost beyond words, she somehow managed to stammer, "Then you wish the babe to be a girl?"

He dimpled. "A girl would be wonderful, though I'm not opposed to a boy. I shall gladly accept whatever you choose to give me."

At that miraculous moment, Jane thought she just might die

of love for him. "Oh, Quentin!" she whispered, impulsively throwing her arms around his neck. "You are the dearest, most wonderful—oh!" She broke off, fiercely hugging him.

He gurgled in response.

She gazed at him adoringly, her arms still snugged about his neck. His face was red, his eyes oddly wide, and—

Oh, heavens! She was strangling the poor man in her delight. Instantly she released him, exclaiming, "Quentin, oh! I'm sorry!" She lightly rubbed his throat. "I truly didn't mean to choke you."

He grinned. "And I truly didn't mind your doing so. If a man must be strangled, how better than by a charming woman's arms?"

Charming? He thought her charming? Jane felt herself grin in return. Charming was a full step closer to enticing than kind, sensible, and nurturing. Perhaps there was hope for her to stir his passion yet.

Flustered by the thought and frantic to cover the confusion it provoked, she said the first thing to come to mind. "How was your meeting?" This evening had been the second of the monthly meetings that Quentin and the farmers had established on the day of the wake.

Though he continued to smile, a shadow darkened his eyes. "Fine. We discussed how best to go about our individual harvests, and where to hire the additional laborers we shall need. Since"—a grimace—"I am so pathetically lacking in experience, the meeting proved most informative for me. Especially since we are to begin the home farm harvest week after next."

"Well, then, it sounds as though the meetings are everything you hoped they would be."

He nodded. "They have proved beneficial to us all. So much so that we plan to expand on the idea after harvest and hold a four-day agricultural symposium to which all the farmers of Worcestershire and its surrounding counties shall be invited. It will give us all a chance to hear other opinions and to learn of the difficulties being experienced elsewhere. No doubt we shall gain valuable new insight and perhaps even find solutions to some of our more perplexing problems."

"That all sounds wonderful, but how will you ever spread the word over so many counties?"

Quentin got to his feet and strode to the sideboard. "We all have friends and relatives in various parts of England. We shall simply write to them and request that they post notices in their villages." After pausing to pour himself a healthy portion of what looked to be brandy, he finished, "I am also considering placing an announcement in *Farmer's Magazine*."

Rather than sprawl on the chaise longue, as she expected him to do, he began pacing before the hearth, now and again quaffing from his glass as he moved.

Perplexed by his sudden agitation, Jane set down her tambour. After watching him for a moment, one during which he developed a most alarming frown, she asked, "Is there something about the idea of the symposium that you find troubling?"

"No, it isn't the symposium, it's—well"—a shrug—"never mind. It's nothing that you need concern yourself about."

"If it's something that troubles you, then I most certainly must concern myself about it. Indeed, I wish to do so. Surely you know by now how much I enjoy helping you?"

His lips curved into a taut smile. "Yes, I do know. Unfortunately, there is nothing you can do to help me in this instance."

"Perhaps, perhaps not. We shall never know if you don't let me try."

He paused, seeming to consider her words as he took a long drink. Finally he lowered his glass and nodded. "All right, then." Resuming his pacing at an accelerated rate, he muttered, "It's my brother, Nicholas. I would like to invite him to the symposium."

She frowned, nonplussed. "Why, I think that a marvelous idea. He sent me the nicest letter welcoming me into the family after we were wed, and his wife sent us that lovely pair of silver candlesticks in the dining room as a gift. I cannot see how inviting him here is a problem unless—" Her heart plunged to the pit of her stomach at that "unless." Swallowing the resulting lump in her throat, she forced herself to finish. "Unless you do not wish him to meet me."

"What?" He stopped abruptly, staring at her as if she'd lost her mind. "Where did you ever get such a harebrained notion?"

She shrugged miserably.

He grunted. "For your information, there is nothing that would please me more than to present you to my brother. I am certain that both he and his wife, Sophie, would adore you."

Slowly, Jane let out the breath she was unaware she was holding and smiled her relief. "Well? Then where is the problem?"

He continued staring for a moment longer, then grunted again and resumed his pacing. "I doubt he would welcome the invitation. We're not exactly on the best of terms."

"I find that hard to believe." She shook her head, truly unable to countenance the notion. "Why, judging from his letter, he wishes only the best for you."

A sigh, a heavy one. "He always did. The problem is, I wished him nothing but ill in return, and never missed a chance to drive the point home. I'm afraid that I drove it a bit too deep six years ago when I tried to spoil things between him and his wife. Since then we have barely spoken." He ran his fingers through his hair, his face a portrait of self-recrimination. "Looking back now, I can honestly say that I shan't blame him if he chooses never to forgive me. My behavior was inexcusable."

"I am certain that you judge yourself far too harshly," she murmured, wishing that there was more she could say. But of course there wasn't.

"No. I doubt I judge myself nearly harshly enough."

Aching at his torment, Jane watched as he tossed down the remainder of his drink. Wanting beyond all else to ease his pain, she gently suggested, "Have you tried telling your brother that you are sorry for your behavior?"

He snorted and shook his head. "Until this evening, I wasn't sorry in the least. I always thought him deserving of the misery I inflicted on him. I was jealous, you see, jealous of the fact that he is the heir and that my parents adore him." He paused in his pacing then to look at her, his eyes pleading for understanding. "I thought his life too easy and privileged, and I resented the fact that he would never have to find his own place in the world as I did, simply because he'd had the good fortune to be born first. It didn't help matters any that he is good and perfect and that our parents are always holding him up to me as a shining example of manhood."

"What changed your feelings?" she softly inquired.

A rueful smile tugged his lips. "Listening to the other men. Many expressed an eagerness to invite their brothers to the symposium, so that they could share their pride in their farms with them. As they spoke, I thought of Nicholas and the attention he lavishes on his own estates, and I suddenly had a longing to do the same. I wanted to share stories, laugh over mutual mistakes, and do all the things brothers are supposed to do together. Beneath my jealousy, I admire him very much and would like to seek his opinion on several matters."

"Then why don't you write and tell him so?" she said, rising to go to him. "Perhaps he feels the same way you do."

"He would have to be a fool to do so, and I can assure you that Nicholas Somerville, earl of Lyndhurst, is no fool."

"A fool is a person who cannot see or accept a gesture of peace from his foe," she countered, coming to a stop beside him. "If your brother is truly as admirable as you suggest, he will see your invitation for the gesture it is, and accept."

"And if he doesn't?" He met her gaze then, naked despair reflected in his eyes.

She looped her arm through his and gave it a hug. "Well, then we shall just have to try again and again until he does. But after reading the letter he sent me, I doubt such an effort will be necessary. If he hated you, he most certainly wouldn't have bothered to send wishes for a long and happy marriage, nor would he have asked me to convey his best to you."

"He did that?" Quentin exclaimed, visibly taken aback.

She nodded. Well, he had conveyed the wishes to both of them, so it wasn't really a lie. Not technically.

"Hmm. And Sophie did send us those silver candlesticks, so she must not utterly loathe me," he mused, a faint note of hope creeping into his voice.

"Exactly. And if you ask me, that note and those candlesticks were their peace offerings to you."

"Perhaps."

"Well, the only way to find out is to send the invitation."

"Of course you are right . . . as usual." To her surprise, he turned to her, and gently cupped her chin in his palm. Raising her face to meet his gaze, he murmured, "My wise, wonderful Lady Jane. What ever would I do without you?"

She thrilled at the tenderness in his voice. "You shall never have to find out, my lord. You need only to look up to find me by your side."

"Do you promise?" he whispered, an odd light flickering in his eyes.

"I promised the Quentin I admired that I would love, honor, obey, *and* abide with him all the days of my life." She dipped her head and kissed his palm. "You are that Quentin now, and

I intend to keep those vows. I shall remain by your side forever and a day, if you wish. You have only to want me there."

His face inched nearer to hers. "I do want you there," he whispered, his face so close to hers now that she could feel his breath fanning across her lips.

For a long moment he lingered, his eyes warm and compelling as they gazed into hers. And she was certain, certain as she was that her name was Jane, that he was about to kiss her.

Excitement at that thought surged through her, making her tremble with anticipation. Yes, please. Please make him kiss me, she prayed. As she watched, feverishly waiting, a shadow passed over his face, and she sensed his withdrawal. Smiling with a sadness she didn't understand, he turned his head and kissed her cheek. "Thank you, Jane," he whispered hoarsely.

"You're welcome," she replied, her lips aching with jealousy of her cheek.

They remained like that for several more seconds, face to face, gazing intently at each other. Then he released her chin and stepped away. Sketching a shallow bow, he murmured, "With your permission, my lady, I shall go write my brother now."

She nodded, barely able to hide her disappointment at his words. At that moment, she would have gladly granted him permission for anything.

Anything at all.

Chapter 13

The dark magic of autumn was upon the countryside by the time the harvest was complete.

Once bright and clear, the youthful colors of summer had ripened into the dying hues of fall, leaving the landscape painted in rich, baroque shades of gold, wine, and bronze. As if to mark the calendar of the season, the first tawny leaves had fallen and now lay like rust beneath the maple, oak, and birch trees; cones hung brown and mature among the ever-green branches of the cedar, pine, and larch. Even the jade-green hedgerows celebrated the time by becoming studded with ruby hips and haws.

Though he had been on the earth almost twenty-nine years, Quentin couldn't recall having ever noticed the change of the seasons before. Now that he did, he decided the pageantry was quite a splendid sight, especially from his current vantage point.

Having been proclaimed Harvest Lord by his two hundred twenty-two harvesters, he rode enthroned atop the last load of crops in the harvest wain, crowned with a circlet of wheat leaves and triumphantly carrying the traditional corn dolly. As dictated by the occasion, the wain had been decorated with flower-twined boughs of oak and ash and was drawn by six colorfully garlanded horses. Around him sat his self-appointed court of twelve, behind him paraded the remaining workers. All sang,

Harvest home, harvest home,
We have plowed, we have sowed,
We have reaped, we have mowed,
We have brought home every load,
Hip, hip, hip harvest home!

The harvesters had been singing the jolly air since the cer-emonial cutting of the last sheaf of wheat, and though Quentin had been unfamiliar with it then, he was now well enough versed in the words to sing along. And sing he did, merrily raising the corn dolly high into the air to dance it around every time they came to the last line.

As a tribute and token of good luck to Jane, ancient Pen-rose Morris, who was said to have been making the Swan-swick corn dollies for nigh onto fifty years now, had skillfully twisted the last sheaf into the figure not of a maiden, as was customary, but of a woman ripe with child. Sun-browned wheat ears had then been added for hair, a bit of gold tinsel for a crown, and ribbons and kerchiefs made up the gown. Quentin himself had added the final touch by tucking a small bouquet of the country flowers Jane so loved into the figure's arms.

As he lowered it again, grinning with the sheer joy of being alive, he pictured how Jane would look when she saw the doll.

She would be delighted, of course. And to him there was no lovelier sight nor any that gave him greater pleasure than Jane's face when she was delighted. She had such a lovely smile, so sincere and easy and filled with such innocent joy that it quite took his breath away to see it. And the way her eyes lit up when she was happy, well, it did the strangest things to his heart, making it hum and sing instead of merely beat. To him, Jane's smile was like a miracle in the way it touched his soul and brightened his life.

In truth, her smile had become the anchor of his day, making him eager to rise in the morning and impatient to rush home to her at night. He prickled with that same impatience now, knowing that she, along with the families of his workers, awaited him in the old tithe barn where she had spent the day directing the preparations for the Harvest Home feast. For him the feast celebrated not just the end of the harvest but the welcome return of his comfortable daily routine with Jane.

Since the onset of harvest several weeks earlier, he had seen far less of his wife than he liked. Oh, she still took breakfast with him as she had before, though it meant that she must rise before dawn to do so, and she often rode into the fields in the afternoon to bring him and his workers cider and ale. Of late, however, he'd been too exhausted to sit with her in the library after supper, and he sorely missed the intimacy of those cozy interludes. The few attempts he'd made to resume them had resulted in his promptly falling asleep on the chaise longue, only to awaken near midnight to find himself covered with a blanket and Jane still by his side, her tambour in her ever-industrious hand.

At those times, as she hushed his apologies with a gentle smile, he would find himself longing to whisk her off to his bed and hold her. Just hold her. To cradle her against him and simply let her soothing presence ease the weary ache from his bones. Unlike all the other women he had ever taken to his bed, who had demanded constant and sometimes exhausting sexual attention, he knew that Jane would understand his fatigue and be content just to lie in his arms.

Well, at least she would be had he not been such a brute on their wedding night. After what she'd suffered at his hands, she would most probably faint from fear should he so much as mention his bed. And he couldn't blame her. If someone had used him in such a monstrous manner, he would have avoided their touch at all costs. So would everyone else he knew . . .

Everyone—except Jane. It never failed to confound him that she didn't shrink from his touch, nor did she balk at touching him. Of course, her touching usually involved treatment of the minor injuries he constantly suffered while attempting to work his estate, and he touched her only when the dictates of propriety required him to do so, such as when he helped her out of the gig or escorted her down the streets of the village.

He smiled wryly at that last, perfectly aware that he lied to himself. His kissing her forehead at the wake had had nothing to do with propriety, and the urge that had led him to kiss her cheek that night in the library had been as far from proper as an urge could be. In truth, as he'd stood there, holding her prettily flushed face in his hand and staring down into her luminous brown eyes, he had been tempted almost beyond endurance to claim her lips with his and ravish her mouth as he had done that fateful night in the Kirkhams' garden.

The only thing that had prevented him from doing so was the way she had trembled when he'd lowered his face to hers. Her faint, almost imperceptible quiver had demonstrated quite powerfully that despite her actions to the contrary, she indeed harbored fear of him. That fear, of course, was of his lust, and any action that might stir it.

Knowing of her fear as he now did, he had taken great pains to hide his growing desire for her, terrified that she would retreat from him completely should he betray it. And aside from his slight lapse in the library that night, he'd done well enough, though he had to admit that it was growing more difficult with every passing day.

For what must have been the millionth time since coming to Swanswick, Quentin cursed himself for treating Jane as he had on their wedding night. He cursed himself not out of a sense of selfish regret—well, at least not wholly—but because he sincerely regretted making her fear passion and thus deprive herself of something that would bring her immense pleasure.

And she would find pleasure in lovemaking, he knew it beyond a doubt. For never in all his years of carnal experience had he met a woman as naturally sensual as Jane, or one so innately passionate. Indeed, the innocent hunger with which she'd responded to his kisses in the Kirkhams' garden had electrified him as no kiss before had ever done, sweeping him away on a mindless sea of desire in which he'd desperately longed to drown.

Had he been as much of a man as he'd thought himself to be at the time, he would have known by the way she stirred him how truly special she was. He would have opened his eyes and seen her, really seen her as he saw her now, and fallen to his knees in worshipful adoration.

Stupid bastard that he was, he'd instead reviled, rejected, and humiliated her in his anger and disappointment that she wasn't Clarissa Edwardes. He had taken the passion she had so joyfully and lovingly offered him and used it as a weapon to kill her desire. It was a crime to have done so, an unforgivable one. He knew that now. If ever a woman was born to love and be loved, it was his sweet Lady Jane. To have made her fear that instinct was the greatest sin of his admittedly sin-riddled life, one that he desperately wished to rectify, but he had no idea how to do so. In truth, he wondered if such a thing were even possible.

As he mused, not for the first time, how such a feat might be accomplished, Samuel Haliday playfully poked him with the handle of a rake, prodding him to rejoin the singing. With a nod and a smile to his friend, Quentin resumed mouthing the words, his mind still on his imbroglio with Jane.

As far as he could see, there was no way to right his

wrong. Well, not unless Jane came to him of her own free will and allowed him to love her as she deserved to be loved. Then he could take her tenderly and skillfully, as he should have done the first time, thus bringing her pleasure and erasing her fears. Since, however, there was as much chance of that happening as of him being crowned king of France, what was he to do?

What, indeed? Absently, he raised the corn dolly for the last line of the song, trying to recall if he'd ever heard of anyone else being faced with his current problem, and if so, how they had resolved it.

Hmm. Well, there was that tale about Lord Innwood. From all accounts, he'd so frightened his bride on their wedding night that she had run home to her mother and refused to return to him. Exactly what had frightened her so, he didn't know. All he knew was that it had taken the man six months of wooing to win her back.

Would wooing work with Jane?

Quentin considered. It might, though he had his doubts. Lady Innwood was a peagoose of a girl whose head was easily turned by bonbons and pretty speeches. He should know, he'd turned it often enough during her first and only London Season. Jane, on the other hand, was cut from an utterly different cloth. Not only was she disinclined toward bonbons, she was far too intelligent to be won over by mere flattery—

Something that presented a most perplexing problem. In the past he'd always used his charm, looks, and, yes, bonbons as a means to his seductive ends. Since Jane seemed immune to all three, what was he to do?

As the heavy wain lumbered off the freshly paved road and onto the dirt lane leading to the tithe barn, he tried to determine what gave her pleasure.

Hmm. Well, she enjoyed her needlework . . . and Scratch. Yes, and she most definitely enjoyed visiting their tenants.

She liked letters from her family, working in her garden, tending to the parish charities, and chattering with the village children. Most of all, she loved anything that concerned their coming child. Indeed, her eyes always shone their brightest when she spoke of the baby. And when he'd presented her with the cradle last week, which he'd had Nathan Quinny carve with flowers and the Somerville crest to match her coverlet, she had even hugged him and quickly kissed his cheek.

He smiled faintly at the memory, both inspired and bemused by it. Was it, then, homely things such as embroidery silk, flower bulbs, and infant frippery that thrilled her as bonbons did other women? Was talk of their coming babe the key to unlocking her heart?

His eyes narrowed in speculation as he gazed at the ancient tithe barn in the distance, its red-stone walls glowing like molten copper in the burnishing glow of the setting sun. They were ideas worth trying, all of them.

And try them he would. He would lavish every color and texture of embroidery silk he could find upon Jane, send to London for the most exotic bulbs and seeds available, and shower her with so many infant gewgaws that they would be drowning in them by the time the babe arrived. Most important, he would make certain to speak of their coming child at least thrice daily and to listen intently when she spoke of it.

If Jane could be won, he would win her. If at all possible, he would start their marriage anew and make certain that she never again rued the day she'd said, "I do."

Thus determined, by the time the wain stopped before the barn, amid cheers and clapping and the lively music of Josiah Plucknett, the village fiddler, Quentin was primed and as anxious as a youth with his first crush to court Jane. The instant he saw her, standing in the forefront of the waiting crowd, leading them in frenzied cheers as she had the day of the duck parade, he understood the reason for his resolve.

He was in love with her.

Love? He blinked his surprise at the realization. He, Quentin Somerville, the king of rakes, in love with quiet, retiring Jane Wentworth? He shook his head in dazed disbelief. Yet, what else could this strange new feeling be, if not love?

He thought for an instant, then grinned. What, indeed?

As he stared down at the object of his desire, so small and dear in her crimson wool pelisse, he found himself wondering not how or when he had come to love her but what had taken him so long to do so. How could he not have loved her from the very instant he saw her?

True, her shyness in company had disguised her kindness and intelligence while she was in town, but how could he not have seen her radiant beauty? Why, just look at her now. She looked like an angel standing there, smiling up at him with childlike excitement.

As he smiled back, wishing that she loved him so that he could kiss her winsomely curved lips, she pulled what looked to be a letter from her pocket and waved it at him. Before he could reflect upon what it might be, his court, led by the leaping capers of Ezra Holt, who he had been told was the perennial harvest court jester, began bowing and gesturing for him to step down.

His heart lighter than it had been since his childhood, Quentin winked playfully at Jane, who blushed prettily in response. Then he descended as majestically as he could manage from the towering heap of wheat. As he stepped from the vehicle, carrying the corn dolly like a scepter, the crowd hushed and Samuel solemnly announced, "Ladies and gentlemen, I give you our Harvest Lord."

All bowed in unison, then gazed at him expectantly.

Easily catching the spirit of the game, he gave the corn dolly a regal wave and proclaimed, "Let the festivities begin."

"Ah . . . not quite yet, my lord," Samuel informed him, slanting a mischievous look at the grinning assembly. "You must first choose and crown a Harvest Lady." He nodded to Anna.

She stepped forward to hand Quentin another crown similar to the one he wore, adding, "You must choose the fairest maid present for the honor, my lord."

"The fairest maid, eh?" he murmured, making a show of searching the crowd. He paused first to consider pretty Tessa Gelder, then moved on to the equally comely Bliss Firkins and to the voluptuous Merry Porrit. Finally he looked at Jane.

"Aha! At last!" he exclaimed, grinning. "I have found the fairest of all, though I fear she is no maid. However, since I shall have none other by my side this evening, I, as Harvest Lord, hereby proclaim Jane Somerville to be my Harvest Lady." With that, he strode over to his wife and placed the circlet upon her becomingly coiffed head.

"Well done, my lord," someone shouted, which was followed by an approving roar of "Hear! Hear! Well done!" and a frenzy of foot stamping. Amid the uproar, he heard Samuel shout, "You must now kiss her to officially recognize her as your lady."

Kiss her? Quentin stared at Jane's face, waiting for it to register dismay at the decree. It never came.

"A kiss! A kiss!" the crowd chanted.

She smiled at the people, then tipped her head back to gaze up at him. "Well, my lord?" she murmured in a strangely husky voice. "We mustn't disappoint our subjects."

"No, of course not," he replied, his own voice sounding foreign in its tautness. In truth, it was he who was dismayed by the notion of kissing her. What if he lost control and kissed her with too much passion? She would be terrified, and the last thing he wished to do was frighten her further.

Yet, to refuse to kiss her would be seen as a rejection by all, and she would be humiliated before half the village and their neighbors. He didn't wish to do that either.

That left only one option. He must bridle his desire and kiss her as chastely as a brother kissed his sister. Praying for the strength to do so, he gently pulled Jane into his embrace. After pausing a beat to steel himself against the lust stirred by simply holding her, he claimed her mouth with his.

A soft gasp escaped her and she quivered at their initial touch, then her arms twined around his neck, forcing him to sustain his kiss longer than he had intended or thought was wise.

As they stood there, lips locked against closed lips, he thought he felt the tip of her tongue sneak out and provocatively trace the line of his mouth. Whether or not she had indeed done so, his response was the same, resulting in a significant and embarrassing tightening in the fit of his trousers. In the next instant she dropped her arms from his neck and pulled away.

Fortunately for him, no one, including Jane, seemed to notice his shameful condition, for the end of their kiss signaled the onset of the festivities and they were swept along in the tide of revelers. As he allowed himself to be propelled into the barn, accompanied by the strains of a gay country air, Quentin pondered Jane's strange response to his kiss.

Though she had gasped and trembled, there had been nothing timid or frightened about the way she'd clung to his neck. And if she'd indeed caressed his lips with her tongue, well, what was he to make of that?

"Quentin! Over here!"

He found the object of his musing standing several yards away, beckoning him to join her and the Halidays at the head table.

He waved his acknowledgment, then worked his way toward them through the crush of merrymakers.

As they had done at the wake, many of the people had donned their best clothes, most of which were quaintly out of date and worn in a queer, piecemeal mix of styles. Rather than finding their display absurd or outlandish, as he would have done three months earlier, he found it charming and savored the carnival air it gave the occasion.

"Well, my lord? What do you think of your banqueting hall?" Jane inquired as he came to a stop beside her.

He glanced about him, then smiled and said, "Magnificent." And it was.

Usually cavernous and bare, the barn had been decked in autumn splendor and transformed into an enormous dining hall fit for the king of the season. Someone, most probably the horde of children who chased willy-nilly through the crowd, had made garlands of leaves and flowers, which now festooned the ceiling beams and walls and twined around the immense lumber piers that supported the arched roof. The long makeshift tables, too, were festooned and practically groaned beneath the bounty of food upon them. Even the rush torches along the wall bore a festive touch, their brackets having been hung with traditional wreaths of hawthorn and evergreen.

"Speaking of magnificent, that is a particularly fine corn dolly you have in your arms, my lord," Anna said.

"Indeed it is, for it is made in the image of our sweet Lady Jane," he replied, holding it up for the women to admire.

Jane studied it for a moment, then made a wry face. "Goodness. I hadn't realized that I'd grown so very stout."

Quentin glanced down at her rounded belly, smiling. "I would use the word 'lush' rather than 'stout' to describe your figure, and since I happen to like lush women," he shrugged, "I find both you and the dolly particularly comely sights."

"You . . . do?" She couldn't have looked more stunned, or pleased, had he informed her that he had just discovered a buried treasure.

"Most definitely," he assured her. In truth, he found her ripeness not just comely but erotic. Voluptuously so.

Anna laughed. "Well done, my lord. Spoken like a proud husband and papa-to-be."

"That is because I am indeed proud, on both counts," he murmured, his gaze still on Jane's face.

Again she looked startled, but only for an instant. Then she smiled as if he'd just handed her the world.

As he smiled back, thrilled to have pleased her, someone shouted, "A toast! A toast to our fine lord and lady. God bless them and their coming babe." The sentiment was echoed in a reverberating roar.

His eyes never wavering from Jane's face, Quentin accepted a tankard of ale from Samuel and lifted it to her in courtly salute. "To you and our babe, my sweet Lady Jane," he toasted. "My God keep and bless you both."

"And to you, my lord," she replied, raising her cup of cider. "May your every harvest be as fruitful as this one."

"May it indeed," he murmured, referring not to his wheat but to the harvest of love Jane had sown in his once barren heart and now reaped in fertile abundance. It was a crop he fervently hoped she would plant year after year, and he looked forward to helping her nurture it. Lightly touching his tankard to her cup, he drank.

The opening toast thus concluded, everyone fell to feasting in earnest. Never in his life had Quentin seen so much food as he did that night, nor had he tasted any better or eaten so much. Halfway through the festivities a gaggle of drunken guisers, all young men dressed as old women and carrying corn dolly ducks, broke into the barn and entertained the assembly with their antics as they stole tarts and pies.

When, at last, everyone had eaten their fill, the toasting resumed, resulting in homage being paid to everything from the weather to the mole on the bosom of a girl named Jennie Hyde. Quentin himself proposed a toast to Jane and her beauty, to which the other men readily drank. They then trooped outside, where they danced the timeless country dances around an enormous bonfire.

The air that night was fresh and crisp, scented with the sharp autumn scents of smoke, earth, and moldering leaves. The moon hung full and orange in the black-velvet sky, wisps of mist crept over the fields like a necromancer's spell seeking restless spirits. Now and again sparks shot out from the blazing bonfire, against which the shadowed figures of the dancers vaulted and twirled, playing out a harvest ritual as ancient as time itself.

To Quentin, there was something unreal about the scene, something mystical and almost sensual. And as he danced with Jane, his feet flying to the animating beat of the music and his soul soaring, he felt as if he were in a dream from which he never wanted to wake.

Feeling suddenly free, of what he didn't know, he executed a brisé, catching and holding Jane's gaze as he turned around her. She was his love and life, the reason for his new-found happiness.

In truth, she *was* his happiness.

She was also the most beautiful sight he'd ever seen, with her eyes reflecting the glow of the fire and her hair ablaze with its color. Looking as she did at that moment, she was the very embodiment of the Harvest Lady, warm, fertile, and seductively ripe.

The Harvest Lady, *his* lady.

Exhilarated by that knowledge, he threw back his head and

shouted his joy, never once missing a step of the lively dance. Another brisé, down the middle, up cast off, right and left atop, and the dance was finished.

Clapping his appreciation of the musicians and fellow dancers performances, he moved to Jane's side and possessively draped his arm around her increasing waist. As he led her over to the bales of straw that had been placed around the fire to be used as seats, one of the harvesters stopped him to proudly inform him that his cousins from Oxfordshire would be attending the symposium.

As the man walked away, Jane gasped and exclaimed, "Oh, my, I quite forgot in all the excitement."

Quentin peered down at her, his smile fading at the consternation on her face. "Forgot what?"

She pulled out the letter she had waved at him earlier. "This." She held it out to him. "It's from your brother."

For a long moment he simply stared at it, then he sighed and took it from her. Turning it over, he fingered the red wax seal, reluctant to break it. Where there was ignorance there was hope, and as long as he didn't know Nicholas's reply, he could hope that he would accept the invitation to the symposium.

As if reading his thoughts, Jane gave his arm a squeeze and murmured, "The answer could be yes, you know."

He smiled faintly at her upturned face. His sunny, ever optimistic Jane. Even if his brother did choose to reject him, he still had her, and she was everything. His heart thus armored, he broke the seal and read the short note.

When he had finished, he lowered it, and she prompted, "Well?"

He returned her gaze somberly for a beat, then grinned. "He's coming, and he's bringing Sophie and their children with him. He seems quite pleased by the invitation and cannot wait to meet you."

She flew into his arms to hug him. "Oh, Quentin. This is indeed wonderful news." As he returned her hug, she whispered into his ear, "Are you as happy as I?"

Wrapped in a euphoric mantle of love and elation, he held her close and whispered back, "Oh, yes. So very happy, my sweet."

Chapter 14

The next three weeks passed in a frantic fit of hustle-bustle. More than three hundred people were expected to attend the agricultural symposium, and the quiet village of Little Duckington was astir with excitement.

The Claypoles, who counted business excellent if they hosted six lodgers a month, scrubbed and painted and refurbished the inn, preparing for the rare influx of guests. The shops, which normally stocked only the most practical of wares, now boasted a dazzling array of luxuries from London, all of which were arranged in their windows in displays calculated to tempt the eye. Even the village green had never looked better, the trees and bushes having all been artistically trimmed into flawless symmetry.

At the abbey, Jane, too, labored, determined to make Quentin proud of his home. Though he hadn't said much about his brother's visit, save that he was glad he was coming, the haunted look in his eyes and his overcritical insistence that everything on the estate be perfect had told her that he was terribly nervous about it. Thus she'd expended all her efforts on the house, attending to every detail herself so as to ensure that there would be nothing to bring him shame.

Now, on the day of their guests' arrival, as she walked about the abbey checking the preparations one last time, Jane had to admit that she, too, was nervous about the visit. It wasn't meeting Quentin's brother, the powerful earl of Lyndhurst, that made her so, though heaven knew she prayed that he would like her. No, it was his wife who worried her. Lady Lyndhurst was said to be a great beauty and beyond elegant. And as Jane knew from miserable experience, such women were often haughty, spoiled creatures who disdained lesser beings. . . .

Such as herself. Oh, what ever was she to do if Sophie proved to be such a woman? Quentin wanted so badly to make a fine impression on his brother, and for his sake she longed to be a credit to him. How was she to do so if the woman scorned her?

Desperately reminding herself of Quentin's promise that her sister-in-law would love her, Jane paused before the hall mirror to check her appearance. She'd worked so hard to make herself look nice, spending more than two hours curling, powdering, pinning, and primping. And when she'd left her chamber she'd thought that she had succeeded. Now, however, as the moment of reckoning drew near, she wasn't so certain.

Her modish Pomona green lutestring gown, which she'd thought so becoming earlier, now seemed a less than ideal choice. Indeed, why hadn't she noticed how its fashionably laced stomacher front emphasized her rounding belly? And her hair—was that ringlet hanging over her shoulder perhaps a touch too girlish for a woman in her condition? Even her naturally pink cheeks, which she had always thought one of her few physical assets, seemed suddenly too ruddy and earthy for good taste. All in all, she was quite out of looks.

Grimacing at her reflection, she turned away. Ah, well, there was nothing to be done about any of it now. His lordship's outriders had already arrived, announcing that the family vehicles were half an hour behind them. According to the clock on the console beneath the mirror, twenty minutes had since passed. It was time to go outside and await their arrival.

Forcing herself to smile and hoping to disguise the fact that she felt as awful as she looked, Jane went in search of Quentin. She found him in the library, sitting at his desk, writing in a ledger. Today he wore his Town attire in honor of his brother's visit, and as she stepped into the room, she couldn't help pausing on the threshold to admire the picture he made.

Perfect, so very perfect. Garbed in a beautifully tailored sea-blue tailcoat, a pale blue-on-white striped waistcoat, and snug white pantaloons, he was the perfect portrait of urbane elegance.

As she stood unnoticed, savoring the sight of him, he reached up and impatiently flicked a stray curl from his forehead. He'd wanted to cut his hair for the occasion, and no doubt would have done so had she not begged him to leave it long, declaring it a crime against nature to shear such lovely curls. To her relief, he'd heeded her argument and had compromised with a ringlet-taming trim. His respect for her wishes had delighted her no end. When she said as much, he replied that he hoped always to please her.

A smile touched her lips at the remembrance of his comment. Of late, he'd done nothing but please her. Indeed, he was the very embodiment of the model husband. Not only was he unfailingly kind and considerate, not a day passed that he didn't bring her a thoughtfully selected gift. Among his most recent offerings were a rocking horse and two stoneware cradle-warming bottles for the babe; a fine set of gardening tools and a new sewing basket for her. He'd even had a handsome collar made for Scratch, one replete with a silver bell and a pendant upon which was engraved his name.

In truth, so courtly and flattering were his attentions that had she not known better, she'd have thought that he wooed her. Since, however, he'd made no romantic overtures, she'd concluded that he was most probably trying to make up for the fact that he didn't love her.

Jane sighed her discouragement. Ah, well. She really shouldn't feel too bad. Despite the disappointing fact that he didn't love her, things between them were still better than she'd ever dreamed possible. After all, he had promised to remain at Swanswick until after the babe was born, and it was clear from his kindness that he cared about her feelings. All in all, she could safely say that she'd made at least some headway in her quest to win his heart.

Her own heart lightening at her acknowledgment of her progress, Jane smiled and said, "It's time to go outside, Quentin. Your brother shall be arriving any minute now."

By his expression when he looked up, you'd have thought that he faced a duel with the finest shot in England. "Yes. All right. Is everything ready?" he murmured, laying down his pen.

"Yes," she replied, stricken to see his hands tremble as he picked up the pounce pot and sanded the ledger page. Oh, her poor, poor love! He was in an even worse state than she. Wanting desperately to soothe his nerves, she added in a cheerful voice, "Things couldn't be more perfect. Not only is Martha cooking your brother's favorite dish, the house looks splendid, the grounds are immaculate, and the sun has come out from behind the clouds to warm the day. His lordship can't help but be impressed."

He eyed her somberly for a moment, then managed a feeble smile. "Indeed he shall be impressed . . . by you. You, my sweet Lady Jane, look beautiful. Is that a new gown?"

She felt herself flush with pleasure at his unexpected compliment. "Yes and no. I purchased it a week before we were wed, but this is the first chance I've had to wear it."

"Well, it is the perfect choice for today."

"It is?" She glanced down at herself dubiously, still thinking that it made her look rather too round.

"Yes." With a nod, he opened the top desk drawer and removed something. Looking up again, he softly commanded, "Come here, Jane. I have a gift for you."

"Another one?" she exclaimed, doing as he bid. "You have quite spoiled me as it is. I cannot imagine what you could have found that you haven't already given me."

"It is something special. Something I should have given you on our wedding night," he replied, moving from behind the desk to meet her halfway. Gazing at her with an odd, almost tender look, he slipped a flat black box into her hands.

She peered down at it in wonder, instantly recognizing it as the sort of case that more often than not held very expensive jewelry. When she simply stared at it, stunned that he would give her such a gift, he urged, "Open it."

When she did, she was struck speechless. It was a necklace and earrings, the equal of which she'd never seen or even known existed. Made of a gold-linked series of square-cut emeralds, each of which was framed in diamonds and hung with an immense tear-shaped pearl, the necklace quite took her breath away . . . as did the matching earrings. "Oh, Quentin," she gasped, unable to say more.

"I take it that you like it?" he inquired with a chuckle.

"It's—it's exquisite," she stammered, her gaze never straying from the jewels. "I've never seen anything like it."

"No, and you're not likely to, either. It has been in the Somerville family for five generations now. My grandmother left this set to me, and her sapphires to Nicholas, specifying that they were to be given as wedding gifts to our brides. She must have had a premonition of whom we would wed, for the sapphires suit Sophie's blond beauty to perfection, and these shall be lovely on you." He lifted the necklace from its white silk nest. "May I?" he inquired.

"Oh, yes. Please," she replied, thrilled that, he thought not only that she was worthy of such a gift but also that she would look lovely in it. "Wearing such splendid jewels shall quite calm my nerves at meeting your brother and his wife."

She felt his fingers pause on her neck. "You're nervous?" There was a trace of surprise in his voice.

"Just a bit," she conceded, wishing that she could take back her carelessly voiced admission.

"Why?" He closed the clasp.

She bowed her head, reluctant to confess her concerns. "It's just that, well—I—I—" She broke off with a helpless shrug.

"Well, what?" he pressed.

"Well, it's just—" She sighed and forced it out. "Your brother is said to be very grand, and your sister-in-law is a famous beauty. I fear that they shall take one look at me and pity you for having been forced to wed me. I do so want to make you proud."

There was a pause, then he commanded, "Look at me, Jane." When she didn't instantly comply, he gently grasped her chin and raised her face. Catching and holding her gaze with his, he said in a firm voice, "You do make me proud. Always. Today shall be no exception. They will take one look at you and think you every bit as marvelous as I do. Indeed, it is you they shall pity for being saddled with a wastrel like me."

Marvelous, her? Her heavy heart lightened at his compliment. Wanting to return the favor, she sincerely countered, "No one could ever pity me for being wed to you. There isn't a kinder, handsomer, or more considerate husband in all of England."

He smiled faintly at her words, his thumb grazing her cheek in a light caress. "A woman like you deserves a fine husband, Jane. One far better than I shall ever be, despite my efforts to be worthy of you." He looked as if he was about to say more, but a footman rushed into the room exclaiming, "My lord. My lady. The coaches have pulled up the drive."

Quentin glanced up, but didn't release her face. "Thank

you, Russell. We will be out directly." Dismissing the servant with a nod, he returned his attention to her. Smiling again, he murmured, "Still worried, sweet?"

She nodded. "Just a little."

"Don't be. You truly do have nothing to fear. I promise. Now why don't I help you put on your new earrings so we can go welcome our guests?"

When Jane was properly bejeweled, Quentin escorted her outside, stopping abruptly on the stoop.

On the drive before them were two beautiful burgundy-and-gold coaches, each pulled by four perfectly matched black horses. A footman had just folded down the steps of the lead vehicle and was now opening the door. The first person to emerge was an exceedingly tall man. As he stepped down, the shoulder capes of his bottle-green greatcoat catching and fluttering in the October breeze, Jane felt Quentin tense beside her.

She glanced up at him. He stared at the man, his expression uncertain and his eyes full of bittersweet longing.

"Your brother?" she inquired softly.

He nodded.

She gave his arm a squeeze. "Well, then, we must go down and welcome him to Swanswick."

He looked at her with eyes like a fox cornered by hounds.

Her heart went out to him. Forgetting her own nerves in her desire to ease his panic, she smiled tenderly and reminded him, "He's your brother, Quentin. If he didn't love you and wish to see you, he would never have accepted your invitation. It isn't as if the symposium is a family affair which he is obliged to attend."

He stared at her a beat longer, then managed a brittle smile. "I suppose you are right."

"Of course I am," she retorted with more confidence than she felt. She'd just caught a glimpse of Lady Lyndhurst, and the woman was even lovelier and grander than she'd imagined. Though the sight made her long to run and hide, she forced herself to step forward and say, "Come along now. They shall think us exceedingly ill-mannered if we linger up here any longer."

His body stiff and his face rigid, Quentin fell into step beside her. As they slowly descended the stairs their guests turned to face them, Lord Lyndhurst looking every bit as tense and uncertain as his brother. The only thing that saved Jane from being in a similar sorry state was her ladyship, who smiled and shot her a look of fond exasperation that clearly said, "Men, silly creatures! Whatever are we to do with them?" Deciding that she might like the woman after all, Jane shyly smiled back.

"Nicholas. Sophie," Quentin finally murmured, coming to a stop before them. He sketched a bow every bit as starched as his demeanor. "Welcome to Swanswick."

His brother stared at him a moment, a faint frown creasing his brow. Then he grinned and pulled Quentin into his embrace. Giving him a hug that looked hearty enough to crack his ribs, he exclaimed, "Glad to be here, little brother. Very glad, indeed."

Quentin visibly relaxed in his embrace. Returning the hug in kind, he retorted, "Not nearly as glad as I am to see you." Though Quentin was counted tall at six feet, his brother topped him by several inches. As he pulled away, smiling broadly, he added, "You don't know how I have longed to see you, Nicholas."

"And you don't know how I have longed to hear you say that," his brother countered. "I have missed you, Quent, more than you shall ever know."

Jane felt a lump form in her throat at the joy on Quentin's face as he clasped his brother's hands, murmuring hoarsely, "Thank you, Nicholas." He didn't need to elaborate on his words. Everyone knew that he was thanking his brother for forgiving him his wrongs and granting him the chance to repair the broken bonds between them.

"Nicholas?" Nicholas raised one eyebrow in mock consternation. "My, my. So very formal. You must get in the habit of calling me Colin again, brother." Breaking into a grin, he turned to Jane and took her small hand in his large one. "I shall expect you to do the same, my dear. We are, after all, brother and sister now." His smile was so jolly that she couldn't help but smile back.

Though not as beautiful as Quentin, Nicholas Somerville was an exceedingly fine-looking man, with his dark eyes and wavy brown hair. Like Quentin, he, too, had a lovely smile and dimples, though his left cheek was marred by a long, thin scar. During a reflective moment one evening in the past week, Quentin had told her about that scar, the result of an accident when he was five and Nicholas was twelve.

At the time of the telling, she'd assumed that he told her as a way of preparing her for the shock of his brother's hideous disfigurement. Now that she met Nicholas, she saw that he'd simply been sharing a memory with her, for the scar was more dashing than alarming. So dashing, in fact, that as he enfolded her in a brotherly embrace, she felt no hesitation in pressing a kiss to the scar as she said, "I am so very pleased to meet you at last, my lord. My husband has told me many splendid things about you."

"Colin, please. Or Nicholas, if you prefer," he reminded her. "We Somervilles do not stand on ceremony with each other."

She smiled and nodded. "Then you must call me Jane."

"Jane it is. And this—" he reached for his wife and hugged her to his side—"is my wife, Sophie. Sophie, this is—"

"Jane. Yes, I know," she interjected, pulling away from him to step toward Jane. With a cordial nod, she clasped both

Jane's hands in hers and held them up to study her from head to toe. After a moment of intense scrutiny, she looked at Quentin and declared, "A fine choice, Quent. I do hope you have the good sense to appreciate her?"

"I can assure you that he does," Jane replied for him, deciding that she indeed did like her sister-in-law. "I couldn't ask for a better husband."

"Or I a better wife," Quentin interposed, moving to her side to wrap his arm about her waist . . . well, what was left of it. Smiling first at Sophie, then at Nicholas, he inquired, "Where is the rest of your family? I have yet to meet my newest nephew."

Grinning, Nicholas turned to the second coach and gestured for the waiting footman to open the door. The man had barely touched the handle when a boy of about five dashed out, closely followed by a girl who looked to be a year younger. Exiting at a more decorous pace was a pretty nursemaid, who carried a plump baby.

The girl, a golden-haired, gray-eyed miniature of her beautiful mother, ran straight to Nicholas, who scooped her up and set her on his broad shoulders. The boy, who resembled his father, went to stand by his mother's side.

Lifting the girl's small hand from his neck to kiss it, Nicholas said, "The little monkey on my shoulder is Isabel, and the gentleman by Sophie is our elder son, Graham." He nodded to the nursemaid, who held up the lovely dark-haired baby for them all to admire. "That young fellow is Christopher, who is six months old this very day."

"Isabel? Graham? You both remember your Uncle Quentin, don't you?" Sophie inquired, smiling at the children.

The little girl nodded and eyed him shyly, while the boy marched forward and sketched a lordly bow. Quentin bowed back, which prompted a grin from the child.

"The pretty lady next to your uncle is your new aunt, Jane,"

Nicholas said, at which the boy bowed again and the girl waved.

Jane smiled, thinking them the loveliest children she had ever seen. Curtsying in response to Graham's bow, she said, "It is a pleasure to make your acquaintance, Graham. Yours too, Isabel." She waved back at the girl. "I do hope you will both enjoy your stay here. Martha, our cook, has baked a batch of gingerbread just for you, and I know several children your ages who are looking forward to playing with you. There is also a pair of ponies in the stables should you care to explore the grounds." The ponies were on loan from Farmer Stubbins, who bred the animals for extra income.

Having thus welcomed the children, she returned her attention to Nicholas and Sophie. "You are no doubt eager to refresh yourselves after your long journey. If you will follow me, I shall see to getting you settled." She then glanced at Quentin, who smiled and nodded.

As he escorted her up the stairs, with Nicholas and his now chattering brood several steps behind them, he bent down and dropped a kiss on her cheek. "Thank you, Lady Jane."

She didn't have to ask him what he meant. Her heart knew his well enough to understand.

The fortnight of the visit whizzed by far too quickly for all concerned, leaving in its wake a treasured collection of fond memories and the mending of the broken bonds between the brothers. Though Jane missed her quiet evenings alone with Quentin, the two couples quickly fell into a pleasant routine that she found most agreeable.

The men, whose first four days were consumed by what turned out to be a wildly successful symposium, passed most of their time riding about the estate and discussing how best to apply what they had learned at the meetings. Promptly at dusk they would return to the abbey for supper, after which they sat before the library fire, brandy in hand, talking of every manly thing from sports to carriages, all the while thumbing through the latest farming publications.

Since the weather had been blessedly fine, the women spent their days picnicking with the children, taking long walks along the autumn-blazed country lanes, stitching their needlework in the garden, and, of course, shopping.

Shopping in Little Duckington had never been better, for along with the mob of symposium visitors came a flood of peddlers, who set up stalls on the village green and hawked a most amazing array of goods. The hamlet took on a festival-like air, which delighted both villagers and visitors—so much so that the symposium was declared an annual event.

For Jane, those two weeks proved particularly satisfying. Not only did she thrill at Quentin's joy in his reunion with his brother, she found a steadfast friend and understanding confidante in Sophie. Indeed, the woman rather reminded her of Rissa, whom she missed terribly, and she had taken to her at once. The feeling proved mutual, and by the end of the second day they were the best of friends. By the end of the visit, Jane felt as if there was nothing she couldn't discuss with her sister-in-law.

And discuss they did. They spoke of the discomforts of pregnancy, which Jane, now in her sixth month, suffered; of childbirth, about which she voiced her fears and Sophie laid them to rest; and of everything else that concerned the feminine heart. The only subject Jane didn't broach was the one that troubled her most: the loveless state of her marriage. And though she longed to confide her problem to Sophie, hoping that she might advise her, she hesitated to do so, uncertain how to introduce it.

As fate would have it—or was it perhaps an answer to her prayers?—the opportunity to bring up the topic presented itself on the last day of the visit. It came about as the women strolled through the garden, clipping the last of the season's flowers. Sophie carried the basket while Jane wielded the shears, an elegant pair inlaid with gold and engraved with a Florentine floral pattern.

As Jane cut several late-blooming roses, thinking that they would be lovely with the asters and cornflowers they had thus far gathered, Sophie commented, "Such exquisite shears. It seems a crime to use them to cut flowers."

Jane nodded, smiling faintly. "My thought exactly. Quentin, however, says that he bought them to be used and insists that I treat them as I would any of my other gardening tools."

"They were a gift from Quent, then?"

She nodded again and clipped a particularly glorious yellow bud. "Your brother-in-law has proved to be a most generous husband. Why, seldom a day goes by that he doesn't surprise me with some sort of gift. I must confess that he quite spoils me."

"Of course he does. It is a man's duty and pleasure to spoil the woman he loves. And I can tell by the way Quent looks at you that he loves you dearly," Sophie commented, taking the bud from her. Carefully laying it in the basket, she added, "To be quite frank, I never thought to see the day that he would so adore a woman. He was a bit of a rake, you know."

Rather than be heartened by the other woman's words, Jane felt strangely deflated. Because she was expecting Quentin's child and they took such pleasure in each other's company, it was naturally assumed that all aspects of their lives were equally perfect. And though she'd initially counted the misperception a blessing, she now found it a curse, wanting to weep every time someone congratulated her upon the blissful state of her marriage. The words, though well intentioned, served only to remind her with heartrending acuity that her marriage was a sham and that her love for her husband would most probably go forever unrequited.

Her expression must have reflected her melancholy thoughts, for Sophie frowned and inquired, "Jane? Is something amiss?"

Oh, how she longed to confess the truth, to share her pain and seek counsel. But she couldn't. She hadn't the strength to utter the words. And so she simply returned her friend's gaze, her tear-glazed eyes mutely begging for the help her tongue could not request.

"Oh, you poor dear. Something is wrong," Sophie exclaimed, her beautiful face becoming marked by distress. "I do hope it wasn't something I said that upset you so?"

Miserably, she shook her head.

"Then what? I mean, if you don't mind my asking?"

Again she shook her head. This time a tear escaped.

"Oh, Jane!" Sophie dropped the basket and pulled her into her embrace. With a sob that gave voice to her heartbreak, Jane buried her face against her friend's Kashmir shawl-draped shoulder and wept in earnest.

"There, there now," Sophie murmured, patting her heaving back. "It's all right. Go ahead and have a good cry. You can tell me your trouble later." After that she simply held her, stroking her back and making soft noises of comfort beneath her breath.

Gratefully, Jane did as she was told. When she had finally cried herself dry, she pulled away with a sheepish smile and apologized, "I'm sorry. I don't know what got into me. I almost never weep."

Her friend smiled kindly and handed her a handkerchief. "If you almost never weep, then something must be terribly wrong for you to do so now." She waited until Jane had wiped her eyes and blown her nose, then inquired, "Are you ready to talk now?"

Jane nodded.

"Good. Shall we sit over there?" She gestured to a stone garden bench set beneath an autumn-dyed maple tree.

When they had brushed the seat free of fallen leaves and were comfortably settled, Sophie took both of Jane's hands in hers and looked at her expectantly.

Jane returned her gaze, so soft and full of compassion, trying to decide how best to begin. At a loss, she shook her head.

Her friend smiled in gentle understanding. "Ah, I see. It is one of *those* kind of problems. Let me guess. It has something to do with Quentin."

"Yes," she admitted in a fractured whisper. "He—he—" —a shuddering sob—"d-doesn't love me."

"What?" Sophie stared at her as if she'd lost her mind. "How can you even think such a thing, much less believe it? I have never seen a man so in love in my entire life. Why, just the way he watches you, as if he cannot bear to take his eyes off . . . and the tenderness with which he treats you . . ." She shook her head, frowning. "Surely you are mistaken?"

"No," Jane whispered, her tears starting anew.

Sophie's frown deepened. "Did Quentin say or do something to make you think as you do?"

"Yes—I mean, no—I mean—" She twisted the handkerchief, struggling to find the words. Finally she blurted out, "It's what he doesn't do."

Her friend's normally smooth brow was thoroughly creased now. "I am sorry, dear, but you really must be more forthcoming if I am to understand you. What exactly doesn't he do?"

"Anything," she murmured, her face burning.

Her friend continued to stare at her, as if still not quite certain what to make of her confession. Then an expression of dawning understanding crossed her face, and she whispered, "Are you telling me that Quentin isn't intimate with you?"

Feeling like an utter failure as a woman, she nodded.

"There, there, now. Not to worry," Sophie soothed, giving her hands a squeeze. "Just because he abstains from the marriage bed doesn't mean that he doesn't love you. No doubt he is afraid to have relations because of the baby. Nicholas was terrified to so much as hug me during my last months with Graham. However, he came around quickly enough once I explained that it was safe for him to love me. Indeed, I went a step further and told him that it was actually good for both the babe and myself that he do so." She chuckled. "There must have been some truth to my claim, for I had an easy labor, and Graham is a most hale child."

Jane smiled wistfully at her words. "If only my problem were so very simple."

"Are you certain that it isn't?"

"Yes." She looked away then, unable to meet her friend's gaze as she confessed, "You see, the problem isn't that—that he has ceased his intimacies. It is that he has never shared them with me. Not truly."

"But of course he has. I mean, he has to have been intimate with you to have planted his seed."

Wanting nothing more than to resume weeping, but refusing to give in to the urge, Jane slowly replied, "There was no intimacy involved in the act. It was planted through a loveless act of mating. Since then, he hasn't so much as kissed me."

She heard Sophie suck in a hissing breath. Before her friend could speak, she turned to her, pleading, "Please do not say anything against Quentin. None of this is his fault. Not truly. He didn't want this marriage. I forced him into it with my deception." She gave her head an adamant shake. "No. If anything is to be said of him, it should be praise for his forgiving nature."

Sophie eyed her with an odd expression. "Quentin Somerville, forgiving?"

She nodded. "Yes. And not only has he forgiven me my trickery, he has shown enormous consideration for my feelings by allowing everyone to believe that our marriage was a love match."

Her friend seemed to consider her words, then slowly shook her head. "How very queer. If what you say is indeed true, Quentin must have changed a great deal since the last time I saw him. The Quent I knew would never have been so very forgiving or considerate."

For the first time since beginning the conversation, Jane smiled. "Yes, he has changed, a great deal."

Again Sophie considered, her eyes narrowing as she digested the information. After a long pause, she softly inquired, "Have you never wondered what might have prompted such a change?"

"Of course I have."

"And?"

She shrugged. "I assumed that it came about as a result of his decision to make the best of matters."

"Simply making the best of matters does not include thoughtfully considered gifts, or lingering glances, or the sort of tenderness with which Quentin treats you," Sophie pointed out. "No. My guess is that Quentin has fallen in love with you."

"What?" Jane stared at her friend in surprise, wanting to believe her theory but too afraid of disappointment to do so. "If that were true, wouldn't he have done something by now to demonstrate his feelings? Something . . . physical? We are, after all, married, and he has every right to touch me."

Sophie shrugged one shoulder. "Well, you know what silly and exasperating creatures men can be, especially strong, proud ones like the Somerville brothers. It took Nicholas an eternity to admit that he loved me. In truth, it is a wonder that we ever got together at all."

"What happened? I mean"—Jane felt her cheeks redden— "if you don't mind telling me?"

"Of course not. You have confided in me, the least I can do is return the favor." Her friend gave her a quick hug. "To answer your question, we confessed our love after I almost killed Nicholas."

"You almost what!" she exclaimed, genuinely shocked.

"Killed him, but I can assure you that it was a mistake."

Jane shook her head over and over again, barely able to believe her ears. "But how—"

"Tarts," Sophie cut in. "Pineapple-apricot ones. I put them on his luncheon tray one day, thinking that he would enjoy them. My Nicholas does so enjoy his sweets." She sighed, as if she still regretted the incident. "What I didn't know at the time was that pineapple makes him deathly ill."

"Oh, the poor, poor man!" Jane ejected, truly distressed by the thought of her kind brother-in-law suffering so.

"Yes. The poor darling had a terrible time of it." Another sigh. "Anyway, I felt so terrible when I went to apologize, that I ended up kissing him. That kiss led to"—she made a dismissive hand motion—"well, you know, during which we confessed our feelings."

"Oh. I see," Jane murmured, and she did. The problem was, she could derive no help for her own situation from the story.

"Do you really see?" her friend inquired softly.

"I think so," she replied, made suddenly uncertain by the other woman's tone.

Again Sophie took Jane's hands in hers. "Tell me, dear, do you love Quentin?"

"With all my heart."

"Have you told him so?"

Jane bowed her head, embarrassed by her cowardice. "I— I cannot."

"Why ever not? There is no shame in loving, you know."

"I know, but—" She broke off, shaking her head.

"But what, dear?"

She looked at Sophie, her eyes again welling up with tears. In a voice that was little more than a broken whisper, she replied, "I cannot because I would die if he turned away." A sob escaped her then, followed by another, and yet another. "Oh, Sophie. Whatever am I to do? I simply cannot tell him, not without being certain first that he shares my feelings. Don't you see that if I tell him, and he feels nothing in return, he might withdraw from me completely?" By the time she had choked out that last line, she was weeping in earnest.

"Yes, I do see, and I understand," Sophie murmured, drawing her back into her embrace.

"Then what am I to do? I love him so!" she sobbed, clinging to the other woman in her desperation.

Her friend hugged her hard and dropped a kiss on her wet cheek. "If you cannot tell him of your feelings, you shall just have to wait for your own pineapple incident."

"What?" Jane pulled back to stare at her friend in horror. "Are you saying that Quentin, too, has a problem with pineapple and that I must deliberately make him ill so that I can apologize?"

Sophie laughed. "No, no, dear. Of course not. As far as I know, Quentin has no trouble with any food. What I am saying is that the right moment to tell him will eventually present itself and that you must make certain to seize it."

"But how will I know when the time is right" she protested.

"Trust me, you will just know."

"But how? How did you know?" She more wailed than uttered the words in her desperation.

Sophie's expression was suddenly far away, and she smiled as if remembering her own moment of truth. Looking impossibly beautiful and radiant, she whispered, "My heart told me."

Chapter 15

"Any news of interest?"

Jane looked up from the letter she was reading to see Quentin standing on the library threshold, dressed for riding. In deference to the brewing storm outside, he wore an ankle-length, chocolate-brown greatcoat, a matching beaver with a wide, rolled brim, and a pair of sturdy top boots, all calculated to protect him should the black clouds make good on their threat of rain.

Smiling her pleasure at the sight of him, she replied, "Elizabeth says that she, Father, and Clarissa will be coming to Swanswick on the twentieth of January to await our child's birth with us. She wants to bring an accoucheur from London, a Dr. . . ." She paused to search the letter for the man's name. "Ah, yes. Dr. Benjamin Glazier. She says that he is all the rage with the *ton* and assists everyone who is anyone in their lying-in. I shall, of course, write back and tell her that I am perfectly happy with the services of our own Dr. Spicer, and that she may thus leave Dr. Glazier in town."

"Perhaps you should let her bring him."

"What?" She looked up in surprise. "But I thought you liked and trusted Dr. Spicer. Indeed, we both agreed that his prescribed diet and exercise regimen have kept me marvelously healthy. Why, just look at me. I have never felt better or been more fit in my entire life."

"I am looking at you, which is why I would like you to

allow your family to bring the man," he replied, an odd shadow passing over his face.

"Oh. I see." She glanced down at herself, feeling suddenly self-conscious at his words. Compelled to apologize for her less than pleasing appearance, she murmured, "I know I haven't been in the best of looks of late, but it is only because the babe has been so very active the past few nights, and I have had little sleep."

"My wanting Dr. Glazier here has nothing whatsoever to do with your looks," he replied, crossing the room in several long strides. "In truth, being with child seems to agree with you, for you grow more radiant every day."

"Then why?" she asked, smiling her gratitude for his compliment. Not that compliments from him were anything new. Of late he'd made a point of telling her each and every day how wonderful she looked, a kindness she very much appreciated in her current ungainly state.

Smiling back, he knelt beside the sofa where she lounged, his touch gentle as he smoothed a curl from her cheek. "I want him here because I shall rest much easier knowing that there is another doctor nearby should Dr. Spicer be unavailable when your time comes, or should a problem arise that requires an expertise he does not possess. I have grown to treasure you and our babe, you know, and I want the best for you both."

Jane felt her jaw slacken at his unexpected admission. "You have?" she whispered, searching his eyes for confirmation of his words. "I mean, do you really treasure us?"

"Very much," he replied huskily. He returned her gaze for several beats, his lips poised and his expression deliberative, as if he yearned to say more. Then an unfathomable emotion darkened his eyes and he looked away.

"Quentin?" she whispered, wondering what it was that haunted him so. Time and again during the past month he had looked at her like that, as if there were something on his mind that he desperately wished to confide. And every time, like this one, he turned away without sharing his thoughts. Haunted herself by what those thoughts might be, Jane softly inquired, "Is something wrong?"

"No. Of course not." He glanced back at her quickly, smiling a smile that did nothing to lift the shadows from his eyes. "Why do you ask?"

"It's just that—" She shook her head, gesturing helplessly. How did she describe what she was feeling? Unable to find a way, at least not without prying into something that he clearly wasn't ready to reveal, she sighed and said, "It's nothing. Just my imagination. I seem to have grown rather fanciful of late."

He frowned and lightly touched her cheek. "Not sleeping would make anyone subject to fancy. Shall I summon the doctor? Perhaps he can give you something to help you rest."

"Oh, no. No." She shook her head, secretly thrilled by his solicitude. "You mustn't trouble yourself. I am fine."

"I can assure you that it shan't be any trouble. I shall simply stop by the village on my way to the Halidays' and send him to you. Of course, if you wish me to remain here—"

"Now you are being absurd," she interjected, loving him all the more for the tender nature of his absurdity. "It is perfectly normal for women in my condition to pass a few sleepless nights—a problem, I might add, that is easily remedied by afternoon naps. So please do go tend to business."

"Well . . ." He carefully studied her face, clearly not convinced of her well-being. "I will go only if you promise to nap while I am gone."

"I promise." *After I finish your birthday gift,* she added silently to herself. She'd had enough fabric left over from his dressing gown to make him a pair of matching slippers, and she needed to finish them before his birthday tomorrow. Fortunately, only an hour or so of work remained to do so, which she could easily accomplish in his absence.

He continued to eye her skeptically for a moment or two, then nodded once. "All right, then, but I shan't be gone long. First, I must check the progress on the dressing of our wheat, then Samuel and I are to ride over to the Stephensen farm to examine a pair of oxen they have for sale. I should be home by midafternoon, at which time I shall be exceedingly vexed if you are not asleep." Fixing her with a look that was no doubt meant to be stern but struck her as endearing, he rose. "Now, if you have no more news from London, I shall be on my way."

Jane glanced at the letter in her lap, her light heart growing heavy. There was one other piece of news, one that she hesitated to tell him for fear of what she might see on his face. Since, however, it was something he must eventually know, she swallowed hard and said, "There is something else . . . it's about Clarissa."

"Oh?"

"Yes. She's . . . engaged." Jane glanced up at him, waiting anxiously for his reaction. He had cared for her lovely stepsister once, perhaps even loved her. Did he still harbor feelings for her?

She might as well have announced the engagement between two strangers for all the emotion he showed. Indeed, he didn't so much as pause in pulling on his gloves as he blandly inquired, "Is she to wed someone we know?"

Jane smiled, beyond pleased by his indifference. "Yes. Lord Crathorne. I must admit that I was surprised by the news, since he wasn't among her admirers during the Season."

He shrugged. "Crathorne is a serious, cautious sort of fellow. No doubt he wished to be certain that she was the woman for him before paying her court. They should suit very well, I think."

"Then you truly don't mind?" she inquired softly. Oh, she

knew she shouldn't ask such a question, but she couldn't help herself. She wanted—no, she *needed*—to be certain that he no longer yearned for her stepsister.

"Mind?" He glanced up with a frown, looking genuinely perplexed. "Why the devil should I mind? I like Crathorne very much, and think that he shall make her a very fine husband."

"It's just that—" She bowed her head over the letter to hide her triumphant smile. "I shall wish to have them for houseguests after they are wed, and I wanted to make certain that you have no objection to his lordship." It was only a partial lie, for she truly did want Rissa to visit.

"You may rest assured that I shall gladly welcome them here anytime they wish to come."

Anytime? Why, he sounded as though he intended to remain at Swanswick forever. Clasping that hope to her heart, she looked up again and said, "Thank you, my lord."

He nodded. "Now, if there is nothing else, I shall take my leave. The storm looks to be moving in fast, and I would like to complete my business before it strikes."

She followed his gaze to the window. The gray sky had darkened to a leaden pewter and the wind lashed at the barren trees. Hating the thought of him being out in such weather, she urged, "By all means, do go." When he didn't immediately depart, she waved her hand to signal that he do so. "Away with you, husband. I shall be exceedingly wretched if you take cold on account of me."

He hesitated a moment longer, as if reluctant to leave her, then nodded and did as she commanded. After a short wait to make certain that he had indeed gone, Jane got up and retrieved her sewing basket from where she'd stowed it beneath the sideboard.

The instant she pulled it out, she groaned. "Oh, Scratch!" Though the cat was presently nowhere in sight, it was apparent from the brown-velvet mouse entangled in her once orderly sewing thread that he had been in the room recently and up to his usual mischief. The thread he'd made mayhem of was, of course, the very thread she needed to complete Quentin's slippers.

For several moments she remained kneeling on the floor, trying to salvage enough to finish the gift. Alas, it was impossible. The delicate silk thread was tangled beyond all redemption. Sighing her exasperation, she sat back on her heels. As much as she hated the idea of going out in this weather, she saw no choice but to drive into the village and buy more.

Hauling herself to her feet, an act that took enormous effort these days, what with the cumbersomeness of her condition, Jane again peered out the window. Though the sky did indeed look ominous, the clouds appeared in no immediate danger of bursting. If she was quick about her errand, she should be back before it rained. Thus resolved, she ordered the gig prepared and sent Jemma upstairs to fetch her warmest bonnet and pelisse.

The trip to Little Duckington proceeded without incident. Once there, she quickly found the required thread in the orderly little draper shop. Pausing only long enough to examine the bolts of trims, from which she purchased several yards of purple and gold ribbon to tie up Quentin's birthday parcel, and to exchange the required pleasantries with the proprietor, the verbose Mrs. Lindley, she was back on the road to the abbey.

She had just crossed Three Duckling Bridge, which spanned the always duck-clogged waterway, aptly named Water Fowl Canal, when—

Neigh! Whinny! Her horse stumbled. Though it righted itself quickly enough, its next steps revealed a pronounced limp.

Concerned, Jane promptly reined it to a stop. Having had

some experience in treating animals, she climbed out of the gig and examined the leg it favored. No sooner had she ascertained the problem to be a stone in the foot than the water-logged clouds burst, dumping their icy contents in a drenching torrent. Though it took her but a moment to remove the stone, she was soaked through by the time she finished.

Shivering now, not only from the dampness but from the wind that cut through her garments like daggers of ice, Jane urged the beast to walk, testing the results of her ministrations. It continued to limp, giving dismaying evidence of a bruise beneath the mud on its hoof. With a sigh, she halted it again. It was apparent that it was in no condition to pull the gig.

Growing colder and wetter by the second, she peered first up the road, then down, praying to see someone she could hail for help. Just her luck. It was deserted as far as the eye could see. Hugging herself in an attempt to ward off the encroaching chill, she wondered how best to proceed.

Hmm. Well, the most sensible thing to do would be to walk back to the village and seek help there. It was but a mile behind her so she would be able to make it there in just outside a quarter of an hour. That decided, she turned her attention back to the horse, which now chomped on a tuft of autumn-browned grass.

Of course, she couldn't leave the animal hitched to the gig. Not in this storm. What if there was thunder and it bolted off in fright across the field? Attached to the vehicle as it was, it could be grievously injured, even killed. Her shivering intensified at that thought, and she guided the rig to the side of the road, where she proceeded to wrestle with the wet leather traces and straps.

She had just freed the beast from its burden and was leading it out from between the gig shafts when two horsemen appeared on the distant rise, coming toward her at an easy canter. She didn't need to see the riders up close to recognize the elegant figure atop the chestnut stallion on the right.

Quentin. And that looked to be Samuel on the gray beside him.

She sagged with relief. Though she normally prided herself on her hearty constitution, she wearied more easily in her present condition, and the simple task of unharnessing the horse had left her impossibly fatigued. Ready to topple where she stood and wanting nothing more than to surrender into her husband's care, she dragged herself to the center of the road, waving her arms to signal her distress.

The men urged their mounts to a gallop at the sight of her, the mighty hooves of their horses kicking divots of rain-saturated earth into the air as they thundered toward her.

Quentin had barely reined to a stop before he was out of the saddle and stalking toward her. Looking furious enough to throttle her, he stripped off his heavy greatcoat and wrapped it about her shivering form. As he roughly moored the buttons, he growled, "What the hell are you doing out in this storm, Jane? I thought you were going to nap by the fire. Indeed, you promised to do so." He more snarled than uttered that last in his ire.

Rather than be intimidated or incensed by his wrath, Jane was thrilled. For it was obvious from the look in his eyes and the head-spinning speed with which he'd bundled her up that he scolded her not out of anger but from worry. His blustering was simply another indication of his growing fondness for her.

Suppressing her urge to smile, Jane snuggled deeper into the folds of his coat, which still harbored heat from his body, and explained as best she could through her chattering teeth. "I'm sorry, Quentin. I meant to keep my promise, truly I did. But Scratch made a terrible tangle of my sewing basket and I needed thread to finish—something I am working on."

"Thread?" His glittering eyes narrowed and the muscles in his chiseled jaw flexed. "You risked life and limb to buy thread?"

She bit her lip and nodded, suddenly aware of how addled her reason sounded.

He muttered an oath, a vivid one. "And here I was just telling Samuel how very fortunate I am to have such a clever wife."

"You—were?" Her delighted query was punctuated by a shiver.

"Yes," he snapped, pulling her against him. Briskly chafing her quivering form through his coat, he added, "No doubt he now thinks me either a liar or a fool."

Jane sagged against him, welcoming both his nurturing ministrations and the shelter his body provided from the storm. "I really am sorry," she murmured against his damp shirtfront, though in truth she wasn't the least bit contrite. Indeed, had she known that he would hold her like this, she'd have gotten caught in a storm long ago.

He snorted. "You're going to be doubly so if you take a chill, which no doubt you shall." A disapproving shake of the head and a scowl. "Just look at you. You're frozen half to death. We must get you home and out of those wet clothes immediately." Without pausing from rubbing her arms, he glanced at Samuel, who stood scrutinizing her horse's hoof. "What seems to be the problem, Haliday?"

"The horse is lame," he replied, without looking up.

"It stepped on a stone," Jane furnished. "I removed it, but the poor beast seems to have bruised its foot."

Quentin shot her a black look. "And that, I suppose, is the reason you felt obligated to stand out here in the pouring rain and unhitch it?"

"Well, yes." Briefly she explained her reasoning, to which Quentin rolled his eyes toward heaven in exasperation. After muttering what sounded like a prayer imploring God to save him from the goosecap foibles of females, he looked back at Samuel and said, "I need to get Jane home. Would you be so kind as to see to the gig and horse for me?"

The man nodded. "Of course, my lord."

Quentin nodded back. "Thank you. I shall send someone around for them later." Without sparing so much as a word to Jane, he swung her into his arms and carried her to his horse.

Though her mind reeled with the intoxicating pleasure of being so near to him, a part of it somehow managed to retain enough presence to make her cry out, "My thread!" as he lifted her into the saddle. She did, after all, still need to finish his gift.

Always the perfect gentleman, Samuel was up in the gig in a flash, retrieving her parcel. When Quentin had tucked it safely in his waistcoat pocket and had climbed up onto the stallion behind her, he murmured, "Jane?"

She nestled against him, savoring his closeness. "Mmm?"

"You say that Scratch is responsible for this debacle?"

"Indirectly, yes," she admitted on a happy sigh.

"Remind me to drown him when we get home." With that, they were off.

Had Quentin not been shivering and so obviously chilled without the protection of his greatcoat, riding in his embrace would have been the most wonderful and romantic experience of Jane's life. As it was, she spent most of the short journey frantically trying to shield him from the wind and rain with her now warm body. Try though she might, her efforts were in vain, for by the time they reached Swanswick his teeth chattered with a violence that made her fear that he would chip them.

Always conscientious of his duties, Lester, the senior groom, materialized the instant they rode up the drive and promptly took charge of the horse as his master dismounted.

Instead of then helping her down, as Jane expected, Quentin merely swept her out of the saddle and carried her up the front steps.

"Put me down, Quentin. I am perfectly capable of walking," she protested, fearing that he might hurt himself. Now almost seven months gone with child, she wasn't exactly light.

He broke off from barking orders to Julius, the second footman, who had the misfortune to be guarding the door at the moment, to cast her a jaundiced look. "Oh, no, Lady Jane. I shan't put you down until you are safely in your chamber before the fire. For once, I intend to see that you obey me." That promise made, he strode across the entrance hall and resumed shouting commands.

Hannah was directed to bring towels and hot bricks, Jemma to fetch tea. Everyone else was brusquely quizzed as to whether or not the fire had been lit in Jane's chamber. Charity, the little maid-of-all-work, who had just emerged from the parlor carrying a coal scuttle, quickly assured him that it had, while Julius darted up to his master and deftly removed his wet hat.

Leaving a trail of rainwater behind him as he went, Quentin whisked Jane up the ornately framed spiral staircase and down the third-floor hallway, pausing only to unlatch her chamber door with his elbow and kick it open. As pledged, he set her down only when they stood before the fire. The chamber itself felt deliciously warm after their chilly ride.

Rather than look pleased by the coziness of the chamber, Quentin continued to scowl, most specifically at her. After several seconds of eyeing her, as if not quite certain what to do with her, he growled, "You need to get out of those clothes. Who helps you dress?"

"Madge."

"Ring for her."

Jane shook her head as she kicked off her waterlogged slippers. "I cannot. She isn't here. It is her half day off and she shan't be back until after six."

He snorted. "Well, then you shall just have to make do with someone else. Who would you like?"

"I don't know," she replied, reaching beneath her chin to untie her sodden red bonnet. The bow had somehow become knotted, and try as she might, she couldn't seem to loosen it.

Quentin made an exasperated noise and pushed her fingers aside. A couple of tugs and he lifted the modish creation off her head.

The *once*-modish creation, she silently amended upon seeing the spoiled silk ribbons and rain-bedraggled plumes.

"Well?" Quentin prompted as he dropped the bonnet onto the hearth.

"Well, what?" she murmured, eyeing the hat with a pang. It had been her favorite ever since Quentin had complimented her on it one afternoon when he'd met her and Clarissa walking in the park.

"Well, whom do you wish to help you undress?" he clarified.

"Oh." She shrugged. "No one. I can do it myself."

"No, you cannot. You couldn't even untie your bonnet, you are shivering so badly." He grasped her wrists and held up her gloved hands to illustrate his point.

Jane's eyes widened at the sight of them. They were shaking, badly. And here she'd thought herself so very warm.

Dropping her left hand to strip the glove off the right one, Quentin ground out, "You have to the count of ten to name a name. If you fail to do so, I shall undress you myself. I will not have you remain in those clothes a second longer than necessary. Not in your delicate condition." He pulled off the glove. "One."

Him, undress her? She felt herself blush, but not entirely from embarrassment.

"Two." He tossed the glove next to the bonnet and began to remove her left one.

Though she found the notion of having Quentin play lady's maid provocative, the thought of actually allowing him to do so left her feeling flustered and abashed. She was, after all, far gone with child, and she had reservations about letting him see her body in such a clumsy state.

"Three." The left glove followed the right one.

What if he took one look at her swollen belly and turned away in disgust? Some men did find women with child repulsive, she'd heard. Despite all his praise about her looks of late, was Quentin secretly one of those men?

"Four." His hands moved to the buttons of his greatcoat.

Was he indeed? she mused, watching him release them from their moorings. Judging from the gentleness of his touch and his lack of hesitation as he unbuttoned the ones over her rounded midsection, she'd be inclined to say no. Still—

"Five," he announced in an ominous tone, liberating the final button. "Six." He removed the garment. "Seven." He dropped it to the hearth next to the bonnet and the gloves.

Dare she let him see her?

"Eight." He worked on the frog closures of her pelisse now.

Did she love and trust him enough to chance such a potentially devastating gamble?

"Nine."

Did she truly believe that he had grown fond enough of her to entrust him with her heart in such a manner?

"Ten." He peeled the soaking pelisse from the sodden cream and gold woolen gown beneath it. Spreading it over the back of a nearby chair to dry, he barked, "Well?"

As Sophie had instructed her to do, Jane listened to her heart.

It said yes. Yes, she did trust him, and yes, she loved him enough to risk anything for a chance to promote intimacy between them. Perhaps the storm was to them what pineapples had been to Sophie and Nicholas. Perhaps, just perhaps, the deeply personal act of undressing her might serve as an impetus to break down their reserve, thus allowing them both to express their feelings. She just hoped that she wouldn't be disappointed at what Quentin might confess his feelings to be.

Praying that she did the right thing, Jane met his gaze and softly replied, "There is no one besides Madge whom I would feel comfortable in allowing to perform such a personal task. No one, that is, besides . . . " She bowed her head, unable to look at him as she whispered, "You."

There was a pause, one that stretched on like an eternity for her. When he finally replied, it was in an oddly choked voice. "Are you certain, Jane?"

She nodded, though she still didn't dare look at his face.

Another pause, followed by a sigh. "As you wish."

As Quentin moved behind her and slowly unbuttoned the back of her gown, Jane wondered at that sigh. Did it bespeak annoyance at being asked to assist her? Or a reluctance to do so? Or could it have been a bit of both? Disheartened by her ruminations, she stood stock-still with her head bowed, suddenly certain that she'd made a terrible mistake.

She was trying to think of a way to rectify it when he inquired, "Should I pull your gown off over your head, or would you like me to drop it so you can step out of it?"

"Over my head, please," she murmured. "I fear that the bodice will no longer slide down over my belly."

Still standing behind her, he gathered up her skirt from hem to high waistline and pulled the gown over her head. She had just raised her arms to allow him to pull them out of the long, fitted sleeves when the babe gave a particularly energetic kick.

Startled, she gasped and clutched her belly, her arms still partially encased in the sleeves of her gown.

Quentin was before her in a flash, grasping her shoulders.

"Jane, what is it? Is something amiss with the babe?" The alarm in his voice was unmistakable . . . and to her, immensely comforting. He must indeed care a great deal to sound so.

Before she could reply and put his mind to rest, the babe kicked again. Again she gasped, this time in amazement. Goodness, but their child was strong.

"Jane . . ." There was a note of agonized desperation in his voice. "Please, Jane. Tell me what is wrong and what I can do to help. "Please." His hands tightened on her shoulders.

She looked at him then. His expression was one of helpless terror mixed with grave concern. Moved more by that expression than by any declaration of love he could have made, she smiled gently and replied, "Everything is fine. The babe just surprised me with its kicking."

"Does it often kick so very hard?" he quizzed, not looking wholly convinced of her well-being.

"Of late, yes. Indeed, it has kicked so much and so hard the past few days that I'm beginning to wonder if I carry a donkey instead of a child. Oh!" She laughed and rubbed her distended midsection. "There it goes again."

He continued to gaze at her face, his violet eyes dark and filled with undecipherable emotion, then he glanced down at her belly. "Is it painful? You know—" He looked up at her face again, his expression uncertain yet full of wonder. "When it kicks?"

She shook her head, as pleased by his interest as she was by his concern. Though he often inquired after her health and spoke of the babe in the abstract manner in which men usually speak of their unborn children, this was the first time he'd ever looked at her belly and directly acknowledged its presence. Wanting to hug him for the joy his doing so brought her, she replied, "No. Oh, no, Quentin. It doesn't hurt at all, it feels strange but wonderful. In truth, I find the movement comforting, for it reassures me that all is well."

Slowly he looked back down at her belly, nodding as if carefully digesting the information.

Emboldened by his interest, she murmured, "Would you like to feel your child move?"

His breath visibly caught and he looked back up at her, his eyes shining and a slight smile curving his lips. "I-Is that possible?" he whispered, as if astounded by the notion.

"With your child, probably so," she replied, freeing her arms from her sleeves and tossing off her gown. Lifting his hand, she placed his palm flat against her chemise-and-petticoat-covered belly. "There. It was kicking me there."

Quentin frowned, his face a portrait of intense concentration. After a moment, he murmured, "I don't feel anything."

"That's because it hasn't moved yet. Just be patient."

One minute passed, then two. Nothing. It was going on four minutes and Jane was about to give up when the babe gave a kick that made her eyes widen.

"I felt it," Quentin exclaimed. When he looked up to meet her gaze, his face was heartbreakingly beautiful with ecstatic awe. "I felt it," he repeated, this time with savage triumph. "And you are right. It feels wonderful. I never knew that a babe stirred so in the womb." As he spoke, it moved again, making him laugh with delight.

"Yes, and it is said that if one presses an ear to the belly of an expectant mother and listens closely, they can sometimes hear its heart beating."

"Indeed?" he murmured, looking sincerely intrigued.

"Indeed," she replied. After hesitating with the last of her lingering uncertainties, she shyly inquired, "Would—would you care to test the theory, my lord?" She held her breath as she waited for his reply. Placing his hand on her swollen abdomen was one thing, pressing his face against it was quite another, especially if he found her condition even the least bit repellent.

But no, you would have thought that she'd just made him emperor of the universe by the expression on his face. "May I?" he exclaimed breathlessly.

At her nod, he fell to his knees. Grinning like a boy who'd just received his first pony, he laid his cheek in the place recently vacated by his hand. Slowly his smile faded, his look of boyish excitement mutating into one of focused absorption. After a moment or two, reverence, profound and rapturous, dawned across his face. "I think I hear it," he whispered hoarsely.

"Do you?" she murmured, the intimacy of the moment giving her the courage to stroke his moist curls. They felt as splendid as they looked.

"Yes. I believe so." He nuzzled his cheek deeper into the damp folds of her petticoat. Meeting her gaze with eyes as brilliant as gems reflecting candlelight, he rather shyly inquired, "Would you think me terribly silly if I spoke to it?"

"Not at all. I do it all the time," she replied, loving him all the more because he wanted to do so.

He smiled at her response, then tipped his lips toward her belly. His gaze still clinging to hers, he whispered softly but distinctly, "I love you."

"You . . . do?" she somehow forced past the lump that had suddenly formed in her throat.

"Yes. Very much."

Tears of joy glazed her eyes. "Oh, Quentin. I am so happy."

"Me, too," he murmured, rising to his feet. As he rose, he searched her eyes, delving into their depths as though seeking something of extreme importance. Perhaps he found what he was looking for, because a moment later he started to speak. "Jane. I have been thinking much of late and . . ."

Whatever he was about to say was interrupted by scratching at the door. His face flooding with frustration, he barked, "Yes?"

"It's me, m'lord, Hannah. And Jemma's with me. I brought ye the towels 'n bricks ye wanted, 'n Jemma's got tea."

Looking as rueful as Jane felt, he sighed and replied, "One moment, please." After glancing about the room, he stalked to the bed and snatched up a woolen dressing gown, which had been laid upon the coverlet along with a nightgown.

When he'd helped Jane into it, he bid the servants to enter. They did so in a frenetic burst of activity that shattered the last lingering fragments of intimacy between her and Quentin. When at last the tea had been set upon a table by the window, the bricks arranged beneath the bed covers, and the towels delivered into Quentin's care, the maids departed.

As the door closed behind them, Quentin again turned to Jane. "We had best get you out of your wet undergarments and into bed while the bricks are hot." Though his tone was kind enough, his manner was impassive, as if the intimate moments before the maids' arrival had never existed.

Wistfully wondering if there was a way to restore their closeness, Jane nodded her agreement. The way he'd looked at her as he'd started to speak, so tenderly and with such naked longing—well, she'd been certain that he was about to open his heart. And then there was the way he'd stared into her eyes as he whispered to their child. Hadn't he seemed to include her in his declaration of love?

On and on Jane mused, remembering every second of the magical moments, trying to read the meaning behind Quentin's every smile and glance, much as a gypsy might read the future in tea leaves.

As she reflected, she mindlessly followed Quentin's commands to raise her arms and duck her head, oblivious to embarrassment as he relieved her of her clammy petticoat and chemise. It wasn't until she felt his hands, so warm and gentle, brush against the flesh of her belly that she returned to the present moment. When she did, her cheeks burned.

What she'd felt was him loosening the drawstring on her drawers . . . which was all she wore, save her stockings. Mortified by the discovery, Jane hugged one arm over her breasts and the other across her swollen midsection, self-consciously trying to hide her distorted body from his sight. The instant she did so, her loosened drawers slipped to her ankles, exposing her completely. Heavens!

"Here," she heard Quentin murmur.

Though the last thing she wanted to do was look at him, Jane glanced up. He held the nightgown that had been laid out with the dressing gown, ready to be donned. More glad to see the simple garment than she'd ever been to see anything in her life, she shoved her head through the presented neck opening and her arms into the long, full sleeves. He, in turn, released the voluminous folds of fabric, which fell modestly over her body.

Still too embarrassed to look at his face, Jane hung her head as he buttoned the front placket. Consequently, she ended up looking at his body. She had no other choice. Truly. His proximity filled her view completely. Oh, and what a view it was!

As she so often did when she knew he wasn't looking, Jane scrutinized her husband's perfect form. And as she always did at those times, she imagined the flesh that lay beneath his clothes.

Hmm. Judging from the strong contours of his torso, she guessed him to have broad, muscular shoulders and a beautifully sculpted chest, rather like the Adonis statue in Lady Saxby's garden. Yes, and his trim waist no doubt tapered into one of those flat, rippling, and utterly fascinating bellies. As for his thighs—

She started to skim down his belly to his thighs, only to stop to stare in astonishment at the area above them. In the place of his usual discreetly manly mound was a pronounced bulge—one that strained fiercely against his trousers and left little doubt, even to someone of her limited experience, what it was.

The knowledge left her breathless. He was aroused. Elizabeth had told her about arousal, about the way men's—ers—grew and hardened when they desired a woman. Yes, and she'd felt the evidence of that when Quentin had taken her.

Could it be that he actually found her desirable in her present state?

Stunned by the notion, Jane stole a glance at his face. It looked tense and strained, as if he were about to pass another stone. Looking away again, she frowned. Well, Elizabeth had said that arousal could be uncomfortable for a man, especially if it went on for a long period of time without relief.

Beginning to feel rather achy herself down below, Jane contemplated, as she'd often done since Sophie's visit, the idea of seducing her husband. Always she had dismissed the notion as ridiculous and impossible. Now, seeing his arousal, she thought it didn't seem at all preposterous. Indeed, it seemed . . . plausible.

But was it?

Obeying Quentin's command to step out of her fallen drawers, Jane decided that it was. She had simply to break through whatever reserve kept him from taking what he so clearly wanted, and then loosen the passion within.

As she pondered how best to do that, he took her arm, saying, "Come." Leading her to her bed, an old-fashioned but immensely comfortable canopied monstrosity of the Italian Renaissance, he said, "You must sit on the edge of the bed so I can remove your stockings. I shall then tuck you beneath the covers and serve you a nice, hot cup of tea."

"And will you join me, my lord?" she inquired, staring up at his strong profile.

"Beneath the covers or in a cup of tea?" he teased, meeting

her gaze with a rakish grin. The instant the words left his mouth, he sobered, as if regretting his joke, and looked away. "I'm sorry, Jane. Please forget I said that. It was a crude jest."

"I didn't mind it in the least," she replied softly. In truth, had she been given the time to gather her wits, she'd most probably have invited him to do both.

"That is because you are gentle and understanding, qualities that make my uttering such a jest all the more boorish."

Trying to think of an appropriate rejoinder, Jane sat on the bed. As Quentin knelt before her to remove her stockings, she couldn't help but notice the look of elevated discomfort on his face, due, no doubt, to the increased tightness of his trousers. As she imagined what it would be like to remove them and release that which strained so hard to escape, he added, "To properly answer your question, Jane, no, I cannot join you for tea. I, too, must change my clothes."

Of course he must, she thought, stricken with sudden remorse. How very thoughtless of her to have kept him in his cold, wet clothes while she played her selfish little game. Unless she wished him to fall ill, which she most assuredly did not, he must remove those clothes, and soon.

Soon? Why not now? The provocative thought sprang unbidden into her mind.

Why indeed? she mused, instantly latching on to it. He'd played lady's maid for her, why couldn't she demand an equal game and insist on serving as his valet? Liking the idea immensely, too much to let it go, Jane braced her courage with another peek at his arousal and blurted out, "No need to leave. I shall help you out of your wet clothes, just as you—you helped me out of mine." So what if her voice broke near the end? At least she'd gotten the words out.

Quentin stopped amid pulling her stocking off her foot to stare up at her. "Pardon?"

"I shall remove your clothes for you," she repeated. "It is

only fair that I do so." This time her voice remained steady, which pleased her immensely.

There was a long, tense pause, during which he continued to stare at her, his eyes filled with an endearing mélange of uncertainty and yearning. Finally he whispered, "Do you know what you are saying?"

She nodded.

His eyes narrowed, as if in doubt. "Are you so certain?"

Jane smiled, her whole body aware of what he asked. "Yes. I am saying that I wish to help my husband remove his wet clothing. Wives do such things, I assume?"

His eyes were little more than slits now, bright, burning ones. "Some do, yes," he replied, his taut voice laden with unspoken meaning. "Are you saying that you are willing to be that sort of wife to me?"

"Not exactly," she replied, still smiling.

He sighed, hard, and pulled off her stocking. "No, I didn't think so, and I cannot say that I blame you. Not after the abominable way I treated you on our wedding night."

"Quentin," she began, wanting to clarify her response.

He cut her off with a fierce shake of his head. "No, Jane. Please let me finish." Another head shake, then, "For what it is worth, and I know it is worth little in light of all that you've suffered at my hands, I truly am sorry . . . for everything. If I could take back all the terrible things I've said and done, and could start our marriage anew, I would." His hands dropped from her foot to ball into trembling fists at his side. "I swear on all that I hold dear that I would."

"Oh, Quentin," Jane cried, moved to the very core of her being. "What I would have told you had you given me the chance is that I am not merely willing to be such a wife, I very much desire it . . . just as I desire you."

"You do?" The look of uncertainty was back in his eyes, this time mixed with hope and the barest dawning of joy.

She slipped off the bed to kneel by his side. "Yes, and if you truly wish to start anew, then we shall make this our wedding night and go forward from here."

"Are you certain?" he whispered hoarsely, desperately searching her eyes. "You aren't . . . afraid of my lust . . . afraid that I might hurt you as I did that first time?"

Jane reached out and caressed his cheek, something she'd longed to do more times than there were numbers to count them. "No, my love. I am not. And do you know why?"

He shook his head.

"Because you are a different man from the one who first took me. You are a tender, gentle, loving man whom I trust in every way." She smiled and lightly traced one of his dimples. "No, Quentin. I have no fear of you."

He returned her gaze for several beats, then looked away, though he didn't pull his face from her stroking hand. His voice broke as he confessed, "You may not be afraid, but I am."

Her hand stilled. "Why?"

"You are so beautiful, so sweet and desirable, and I want you so very badly. Too badly, I fear. I am frightened to so much as kiss you for fear that I will lose control and ravish you as I did before." He met her gaze again, his eyes clouded with apprehension and misted with pain. "I so want to please you, to show you all the joys of the marriage bed. I am just not certain that I'll be able to bridle my lust enough to do so."

She smiled gently, her heart swelling with tenderness. "I am willing to take the chance if you are."

"But what of the baby? Isn't there a danger that it might be harmed if I love you?"

Jane laughed softly, as much from delight at his concern as at the absurdity of it. "Oh, no, my lord. I assure you that you shan't harm either of us. Indeed, I have it from a very reliable source that it is actually good for us to be loved. So, you see, you truly have nothing to fear."

He opened his mouth to speak, but she waved it shut again, saying, "And do not ask me if I am certain. I am. I promise." Smiling with all the love, desire, and hope for their future that she felt inside, Jane leaned over and twined her arms around his neck. "Now kiss me before I change my mind."

With a muffled cry, he obliged, pulling her into his embrace to kiss her with a thoroughness that left her limp and quivering.

It was a glorious kiss, even more glorious than the potent ones they had shared in the garden. For this time as Quentin's mouth melded with hers, Jane felt not just desire radiating from him, but love. She could sense it in every tingling brush of his lips, she could taste it in every heated thrust of his tongue. And the way he held her, so gently and with such reverence, made her feel deliciously cherished.

Happier than she'd ever been in her life and wanting to demonstrate her own love for him, Jane roused herself from her voluptuous stupor and returned his kiss in kind.

Careful, Quentin cautioned himself, abruptly pulling his lips away. One more kiss and he would lose himself for certain. The way Jane moved her mouth against his, so hungry to give and receive pleasure, inflamed him in ways that were unbearable in his painfully aroused state. Indeed, his loins felt seared to ashes, and his male parts throbbed in a way that boded ill for his control.

As he fought hard to calm himself, sucking in deep, shuddering breaths and silently singing the harvest song, Jane opened her passion-drugged eyes and murmured, "Quentin? Is something amiss?"

He smiled tenderly, thinking that he'd never seen anything so very lovely as Jane's face at that moment. "Of course not. With you in my arms, what could possibly be amiss?"

"It's just that, well, you pulled away so suddenly, I thought . . ." She bit her kiss-swollen bottom lip and looked away.

"Thought what?" he queried softly.

"That . . . that you had c-changed your mind about wanting me."

He chuckled and shook his head. "Oh, no, sweet Lady Jane. I shall have to be dead and in my grave in order not to want you. I stopped because I want you too much. Had I continued, I most certainly would have lost control."

"Oh, I see." By the glance she slanted at his trousers, it was obvious that she did see. After staring at his arousal for some time, she looked back up at him and murmured, "It must be terribly uncomfortable. I mean"—she blushed and gestured at his groin—"your trousers being so tight and all. And wet. Yes, you must be chilled through."

"I can assure you that I am not the least bit cold down there," he replied, charmed by her flustered babbling.

"Perhaps not now, but you no doubt shall be soon, and it would never do for you to take a chill. Why, you might even catch cold!"

He chuckled again and dropped a kiss on her prettily flushed cheek. "Oh, I don't see much danger in that. I have yet to hear of a man catching a cold in that particular part of his anatomy."

Her color deepened. "No, uh, of course not. What I meant was that—that you need to get out of all your clothes. The cumulative chill of your garments could be enough to give you a terrible lung infection. I have seen it happen before."

"Have you indeed?" he countered, amused by her attempts to rationalize her eagerness to see him naked. Pleased that she desired him so, and feeling somewhat more in control now, he added, "Well, in that case, I must bow to your greater wisdom."

Odd, but now that she was finally going to get her wish of seeing Quentin's body, Jane found herself unexpectedly bashful. This time, however, unlike all the previous times when she had lost her nerve, she refused to give in to her shyness. Thus, she stiffened her spine and said, "We shall start with your boots."

He nodded. "As you wish. You are in command."

She nodded back, not so certain that she wished or even knew how to lead. Not in matters such as these. Nonetheless, she said, "You must sit on the bed so I can pull them off."

Quentin stood and helped her up, then sat as directed and stuck out his feet. She grasped his rain-splotched right boot and tugged it off. She'd often helped her brother remove his boots when they had lived at the vicarage, so it was a task she gladly and easily performed. When she had divested him of his left one and set the pair before the fire, he murmured, "What next?"

"Um . . ." She glanced at him, looking so handsome and rakish, half sitting, half lounging on her bed. Tempted by the sight to wantonly jump on him and rip off his clothes, she bit her lip and mumbled, "Your coat. We shall start at the top, nearest your lungs, and move downward."

And that is exactly what she did. Directing him to stand, she stripped him first of his wet coat, then his damp waistcoat, and finally his sodden shirt. As she removed the last, she found herself barely able to work the buttons, so badly did her hands tremble from anticipation. At last, at long last, she was going to see what lay beneath his clothes.

To her delight, he was every bit as exquisite as she'd imagined. His shoulders and arms were gloriously muscled, his chest magnificently sculpted and defined. Yes, and his lean midsection was just as rippling and fascinating as she'd hoped, perhaps even more so. Something that did take her by surprise was the glowing splendor of his skin. It reminded her of expensive silk satin, dyed a pale shade of honey. That a man could have skin so very perfect in both texture and hue was nothing short of a miracle.

Jane reverently touched his chest in awe, thrilling at the tickling crispness of the hair sprinkled across it. Lightly outlining the dramatic contours with her fingertips, she whispered, "Beautiful. Oh, Quentin, you must be the most beautiful man in the world." She shook her head, still unable to believe her eyes. "Just look at you. You are so perfect."

"I would rather look at you," he murmured, pulling her against him to reclaim her mouth with his. She kissed him back, moaning her delight as she twined her arms around his waist and stroked his impossibly smooth back.

For several moments they remained like that, teasing, tantalizing, and stimulating each other with their lips and tongues. Then Quentin pulled away, groaning, "Enough, Jane. Can't you feel how much I want you?" He demonstrated by pressing his groin against her belly.

Her eyes widened at the feel of it. "Oh, yes. I do feel. How very wonderful."

"Yes. It is wonderful that I am fortunate enough to have such a lovely and desirable wife," he countered, pulling away again.

"Quentin?"

He looked up from trying to ease the fit of his trousers. "Yes, my sweet?"

She bit her lip, then shyly confessed, "I, too, feel all tight and feverish—down low."

He smiled tenderly. "Would you like me to tend to you there? As your husband, it is my duty and privilege to do so."

Jane felt herself turn scarlet at his offer. "No—not yet. I am rather—enjoying the sensation." Goodness! She was beginning to sound every bit as wanton as she felt. What he must think of her!

What Quentin thought was that she was impossibly sweet and alluring. Indeed, it took but a single, innocent touch from her to inflame him in ways that other women's carnal caresses never had. And right now, the way she stroked his chest was driving him mad.

As he struggled against his ungentlemanly urge to ravish her where she stood, her fingers suddenly changed direction and traced downward. Over his ribs and midsection they trailed, tickling him in a way that made him moan aloud. When they finally came to a rest, it was at the waistband of his trousers.

For several groin-wrenching moments she lightly outlined where flesh met fabric, then her hands moved to the buttons of his falls, and she released him. As he sprang forth, hard, hot, and visibly pulsating with need, she froze, gaping at him in blatant fascination.

He, too, froze, his breath catching in his throat as he braced himself for her touch. Oh, it wasn't that he didn't want her to touch him there. He did. It was just that he was terrified that he would lose himself if she did.

To his relief, she grasped not him, but the top of his wet trousers, which she slowly peeled off his body, taking his stockings down with them. Exhaling the breath he'd been holding, Quentin lifted his feet to allow her to remove the garments.

When he at last stood naked and impossibly aroused before her, Jane murmured, "Is it all right if I touch your—er—" she gestured to his swollen sex.

Though he was not at all certain that he could bear her doing so, he was unwilling to deny her the exploration she so obviously longed for, so he nodded.

She smiled faintly, then reached down and lightly traced his length. He gasped in shock, gritting his teeth as his hips jerked in savage response. Undeterred by his reaction, she encircled him, squeezing experimentally as she stroked downward.

A strangled cry escaped him, and again his hips thrashed, this time with a violence that almost brought him to his knees. He couldn't take it, damn it! He simply couldn't! The torment was too much for him to bear.

Before he could recover enough to put a stop to her overly stimulating inspection, her hands were again on him, curiously examining his sheath and lifting it to probe the taut pouch below.

Choked with lust and paralyzed by erotic sensation, he stood helplessly frozen in place, his hips writhing convulsively as she fondled him to her heart's content. He had just felt the telltale moisture that always preceded his release and had braced himself for the shame of losing himself, when her hands dropped away and she said in a strangled voice, "I—I am ready for you to tend to my—well, you know."

Indeed he did, and the thought of doing so did nothing to relieve the devilish heat he was in. Nonetheless, he delighted in the chance to gift her with her first womanly rapture, and he gladly suffered the torment it gave him to take her in his arms again.

After thoroughly kissing her, he unfastened her nightgown buttons, lightly pressing his lips to each silken expanse of skin as it was exposed. Slowly, ever so slowly so as not to rush her or drive himself over the edge, he bared her breasts.

They were beautiful—she was beautiful—so very ripe and lush and blooming with femininity in her pregnancy. Though he'd never been attracted to women in her condition, thinking them ungainly and misshapen, he could barely keep his hands off Jane. Indeed, he wanted to kiss and caress every burgeoning contour, to explore the magical wonders of the fertile body that grew his child.

Determined to do exactly that, Quentin lifted the gown

over Jane's head and tossed it aside, then laid her gently upon the bed. The contrast of her pale ivory skin against the deep ruby of the damask coverlet presented a picture of timeless splendor that made him wish for skill with paint and canvas so he could preserve it forever.

Since, however, he possessed no such talent, he etched the picture upon his heart, then climbed onto the bed beside her. His touch worshipful and his lips adoring, he kissed and caressed and tasted every irresistible inch of her. By the time he reached her thighs, she lay writhing and moaning her need.

Smiling his satisfaction at her response, Quentin kissed her upper thighs, then opened them to reveal the treasure between them. That she desired him as much as he did her was apparent from the glistening moisture there. Wanting nothing more than to mount her and bury his aching male sex in her soothing female places, Quentin lightly ran his finger over her, parting her need-swollen flesh.

Jane arched up, crying out at the resulting sensation. Elizabeth had said that it would be wonderful, but this—oh, this!—was beyond all description.

For several electrifying moments he continued to touch her there, now teasing, now stroking, now deeply caressing. Her nether regions melted and pulsed. Then he dipped his head and kissed her.

Sobbing with joyous abandon, she surged against his mouth, mutely begging for more. And, oh! He gave her just that, pleasuring her with a skill that made her scream with shattering urgency. Over and over again he brought her trembling to the edge, rendering her breathless as he kissed her everywhere except the place that throbbed furiously from his neglect.

"Quentin! Oh, Quentin! Please!" she moaned, desperately trying to guide his head to the aching bud.

He chuckled. "Well, since you said please—" and flicked his tongue over it.

She cried out, her legs straining apart in her pleasure. Again he licked her there, then again and again, his tongue masterfully bringing her undreamed-of bliss. And then—then—

Her whole being exploded into unearthly ecstasy.

"Oh, Quentin," she sobbed, when she at last fell back against the bed. "I have never felt anything like that in my life."

"I take it, then, that you approve and would like to repeat the experience sometime?" he inquired, crawling from between her legs to clasp her in his embrace.

"Oh, yes," she sighed, nuzzling against him. The instant she did, she felt his engorged sex brush against her thighs. Pulling back to peer down at it, she murmured, "We really must do something about that. If you ache anywhere near as badly as I did, you must let me tend to you immediately."

He grimaced down at himself. "Now that you mention it, I do ache rather badly."

"Well, then—" She pushed him over onto his back.

Before Quentin quite knew what was happening, Jane was returning his favors, kiss by stimulating kiss, caress by bedeviling caress, touch by electrifying touch. When she finally worked down to his manhood and started to tease it with her tongue, he could bear his urgency no longer.

"Jane—I—I—no—" he moaned, pulling himself from her grasp.

She peered up at him, stricken. "You don't like that?"

"I love it," he gritted out, hauling her up from between his legs.

"Then why—"

"Because I love doing this more, and am in no condition to do both right now, that is why," he replied, gently wrestling her to the mattress. After stroking her between her legs to make certain that she was wet and ready to receive him, he carefully eased inside. Tenderly kissing her lips, he whispered, "If you feel even the slightest pain, tell me immediately and I shall pull out."

She grinned like a cat with a particularly large saucer of cream, and wrapped her legs around his hips. "It doesn't hurt a bit. It feels splendid." To demonstrate the truth of her words, she arched up and took him deeper.

The resulting sensation snapped the last of his control and he plunged all the way in. When she moaned and writhed against him in impassioned response, he began to move. She soon caught his rhythm and moved with him in perfect synchrony. As their passion escalated, so did the frenzy of their bodies, making them thrash wildly with pleasure as they raced closer and closer to what they sought. When they, at last, found it, they did so in rapturous harmony, crying out in a duet of shared bliss as they climaxed in each other's arms.

As Jane fell back upon the mattress and Quentin beside her, mindful, as he had been during their passion of the danger of crushing her belly, she whispered, "Oh, my! That was even better than what you did before it. I could do that every day forever."

Grinning, Quentin propped himself up on his elbow to look down at her love-flushed face. "Only forever?" he teased. "And here I thought that you'd enjoyed yourself."

She returned his gaze for a moment, her expression suddenly thoughtful. Then she threaded her fingers through his curls and pulled his lips to hers. "You are right, my lord. It is wonderful enough to do forever and a day."

Chapter 16

J ane pressed her face to the coach window, peering out at the winter wonderland beyond. It had snowed lightly but steadily for a week now, leaving her world blanketed in a glistening white mantle embellished with snow-flocked evergreens, icicle-draped cottages, and frozen ponds that reflected the pale winter sun like looking glasses in feeble lantern light.

It was perfect, exactly how she'd hoped it would be for her first Christmas with Quentin. Not that its perfection surprised her. Her whole life had been more perfect than her fondest dreams since she and Quentin had made love the month before. For from that day forward, she had become his wife in every rapturous sense of the word, and he the most attentive and protective of husbands. Indeed, he seldom let her out of his sight these days, claiming her to be far too reckless of her condition to go about by herself. Thus he insisted on accompanying her everywhere she went and was constantly underfoot at the abbey, scolding her for working too hard and urging her to rest.

Of course she enjoyed having him with her. However, his continual presence did pose one problem: that of finding enough time alone to finish her Christmas gift to him.

Because he so adored the dressing gown she'd made him for his birthday and refused to wear any other, she'd made him a second one from a length of wine velvet she'd had Rissa send her from London. With Sophie's help, she had completed it just this morning, while he and Nicholas were out selecting a tree from which to have the Yule log cut for tonight.

Sophie and Nicholas, along with their children, had arrived yesterday to spend Christmas with them, and had announced their intention to stay on until after the babe was born. Having them there simply added to the bliss of her life.

Right now, Jane and Sophie, snug inside the Somerville coach, were on their way to Little Duckington to do some last-minute shopping and to bid the villagers a merry Christmas.

Like the countryside, the village presented a charming vision of Christmas with its snowcapped cottages and icicle-festooned shop signs. People bundled up in heavy coats and colorful scarves hastened along the walkways, many bearing armloads of greenery with which to deck their homes. Even the churchyard, which was normally a bleak picture in winter with its grim gray tombstones and barren black trees, looked nothing short of festive on this day before Christmas with its graves adorned, according to ancient tradition, with holly wreaths tied up with red ribbons.

"Oh, look! Ice skating!" Jane exclaimed, as they passed the village green. Someone had swept the frozen pond clean and what looked to be half the village now glided upon it. Turning to Sophie, she pleaded, "Please, do let's stop and watch a while. I used to love skating when I lived in Oxcombe village, and I so miss it. Indeed, it never seems quite like Christmas without taking a turn or two about the ice."

Sophie laughed and signaled their driver to stop. "I, too, adore skating. Who knows? Perhaps one of the villagers will take pity on us and offer to lend us their skates for a turn."

Jane smiled at the thought of what Quentin would have to say about her taking to the ice. She giggled. On second thought, he probably wouldn't say a word. He couldn't. He would be too busy suffering a fit of apoplexy. Since, however, he wasn't there . . .

"I shall keep my fingers crossed that they do," she gaily replied.

The air outside was cold and fresh, freezing their breath into ghostlike puffs as they hurried across the snow-shrouded green. Though large with child now, Jane often found herself restless for exercise and longed for something more vigorous than the short, sedate walks about the Swanswick park that Quentin allowed her. Thus, she was exhilarated by the possibility of skating.

As they made their way the short distance to the pond, they were hailed from all sides by villagers, who easily recognized her short, round form and Sophie's statuesque one. With her uncommon beauty and gentle wit, her sister-in-law had made a most favorable impression on the denizens of Little Duckington during her first visit, and they all looked pleased to see her again in their midst.

They had just sat down on one of the bales of straw that served as benches and had accepted a cup of hot spiced cider from Lallie Nobbes, the baker's wife and mother of four of the younger skaters, when Willy glided up to them. Like all the skaters, his nose was bright red and framed by a matching pair of cheeks.

Snatching off his oversized cap, the hue of which perfectly matched his nose and cheeks, he greeted them, "Merry Christmas, Lady Jane, Lady Lyndhurst."

"A merry Christmas to you, too, Willy," Sophie and Jane returned in unison. Sophie, who had been enchanted with the boy on her first visit—a feeling that Willy returned in full measure—inquired, "How is the ice today, sir?"

"Smooth as glass," he replied with a grin. "Do ye skate?"

Sophie smiled back. "Indeed we do, both of us. Your lady

and I were just saying how it didn't seem like Christmas without a turn on the ice. Too bad we didn't think to bring skates."

As Sophie had no doubt expected, the boy hastily offered, "Ye can take a turn on mine. I'm tired and was gonna sit fer a while anyhow." To illustrate the earnestness of his claim, he sat on the bank near their feet and unbuckled his wooden skates with their iron blades. Holding them up, he queried, "Who wants ta' go first?"

"You go on," Jane insisted to Sophie. Now that she was actually faced with the opportunity to skate, she wasn't so certain that she should. If she fell, she most probably wouldn't be able to get up again without assistance, what with her belly and all. And there was a good chance that she would fall, considering the disproportionate amount of weight she carried in front.

As if reading her thoughts, Sophie murmured, "You shall be fine. I skated in my eighth month and did so quite gracefully, if I must say so myself. Indeed, I felt far less clumsy on the ice than I did on solid ground."

"Nicholas let you skate?" she exclaimed, wondering how two brothers could be so very different.

The other woman laughed. "Heavens, no! He doesn't know about it, and you mustn't tell him, just as I shan't tell Quentin on you. As you well know, Somerville men are unreasonably protective of their women."

"Yes. Well—" Jane eyed the skates with longing. "I suppose it shan't hurt to take one turn if I am careful. After all, Dr. Spicer did say that I am in plump currant." She nodded thoughtfully, then smiled. "Yes. I do believe that I will take a turn."

With Willy's solicitous aid, the skates were soon strapped to her boots and she was helped onto the ice. After standing stock-still for several moments, paralyzed by second thoughts, she warily took a gliding step. Hmm. Sophie was right. She didn't feel so very clumsy. Smiling at her discovery, she propelled herself another short distance, then another, still prudently exercising caution.

After testing her abilities with several more investigative spurts of motion, she felt comfortable enough to make a full rotation around the pond. When she had done so without incident, she tossed aside caution and skated with the joyful abandon of a twelve-year-old, even venturing a twirl or two. She had just glided around the pond backward when Sophie skated to her side.

Grasping her friend's hands to whirl her about, Jane exclaimed in delight, "Where did you get the skates?"

Sophie nodded toward the bales they had vacated, upon which now sat Willy and his best friend, Davy Matthews, the cobbler's son. "Davy insisted that I borrow his and join you on the ice. I think it amuses him and Willy to see noblewomen carry on like hoydens."

"No doubt," Jane agreed with a grin. Slanting a mischievous look at the boys, who sat drinking the mugs of cider they had abandoned, she murmured, "Shall we show them how very indecorous ladies can be?"

Sophie grinned back. "But of course."

After taking several turns about the ice, weaving in and out between the other skaters in a wild game of tag, they glided to the center of the pond. Locking hands, they proceeded to spin, picking up speed with every rotation. So fast did they whirl that all Jane could see of Sophie was a blur of her bright-blue cloak, closely chased by a flash of her own crimson one. They had just stopped and had fallen into each other's arms, laughing and impossibly dizzy, when someone called their names.

They glanced over at the bank and saw their husbands, their handsome faces marked with infuriated disapproval.

"Oh, blast! Whatever are they doing here?" Sophie murmured, pulling her fur-lined hood back over her head. "I thought they were attending to the Yule log."

Jane shook her head and tucked her hair, which had come loose during their spinning, under her down-trimmed bonnet. "I don't know, but by their faces, we look to be in the briers with them."

Sophie considered her husband's thunderous face for a moment, then turned back to Jane, grimacing. "Indeed we do." A sigh. "Ah, well. I suppose we should go and get our scolding over with."

"I suppose so," Jane agreed, disappointed to see their fun come to an end.

Exchanging a look of long-suffering martyrdom, they joined hands and skated toward the edge of the pond. They were almost there when—

Smack! "Oomph!" A boisterous group of boys, who had taken their cue from their lady and now played a harum-scarum game of tag, plowed into them at breakneck speed.

Crash! Jane was slammed to the ice, crushed beneath the children as they fell in a pile upon her, while Sophie was thrown several feet away.

"Good God, Jane!" Jane heard Quentin shout through the befuddlement of her stunned daze.

"Ow, me lady! O-w-w! I'm sorry! Are ye kilt? Ow! Ow! Ow!" her assailants keened, dragging themselves off her.

"Stand back, damn it! Let me through," she heard Quentin roar. In the next instant she felt herself being gathered up in his arms. "Jane, love? Are you hurt?" he murmured, pushing back her bonnet, which had been knocked over her face.

Jane squinted at him through a swirling constellation of stars. His eyes were wide and dark with panic, set in a face drained of all color. In short, he looked terrified. Frowning and shaking her head to clear it, she muttered, "I don't think so."

"Are you certain? Can you move everything without pain?" he pressed fearfully.

Dutifully she wiggled everything that could be wiggled, then nodded her now clear head. "Aside from a bruise or two, I seem to be fine." As she said the words, she suddenly remembered Sophie, whom she feared might not have fared so well. Indeed, the last she'd seen of her friend, she'd been flying through the air headfirst. Worried that she was badly hurt, perhaps even dead, Jane tried to sit up, exclaiming, "Sophie! What about Sophie?"

Quentin gently forced her back down again, then looked in the direction that Sophie had been thrown. After signaling to his brother, he nodded and said, "She's fine, too, though I must say that it is a wonder that neither of you was seriously injured. Especially you. Must I remind you, madame, that you are with child, and are thus in a delicate condition?"

"Believe me, you needn't remind me," she muttered, shifting into a more comfortable position. Well, at least as comfortable as she could get while carrying what felt like an anvil in her belly . . . a kicking anvil, she added silently, grasping her belly.

The alarm flew back into Quentin's eyes. "Is something wrong with the babe?"

"No. Of course not," she replied with fond exasperation. It was his favorite question of late, one he asked if she so much as scratched the itchy, overstretched skin on her belly.

"Are you certain?" Favorite question number two.

She smiled wryly and nodded. "Aside from my backside being frozen from lying on this ice, the babe and I are both fine. Now, if you don't mind, I would like to get up."

As Quentin helped her to her feet, almost coming to grief himself a few times as his boots slipped and slid about the ice, Jane stole a glance over to Nicholas and Sophie. Nicholas appeared to be scolding his wife, who simply looked amused by his lecture and silenced him by pressing a kiss to his lips.

In the end, it was the women who wound up helping their husbands off the pond. Though the men had made it onto the ice easily enough, driven as they were by their panic to get to their wives, they had a devilish time getting off it again in their slippery boots. Quentin fell twice, badly bruising his tailbone, and everyone lost count of how many times Nicholas hit the ice. Whatever the total, he was limping by the time he stepped onto the bank, wearing a scowl identical to that of his brother.

After the skates had been returned to their rightful owners and the men had hired someone to deliver their mounts to the abbey, they helped their unrepentant wives into the coach. The instant their backsides hit the seat, they began to ring a peal over the women's heads. They continued to do so the entire trip home, taking turns in stating their grievances and nodding like a jack-in-the-box on a loose spring as the other spoke.

Stern though the scolding was, it was clear that it was given out of love, so the women simply smiled and murmured an occasional "Yes. Of course. It shan't happen again," all the while exchanging looks of veiled amusement.

They were within sight of the abbey when a sharp pain suddenly knifed through Jane's lower back, doubling her over and bringing Nicholas's lecture on the duties of a proper wife to an abrupt halt.

"Jane, love. What is it?" Quentin cried, an urgent inquiry echoed by the remaining Somervilles.

As quickly as the pain struck, it subsided, leaving in its wake a dull ache. After waiting several tense beats to assure herself that it was indeed gone, Jane slowly straightened up again, catching the breath she had lost in her surprise.

"Jane?" Quentin prodded, frantically.

"It's—it's nothing," she murmured, shaking her head. "Just

a pain in my back. No doubt it is due to supporting so much weight in front. I feel fine now."

Quentin continued to frown, his brow creased with concern. "After the fall you took, we should send for Dr. Spicer and let him determine whether or not you are indeed fine."

Again she shook her head. "No, no. I hardly think it necessary. The pain didn't amount to much."

"Be that as it may, Jane, Quentin is right. You should be examined," Sophie chimed in. "You did take a nasty spill."

Another head shake from Jane. "I appreciate everyone's concern, truly I do, but I am fine. Besides, it is almost Christmas Eve, and I hate to disturb the doctor for what I am certain is no reason." When Quentin seemed about to argue further, she decided a change of subject was in order and hastily added, "Speaking of Christmas Eve, what were you men doing in the village? I thought that you were going to spend the day procuring our Yule log."

"We have one," Quentin replied, his brow not clearing. "When I asked Nathan Quinny and his apprentices to help us cut the one we had selected, he insisted on giving us a fine oak log left over from the tree he'd cut to make our babe's cradle. He claims that burning it as a Yule log will bring extra blessings to our child."

"Yes, and we had just finished treating him to a pint of ale at the inn when Joel Claypole came in from skating with news of your mischief." This was from Nicholas, who eyed his wife in a way that clearly informed them all that she hadn't heard the end of the matter.

Sophie sighed her exasperation. "I hardly think it fair or correct to term a few turns about the ice 'mischief.'"

"The reckless manner in which you were skating can most definitely be termed mischief, just as your allowing Jane to join you in your folly can be labeled both dangerous and reckless," Nicholas shot back.

Refraining from rubbing her sore lower back for fear of making even a bigger hill than had already been made out of the skating molehill, Jane said, "Please don't blame Sophie for my actions, Nicholas. I was the one who insisted that we stop at the green, and it was she who joined me on the ice."

"Well, it hardly matters now who is responsible," Quentin retorted, as the coach pulled to a stop in front of the abbey. "What is done is done. If you both promise that you shan't do anything like that again, we will let the matter drop. Is that amenable to you, brother?" He glanced at the other man, who nodded.

"Jane?" He looked first to her for a promise, which she gave with a nod. Then to Sophie, who smiled faintly and murmured, "You have my word, Quent. I shan't allow Jane to do anything more vigorous than lift a sewing needle until after the babe is born."

Satisfied, he nodded. "Now that that is settled, I suggest that you women rest for the festivities this evening. No doubt you are weary from your—ah—misadventure."

Jane readily agreed. Bed did sound wonderful. No doubt a nice nap, burrowed between the warm covers of her cozy bed, would be just the thing to soothe the nagging ache in her back.

Christmas Eve arrived, bringing with it the sacred, time-honored traditions Jane so loved. A fat red Yule candle was lit in the window at dusk, followed by the ritualistic placement of the gaily decorated Yule log. As dictated by legend, the roots of which were lost in the dark mists of antiquity, the log was ceremoniously kindled with fragments from Swanswick's last Yule log, the charred remains of which had been carefully preserved by Owen and Martha. Given to superstition, the couple had taken care to burn a log at the abbey every year, despite the lack of a master's presence, wishing to secure blessings for all who lived on the estate.

This year there looked to be blessings in abundance. Not only did the estate have a master who cared for both the people and the land, it had a loving mistress and an heir on the way. The harvest had never been better, and there was great hope for an even finer one the following year.

Swanswick Abbey was truly and greatly blessed.

As Jane sat at the foot of the feast-laden dining table, watching Quentin laugh at the antics of the mummers, who ran about the table playing out the story of Saint George and the dragon, her joy knew no bounds.

Christmas was a time of hopes and dreams, a time to make wishes and trust them to come true. Her wish was that she and Quentin would be as happy as they were tonight—for forever and a day. That had also been her wassail toast—happiness, for forever and a day. And there wasn't a doubt in her mind that it would come true.

"Oh, no!" little Isabel squealed, her plum pudding–smeared face reflecting her despair as the valiant Saint George, a youth armored in gold foil, fell beneath the dragon's assault. The dragon, a particularly imaginative creation with its forked green and red linsey-woolsey tail and papier-mâché head, pounced on the fallen hero with fiendish glee.

Smiling, Jane took the child's small, sticky hand in hers and gave it a reassuring squeeze. "Look, Issy, it's the doctor." She nodded to a comical fellow who now hopped frantically around Saint George, brandishing a jug marked "Magic Potion."

Though not part of the classic tale of Saint George and the dragon, the doctor, with his capers and magic potion, had become a beloved part of mummers' shows throughout England and was more often than not included in the play. As had become usual, the doctor of this particular performance pried open Saint George's mouth and poured in some magic elixir, which brought the man sputtering back to life. The dramatic flailings of George as he revived, not to mention the comical victory dance performed by the doctor, never failed to make their audience roar with laughter.

This audience, which consisted of the Somervilles, their servants, and the Halidays, was no exception. They came laughing and applauding to their feet the instant Saint George stirred. Jane, too, jumped up, only to fall back into her chair as she suffered another stabbing pain in her back. This time, however, instead of subsiding, it knifed through her belly.

"Jane?" she heard Sophie call over the din.

Jane glanced up at her friend, who sat to her right. Not wanting to spoil the festivities, she smiled and nodded.

Though her back had continued to ache despite her nap and a long soak in a hot bath, this was the first real pain she'd experienced since the one in the coach. Thus she wasn't unduly alarmed. No doubt she had stood too abruptly to allow her additional weight to properly distribute itself. When she glanced at Quentin, she saw that he too looked at her and she could tell by his expression was about to rush to her side.

Wanting to reassure him as well, she again smiled and nodded, then pushed back her chair and forced herself to stand. She was halfway to her feet when she was besieged by another pain, this one worse—far, far, worse—than the previous one. Feeling as if her back were breaking and her womb being torn asunder, she fell forward, spilling tears of pain as she sank to her knees.

"Jane!" Sophie cried, kneeling beside her. "Oh, Jane! Is something amiss with the babe?"

Before she could answer, she felt a rush of heated dampness pour from between her legs. The blood-tinged liquid soaking the skirt of her holly-printed gown provided an ominous reply.

Chapter 17

"What the hell is taking so long?" Quentin growled, pausing in his pacing to glare at his brother as if it were he, not the baby, who was guilty of delinquency.

Nicholas returned his brother's glare with a look of sympathy, knowing all too well what he suffered. He, too, had been a dreadful bear during his wife's three confinements, growling at everyone who came near and snapping off the heads of anyone who dared to try to pacify him. Indeed, so insufferable was he, it was a wonder that his entire staff hadn't quit and that both his friends and family hadn't abandoned him.

But of course they hadn't, just as he wouldn't abandon Quentin, no matter how surly and unreasonable he became. Like those who had lent him support during Sophie's confinements, he loved his brother and would stay with him, no matter what he said or did. And when this was over, there would be no need or expectation of apology for anything. All hasty words would be forgotten in the rejoicing over the arrival of the newest Somerville.

Watching as his brother ran his fingers distractedly through his long curls, Nicholas replied, "It has only been two hours, and as the accoucheur told you the last time you pestered him, these things take time. Indeed, Sophie labored seventeen hours with Graham, which we were told is a remarkably short time for a first birth. Besides, the doctor said that things are progressing well enough and that he sees no need for alarm, despite the fact that the babe is arriving a month early."

"I know, I know," Quentin muttered, dragging his fingers through his hair again. "I'm sorry for being so bloody-minded. It's just that—"

"No, Quent. Don't apologize," he cut in, rising from his chair by the library fire to go to his overwrought brother, who paced before the snow-flocked windows. Firmly grasping his shoulders to stop him, he softly chided, "Never apologize for worrying about the ones you love. It is right and good that you do so, and I would be most disappointed in you if you weren't in a stew."

"Being in a stew is one thing, but—" Quentin shook his head, shamefaced. "I don't know what has gotten into me. Everything everyone says or does this evening makes me snappish, and I cannot seem to control my churlishness."

"All good husbands are churls during their wives' confinements," Nicholas reassured him. "Any man who has gone through what you are going through now will tell you that it is so."

"You too?"

"Me too," he confirmed.

Quentin smiled faintly. "Somehow I cannot imagine you, the soul of all that is polite and correct, worrying yourself into a froth of rudeness."

"Believe me, I did. Indeed, Sophie's accoucheur said that he'd never seen a less patient father than I." He chuckled. "Less patient. Ha! With such tact the man should have been a diplomat."

Another brief smile from Quentin. "Were you really that bad?"

"Probably worse, but tetchiness is to be expected at such times, and no one thinks any worse of a man for behaving so." Nicholas released his brother's shoulders to clap him on the back. "Now, what say you to a nice glass of brandy? It is no doubt going to be a long night, so you had best reserve your strength."

"I suppose you are right," Quentin admitted, though his worry-creased brow still didn't clear.

"Of course I am. Don't forget that I have been through this three times before. My suggestion is that you have a drink with me by the fire and try to settle your nerves. No doubt Jane will be calling for you soon, and it would never do to let her see you in such high dudgeon." That recommendation made, Nicholas gave one of his brother's tousled ringlets a fond tug and nudged the conversation in a more lighthearted direction. "Speaking of appearances, you look like a pirate. Do they not have barbers in this part of England?"

Quentin smiled ruefully and ran his hand over his bohemian mane, as if reacquainting himself with its length. "Oh, we have a barber. A fine one, in fact. Unfortunately Jane refuses to allow me to utilize his services. She likes my hair long and claims that it would be a crime against nature to cut it."

Nicholas laughed heartily at his response. "I should have guessed. The ladies always did have an inordinate fondness for those curls of yours," he commented, guiding his brother to one of the two leather wing chairs before the fire. "Do you remember the dreadful poetry Lady Ogilvie used to write about them?"

Quentin grimaced as he sat down. "How could I forget lines like, 'Curls that render pearls jealous of their splendor'?"

"How, indeed?" he countered with a chuckle. "My favorite was always, 'Glistening ringlets, coiling like stringlets of silk. Ding, ding—'"

"'—sing the bells. Today I wed my love with his springy, ringy curls,'" Quentin finished for him. He groaned. "Thank you kindly for reminding me of something I have tried very hard to forget."

Laughing again, Nicholas went to the sideboard to pour them each a drink. "If Jane adores your curls as much as you say, I suppose we should count ourselves lucky that she isn't inclined toward poetry. Or is she?" He cast his brother a droll look of inquiry.

A firm head shake. "I should say not. Jane is a most practical and sensible creature. However, should she someday choose to try her hand at verse, I shouldn't be at all surprised if she did so quite admirably. My wife is an amazingly intelligent woman with the most astounding talents. I have yet to find anything that she doesn't do superbly."

Nicholas smiled approvingly at his brother's boast. "Spoken like a true Somerville husband. Mother always said that Somerville men make the proudest and most devoted husbands in the world. No doubt she would be thrilled to hear you sing such high praise for Jane. Father, too. They were both very taken with her at your wedding." Picking up the two glasses into which he had poured generous measures of brandy, he added, "But, of course, I needn't tell you how they feel about her. They have never been shy about voicing their thoughts."

"Yes, well, that, too, is a family trait," Quentin retorted, accepting the drink Nicholas offered him. "I am certain that you heard that I didn't exactly share their admiration for Jane at first, and minced no words in pointing out the fact to them."

"Mother did mention something, yes," he murmured, taking the opposite seat.

Quentin chuckled darkly. "After what I said, I can just imagine what that something was."

Nicholas shrugged and took a sip from his glass. "She didn't say much, really. Just that you accused them of ruining your life by forcing the match."

"Well, I most certainly believed that to be true at the time. I see now that they most probably saved it."

Nicholas glanced quickly at his brother, taken aback by his admission. "How so?"

Staring into the fire, Quentin quietly replied, "You remember how I used to be, how terribly bitter and angry I was all the time." It wasn't a question, it was a sad statement of fact.

Nonetheless, Nicholas felt obliged to respond, which he did with a simple "Yes."

Quentin nodded. "That anger stemmed from my resentment of being born a second son. Indeed, not a day passed that I didn't curse fate for dealing me what I saw as a grossly unfair hand in life. For me, being born second meant being second-best in everything, second even in our parents' hearts. I felt inferior and unwanted, like I had no real purpose or place in life. I was certain that without a title and a fortune I had no chance of ever attaining respect or happiness . . . or love." A shrug. "You know how things are in the *ton*. A second son is good enough for a flirtation, but little else."

"You greatly underestimated yourself, especially in that last," Nicholas interjected. "I may have a title and wealth, but I don't recall any woman ever writing poetry about my charms."

His brother shrugged again. "Pretty looks are all good and fine when it comes to infatuation, but they are a poor recommendation for a husband if the man behind them has nothing more to offer."

"I doubt if Jane would agree with your harsh appraisal of yourself," Nicholas shot back, shocked by his brother's poor opinion of himself. "She seems to find much to recommend you, and as you said yourself, she is an inordinately intelligent and sensible woman."

"Yes, she is." Quentin smiled gently, his face reflecting the depth of his love for his wife. "You asked how being forced to wed her saved me? The answer is, by showing me what it means to love, really love. Loving Jane has made me stronger, wiser, and better. It made me put away my reckless, selfish, and self-destructive ways in the quest to be worthy of the honor of being her husband. In short, my Jane's love has made me into a man, a real one, one who, for the first time in my life, I am proud to be."

"For what it is worth, I, too, am proud of the man you have become. More so than you shall ever know. You are a credit to the Somerville name, and I am delighted to call you brother," Nicholas said with heartfelt sincerity. Raising his glass, he toasted, "Here is to you, Quentin, the noblest man I know—titled or untitled—and to your wonderful Lady Jane. May you both always be as happy as you are now. Forever."

"And a day. Forever and a day." Quentin smiled. "My Jane has also made me greedy for her love."

"Forever and a day, then," he echoed, to which they both drank.

One hour passed, then another, as the men lounged before the fire. Sometimes they reminisced about their past, laughing over boyhood mischief and putting to rest forever that which had torn them apart. Other times they spoke of the future, making plans that included each other and adding yet another fortifying link in their ever-strengthening bond of brotherhood. And sometimes they simply sat there, easy in their companionable silence.

Midnight came and Christmas was born, a birth that passed unnoticed and unheralded by all but the tolling hall clock. Sometime around two, when there were still no news of Jane, Quentin went up to her chamber, only to be sent away again with the calmly uttered statement, "Things are going as well as can be expected," from the accoucheur and a gentle admonishment to rest from Sophie.

But of course he didn't rest. He couldn't, not until Jane was delivered and in his arms again. Thus, he spent the dark hours until dawn wandering about the hushed abbey, feeling lonely and lost and more grippingly afraid than he'd ever been in his life.

In truth, he'd gotten so used to having Jane by his side, to having her to turn to whenever he needed comfort or companionship, that he didn't know what to do or where to go. And so he moved restlessly from room to shadowed room, touching everything and anything that belonged to her, desperately seeking the solace of her gentle presence.

In the formal parlor he held the gloves she had left atop the pianoforte, again seeing her bright smile as she stripped them off to play the carols they had sung at dusk. In the library, where Nicholas now snored softly before the dying fire, he sat in her sewing chair, clasping her beloved tambour to his heart, remembering all the times he had looked up to find her by his side holding it. And then he came to the entry hall anteroom, where he found her favorite red cloak. That he buried his face against, inhaling the lingering sweetness of her scent and sobbing his worry into its soft folds.

As if sensing his troubled mood, Scratch followed him about the house, rubbing against his leg and purring, as if in reassurance. Quentin, in turn, picked the cat up at every stop, sometimes absently scratching it between its ears, other times confiding his deepest, darkest fears to it.

Finally, after what had seemed to Quentin a year of haunted midnights, day broke, bringing with it the faint music of carolers, who woke the countryside with their song. At first far away and as ethereal as angels on the wind, the voices gradually drew closer, growing corporeal as they drew near.

For a long while Quentin stood motionless at the frost-misted window of the family parlor, listening and watching as the children trooped up the snowy drive. The rising sun blushed the whitewashed landscape with shimmering shades of rose and burnished gold, giving the wintry scene the idealized look of a picture, painted to capture the perfect Christmas morn. And indeed it would be perfect had Jane been by his side, standing warm and safe in the curve of his now empty arm.

The children had just assembled at the foot of the front steps when someone softly uttered his name. He turned to find Sophie standing on the threshold, looking as tired and rumpled as he felt. There was something about her face in the feeble morning light, a strain about her eyes and a tautness to her smile, that made him cry out in alarm. "Jane! Is she—"

"Jane is doing as well as can be expected," she gently interjected. "As you know, she's rather slim through the hips, and her contractions aren't as strong as Dr. Spicer would like. But she is coming along . . . slowly."

"But she shall be all right . . . she and the baby?" he pressed, rushing across the room toward her.

She nodded. "Yes. Of course."

For a brief moment Quentin searched her gray eyes, seeking unspoken fear. When he found only weariness, his shoulders slumped.

She smiled and squeezed his arm. "You look tired half to death, Quent. You should try to get some rest."

"Maybe later, but right now I would like to see my Jane. Since all is well, do you suppose the doctor would permit me a visit? I very much want to wish her a Merry Christmas." He smiled and nodded at the window, from below which the strains of "God Rest Ye Merry Gentlemen" drifted. "It is Christmas Day, you know."

"Yes, it is," she replied, smiling back. "The carolers are what brought me here. I was looking for a footman. Jane asked that I have someone give them sweets and then direct them around to sing beneath her window. She also asked that I instruct your valet to invite you to join her as soon as you rise for the day." A laugh. "I told her that you'd most probably never gone to bed and were up pacing holes in all the carpets. Since I am correct, I see no reason why you shouldn't go to her now. I believe she has a gift she wishes to give you."

For the first time since Jane had collapsed the night before, Quentin smiled a truly glad smile. "I shall go to her directly. First, however, I will see if I can't find a footman for you."

He found several footmen in the kitchen, all of who looked tired and rather grumpy, no doubt from having drunk one too many Christmas toasts in the servants' hall. After relaying Jane's instructions, he rushed upstairs again to fetch his gifts for her. Ignoring his valet's suggestion that he wash, shave, and change his clothes before visiting his wife, Quentin hurried off down the hall to the room where Jane awaited him.

Sophie had apparently gone to greet Christmas morning with her family, for only Dr. Spicer was in attendance when he arrived. The doctor, a kindly man with intelligent green eyes and a gentle, careworn face, greeted Quentin with a smile when he entered the room. "My lord," he murmured, looking up from his task of arranging his instruments on a table beside the hastily erected birthing cot.

Since the cot was empty, Quentin looked toward the bed where he and Jane had passed so many pleasurable nights together. She lay on her side facing away from him, gazing at the row of casement windows beneath which the carolers now sang. Wanting nothing more than to climb beneath the covers and hold her, he quietly inquired of the doctor, "How does my lady?"

"As well as can be expected" was the inevitable reply.

He grunted his impatience. "Which means?"

The doctor shrugged. "Which means that there is nothing for us to do but wait. Should things progress as I hope, you shall be a father by late afternoon."

Before Quentin could quiz him as to the nature of that progress, Jane lifted her head and called, "My lord?"

"I'm here, love. Come bearing gifts and Christmas greetings for my lady fair," he replied, rushing to where she lay.

She grimaced. "I'm afraid I don't feel so very fair at the moment. Indeed, if I look even half as dreadful as I feel, I must be a fright."

"Never," he countered gallantly, dropping to his knees to press a kiss to her lips. "You could never look anything but beautiful to me." And it was true. Even pale, with her face drawn and her usually bright eyes dulled from exhaustion, she was still the loveliest creature in the world to him. So lovely, in fact, that he couldn't resist stealing another kiss.

"And how are you faring, my lord?" she inquired, when he reluctantly pulled away. "You look as though you didn't sleep a wink all night."

He set his offerings on the edge of the bed and smiled ruefully. "How could I sleep, knowing that you are suffering?" Sobering at the thought of her pain, he gently cupped her ashen cheek in his palm, whispering, "Has it been too terrible . . . the pain?"

She nuzzled against his hand with a sigh. "No worse than I expected. Elizabeth wrote me about childbirth, and Sophie answered all my remaining questions. Knowing what to expect when has done much to alleviate my fears."

"Well, I wish someone would take pity and explain things to me. I've been in a lather of nerves awaiting word of you."

She smiled faintly. "You have?"

He nodded. "Indeed, it has taken all my restraint not to burst in here and carry you off. It sounds harebrained, but I have the queerest notion that as long as you are where I can see and touch you, I can somehow protect you from harm."

"I feel the same," she whispered, touching his cheek with trembling fingers. "Will you stay with me as long as the doctor allows?"

He smiled and kissed her hand. "To hell with the doctor. I shall stay as long as you wish."

"Forever and a day?"

"Even longer if you wish."

To his pleasure, she giggled. "All right. Then I wish you with me as long as there is an eternity and—oh!" She abruptly clutched her belly, her face contorting into a mask of raw pain.

"Jane?" he cried, looking frantically at the doctor.

The man was by her side in a flash, speaking softly and bidding her to take a deep breath.

Desperate, so terribly desperate to do something to ease her suffering, Quentin snapped, "Surely you can do more than just talk, man. There must be something you can give her for the pain."

The doctor shook his head, his expression regretful. "There is nothing. And unfortunately, the pain will have to get worse before it can get better. Her ladyship has yet to have any truly powerful contractions, which she must, of course, have to push the babe into the world."

"And when exactly can we expect those?" he growled, possessed of a sudden, irrational urge to throttle the man.

Apparently the accoucheur was as used to churlish husbands as Nicholas predicted, for he seemed utterly unperturbed by Quentin's threatening demeanor. Still smiling encouragingly at Jane, who actually seemed to be easing beneath his coaxing, he replied, "Hopefully within the next few hours."

"Hopefully?" Quentin snorted his frustration. "And if they don't come?"

"Why, then I shall administer ergot."

"But if—"

"For goodness' sake, Quentin. Stop plaguing the poor man," Jane chided, unclenching her teeth to expel what sounded like a sigh of relief. "Pain is a natural part of child-birth, and there is no help for it. Now let us exchange gifts before the real pain starts and I am unable to enjoy mine."

At Quentin's insistence, Jane opened her gifts first. There was an exquisite gold and enameled watch and chatelaine that she had coveted since first seeing it featured in *Lady's Magazine*, an ermine-trimmed hood to match her favorite red cloak, and a beautiful sandalwood fan painted with the country flowers she grew in her garden. He'd even remembered tokens for the babe: an ivory comb and brush set and a cunning arrangement of silver bells and animals, which was to be hung over the cradle to amuse the child.

"Oh, Quentin. They are all too wonderful," she exclaimed, glancing from one gift to the other, as if loath to admire one in favor of the others. "I am afraid that my gift looks quite mean in comparison to such richness."

Quentin smiled at her delight, pleased to see a faint flush of color rise in her pale cheeks. "Nonsense, love. I shall think anything you give me splendid, because it comes from you."

Had it not been for the ashen cast to her skin and the lines of fatigue about her eyes, Quentin would have judged his wife quite well by the grin she gave him then. "We shall see," she declared. "You will find your parcel beneath the bed."

Her gift to him was a stunning wine-velvet dressing gown, which was every bit as wonderful as the purple one she had made him for his birthday. And she'd made this one as well, he could tell from the neat stitching and the superbly embroidered Somerville crest on the left breast. Nobody in the world sewed as beautifully as his sweet Lady Jane, and he told her so in no uncertain terms.

As he'd hoped, she was thrilled by his sincere praise. Beaming her pleasure, she insisted that he strip off his rumpled coat and waistcoat right then and there to check the fit.

Of course it, like everything else about the garment, was perfect.

"Thank you, my sweet. I adore it," he murmured, sealing the declaration with a kiss.

The rest of the morning passed in a haze of loving words and whispered reassurances, punctuated by labor pains, which Quentin, through Dr. Spicer's instruction, helped Jane weather. With the good doctor's permission Sophie brought Nicholas for a visit at midday. The latter came bearing an extravagant bouquet of fresh flowers, the origin of which he refused to reveal, though everyone teased and teased to find out.

Midday quickly waxed into afternoon, afternoon waned into evening, the lengthening time bringing with it a steady increase in Jane's pains. Though it tore at his heart to see his beloved Jane suffer so, Quentin remained steadfastly by her side, holding her hands and murmuring his love during her contractions, and gently sponging her sweat-drenched face when she lay drained and quivering in the aftermath.

Several times during the day both Sophie and Jane's maid, Madge, had tried to relieve him of his nursing duty, but he refused to go, staunchly determined to remain by Jane's side. Forever and a day, that was how long he had promised to stay there. And unless she bade him go, that was how long he would stay. He even stayed while the doctor examined her, though it took all his self-restraint not to punch the man when she sobbed her pain at his prodding.

It was during one of those examinations, just as the candles were lit and the pale winter sun slipped below the stark white horizon, that Quentin experienced his first, horrible inkling that all was not well. Rather than calmly and matter-of-factly going about his business as he had the times before, the doctor drew back sharply at whatever he saw, then narrowed his eyes and leaned further beneath the coverings to do something that made Jane cry out in agony.

Not wanting to alarm Jane, who was now too spent to do more than weep weakly at her pain, Quentin stifled his urge to grill the man. Though it almost killed him to do so, he waited until the doctor had finished, then followed him across the room, where he finally aired his concerns.

Grasping the man's arm to lead him yet further from the bed, he said in a low voice, "Something is amiss, Dr. Spicer. I can see it in your face."

Casting an anxious glance at the bed to make certain that they weren't being overheard, the doctor softly replied, "You are correct, my lord. There is something amiss. The babe is trying to make an unnatural presentation."

"Unnatural presentation?" Quentin repeated, his eyes narrowing. "Are you saying that the babe is in a breech position?"

The doctor sighed. "If only such were the case. A breech would be a much simpler problem to correct. But no." A head shake. "It is in a transverse lie."

"Which means?"

Another sigh. "It is lying crosswise in the womb instead of lengthwise." He illustrated with his hands. "Instead of presenting itself head first, the arm and shoulder were in the birth canal at my last examination. Of course I pushed them back up, but, well, unless her ladyship can produce hard enough contractions to push it into the proper position, I shall be forced to reach inside her womb and turn it myself. The process is called version."

"Version." The word hit Quentin like a punch in the gut. Though he knew little about the subject of childbirth, as did most men, he'd heard about the horrors of version. One of his friend's wives had had to undergo the hellish procedure, and the young husband had wept with angst as he'd recounted the hideous screams and tortured pleas for death that had come from the room during the operation. And though the woman had been delivered and had eventually recovered, the husband lived in fear of ever touching her again, terrified that she would someday have to go through another such atrocious ordeal.

Just the thought of his Jane suffering such torment made him want to scream his anguish. Feeling as though he were about to shatter into pieces, Quentin closed his eyes and raggedly whispered, "Is there nothing that can be done . . . besides version?"

"Perhaps. I am going to administer ergot now. Ergot increases contractions, and sometimes that increase is enough to turn the babe."

"When will we know for certain?" Quentin inquired, looking back at Jane, who had begun to writhe and moan.

The doctor, too, gazed at her, frowning. "By midnight. If I see no improvement, I shall be forced to perform the version then. Your wife will have been laboring for at least twenty-seven hours at that time . . . most probably closer to thirty-four or thirty-five, judging from what she told me about the pains she suffered yesterday afternoon. I fear waiting any longer if you wish this babe to be delivered alive."

And so the ergot was given, then Quentin and the doctor began their grim vigil. Sophie, who had returned to the room shortly after the drug was administered and had been given the horrifying news, now sat with them, adding her prayers to theirs. As for Jane, in her exhausted misery, she was beyond wondering or even caring about their morose mood.

Slowly the evening hours crept by, deepening into what for Quentin was the blackest of nights. As promised, the ergot increased and strengthened Jane's contractions, sending her into what seemed to be an endless convulsion of pain. Twice during that time the doctor examined her, only to frown and shake his head in response to Quentin's querying looks.

Then midnight came. This time after examining Jane, the

doctor pulled Quentin to the far side of the room, his expression bleak. "I am sorry, my lord, but the babe seems to be wedged in position. Our only hope of saving both mother and child is—"

"Version," Quentin finished for him, closing his eyes in his anguish as he said the word.

"Yes. At this point I see no alternative but to turn the babe to a feet-down position and pull it out by the legs. Your wife is far too weak to help push it out now, and she will most certainly die undelivered unless we do as I suggest."

"But she will live if we do the version?" It was more a desperate plea than a question.

The doctor sighed, his face looking suddenly haggard. "She shall have a chance, as will the babe. It is the best I can promise in such a case."

"Then you must do it." This was from Sophie, who had joined them unnoticed and now stood by Quentin's side. Giving his arm a gentle squeeze, she added, "If there is any chance at all, we must take it."

Of course she was right, and Quentin knew it. And though he hated to see Jane, who had already suffered so very much, go through such a hideous ordeal, he would do it. He loved her too much to let her die without a fierce fight for her life. And so he closed his eyes to halt the flood of tears that threatened to fall and raggedly inquired, "What do we do first, doctor?"

"We need to move her to the birthing cot, then we must find someone to hold her steady while I do the procedure. Despite Lady Jane's weakness, I can promise that she will fight like a she-devil once I get started." He glanced at Sophie. "Perhaps you, Lady Lyndhurst and her maid—Madge, is it?—would be best for the task. She seems to trust you both and—"

"If anyone is to hold her, it shall be I," Quentin cut in.

"You?" The doctor looked at him as if he'd quite taken leave of his senses.

"Yes," he confirmed. "I am her husband, after all."

"Indeed you are, which makes you imminently unsuitable for the task. In my experience husbands grow as distraught as their wives during the procedure and end up being more a hindrance than a help." The man shook his head. "It is best that you wait outside."

"Perhaps the doctor is right, Quent," Sophie murmured. "As much as you love Jane, it shall most probably be more than you will be able to bear to see her in such pain. Go sit with Nicholas. I promise to see our Jane safely through this."

Stubbornly, Quentin shook his head. He had promised Jane that he would stay with her, and he'd be damned before he'd break that promise. In a tone that brooked no argument, he said, "I am staying, and that is that. I do agree, however, that Lady Lyndhurst should remain, for it shall no doubt comfort my wife all the more to have her dearest friend nearby." He paused a beat to look first at the doctor, then at Sophie. When neither tried to naysay him, he added, "Now, shall I carry my wife to the cot?"

The next few minutes slipped by in a haze of dread as they prepared for the ghastly task before them. To Quentin's everlasting thanks, Jane was almost insensible in her pain and exhaustion, and was thus unable to grasp the horror of what awaited her.

All too soon—at least for Quentin—they were ready to begin.

What followed was worse, a thousand times worse, than Quentin had imagined. Every agonized scream from Jane, every desperate struggle and piteous plea for the doctor to stop slashed his heart, making him long to curse and rage against the heavens above for their cruelty in allowing someone as gentle as Jane to suffer such torment.

But of course he didn't give in to his urge. He couldn't. He had to be strong for Jane. And so he smiled, though he wept and wailed inside, crooned reassurances in which he held no belief, and made promises he knew were beyond him to keep, all the while holding her small, pain-wracked form in a firm grip.

After what seemed like a lifetime, Sophie called out from her station beside the accoucheur. "It is almost over, dear. The babe is turned and the doctor has just found its feet."

"How long?" Quentin gritted out, releasing one of Jane's arms to mop the sweat from her pain-contorted face.

"Only a few moments," the doctor replied, without looking up. "It's coming now."

"Yes, it is coming! I can see it!" Sophie exclaimed excitedly. Several seconds elapsed, during which Jane screamed as if she were being torn asunder, which no doubt she was, then her wails were joined by those of their newborn babe.

"Jane, love! Do you hear?" Quentin cried, kissing her damp forehead. "Our babe is here!"

She took several sobbing breaths, then hoarsely whispered, "Is . . . is all well with it?"

Quentin repeated the question to the doctor, who nodded at Sophie and said, "Why don't you see for yourself?"

Smiling as proudly if it were she, not Jane, who had borne the child, Sophie carried the naked babe to them, announcing, "My lord, my lady. Your daughter."

"A girl?" Rather than look at the child as Sophie laid it beside her, Jane gazed soberly up at Quentin. "I hope you don't mind so very much that it isn't a son, my lord."

He grinned, more pleased by his new daughter than he would have been by a dozen sons. "Of course not," he exclaimed, taking one of the infant's impossibly tiny hands in his. "In truth, I was rather hoping for a girl."

"You . . . were?" For the first time since giving birth, Jane smiled. It was a feeble smile, but one that reflected true joy.

He nodded. "I prayed for one every night."

"Prayers that you shall most probably regret in seventeen or eighteen years," Sophie chimed in with a laugh. "Even as a newborn, your daughter shows uncommon beauty. You, my lord, are going to have a devil of a time fighting off all the bucks who shall be clamoring to court her."

"She is lovely, isn't she?" Jane whispered, stroking the babe's cheek with trembling fingers.

"Almost as lovely as her mother," Quentin replied, kissing his wife's pale cheek. "Thank you, my love. You've given me a Somerville truly worthy of the name."

"Speaking of names, what shall you call her?" Sophie inquired.

"Love?" he murmured, deferring to Jane.

"Flora Grace," she replied without hesitation. "I always thought that if I had a daughter, I should very much like to call her Flora. And Grace was my mother's name. So if you have no objections, my lord, that is what I would like to name her."

He shook his head. "None at all. I think Flora Grace a perfectly lovely name."

"Flora Grace Somerville," Sophie tested. She nodded. "Very pretty indeed."

Certain that he'd never been so very happy in his entire life, Quentin looked at the doctor, who still tended to Jane. "All is well with my wife, I assume?"

He nodded. "The afterbirth is a bit slow in coming, but that is to be expected in these cases."

"Since all is well here, why don't you introduce our new daughter to her uncle, love?" Jane suggested. "No doubt he feels quite left out."

Quentin smiled tenderly. His darling, selfless Jane. Even

after all she'd endured, she still worried about the feelings of others.

"Yes, do," Sophie chimed in. "Nicholas has been pacing a hole in the library carpet since nightfall, and I am certain that he is frantic for news."

"Well—" Quentin glanced uncertainly at the babe. She looked so small and fragile, as if she would break if he picked her up.

As if reading his thoughts, Sophie laughed and said, "Never fear, Quent. She's much sturdier than she looks. Just let me wash her up a bit and wrap her in her swaddling, then I shall show you how to hold her."

At Jane's nod, he sighed and said, "All right, but only if the doctor is certain that he shan't be requiring my assistance."

The doctor gave a dismissive wave. "Do go show off your babe, my lord. Lady Lyndhurst and I can take care of matters here."

And so after Sophie had sponged off the babe and wrapped her in warm swaddling, Quentin gingerly carried his daughter to the library. So tiny and delicate did she feel in his arms that he was certain she would shatter if he so much as jostled her.

Nicholas, of course, was long past such foolishness. The instant Quentin introduced him to his new niece, he swept her out of her father's arms and carried her to the light. Holding her with practiced ease, he took careful inventory of her features, after which he declared her the finest Somerville yet.

They were engrossed in deciding whether Flora's tiny nose was that of a Somerville or a Wentworth, when Sophie rushed into the room. She didn't have to speak for Quentin to know that something was terribly wrong. Her blood-splattered skirts and grief-stricken face conveyed the message more powerfully than words.

"Jane?" Quentin croaked, choking on his sudden terror.

"Oh, Quentin." She shook her head over and over again,

tears spilling down her pale cheeks. "T-The afterbirth came j-just after you left and—and—" Her voice fractured with a sob. For several interminable seconds she fought to repair it, then continued in a splintered whisper. "The c-contractions needed to stop the bleeding d-didn't come until a couple of minutes later, and—and she suffered a terrible hemorrhage. She—"

Quentin didn't stay to hear her finish. He couldn't. He didn't want to hear that Jane, who only moments earlier had been smiling radiantly at their newborn daughter, was . . .

No! his mind screamed. Jane was fine . . . she had to be.

Fueled by panic, he bounded up the stairs, taking them two, sometimes three at a time, sobbing Jane's name as he went. Flinging open the chamber door with a violence that slammed it against the wall, he dashed into the room, roughly shoving aside the doctor, who stood grave and mute at the blood-soaked cot.

"Jane. Oh, my love," he cried brokenly, collapsing to his knees beside her. Drawing her head and shoulders into arms that were suddenly weak and trembling, he hugged her against his chest, gently cradling her as he buried his tear-streaked face in her sweat-matted hair.

God help him! She was cold, so very cold. And limp, as if her bones had seeped out with her life's blood.

Despair shrouding him like a pall on a coffin, he gently turned her head to nuzzle his face against hers, praying to feel the warmth of her breath stir against his cheeks as it did when they kissed. After several shattering seconds, he pulled away again.

For a long moment he sat staring into her still, white face, remembering her gentle smile and the spirited brightness of her eyes. Pained beyond tears by the memories, he clasped her again to his breaking heart, whispering, "Forever and a day. You promised me—forever and a day."

Chapter 18

"My lord, please. You mustn't move her about so. You might start the bleeding again. She is to be kept absolutely still if she is to have even the slightest chance at recovery," the doctor cautioned.

Quentin glowered at the man, the words slow in penetrating the dense fog of his grief. When they did, he croaked, "Recover?"

The doctor sighed and wearily rubbed his bloodshot eyes. "I am not going to lie to you, my lord. Your wife is in a bad way. Very bad, indeed. As you yourself can see, she is more dead than alive. Indeed, her pulse is so weak and her breath so faint that I too thought she was dead for a moment."

"Yes . . . but she is alive," he mumbled in a dazed tone, barely able to believe his ears. "Alive." He sobbed his jubilation and pressed a kiss to her still lips, silently giving thanks.

"Alive, yes."

"And she will recover?" He glanced pleadingly at the doctor, mutely begging him for hope.

The man's fatigue-drawn face softened a fraction, and he even managed a small smile. "Were she anyone else, I would say no. But your lady, perhaps. That she has survived thus far is a miracle."

"What must be done to give her her best chance at life?" a new voice interjected.

Quentin looked toward the door to see his brother standing

there, so strong, cool, and commanding, looking every inch the powerful earl that he was. Having him there, seeing his strength and knowing that he had come to share it kindled a comforting ember of warmth in the desolate iciness of his despair.

In that brief instant their gazes met, Quentin's bleak and desperate, Nicholas's reassuring and promising hope, then Nicholas strode into the room. "Just tell us what we must do, Dr. Spicer, and it shall be done. We will do anything to save our Jane," he said, stopping beside Quentin, who was still on his knees cradling Jane. Nodding once at the doctor to substantiate his claim, he crouched down next to his brother, draping his arm around his shoulders in fortifying unity.

The doctor smiled, as touched by Nicholas's brotherly gesture as Quentin was. "As I said, she must be kept still and quiet, though in her current state I doubt the latter shall pose any difficulty. Aside from that"—a head shake—"there is little we can do beyond hope and pray. If the bleeding doesn't resume and we can get nourishment into her, she might recover in time. My suggestion is that you hire a nurse experienced in the care of cases such as this . . . perhaps Mrs. Risby of Snodsbury, if she's available. She's proved herself quite competent in the past."

"If you would be good enough to give me directions to her home, I shall go for the woman posthaste," Nicholas declared. Giving Quentin's shoulders a squeeze, he added in a low voice, "Never fear, she shall be available to nurse our Jane. I promise."

Quentin smiled faintly and nodded. There wasn't a doubt in his mind that his brother would keep his promise.

Nicholas nodded back. "You also needn't worry about Flora. Sophie has put her in the care of our wet nurse. Since Christopher is almost weaned now, she has plenty of milk to spare." He looked over at Dr. Spicer. "Is there anything else that needs doing before I leave for Snodsbury?"

The accoucheur shook his head. "No, nothing. Aside from bathing her ladyship and putting her into bed, there remains little we can do. I sent Madge for hot water and fresh linens, and Lady Lyndhurst is to return after she takes care of the babe. Between the three of us, we should be able to manage well enough."

"What about you, Quent? Anything you need?" he murmured.

Quentin looked up from Jane's face, so white and beloved, to meet his brother's gaze. There was compassion in Nicholas's dark eyes, and worry, and steely determination. There was also love, so much love that Quentin knew if he asked him to ride to the ends of the earth for him, he would do so without hesitation.

Rendered mute by his own love and blinded by his tears of gratitude, he shook his head, desperately wishing that he were stronger so he could express his emotions.

Apparently his feelings showed on his face, for Nicholas whispered, "It's all right. You needn't say anything. I know." Giving his shoulders a final hug, he stood up. "I shall return as soon as possible. Now, Dr. Spicer, if you would be so kind as to give me directions?"

At that moment Madge bustled into the room with two buckets of steaming water, followed by Hannah, the chambermaid, her arms loaded with linens and towels. Bringing up the rear was Sophie, who promptly chased the men out of the room, informing them that bathing Jane was women's work.

Though Quentin was loath to let his wife out of his sight, terrified that she would take another, and this time fatal, turn for the worse if he left her, he finally allowed Nicholas to lead him away. For the next half hour he numbly shadowed his brother, following him about like a lost puppy as he ordered his footmen awakened and his coach prepared, not knowing what else to do with himself.

As they stood silently at the front door, waiting for the coach to be brought around, Nicholas pulled him into a hug, gently chiding, "Do try to rest while I'm gone, little brother. It shan't do Jane a bit of good for you to wear yourself ill with worry."

Quentin smiled wanly at the brotherly speech. "I know."

"So do I," his brother retorted wryly, pulling away. "I know that you shan't heed a word I say. Not that I blame you. I doubt I would be able to rest either if it were my Sophie lying up there. Still, do promise me that you will try."

"I will try," he vowed, though they both knew he lied.

The coach pulled up before the door then, its lanterns glowing like spectral mist through the snow that fell from the predawn sky. Nicholas was down the steps in a flash, his greatcoat capes dancing on the arctic wind as he went, flapping and fluttering about him like the wings of an angel in flight.

An angel of mercy, hastening to bring deliverance to an innocent sufferer.

Smiling faintly at his fanciful thought, Quentin waited there until the vehicle had disappeared into the night, then went back upstairs. Once there, he haunted Jane's chamber door until it at last opened and the servants departed, carrying basins of red-tinged water and a mountain of bloodstained linen.

"Quentin," Sophie greeted with a weary smile. "Is Nicholas off, then?"

He nodded. "Yes. And Jane? How is she?"

"No worse. If you feel up to helping him, Dr. Spicer could use assistance in transferring her to the bed."

Of course he helped, thrilled to do something, anything at

all, to aid in Jane's comfort, though he knew that she was beyond all awareness in her unconsciousness.

When at last they had her tucked beneath the fresh coverings, with her icy body surrounded by hot bricks, Quentin knelt beside the bed, hovering protectively over her still form as if in doing so he could somehow secure her fragile hold on life. And it was fragile, terrifyingly so. He could see it in her face, as pale and sunken as that of a wax death effigy. He could feel it in the faintness of her breath and the threadiness of her pulse.

His love teetered on the brink of death, and there was nothing he could do to draw her back.

Abysmal despair seeped into his soul at his helplessness, leaving him leaden, hopeless, used up. Feeling as though he sank into a bottomless morass of pain, he laid his head on the pillow beside hers, brokenly sobbing, "Please don't leave me, Jane. Please! Don't you know that you are everything to me? You are my peace . . . my sanity . . . my conscience. You are the soul I thought I'd lost years ago, the heart I never knew I possessed. You are all that is good and pure and wonderful . . . my light . . . my angel . . . my salvation."

By now tears rolled freely from his eyes, scalding his cheeks with their bitterness. "You, my love, are my life, and I shall most certainly die without you."

He raised his head then, sniffling as he gently stroked her hair back from her face, remembering with heartrending clarity all the times he'd touched it so in the aftermath of their lovemaking. Again he saw her smile, blissful and filled with awe at her rapture. Again he saw the radiant flush of her cheeks and basked in the luminous warmth of her eyes. Again he heard her voice, low and husky with pleasure, telling him that she loved him.

The memory shattered him, leaving him cut, bruised, and bleeding inside. Mute in his agony, he slowly crumpled into a heap by the bed, curling tightly into himself to hug his knees to his aching chest. Drily weeping, soundlessly keening, he lay there waiting.

If death came for Jane, it would have to take him as well.

"I don't know who looks worse, him or her," a strange voice declared, invading Quentin's exhausted slumber. In the next instant someone shook him, gently but insistently, and he thought he heard his brother call his name.

Distanced from time and place by his sleep, he frowned, struggling up through the sea of murkiness that was his mind. When he at last broke the surface into consciousness, he opened his drowsy eyes to find a stranger hovering over him.

Blearily he peered at the woman, a jolly-looking soul with a round, rosy face framed by a neat lace cap, trying to recall where he was, and why. When he did remember he bolted upright, crying, "Jane!" only to fall back again when his head slammed into something hard.

A loud yelp and quick glance told him that something was a jaw, Nicholas's to be exact, who had been kneeling over him, shaking him awake.

"Bloody hell, Quent. I always knew you had a hard head. I just never knew how very hard until now," his brother gritted out, falling back on his heels and massaging his abused face.

"Jane?" Quentin inquired anxiously, though he did have presence of mind enough to cast his brother an apologetic look.

"Dr. Spicer says that she's the same, though I think that her breathing seems stronger." This was from Sophie, who had appeared beside the woman, with the good doctor looking on from over her shoulder. "Never fear, Quent," she continued. "We kept a close watch on her while you slept. We considered waking you and sending you off to bed where you would be comfortable, but—" she shook her head—"if you are anything like your brother, you would have refused to go, so we let you sleep where you dropped."

With Nicholas now safely out of head shot range, Quentin again sat up, resisting the urge to moan aloud at the soreness of his muscles. As he stiffly pushed himself to his feet, Sophie added, "As you no doubt guessed, Quent, this is Mrs. Risby, the nurse. And this, Mrs. Risby, is Lord Quentin Somerville, your patient's husband."

"Of course he is," the woman declared briskly. "Who else'd be snoring away on the floor beside her ladyship's bed? See it all the time." She made a clucking noise and shook her head. "Well, there won't be any more need of doing that again, my lord. Not with me here. You tend to yourself, and I'll tend to your lady. Now if you gentlemen'll be good enough to excuse yourselves, I'd like to get to work. Her ladyship looks in dire need of my services."

"Then you can help her?" Quentin inquired hopefully, deciding that he rather liked the no-nonsense nurse.

In a manner that could best be described as bustling, the woman moved to the bed, where she first felt Jane's pulse, then checked her for fever. "I've seen better," she pronounced with a shrug. "Seen worse too, and pulled 'em through. My guess is that she'll live, though it'll be a goodly while before she's back to herself." Another shrug. "Only time will tell if I am right, of course."

One day passed, then another and another, all of which Quentin spent haunting the sickroom. For hours on end he would sit by the bed, watching as the nurse patiently spooned tiny amounts of broth between Jane's still, cracked lips, coaxing and crooning to her to swallow as if she were her own child. He tarried there not just to be near Jane, though that in itself was reason enough, but because Mrs. Risby gave him hope.

During those dark days, throughout which there appeared

to be no change in Jane's condition, it was only the nurse's constant pointing out of small but encouraging signs of improvement that kept him from going mad with worry.

On the first day, as he knelt by the bed, weeping in despair, the woman lifted Jane's hands to show him the color beneath her fingernails, calmly explaining that it indicated a renewal of her lost blood. The second day, she displayed the faint but definite pinkening of Jane's formerly blanched gums, proclaiming it excellent progress. And on the third one, she allowed him to spoon his wife some water, directing his attention to the way her tongue now weakly lapped up the moisture.

"Patience," she gently chided him each time. "To have hope you must first have patience."

And their patience did pay off in hope, for late on the fourth day Jane stirred, and even made a soft sound. She didn't, however, open her eyes until the eve of the fifth day. When she did, Quentin was at her side, ready to welcome her back to the world of the living.

"Quentin?" she hoarsely whispered, frowning as if she couldn't quite recall where she was or why.

"Here, love, always here. Forever and a day, remember?" he murmured, falling to his knees to drop a light kiss on her lips.

She smiled. It was a frail smile, true, one that trembled from the effort it took to form it, but to Quentin it was the most glorious smile in the whole world. "Yes . . . of course I remember. How could I forget? But"—her brow creased again—"I feel so weak and queer."

"Of course you do, love. You've been terribly ill for almost a week now. You lost far too much blood after—"

"The baby . . . yes. I remember now." Another weak smile lit her wan face. "Our daughter. She . . . she is well?"

Quentin grinned, barely able to contain his elation at seeing his Jane smile at him again. "She grows plumper and prettier every day. Sophie's wet nurse has been taking excellent care of her. Well"—a chuckle— "she and little Izzy. Isabel is quite bewitched by her new cousin and has adopted her as her own. Would you like me to bring Flora to you so you can see for yourself?"

"Perhaps in a few days, when her ladyship is stronger," Mrs. Risby interrupted, coming to stand next to Quentin. "Right now she needs rest, and plenty of it."

"But that is all I have been doing," Jane protested weakly.

"You have been mending, not resting. Mending takes all one's strength, which you must regain through rest," the nurse informed her firmly.

When Jane looked about to argue, Quentin laughed and said, "Do not waste your time debating with Mrs. Risby, love. The woman is an utter dragon. She is also a fine nurse, whom I trust implicitly, and if she says you must rest, then rest you shall."

From that day forward Jane's health rapidly improved. So rapidly, in fact, that even Mrs. Risby was amazed. Despite her astonishing recuperative powers, Quentin demanded that she take her recovery slowly and insisted on treating her as if she were the most delicate and precious treasure in the world, which to him she was. Thus her next weeks were spent being pampered and coddled by everyone at Swanswick, including Sophie and Nicholas, who stayed on to keep her company.

As promised, Jane's father, stepmother, and stepsister arrived near the end of January, fully expecting to assist in the birth of the babe. When they learned what had happened, the latter two gave Quentin a fearsome tongue-lashing, distressed that he hadn't thought to summon them sooner. From all appearances, they had yet to forgive him when they departed again two weeks later, though he had repeatedly and humbly apologized.

As the weeks progressed and Jane grew stronger, the women from the village and cottages, and some of the children too, came to visit, bringing gay gifts and filling the abbey with laughter. It wasn't, however, until the first day of April, by which time Jane was ready to go mad from the smothering tedium of her prolonged convalescence, that Mrs. Risby and Dr. Spicer finally declared her mended.

On that happy day, as she lounged contentedly in bed, waiting for Madge to prepare her bath, Quentin strolled into the chamber carrying Flora. She smiled at the sight of them. So besotted was Quentin with his daughter that it was becoming increasingly rare to see one without the other. As he'd so often done during her convalescence, he brought the babe to the bed, where he carefully placed her in her mother's arms, then stretched out beside them to admire the picture they made.

To Jane's delight, Flora showed every sign of favoring her beautiful father in both coloring and features, though Quentin stoutly maintained that the brightness of her blue-violet eyes, the soft curve of her rosebud lips, and the sweetness of her nature could only have come from her mother.

That morning, as Jane lay admiring her daughter, wanting to burst with pride as she always did when she gazed at what her and Quentin's love had created, Quentin murmured, "When you feel up to a bit of revelry, I thought we would have a feast."

She looked up, still smiling her motherly pride. "A feast?"

He nodded. "To celebrate the birth of our daughter. I want to have a grand affair with all our friends, tenants, and family members present." He smiled wryly. "Speaking of family, do you suppose Elizabeth and Clarissa have forgiven me yet?"

She laughed. "Oh, yes. After explaining how very distraught you were over my illness, they now think you a stellar husband."

"That wasn't the impression they gave me during their visit," he retorted with a grimace. "There were several times when I thought that their gazes alone might flay me alive."

Again she laughed. "Well, they couldn't let you know how easily they had forgiven you, now, could they? Why, you might not have learned your lesson properly, and thus forget them in the future should something happen again."

"You can assure them that I learned my lesson, and very well, thank you kindly," he countered with a chuckle. "Indeed, should the house catch fire I shall most certainly take the time to write them before escaping the flames." He sobered then. "You aren't saying that they have forgiven me just to save my feelings, are you?"

"Of course not. If you want proof, you may read Rissa's last letter. In it she expresses hope that her Lord Crathorne will love her to distraction, as you do me."

"In that instance, you must tell her to bring her husband-to-be to the feast so I can instruct him on the finer points of being a doting husband," he replied, raising up on his elbows to peer at their daughter, who had just yawned.

"Then you are serious about the feast?"

He glanced at her sharply, frowning. "Of course. Why wouldn't I be serious?"

She shrugged. "It's just that such celebrations are usually reserved for the birth of an heir. And—" She slanted him an arch look. "You shall have an heir one day, my lord. I promise. Dr. Spicer says there is no reason in the world I cannot give you more children."

He paled to ash at her words. "Oh, no, Jane," he growled, shaking his head. "I shan't risk your life for an heir. I am perfectly content with our Flora."

"Well, I'm not," she declared, stubbornly. "I want her to have brothers and sisters, at least half a dozen of them."

"Half a dozen?" He paused a beat, clearly taken aback by the notion. Then he chuckled. "Greedy little wench, aren't you."

"Only when it comes to you." She lifted her head to kiss his lips. "I want several boys just like you to love." She kissed him again. "Everyone says that it is possible, even Mrs. Risby. She agrees with Dr. Spicer that it is extremely rare for a woman to suffer as I did twice, and that my next babe shall no doubt come with ease."

"Well . . ." he mused, clearly unconvinced.

"Please, Quentin? I'm not suggesting that we try again now. But someday. It means so very much to me. Besides—" she gazed lovingly down at their daughter, who had drifted off to sleep in her arms. "I shudder to think of how very spoiled Flora will be if we do not give her at least one brother or sister. You do so overindulge her."

"Yes. And I plan to continue indulging her, just as I plan to indulge you and whatever other children you might someday give me."

"Then you agree?" Her lips curved into the smile he so loved. "We can have more children?"

"Have I ever been able to deny you anything when you smile at me like that?" he inquired, shaking his head at his own weak will. "I suppose that if Dr. Spicer thinks it safe, we might try again—someday." As she moved to kiss him in her delight, he stopped her, sternly reminding her, "I said *some-day*. We shan't try again until we are absolutely certain that you are healed. That might be a great while longer yet, you know."

"Yes. Of course, my lord. Anything you say," she murmured obediently, shifting the baby to free one arm. Coiling it around his neck, she pulled his face close to hers. Now lip to lip, she whispered, "Until that time, you won't deny me your kisses, will you? I can assure you that I am quite well enough for kissing."

"Kisses shall be free to you for the taking, my love. All you shall ever want, whenever you want them," he vowed. With that, he tenderly fulfilled his promise.

Epilogue

Mother Nature, too, celebrated with them that day. Or so it seemed to all present at the feast celebrating Flora's birth. After a week of gentle showers the rain clouds suddenly cleared, leaving in their wake an impossibly blue May sky. Even the guinea-bright sun cooperated with the occasion, shining bright and agreeably warm, bringing cheer to all it touched.

As he had in the fall, and then the winter that had followed, Quentin now took a moment's respite from the blinding bustle of everyday life to see and appreciate the glory of the early spring. Wondering how he could have let so many seasons change and pass through his life completely unnoticed, he stole away from the feast, which was being served as a picnic in the Swanswick park, and climbed to the top of a rise a short distance away.

It was almost quiet there, peaceful, the only sound being the muted laughter of the revelers that carried on the soft, fragrant wind. Inhaling the green, earthy scents, he looked around him, his heart swelling with pride at what he saw.

On and on, seemingly forever, stretched fields, meadows, pastures, and woods, all his, all touched by the magical bounty of spring. There was yellow charlock and blue speedwell nestled among the sproutlings in the neatly plowed fields; spiky purple orchids, drooping golden cowslip, and delicate white stitchwort, clustered, swirled, and dotted the verdant green vistas of meadows and pastures. The hedgerows, too, abounded with color, the blackthorn hedges in white, raggedly bordered by wild violets.

He had just crouched down to pick a bouquet of the dainty buttercups and primroses blooming at his feet, knowing how much Jane adored them, when he heard the soft whisper of footsteps. Glancing up, he saw his father approaching.

Smiling faintly, he stood. "Father," he murmured with a cordial nod. His parents had arrived late the night before, having been delayed by a problem at their Somerset estate. Thus, he had yet to speak with them except for a few hurried words of welcome.

His father nodded in return and came to stand beside him.

For several moments neither of them spoke as the marquess studied first his son, then the lands about him. In the past such scrutiny had always unsettled Quentin, making him angry and tense, certain that his father searched for yet another failing for which he could criticize him.

Now, however, he felt nothing but a quiet sense of pride, which came from the empowering knowledge that his estate, his life, and he himself were the best he could make them. For the first time ever, he had done something of which he was truly proud, something that manifested itself in the estate, his person, his marriage, and his child.

That something was his love for Jane.

She was his driving force. It was she whom he sought to please; she, he wished to make proud; she, for whom he had at last grown up and become a man. If that wasn't enough for his father, then so be it. If it was enough for Jane, then it was enough for him.

Rather than watch his father's face as he studied the land, trying to gauge his expression as he once might have done, Quentin resumed his own observation. He was just admiring the gliding splendor of an orange-tip butterfly when his father murmured, "I'm proud of you, son."

Quentin smiled faintly, though he didn't look away from the butterfly. "I'm proud of myself," he admitted.

"I know. And I am glad." There was brief pause, then, "You are content, too, aren't you?"

"Yes. Oh, yes." Quentin turned to his father, wishing that he had the words to express how very content he truly was. Since none seemed quite eloquent enough, he simply said, "I never knew that there was such happiness to be found in this world as I have found with my Jane. But you knew, didn't you? That is why you sent me here." He cocked his head to the side in query, his smile broadening a fraction as he awaited a response.

"I hoped," his father replied quietly. He took a deep breath, closing his eyes as if savoring the spring perfume. Then he added, "I saw in Jane the peace you so desperately needed, and I hoped that you would find comfort and strength in it. As you have clearly discovered for yourself, your Jane is a rare treasure. Her preciousness comes not from doll-like beauty or the empty wit so prized by the *ton*, but from a gentleness of spirit and a genuine goodness all too rarely found these days. My only hope now is that you will cherish her as she deserves to be cherished."

"I do and I will. You may rest assured that I shall love and cherish my darling Jane forever." He grinned and softly added as an afterthought, "And a day."

His father frowned. "Pardon?"

He shook his head, laughing softly. "Nothing. It's just something Jane and I like to say."

His father smiled and nodded, as if he understood exactly what he meant. "You are probably wondering why I followed you out here."

Quentin shrugged. "Not really, though I am glad you did."

"As am I." Neither felt need of an explanation as to why the other was glad. As if in acknowledgment of their understanding, his father nodded, then continued, "I just wanted to tell you that you are free to enjoy the Season now if you wish. You shall find all doors again open to you."

"The Season?" Quentin repeated blankly. It had been a long while since he'd thought of London or the pleasures of the Season. Now that he did, neither seemed particularly enticing. Not compared to what he had here.

"Quentin? Oh, there you are! We have been looking all over for you." Quentin turned to see Jane walking toward him, looking beyond beautiful in her pink silk gown with Flora in her arms. Smiling with a radiance that made his heart turn cartwheels in his chest, she added, "It is time for Flora's nap. I thought you might like to kiss her before her nurse takes her."

"Indeed I would," he murmured, kissing Jane's lips as she came to a stop before him. As he took his daughter in his arms, his father said, "I was just asking Quentin if he was bringing you to London for the Season. It has started, you know, and promises to be most entertaining. Or so I have heard."

Having carefully nested the babe in his right arm, Quentin reached over and pulled Jane into the crook of his left one. Hugging her close to his side, he replied, "I shall do whatever my darling wife wishes."

She smiled, though the radiance of that smile was dimmed by a faint shadow. "Of course we must go. I know how very much you love the parties and company of the *ton*," she replied.

Quentin gazed down into her warm brown eyes, aching with tenderness at her unselfish response. Dipping down to drop a kiss on her forehead, he replied, "The only company I truly wish is that of the ones I love most, you and Flora. As for the parties, well, I find the gay village affairs much more diverting than anything in Town."

"Are you certain?" she murmured, anxiously searching his eyes.

He nodded. "Yes. I have everything I shall ever want and need right here, my love." And it was true. She was all he would ever need.

For forever and a day.

For only $3.99 each, they'll make your dreams come true.

LORDS OF MIDNIGHT

A special romance promotion from Signet Books—featuring six of our most popular, award-winning authors...

Lady in White by Denise Domning
❏ 0-451-40772-5

The Moon Lord by Terri Lynn Wilhelm
❏ 0-451-19896-4

Shades of the Past by Kathleen Kirkwood
❏ 0-451-40760-1

LORDS OF LOVE

A Perfect Scoundrel by Heather Cullman
❏ 0-451-19952-9

Jack of Hearts by Marjorie Farrell
❏ 0-451-19953-7

The Duke's Double by Anita Mills
❏ 0-451-19954-5